The
Hucksters

By Frederic Wakeman

SHORE LEAVE

THE HUCKSTERS

The Hucksters

by

FREDERIC WAKEMAN

Rinehart & Company,
Incorporated
New York   Toronto

To
JED HARRIS

The
Hucksters

[CHAPTER I]

VICTOR NORMAN CAME AWAKE QUIETLY AND LOOKED AT HIS watch. Twenty after nine. He glanced at the mussed but empty twin bed beside his, picked up a cigarette, then put it down. He was against smoking before breakfast, on the theory that it promoted ulcers.

Marguerite came out of the bathroom in her slip, looked around for her dress and began to put it on.

"Good morning," Vic said.

She wriggled her head through the neck of the dress. "Oh, I waked you up! I'm sorry, Vic. You needed the sleep."

"So did you. Anyway, I have to see a man this morning." He picked up the phone and asked for room service. "What'll you have for breakfast, Marguerite?"

She took her coat from a closet.

"Nothing, dear. I'm late for work as it is."

He ordered breakfast for one, listened to room service tell him how tough things were in the Waldorf nowadays and it might take some time to find a waiter to bring the food up.

"Well, do your best. And send a *Times* along, please."

Marguerite said, "I gotta go, honey. I'm late."

"I had a wonderful time, Marguerite. I'll call you."

"You going to stay in New York? Or are you going back to Hollywood?"

3

Vic said he didn't know. "I'm looking for a job here though."

Marguerite hesitated at the door. "Well, it was nice to renew old acquaintances, Vic. It really was nice. I had fun!"

"So did I, Marguerite."

Vic was glad to see her go. He had gotten a little drunk last night and called her out of hunger. But all night is a long time to spend with an old friend and it was a relief to be at liberty again.

He climbed out of bed, showered, shaved, and put on his underwear. He found the Manhattan phone book, located a number, and looked at himself in the bathroom door mirror while waiting for the operator to dial it.

He looked thin and promised himself to eat, sleep and live more reasonably.

The waiter knocked and he said "Come in," signaling where he wanted the breakfast table set up.

"Hello," he said. "Mr. Kimberly, please." Then to Kimberly's secretary, "This is Victor Norman." She said that Mr. Kimberly was talking to a client and he told her he'd wait.

He signed the check for the waiter, who left the room. His suite faced south, and far downtown he could see the towers of Wall Street. Ever since 1929 he had always thought they looked like a graveyard, although he hadn't been in the district three times in ten years and had almost no idea of what went on down there.

"Good morning, Mr. Kimberly," he said. "Yes, I'm ready anytime you are. . . . I'm at the Waldorf. . . . Forty-five minutes is fine. . . . No, I haven't seen it yet. . . . The *Times*, you say? Fine, sir. Be seeing you."

He sipped his orange juice and looked at the *Times* front page. The war in Europe was going well, Patton's Third Army had driven twenty-one miles further into Germany, the Germans were being forced into acts of military desperation, the Russians were fighting in the Viennese suburbs. In the Pacific we were cleaning up resistance on Okinawa.

He turned to the advertising notes in the business section

to read what they had to say about him. The *Times* had printed it almost word for word the way he'd phoned it in yesterday:

> VICTOR NORMAN who arrived in New York from Paris last week, today announced his resignation from the Office of War Information, Overseas Radio Division, and stated his plans to return to commercial radio work. Mr. Norman, prior to his OWI appointment early in 1942, was head of the Hollywood office of the J. B. Ritchey advertising agency, and before that was radio director of the New York office of the Pratt and Birch agency. His OWI duties have taken him to Africa, Italy, the Near East, London, and Paris, where he was last stationed.

He finished breakfast and began dressing, very carefully, for this was an important meeting. He looked at his suits, narrowed his choice down to a flannel and a sharkskin. Both suits had cost one hundred and fifty dollars, and he debated which one better looked the price. He decided on the sharkskin.

A white unhollywood-looking shirt, of course. He wanted to look sincere and businesslike. Most of his ties were strictly from Charvet and Sulka and the Countess Mara. Far too loud for a really sincere person. So he put on a plain black knitted one, and finally the shoes he'd bought in London. Those shoes were the goddamnedest sincerest looking shoes in all of New York.

He left his Louis XVI suite, plunged downwards into the convention-loving lobby of the Waldorf, and strolled out into the bright March morning, walking westward across Park Avenue towards Radio City, to the offices of Kimberly and Maag. Plenty of time and cabs were hard to get.

Like many a midwesterner he had long ago chosen to ignore his birthplace, and to forget, literally, the home soil in which his roots had once been deeply planted.

Now, wherever he was, he claimed New York and New York, more than any other place on earth, claimed him.

This morning there was a tense but good feeling of being

home again, and he savored those luxurious signs of home which, even in wartime, had not disappeared from this part of the city, his part of the city, the high rent, expensive, snobbish, hustling, gossiping, drinking, conniving, show-offy east side.

The doormen still looked deferential and tip-hungry; the women still wore nylons, walked little dogs, went to extraordinary lengths to emphasize their usually undersized breasts.

He liked the rich smell of them as they passed by; thought them the most beautiful, desirable women in all the world.

It's because I've been away so long, he thought, and then he admitted to himself that it was not a sincere thought because he had always felt that way about New York women. Never for a long enough time to get a fix on anyone of them, because he was a bachelor addicted to brief romances and a radio man afraid of long term contracts.

A splash of color in the window of a temple devoted to the cravat stopped him cold. The glass reflection of his own black string tie helped him make up his mind.

Vic went in the shop and told the rather precious young person, whose reason for being out of uniform was as obvious as the perfume which cloyed the air around him, that he wanted to see the tie in the window.

It was hand-painted, rich, and very, very sincere, being priced at thirty-five dollars.

Vic opened his billfold. Two twenties and a ten. And incidentally, all the money he owned.

He paid the clerk, put on the tie, and walked, faster now, to Rockefeller Plaza, past the ice-skaters and into Radio City's central building.

The reception room of Kimberly and Maag was decorated in English 18th century. A gracious lady sat at a very fine inlaid Sheraton desk. There was a breakfront with old books in it. Vic had seen worse breakfronts on his OWI weekends at English castles.

She called Kimberly's secretary on an interoffice phone.

"He's talking to Chicago," she reported. "If you'll just wait a few minutes."

Vic sat down, looked at a morning paper with specious interest.

He was a little tense. He never hunched his coat over his shirt collar or fumbled with his tie except when he was nervous. He really needed this job.

But I can't afford to show it, he thought. He'd hired enough men himself to know that the minute an applicant showed job-hunger, his chances went way down. The best time to get a job was when you didn't need one. Then you showed you didn't give a damn and that made them hot to hire you.

He walked casually around the reception room, looking at magazine advertisements in rich, carved frames. These represented the agency's clients. Coffee . . . cigarettes . . . soap . . . there were about fifteen of Wall Street's biggest blue chips. He guessed Kimberly and Maag ranked about second or third in the ad agency field. Probably collecting their fifteen percent commission on thirty-five or forty million dollars a year.

"Mr. Kimberly will see you now," the receptionist said. . . .

Kimberly stood up to shake hands. The first thing Vic noticed was his black tie.

We're all a bunch of hustlers and connivers in this business, Vic thought. But this man Kimberly is a very high class type. He looked *in place* in this big walnut office, with its real Chippendale chairs and Kirman palace rug. Only the fireplace was a fake, but a very good fake. You can't have everything, even in Radio City.

"Hello, Mr. Norman," he said. And "I hope all this plush doesn't annoy you. I'm just a country boy myself, but my wife likes this kind of crap. And I must admit it impresses some clients. Please sit down. Cigarette?"

Vic sat down. "Thanks. I'll smoke my own. They're too hard to get nowadays."

He pulled out a pack and Kimberly said, "I see you're

smoking our brand." He meant the brand for which his agency handled the advertising.

"I had to go to three night clubs last night, before I found 'em. Cost me a buck, just to impress you."

Kimberly laughed. "I see OWI didn't make you lose your sixth sales sense."

A phone rang. Kimberly picked it up. "Excuse me. . . . Hello. Oh, good morning, Mr. Evans. . . . Well, sir, I thought it was an average good show. . . . If I were rating them, I'd say it was ten percent worse than last week's show, and fifteen percent better than the week before. . . . Yes, Mr. Evans, I did sense that the orchestra was a little off the beam. Too much spinach on "Accentuate the Positive?" . . . Yes, I see now exactly where they got off the beam. . . . You bet I will, sir. . . . I'll goose the entire cast. . . . No, no, Larsen didn't have a thing to do with it. . . . He's definitely off all your shows, Mr. Evans. . . . And I can see now why he should be. . . . You're 100 percent right. . . . Right. . . . Check. . . . We'll be seeing you tomorrow. . . ."

He hung up and walked over to a bathroom, leaving the door open. There was a medicine cabinet filled with bottles. He picked up a spray and used it on his throat.

"Been feeling a little rocky. Probably need some sulfa. Feel like I'm running some temperature."

He came back and sat down, not at the desk this time. "That was Evan Llewelyn Evans. Our Beautee Soap client. Know him?"

"I guess everybody in radio knows him by reputation," Vic said. "But I never met him. He must be quite a character."

"He's not really the ogre that gossip makes him. But you know how it is. A man that important—well, when I sneeze, it's just a sneeze. But when he sneezes, it causes tremors in Wall Street, Hollywood, and even on Main Street in Pessary, Ohio."

"I guess you can afford a few earthquakes on his billing."

"Yes, it's crowding ten million this year."

The phone rang again. "I'm not in to Hollywood," Kimberly said into it. "Tell them to stop bothering me for ten minutes."

"I don't know what happens to our men when we send them to Hollywood—but they suddenly turn into maniacs."

"It's the clothes they wear," Vic said. "I've noticed it too. They try to live up to those Hollywood styles. It's hard to think straight in purple slacks and pink shirts. I tried it once and I know."

Kimberly finally got down to business.

"Now, Mr. Norman. I understand you've left OWI and want to get back into the agency business."

"Right."

"Well, we know you by reputation of course, and we're flattered you'd call on us. How come you left OWI?"

"Because the war's over."

"You mean really?" Kimberly was fascinated with this news coming, as it were, direct from headquarters.

"That's right. This is an air war and a production war, Mr. Kimberly. Sure there'll still be a lot of big battles, and the communiques will make them sound decisive. But it's just street cleaning. Nothing else. The war in Europe was over with the Normandy landing."

"But how about Japan?"

"The war's over there, too. I wouldn't want you to quote this, but I think there's a very good chance of Japan falling before Germany does."

"Really? That is interesting. So you left OWI because you feel the war is over."

"Maybe it's only a convenient reason, Mr. Kimberly. Actually, a man in OWI is only halfway in war, and it's no damn good. I'm 4F and after they turned me down, I sought overseas propaganda as a reasonable facsimile. But it wasn't."

Kimberly said soberly, "I almost enlisted. Could have been a lieutenant colonel. Probably a full colonel by now. Then I figured, how can I leave all these people? Eight hundred of them dependent on me. The damn place'd fall apart. I was thirty-eight then."

"I know how you felt. I was thirty-two when it started." And then casually, almost as if speaking to himself, he threw away the next line, "Earning twenty-five thousand a year, not including bonuses." He got back on the subject and stated vigorously, "But combat is the core of war and they turned me down. So when I started to work with OWI I began to hate myself and then quite naturally the work I did. I began to think the only good propaganda was a big victory—and that no other propaganda can ever compensate for lack of victory. In these times only a middle-aged man can think of words as bullets. Anyway, I felt useless and, well, not functional. So I said to hell with it."

Kimberly got down to business again. "What kind of job are you looking for?"

"Any kind. So long as it pays twenty-five thousand a year to begin with, and the promise of more. Much, much more."

Kimberly laughed. "You lay it right on the barrelhead, don't you? Well, I know a lot about you. I talked with Ritchey. They'd take you back."

"I'd rather work here."

"Why?"

"Because you're a damned smart operator. I know. I've bucked you in a lot of talent deals."

Now this was certainly being sincere.

Kimberly said, "I wish I had a top spot for you in my radio operation, but frankly I haven't a thing. Maag, my partner, runs the Hollywood radio end."

Vic wished he hadn't bought that tie. Kimberly paced around the office. Young, intense, handsome, with an engaging stylized frankness, he made you feel as if you were being let in on a state secret when he asked the time of day.

"I'm having quite a problem filling jobs for returned veterans now. Nothing big, like your kind of job, of course, but it's quite a problem. They don't seem able to readjust to this business. Object to irritating radio commercials, that sort of thing. Some are really psychiatric problems. . . ." He laughed. "I should talk. I've been psycho-analyzed twice."

"I don't think you'll have that problem with me," Vic said. "I don't like to work, so I work for one reason. To make money. I'm not mixed up about what it takes to make money in this business. Certainly not more than average brains. That's me too, you know. But a man's got to look bright, act like a Racquet Club member even if he isn't, have two to three simple but good ideas a year, learn how to say yes sir all the time, and no sir once in a while, and ever so often have guts enough to pound a client's desk and tell him that's the way it's gotta be. . . . That's all there is to it."

"You sound like Evan Evans," Kimberly said. Then he snapped his fingers. "I've got it. You're a radio man. But there's no reason why you shouldn't become an account executive. Especially when the account has three nighttime and two daytime radio shows."

This was the thing Vic had been afraid of. Kimberly walked over to him, placed a hand on his sleeve. He spoke with charged excitement, in transports over his brilliant new idea.

"How," he said, very slowly and with great emphasis, "how would you like to be the account executive on the Beautee Soap account?"

Vic thought it over. "How long did it take the current AE to get himself cut off at the pockets?"

"Seven months and fourteen days, to be exact. But you're different. He was a goon. Scared to death all the time. I've got a hunch the Old Man'll react to you. He works entirely by instinct you know. He'd take to you. . . ."

"For how long?"

"Well, he took a shine to me twelve years ago. I was just an assistant account executive. And he put me in the agency business. It was the only account I had when I opened up shop. I didn't know a damned thing about radio, so I took Maag in as full partner."

Vic stood up, looked out of the window at St. Patrick's
cathedral, down on the skaters.

"I don't know," he said slowly. "I really don't know. A
friend of mine tried it once with the Old Man. Jay Kulmer.
Evans broke him. Really cracked him."

"Jay was always afraid of him, too. It's good pay. It's—"
he paused a split second—"it's more than you're asking."

"How much?"

Kimberly hesitated only a second, then gently dropped
his answer in Vic's lap. "Thirty-five thousand a year. And a
fat bonus. And maybe some stock after a year. And a big
expense account to help out with income taxes."

Vic was sitting on a corner of the desk. Kimberly was
over by the fake fireplace. Vic glanced down at a memo on
Kimberly's desk. On Beautee Soap stationery. Office of the
President. "Dear Kim: Your man Larsen has once again proved
his total unfitness to stay on the beam. . . ."

Kimberly said, "Say, that's quite a tie. Must have cost
plenty."

"I thought you'd like it."

"What?"

"Nothing. When do I start?"

Kimberly hurried to congratulate him. "I knew you'd take
it. When can you start? I want to introduce you to the Old
Man as soon as possible."

"I just got an idea for a good soap commercial," Vic said.
"A hot flash. Why don't we put it on a record and play it for
him at the first meeting? Might impress the old son of a
bitch."

Kimberly was enthralled. "Now that would really bowl
him over. I think it's a great tactic. Do you want to see your
office? It's not quite, but almost as fancy as this one. As
Beautee Soap account executive you'll rank next to me in the
office, but if you tell that to any of our vice-presidents on the
Plans Board I'll deny I said it."

"No hurry, I'll find it tomorrow."

Kimberly thought that was better. "Larsen may still be there, anyway. Might be awkward."

"So long," Vic said.

"So long. I want to call Maag on the coast and tell him the good news. By the way, do you need any money? Excuse me for asking, but the OWI isn't noted for . . ."

Vic looked at Kimberly, gauging him. He needed ready cash very badly, but this was one morning he had to be sincere. So he said, "Money? No, of course not." He decided not to thank him, either. "Good-bye, Mr. Kimberly."

"Let's make it Kim. Good-bye, Vic"

The phone rang. "Excuse me," Kimberly said. It was Maag in Hollywood. The time was to come when it would be impossible for Vic ever to think of Kimberly without a phone in his hand. Another phone rang. "Good-bye," Vic said. "This must be the only telephone booth in the world personally furnished by Mr. Chippendale."

Kim waved appreciation at the gag and said, "Morning, Tony. The new Beautee Soap account executive just left my office. It's . . ."

Victor Norman gently closed his new employer's door.

[CHAPTER II]

MISS RICHARDS WALKED INTO MISS HAMMER'S OFFICE WITH AN air of great expectancy.

"Well, I guess it's a deal, Louise," she said. "Mr. Norman's in with Mr. Kimberly now. He's meeting the Plans Board."

Louise Hammer was, naturally, all ears, being Larsen's former secretary, and certainly in line to be Norman's secretary, knowing as she did *everything* about the Beautee account.

"I haven't even seen him yet," she complained. "What's he like?"

He was very handsome, for Miss Richard's money. "You know, thin and dark and tall. He's quiet, not gushy like most of them. He still has hair, and I don't think he's got ulcers yet. At least he doesn't look like it."

"Don't worry, he will. They all do," Miss Hammer said. She was a smart-looking business girl, while Miss Richards was a plain-looking business girl. "I'm dying to see him."

Miss Richards looked around cautiously. "Did Larsen say he was coming in today? Mr. Kimberly asked me to find out."

"He cleaned out his desk last night. No, he won't be back. Poor Mr. Larsen," Miss Hammer looked troubled. "When I think of all the nights we stayed here trying to do things so perfectly that even Mr. Evans couldn't complain. Do you know I worked fifty-eight hours last week?"

"Maybe Mr. Norman will be easier. I hope so."

14

"They all are at first. It's only when he starts picking on them. They get desperate. Mr. Norman'll be my fifth Beautee account executive."

Miss Hammer's fifth account executive walked in at that point. Miss Richards said "Oh, excuse me," and disappeared.

"Good morning," Vic said. "I guess you're Miss Hammer. I'm Vic Norman and looking for a secretary, if you'll put up with me."

He was cute as could be, and Miss Hammer said she hoped she could please him.

He sniffed. "What's that perfume smell? It's the same in all the offices."

"Oh, it's Beautee toilet water," Miss Hammer said. "All the secretaries use it. Mr. Evans sends each of us a dozen bottles for Christmas."

"It's very lovely," Vic said. "Very lovely."

He invited her into his new office to talk things over.

It was a nice office with all traces of Mr. Larsen thoughtfully removed. There was even a brand new calendar. It looked just like the office of a thirty-five thousand dollar a year advertising executive.

"How about it," he said, sitting down at the desk. "Do you find it pretty rugged? Your job, I mean?"

"It takes a lot of hours, but I love it," she said. "Now that I'm in radio, I don't see how I could ever do anything else again. Even if I do have to work nearly every night."

"That's got to stop, Miss Hammer. The night work. My father used to say hard work never got anybody anyplace. The important thing is to be sincere. That's what he said."

Miss Hammer laughed. "I'll try not to work too hard."

"And another thing," Vic told her. "I'll let you in on a little secret. I don't know anything about this business. So all these experts who work for you and me now . . . I mean the radio producers, art directors, script and copy writers . . . don't let them guess how little I know."

Miss Hammer thought that was too hilarious. Everybody in radio knew Mr. Norman's reputation.

"It's a fact," he said. "Meantime, will you get this radio commercial mimeographed into scripts and ask one of the producers to see me. I want to cut an audition record of it this afternoon, and we have to do some fast couchless casting."

Miss Hammer scanned it. "Oh, it's clever," she said. "But that colored maid part. I really would sincerely advise you to cut that, Mr. Norman. Mr. Evans doesn't care for—you know—colored people."

"Now you're being too sincere, Miss Hammer. Just get it mimeographed as is, please."

"Mr. Greene, he's the copy head on printed advertising for Beautee, wants to see you, first thing. He's got some kind of crisis."

"Another thing, Miss Hammer. We can only afford three crises a day around here. Anymore than that gives you ulcers. Tell Mr. Greene to come in anytime. . . ."

Vic talked to Greene who spoke in a jargon about low readership figures because Mr. Evans wouldn't let them use modern editorial techniques. "You've got to trick people into reading ads," he explained. "Mr. Evans always wants to hit them over the head. If you would just try to sell him on some of our new approaches . . ."

"I don't know," Vic said. "In this business it's hard to argue with success."

Next Vic saw two radio producers. After that, he walked into Kimberly's office.

"Kim," he said, "I think I'd better tell you the conditions I want to work under."

Kimberly looked at him with a brief flicker of worry, then settled back and said: "Shoot."

"I've just talked to some of the people on the account. They're too damn taut. Almost hysterical."

"Really. What's happened this time?"

"Nothing. You know what I mean. They're all frightened of that Old Man. They're afraid he'll crucify them on a minute's notice."

"He doesn't operate that way," Kimberly had a finger on

his wrist and was looking at his watch. "Ninety. Not bad, considering all I drank last night. Why Evan Evans doesn't even know such people exist."

"That's not the point, Kim. You're a little taut, too. I don't know the Old Man yet, but I bet he takes advantage of it. All I want to do is to get people relaxed. Dammit, nobody does good work in that hysterical state."

"How you going to do all that, Vic? Frankly, I'm curious."

"By being relaxed myself. I want to seem to them not to give a damn about this job or old man Evans or you. I think we'll get better work out of them."

Kim thought it over. "Hmmm. I see the psychology . . . rather the psychiatry of it. Just so Mr. Evans doesn't get wind of it. He'll think you're not interested. I'm sure he has spies planted all over the agency."

"He'll think I'm interested all right. I'm just telling you so you'll know what's cooking when you begin to hear about the sloppy unbusinesslike way I'm running things."

"Okay, partner," Kim said. "You know you're the only man on that account I've ever had any real confidence in, so what you say goes. Come on, let's get downtown. You can be as relaxed as you want to, just so long as you keep the Old Man happy."

"I'll get Old Doc Norman's little wonder commercial," Vic said. "Meet you at the elevator."

On the way down to Wall Street, Kimberly briefed Vic and tried to keep calm. He was very nervous.

"I wish I'd had a chance to hear your commercial record. It's all right, isn't it?"

"Stop worrying," Vic said. "Sure it's all right."

"Now don't get nervous, Vic. It'll be a big meeting. I really should have found time to listen to that record."

Kimberly never had time to hear or read anything. So as a result he was always selling things which were put into his hands, but of which he had no knowledge. Vic had heard a story of how he went to a sponsor all primed to sell a quiz show, but the audition had been for a cops and robbers show and he had to play the record in some embarrassment, after a preamble on the merits of quiz shows.

"This," Kim explained, "will be what Mr. Evans calls an indoctrination meeting. He'll have all his key people there, and he'll tell you his philosophy about advertising."

"Most clients take you through their plants. I like this way better," Vic said. "Who's going to be there? I'm lousy at names."

"So's Evan Evans. Maybe that's a good sign.

Kimberly pulled out an envelope and drew a rectangle. "That's the board table. Beautee follows strict protocol. Mr. Evans will sit at one end, and I'll sit at the other. You'll sit on my right and Paul Evans, that's his son, will sit on his right. Paul is the heir apparent. He won't give you any trouble. Then on Mr. Evans' left will sit Irving S. Brown, the executive vice-president. Evans has paid him up to $250,000 a year, with bonuses. Next to Brown comes the wartime advertising director, a woman named Regina Kennedy—somewhat of a problem, too—his regular man for the job was drafted and he said to hell with hiring any more men. So he took the chap's secretary and made her advertising director at $20,000 a year. It doesn't make any difference, really, because Old Man Evans is the advertising director in every respect, as you'll soon find out. And, oh yes, standing to the left of Mr. Evans will be his assistant, a little fellow named Allison who's really a glorified secretary. He makes $30,000 a year."

"Am I supposed to look bright?" Vic asked. "Or does that call for a bigger salary?"

"No, just look deferential for the time being. Watch me. I'll cue you. One thing, nobody ever disagrees with Mr. Evans. I mean you just don't tell him he's wrong. Nobody ever has. And I guess nobody ever will."

The cab pulled up at the building. The two ad men went in, Vic carrying his commercial record.

"I'll see him alone, before the meeting. But first I'll introduce you to Allison and Miss Kennedy."

The executive office of the Beautee Soap Company had a

rather unusual feature. All the executives, except Mr. Evans, sat out in one huge room, with their secretaries sitting at identical desks opposite them. The room was plain, with severe light wooden desks, metal wastebaskets, nameplates, ash trays, in fact every bit of furnishing, all standard. The vice-president in charge of sales had the same setup as a junior clerk, despite his $100,000 salary.

Three signs, all neatly lettered in identical frames were repeated many times on the walls and pillars of the big room. They read:

Get it in Writing

If we could make Beautee Soap
any Better—we would

Our reputation has always been
for Courtesy at all times.

Kimberly introduced Vic to Miss Kennedy and Mr. Allison. He then left to see Mr. Evans.

Allison suggested waiting in the board room "Where we can talk."

The board room was heavy with mahogany and tradition. They even had brass cuspidors left over from the first Evans regime, the Old Man's father and founder of the company. A nineteenth century magazine ad on Beautee Soap was framed over the fireplace. Vic laid his commercial on the record player. He waited for Miss Kennedy to select her chair, which was just where Kimberly said it would be. Then he sat in his appointed place. Allison paced around the room, looking out the door on every trip past it.

"I thought the Figaro Perkins show was very good last night," Vic said, just to make some conversation.

Miss Kennedy passed. "Has Mr. Evans given you his script on it yet?" she asked Allison.

He said no. Vic asked Allison what he thought of the show, and he passed too.

Apparently, no one had an opinion on anything until The Opinion got to them.

"One thing," Miss Kennedy said. "On the commercials. I think Mr. Evans is getting pretty tired of that high soprano female voice. I think you should goose the producer on it, Mr. Norman. Mr. Evans likes deep female voices."

"That's right," Allison said. "Keep 'em on the beam up there at the agency. Down here, we take the view that we either know where we're going—or we don't. And once we know where we're going, the only problem then is to stay on the beam."

"I'd goose them all a little, if I were you," Miss Kennedy said. "The last regime was well—you know, lax."

Just to impress them, Vic whipped out a pad and wrote "soprano" on it, thinking the poor little girl was probably sleeping with the producer. Then he wrote the word "goose." The idea of goosing a soprano almost broke him up, but he kept his self-control and played it straight and sincere.

"I have a new commercial idea here on a record," he said. "We thought we might play it for Mr. Evans at the meeting, but I'd appreciate your opinions beforehand."

So he played the record.

"Interesting," Miss Kennedy said. "But what do you think about that—you know—policy matter, Mr. Allison?"

Allison explained the policy matter. "That colored voice, I'm not so sure about that. I mean not as advertising but from Mr . . . I mean the, ah, policy point of view. I don't . . ." He looked out the door and was either galvanized or goosed into action. "Here he comes."

Miss Kennedy jumped up. So Vic stood up too. Allison reached his customary place and froze into position as Evan Llewellyn Evans, up to and including his famous straw hat, came in, followed by Kimberly and two other men.

All stood rigidly at attention until Mr. Evans sat down, at the head of the board table. Then Kimberly said:

"Mr. Evans may I present Mr. Victor Norman. And Mr. Paul Evans and Mr. Irving Brown."

Vic stepped forward to shake Mr. Evans' hand, but was warned back by Kimberly. Apparently the old man's hand was unshakable. Vic did shake hands with Paul Evans and Irving Brown. And they all sat down, except Allison who remained standing back of the Old Man's chair.

The feeling of tenseness in the room was extraordinary. All eyes were fixed on the old man at the head of the table. He sat, looking down at the table, and there was great silence for what seemed like two or three minutes.

It gave Vic a chance to look his new client over. So this was Evan Llewelyn Evans, advertising and radio genius, scourge of account executives. The man who had paid one million dollars for a comedy show, then canceled it after one program because the gagwriters had put in one off-color joke. The man who had built and broken more stars than anyone else in radio. The man who had fired a world famous Metropolitan Opera soprano because she wouldn't sing "Some of These Days."

He was a small man, almost dainty, with tiny graceful hands. He was in his middle fifties and looked older. He raised his head suddenly, staring across at Kimberly, and Vic saw that his eyes were a snapping blue.

And his clothes. Vic had heard about the way he dressed, but it didn't seem possible. He wore a black alpaca coat, a white linen vest, and a bandanna kerchief tied around his neck. Yes, a bandanna. Under it was a starched collar with a gleaming gold collar button, but no tie. He carried a fine white handkerchief in his sleeve. And wore an old straw field hat, indoors and out, winter and summer. He was certainly the General MacArthur of the ad game, Vic thought. His clothes suggested more than mere eccentricity. No doubt about it, he was a showman.

In the expressive silence, Mr. Evans raised his straw-covered head once more, hawked and spit on the mahogany board table.

No one spoke. Very deliberately, he took the handkerchief

out of his sleeve, wiped the spit off the table, and threw the handkerchief into a wastebasket.

"Mr. Victor," he said.

Allison leaned down and whispered.

"Mr. Norman," he said, shouting in a deep bass. "You have just seen me do a disgusting thing. Ugly word, spit. But you know, you'll always remember what I just did."

Taut silence.

Then Mr. Evans leaned forward and whispered hoarsely, "Mr. Norman, if nobody remembers your brand, then you ain't gonna sell any soap."

Pregnant pause.

"Mr. Norman, that's what we're in business for—to sell soap. Beautee soap. I don't want you to ever forget that. You got to eat, drink, sleep and yes, by God, dream soap. Because even if you build the most glamorous, high Hooperating show on the air—it ain't gonna do us a damn bit of good unless you figure out some way to sell soap on it. You gotta make the people remember you. Check?"

"Check!" said Mr. Kimberly.

"Check," said Mr. Brown.

"Check," said Allison, almost in unison with Miss Kennedy. Only son Paul and new-man Vic failed to echo it.

"And the way I look at it. You got your people and I got my people. And we both gotta keep goosing 'em to make 'em sell more soap. Beautee soap."

He made a goosing motion.

"Right?"

"Right!" they all said again, following the chain of command. It was a ritual.

"Now one other thing, Mr. Forman."

Allison leaned down and whispered again.

"Now one other thing, Mr. Norman. I believe in selling by demonstration. Any other way . . ."

He looked around, found a water carafe at his right, grasped it.

"Any other way," he repeated, turning the carafe upside down on the board table, "is all wet. See what I mean?"

The water ran on Brown and Regina Kennedy. Neither made a protective motion. Allison leaned forward and mopped up with his two handkerchiefs. Evans watched dispassionately until Allison had finished. Then he leaned forward again, this time hoarsely whispering.

"Also, Mr. Norman, this company gives your agency ten million dollars a year to spend in advertising. And do you know why? I'll tell you a secret about the soap business, Mr. Norman. There's no damn difference between soaps. Except for perfume and color, soap is soap. Oh, maybe we got a few manufacturing tricks, but the public don't give a damn about that. But the difference, you see, is in the selling and advertising. We sell soap twice as fast as our nearest competitor because we outsell and out-advertise 'em. And that gets me to an important part of this meeting."

He blew his nose loudly and continued.

"We get our results by work. By chin-chin and by compass direction. When we want something, we work it out. When we don't know where we're going, we chin-chin until we do. That's the time for ideas, suggestions, new plans. But once the compass points north and we know where we're going, we stay on the beam. And we don't want anybody associated with us who's off the beam. I ain't interested in ideas that are off the beam and I ain't interested in people that are off the beam. Check!"

"Check," went around the board table like a whipcrack.

"Example, Mr. Norman. Last night on our Figaro Perkins show, that orchestra kept putting spinach into the music. By spinach, I mean off the beam, off the melody. Now I like my music played on the beam, and fast and loud. I think that's the way the public likes it too. These newfangled bands are all creampuffs and strings. Wet dream music, I call it, with apologies to Miss Kennedy. I say to you, Mr. Norman, get that buffoon Larsen's band off that show. Right?"

"Yes, sir," said Vic, and whipped out his notebook. He wrote, "New band, Figaro Perkins show."

The Old Man got up. "That's about all I had to say. Except"—he took off his alpaca coat, walked around and put it over Vic's shoulders—"except I want you to realize you're wearing the Beautee soap coat now. I hope it fits you well."

"Thank you, sir," Vic said.

"Remember, two things make good advertising. One, a good simple idea. Two, repetition. And by repetition, by God, I mean until the public is so irritated with it, they'll buy your brand because they bloody well can't forget it. All you professional advertising men are scared to death of raping the public; I say the public likes it, if you got the know-how to make 'em relax and enjoy it."

Kimberly said, "Mr. Evans, it may interest you to know that Mr. Norman sat up all night last night, working out a twist on your present commercial idea. And if you want to hear it, we've got it here on a record. Of course, it may be a little off the beam, as Mr. Norman had not had the privilege of hearing your indoctrination ideas before doing it. But . . ."

Mr. Evans said, "I'd love to hear it."

Vic went to the record player. "I might say that I got the idea from reading something that was attributed to you. So if it's good, I can only be proud to say I shared the work with you, Mr. Evans."

He played the record. It was quite a scene. These seven people in the board room, their combined incomes totaling at least a million dollars a year, listening to the chattering radio commercial as if it were the fifth act of *Hamlet*. Five of them listening grimly, critically, but above all cautiously, never showing by any expression the faintest sense of liking it. Waiting for the Old Man. Standing by for The Opinion.

The actors were good, and it was a professional job:

VOICE: Beautee is as Beautee does.
COLORED MAID: (Chuckling) Love that soap.
ANNOUNCER: You know friends, they say Hollywood

is the place where the stars worship
Beautee. How about it, Miss Wanda
Jean? You're just about Hollywood's
loveliest new star, so you ought to know
something about Beautee.

WANDA JEAN: Right you are, Bob Allen. Hollywood *is*
the place where the stars and their per-
sonal maids worship Beautee.

COLORED MAID: Love that soap.

WANDA JEAN: Why, in my forthcoming technicolor picture, "The Stars Stopped" produced by
GRM, I do believe everyone in the cast,
including myself, used the Beautee Soap
Beauty treatment.

ANNOUNCER: Yes, next to the Trocadero, it's Hollywood's favorite bar.

WANDA JEAN: It's *my* favorite bar.

COLORED MAID: Love that soap.

ANNOUNCER: So why not take a Beautee tip from
gorgeous GRM starlet Wanda Jean. And
remember, 81% of Hollywood's loveliest
Beauties use Beautee soap.

VOICE: Beautee is as Beautee does.

COLORED MAID: Love that soap.

When it was finished, there was the deep silence of waiting, which funneled into intense concentration on Evan
Llewelyn Evans. Finally he raised his head and said, "Play it
again."

Vic played it again.

Evans said, "What do you think, Mr. Norman?"

Vic said instantly, "One thing, it's as simple as soap."

Evans chuckled, lifted his straw hat. "I like it. I take off
my hat to you. Only I'd cut that line about it being Hollywood's favorite bar, next to the Trocadero. Dammit, Beautee
is not second best to nothing. It is Hollywood's *favorite* bar
and don't you ever forget it. Check?"

"Check," Kimberly said. "Now that you've sharpened it up by cutting out that second-best reference, I'll buy it."

Irving Brown said, "Just what it needed. I knew it needed a little something, and Mr. Evans put his finger right on it. Excellent!"

Regina Kennedy said, "I knew Mr. Evans would like it. I'd heard it before and approved. I was a little afraid of the colored maid, though. Clever, but—"

Evans spoke to her as if to a small child.

"I don't think you quite get what's in Mr. Norman's mind on that colored maid, Miss Kennedy. He not only relates a familiar saying to our product, but he's thinking of appealing to the colored market, while at the same time appealing to the white market because she's obviously a lady's maid. And Beautee soap is a lady's soap. The lady's maid becomes a servant to the soap that's aristocratic—Beautee soap. It's really part of our quality story."

Mr. Brown said, "I really hadn't noticed it until you pointed it out, Mr. Evans, but it does exactly that."

Paul Evans said, "I don't quite see it."

"You wouldn't," the Old Man grunted. "Do you see it, Miss Kennedy?"

"Perfectly," Miss Kennedy said. "It'd make me buy Beautee soap."

"Put it on the air, effective with our Friday show. Put it on every show twice, with different movie stars of course. Mr. Norman, I can see you"—Evan Llewelyn Evans paused, reached in his mouth, jerked out a bridge of teeth and stuck them under Vic's nose—"I can see you've already got your teeth in our problem."

He put his teeth back in his mouth, and painfully stood up. The others jumped up in unison.

"See what I mean?" he said.

The meeting was over.

[CHAPTER III]

THE TWO AD-MEN STOOD ON A CURB IN WALL STREET AND whistled vainly at cabs.

"If I spent as much time looking for business as I do looking for cabs I'd be grossing fifty million a year," Kimberly complained. He advised Vic to plan on leaving a full half hour before any of his appointments with Evan Evans. "It's impossible to tell him you couldn't get a cab. He just can't understand things like that."

"He'd probably blame you for not buying me a cab, to be used exclusively for trips to the Beautee soap company," Vic said.

"Hey, that's not a bad idea." Kim raced out into the snarled traffic to compete for an empty hack, but an executive-type man in a Brooks Brothers suit beat him to it.

He bitterly returned to the curb and Vic said, "That's Wall Street for you . . . these bloated capitalists are reduced to stealing cabs yet. Shall we try the subway, Kim?"

"I won't ride uptown in the subway," Kim said. "I'll kill myself first."

So Vic wandered to the corner and proudly returned with a cab. Sitting down made a lot of difference.

"I'm feeling capitalistic again," he told Kim. "Now that I've got a cab of my own I don't hate anybody."

Kim slumped back on his neck and pulled up the jump-

27

seat for his feet. "God, I'm tired. What a day. Anyway, I've found something that upsets you. At last. Taxicabs. It makes me feel better about my own intolerances."

"I'm only intolerant when I'm inconvenienced," Vic said. "I only hate the Catholics when their damn parade keeps me from crossing Fifth Avenue on St. Patrick's Day. And my anti-semitism is confined just to Yom Kippur and Rosh Hashonoh when they close the shops and I have to walk blocks for my *New York Times.*"

Kim chuckled. The afternoon had made him even fonder of Vic. "I was just thinking. You're a very cool character. It's very revealing to me that you haven't said one word about the meeting."

"Why should I? It's over."

"I should think you'd like to hear my analysis of how you stacked up with the Old Man."

"Sure. Go ahead."

Kim forgot his fatigue and sat up, brisk and elated. "Like that." He made a circle with his thumb and forefinger.

"One hundred percent pluperfect." He laughed happily. This was a big day. The new man had made good. "I knew it all the time. I had an intuition you'd click just like that." He made the circle again. "I've never seen him so pleased with a new account executive."

"And you've seen plenty of 'em, all right."

"That commercial. It was a stroke of genius. 'Love That Soap.' I wish I'd thought up that one." Then he said quickly, "No, I don't either. I'm glad you did."

"He's a real comedy character," Vic said. "I'd like to have an option on him for radio. Pictures, too."

"I wouldn't call him a comedy character," Kim said soberly. But he quickly shifted his spirits back into high gear. "What do you say we play hookey and not go back to the office? I feel like celebrating with a drink."

Vic looked at his watch. "It's six o'clock. How can anybody play hookey from the office at this time of night?"

"You just don't know me," Kim said. "I seldom get away

until eight. Eight A.M. till 8 P.M., that's my normal schedule. Driver, the Stork Club. Not that I'm trying to steer you along my path."

"Not at eight in the morning, you won't," Vic assured him. "Only scrubwomen and presidents have any right to be in business offices at that time of day. I'm not even that lowest form of agency life, a vice-president. But don't think I'm punching for it. I'd turn it down if you offered me one."

But that was a concept foreign to Kim and he wrote it off as just a gag. He said, "Don't worry, Vic, you will be soon, if you keep this up." Then he said reflectively. "With you on the job maybe I won't have to work so hard now. Larsen was so damned incompetent on the Beautee account that I had to spend all my time placating the Old Man. Larsen got so he couldn't even make a decision on where to eat lunch."

Vic asked Kim what Larsen was doing.

"Poor Larsen cracked," Kim said. "He's got a persecution complex. Thinks I didn't support him with Evans. He was no executive and he didn't belong in that job. It was too big for him. But the Old Man met him, liked him, and insisted I give him the job. I knew what would happen. But what could I do?"

"Is he really cracked up?"

"His doctor says it's a nervous breakdown, but I'm putting him in the hands of my psychiatrist to make sure. I'll let you know what the diagnosis is. I'm paying the bills, of course."

"It's nice to know there's a free psychiatrist around, if I ever need one," Vic said.

Kim said cautiously, "This doesn't bother you, Vic?"

"About Larsen? Look, Kim, don't worry about me. That Old Man won't ever get to me because I don't give a damn. I want you to know I'm very sincere about that."

Kim slapped Vic's knee appreciatively. "I do know that. That's why I hired you. Yes, I'm going to have more time now, you're going to give it to me. Maybe," he said thoughtfully, "enough time to get some new business. K and M could use a big new account or two."

At the Stork Club, Kimberly and the headwaiter greeted each other with gravity and mutual respect.

"The Cub Room, Mr. Kimberly?"

"I think so, Joseph, Please."

"Fine. I can give you your usual table."

Kim said, "Joseph, this is Mr. Victor Norman, a new associate of mine." He handed the man a ten dollar bill.

The man said, "I remember Mr. Norman from years ago. We'll be glad to take care of you, anytime, Mr. Norman."

"Gee, thanks," Vic said. He said it in such a way that when they sat down Kim felt impelled to explain the New York night club situation as it now stood.

"All this war money has made New York a boom town," he said. "You can't get tables at the good places unless you're known. They keep you standing around for hours if you don't butter them up once in a while. If you bring a client in, it's worth it. That kind of crap impresses clients, especially the out-of-towners."

"I'm not even a client," Vic said, "and I'm impressed."

"I hope you don't disapprove of slipping a headwaiter a tenner once in a while."

"I approve. Especially when it's your money. The whole thing fits right in with my theory."

"What theory? Waiter, a double scotch, please. What's yours?"

"Single scotch. With water."

"What theory?"

"My theory of making friends," Vic said. "I am a man of many friends. They get me railroad reservations, hotel rooms, steak, scotch, all sorts of friendly things. But is it because of my personality? Because they like me? No. I just give them money. The cleanest, simplest basis of friendship you can find."

The headwaiter bustled up and plugged in a phone, placing the instrument in front of Kimberly.

Vic said, "I didn't hear you order this gadget. Tell him to give it to some talent agent."

"I can't. It's a standing order, wherever I go. I have to let them know where I am, every minute. You'll have to do the same now."

"Some of the places I go, I wouldn't want it known."

Kimberly laughed. "You, too? Well, I must tell you that when a certain client gets an idea, he's got to talk about it, whatever the hour of the day or night. You'll find out."

Kim finished his drink. "Waiter, another double here. How about it, Vic?"

"Single's fine."

"Oh, make it a double anyway. Saves time."

"All right. A double."

"You have to drink doubles nowadays," Kim said, picking up the phone. "This nonsensical midnight curfew won't let a man get slowly drunk anymore. Not enough time."

He asked for a Butterfield number, and covered the phone as he waited. "I want you to consider this a top military secret, as it wouldn't help my reputation, bad as it is. But you look like a man who isn't shocked by anything."

Vic made an expression to confirm the statement.

"Excuse me," Kim said. He spoke into the phone. "Hello, lover. How's Kimmy? Have you taken his temperature? One degree, huh. Well, I don't think it's at all serious, lover, but you'd better have the doctor over, No, I haven't felt at all well today. Been running a little temperature myself. I'm going to stop by Harry's office tomorrow for a thorough checkup, if I get time. Well, right now I'm at the Cub Room with Mr. Victor Norman. Say, I've got a great idea. Wait a minute." He held the receiver away from his mouth and said, "How would you like to have Maggie, that's Mrs. Kimberly, come down and we'd all have dinner together?" Naturally, Vic said "delighted," and Kimberly made the date with his wife.

Kim said "good-bye lover" and hung up. "What was I saying? Oh yes . . ." he discreetly lowered his voice. "One afternoon, not so long ago either, I was doing a little extra-curricular work. Of course I had to leave the phone number with my secretary, and you know, that old so-and-so Evans caught me right at the worst moment for an interruption. You'd have died. There I was, talking about newspaper coverage in this dame's bed. She could have killed me."

He paused, weighed the effect of the confession on Vic. "Does that disgust you?"

"It tempts me," Vic said. "If I'm not around in the afternoons, just remember that what's good enough for the boss is good enough for me."

"Years ago," Kim said, "Evan Evans used to cut quite a swathe himself. But now his age, his liver, and probably his prostate gland have reformed him. And you know there's nothing quite so sanctimonious as an over-age rake. That's why we have to be so careful not to let him get wise to any of our peccadilloes."

"Where does Maag fit in with him?"

"He doesn't," Kim said. "Maag divides his time between here and the west coast. But when he's here he concentrates on the other New York clients." He sighed. "I wish I had Maag's freedom. Mr. Evans keeps me pretty well staked out. I can't even leave town, except when he's on vacation. So Maag runs all the radio shows in Hollywood."

"Incidentally, on that Figaro Perkins show we could use a new singer as well as a new band. I think she stinks."

Kimberly put down his glass. "I hope there's not a microphone in that flower bowl. Miss Steele is a great favorite of Mr. Evans. But don't get me wrong. Only as a singer. She sings loud, you know. Mr. Evans likes loud singers."

"In that case, I think she's terrific. Although it is a shame she can't sing."

Vic was feeling the scotch. Kim drank steadily, never showing it.

"Looking back over the meeting," Kim said, "perhaps you'd like to hear a few comments. Just to give you a better understanding of the entire Beautee picture."

"Sure," Vic wished that Kimberly would take off his overalls. Hell, it was almost seven and here he was, trapped in the Stork Club, waiting for the whistle to blow.

"Naturally, I watched you very carefully today. I hope you understand on a thing as important as this that I'd want to."

"Sure."

"And I've never seen an easier, more relaxed performance. For a first meeting, it was miraculous."

"Thanks."

"I know what an ordeal it is, Vic, and I envy the way you handle yourself."

"You embarrass me a little." Vic said. "Compliments bother me."

"Sorry. I'll remember that." Vic had put Kim on the defensive and he was not too confident about finishing what he'd started to say.

So Vic said, "I only wanted you to know that if you have any criticisms, Kim, you don't have to give me the old build-up first."

"No criticisms," Kim said. "Just a couple of minor suggestions. Let's have one more round before Maggie comes."

That was fine with Vic.

Kim continued. "Point one, you impress Evans by being so easygoing. You give him the feeling of being in command of yourself. But occasionally this afternoon I got the feeling that you weren't listening to him. I sensed that feeling in him, too."

"I can't understand how you felt that," Vic said. "I heard every word he said. I'll try to stop daydreaming in front of him, Kim."

"If you just heighten the appearance of taking in everything he says—not too obviously—I think it's slightly better strategy with him."

"You said you noticed a couple of things. What's the other one?"

"This is really minor. Those stooges, Brown, Allison, Kennedy, Paul Evans. They don't mean a thing in the final analysis. It's a one man show, you saw that. But if those little people don't like you, they can make it damned annoying. You see, they've nothing to do but needle and criticize—"

"And goose," Vic said.

"Right. So it's better tactics to act as if they were important. To do little things that make those nobodies feel like somebodies. This afternoon, I noticed a rather contemptuous look on you several times when you were discussing things with them."

"Are you sure it wasn't pity?"

Kim said, "I just thought I'd mention these little things. I hope you're not offended?"

"No. I understand."

"I knew you would," Kim was relieved.

"Right." Vic almost added "Check" but did not because he felt it might unnecessarily hurt Kim, for whom he was beginning to have understanding, affection and, after this meeting today, great sympathy.

"I wish I hadn't called my wife," Kimberly complained. "I'm beginning to feel like going out on the town. By the way, Vic, are you married? I never thought to ask."

"Nope. Not even divorced."

"I hope you enjoyed the women in Paris."

"I did. Especially those who still had hair."

"My psychiatrist tells me I'm a sex maniac. But I told him that I doubted if bulls and rabbits had Oedipus complexes."

"I must have missed a line."

"No, I left out two consultations." He stood up. "Had to. Here comes Maggie. Mrs. Kimberly, this is Mr. Victor Norman."

Maggie Kimberly shook hands. She was a Park Avenue housewife, complete with the mink coat and the diamond brooch. Pretty but not flashy. Thirty-five. Refined. Nice figure. Most presentable.

She kissed Kim, and spoke gaily with the high, clear projected voice of an assured Park Avenue woman.

"Darling. How did it go today?"

"For me, as usual. But Mr. Norman was sensational."

"Anything exciting happen?"

"No. Waiter, an iced dubonnet for Mrs. Kimberly. Two more of the same for us."

She let Vic help her with her mink coat. She sat down and said brightly, "Did I keep you waiting long, darling?"

"No. Just long enough for a drink or so."

"With the accent on the 'or so,' I'll bet. You men always try to relax too fast."

"Maggie thinks I work too hard," Kim explained. "But when she asks me what I did to get so tired, I can never remember. I guess I don't really work very hard after all."

"You answer the telephone," Vic said. "That's work."

"He's just joking," Maggie said to Vic. "You really work very hard, don't you, darling? But he never will tell me anything about it, Mr. Norman. Do you ever tell your wife anything about business?"

"Mr. Norman has no wife, lover. But tell us about your day."

She sighed. "I had a fuss with that teacher again about Kimmy. I think we ought to take him out of that awful school, darling. They simply refuse to use modern methods of training children. And it's doing something to Kimmy's personality. They're making him rude and unmanageable."

She turned to Vic. "Do you have any children, Mr. Norman?"

"Lover," Kim explained to her in a fatherly manner, "Mr. Norman has no wife. Remember? Therefore, no children he could discuss in the Stork Club. Also for your information, Mr. Norman is the new account executive on the Beautee soap account."

"Oh, isn't that grand," Maggie said. She was sipping delicately at her dubonnet and now she raised the glass. "Congratulations. And how do you like Mr. Evans? I think he's just precious. The most fabulous man, really."

"I don't know yet," Vic said, "I'm still very wet back of the ears. Kim, are you going to use that thing again?"

"I'm just calling home to see if anything's happened," Kim said.

"You know, Mr. Norman," Maggie said, "sometimes I think Kim should have married Mr. Evans instead of me. They see so much more of each other than we do."

Kim hung up and said, "I'm getting hungry. Where'll we eat? Any ideas, Vic?"

Vic said he hadn't been back in New York long enough to know where the food was.

Maggie said, "War has done the queerest things to Kim's eating habits. All he ever wants now are restaurants that'll give him steaks, butter and hollandaise sauce."

"And a chair to sit in, but quick," Kim added. "Say, how about the Casablanca? They'll give me steaks there."

So they went to the Casablanca and the telephone came for Kim, who duly informed his servant of his whereabouts. Maggie and Vic were studying the meatless menu, but Kim commanded them to ignore it and ordered steaks which turned out to be fine steaks.

Vic said, "These must be pre-war steaks."

Kim said, "It's a celebration. We're celebrating Victor Norman day in Wall Street." And it called for champagne from France.

"California champagne is all right for Frenchmen and the ad-men who have the account," he said. "But not for us."

Vic liked the idea of champagne. "I don't know why, but I'm in a drinking mood tonight," he said. "Maybe you'd better pin my address on my lapel."

"Don't try to keep up with Kim," Maggie warned. "It might prove disastrous if you're not used to drinking."

"I have to drink enough for both Maggie and me," Kim said. "She fakes her drinking."

"When I married into a Presbysterian minister's family," Maggie said, "I thought I was going to spend my life serving lemonade to nice old ladies, didn't I, darling?"

"I don't exactly know what you thought, lover. But you look very fetching tonight. Very sleepable-with."

"Darling! You'll shock Mr. Norman."

A floor show was desperately trying to dazzle the noisy diners, and Kim pointed to the stage.

"Now that is something I would really call sleepable-with. Lover, don't you think she's very sleepable-with?"

Maggie said, "You must be a little tight, darling. I must explain something to Vic, darling. Every time he gets a little tight he thinks all women are sleepable-with."

"Anyway she is," Kim said. "Wouldn't you say so, Vic?"

Vic's back was to the stage, so now he turned around to look and it was Jean Ogilvie.

She was just beginning to sing one of her pert, risqué little songs. Charming and intimate.

She looked very appetizing, clinging to the microphone and making musical jokes in a small, well-styled voice.

Then she sang some torchy ballads. She'd changed her style since Vic had last heard her, now belonging to that school which sings as if suffering from a gastro-intestinal upset, with face and mouth writhing in a tortured but rhythmic manner, and the tones throbbing with pain.

She closed her act with an imitation of Frank Sinatra that killed the people.

Vic knew she had seen him, so he didn't send the waiter for her after she made her exit.

She immediately came to his table.

"Vic darling," she said. "You mad character." She kissed him. "I thought you'd died or something."

She met the Kimberlys, sat down and found out about Vic. It was wonderful, simply wonderful, their both being in New York. She was mad about New York after horrible, horrible Hollywood. She'd sat out her picture contract at Romanoff's, waiting for a musical that never got written. And she'd always been mad about Vic. He was such a mad character. Let's see, it'd been four years since they'd seen each other, hadn't it? God, the time.

"How do you know he isn't married, after four years?" Kimberly asked.

But Jean Ogilvie was sure he had not done such a thing. "Not my Vic," she declared. "He's a swivel neck, the bastard. You know, he's the type strange women send notes to in cocktail lounges."

"That was the only time in my life, that once when I was with you," Vic said. "And besides, she was forty and drunk."

"I'm just now beginning to appreciate what a boy wonder I hired," Kim said. "I feel like some more champagne. Waiter, another bucket."

"Darling," Maggie was firm. "You know you'll only feel terrible tomorrow. We'd better go home. Kim gets up at six-thirty regardless of what time he goes to bed," she explained.

"Why aren't you on the radio?" Kim demanded of Jean. "Or in pictures? You're pretty terrific, you know."

"Just show me how," Jean said.

"That's easy," Kim said grandly. "Just by accident we have at our table one of the biggest radio men in the country. Miss Ogilvie may I present Mr. Norman whom I believe you've already met."

Vic was annoyed. You couldn't talk that way to talent, drunk or sober.

"We'll see," he said. "How long you been here, Jean?"

"Don't change the subject, honey," Jean said.

"Miss Ogilvie," Kim said, "why don't you make Vic put you on the radio? I think you could sell soap."

"Darling, she certainly has sold you," Maggie said. "Now why don't we run along and let these two talk over old times?"

"Please stay," Jean begged. "I promise to sing some different songs for my next show. You want to stay, don't you Mr. Kimberly?"

But now Kim was a martyr. "I'll be a martyr. But only to keep my newest and best employee happy. I know you've got a lot to talk about. Did I say talk? Excuse me, Miss Ogilvie, but somehow it's hard to associate mere conversation with a creature as gorgeous as you."

"Come on, darling," Maggie fled into her mink coat quick as any mink. "Good-bye all. See you later."

"Your new boss is a nice man," Jean said. "Is it a big company?"

"One of the biggest."

"Easy money, sounds like," Jean said. She patted his hand. "Hello, you mad character."

"Hello. No, not easy. It's one of those things where you sometimes wonder if there's enough money in the world to pay for it." He threw himself back into her mood. "My God, Jean, I damn near fell in love with you, even if you are a singer. You're what I'd call a nice piece of talent."

"You're sweet."

"How's it going?"

"Okay. They pay two-fifty here and I do a sustaining on the radio. Do you think I'm good, Vic?"

"You sounded damn good tonight, baby. I'll catch your sustaining show and see how you come over the air."

"You think you might really get me a job on a big radio show? God, if I could only get out of this dump."

"Who owns it?" Vic sniffed the air. "Frankie Powell?"

"Yes. How did you know?"

"I been in so many of these joints, I can smell the ownership. These retired racketeers keep changing the names, but they can't change the smell."

"How much trouble would it take to get me a good radio job?" she asked.

"Jean, you're very beautiful and you tease and charm the people but you haven't really got very much sense. Anybody knows that to get a good radio job you have to be sincere—"

"What do you mean, sincere?"

"Well, like sleeping with people who can give you radio jobs."

"Okay," she said. "When do we start?"

"Later," he said. "I like your hair. It used to be black. Bright red hair becomes you. Your face is still soft and sweet enough for it."

She wore it in a long pageboy style and she reached back

and brought a handful of hair around where she could examine it critically.

"It's a little flashy. But in this business, honey, you gotta have flash."

She patted his hand tenderly. "I never thought I'd see you again. It's been years. Remember the first time?"

"Sure, it was at the old Tropics. They've changed it into a studio for a breakfast club radio show. A good saloon ruined."

The memory made her sigh. "God, I was a mess in those days."

"You were fine. You were an artless little girl and I liked you. You told me about your family. I liked them too. How are they?"

"Father's still busheling on weekdays and painting Prospect Park landscapes on weekends." She laughed. "No, he's graduated to nudes now."

"I hear a touch of RKO oxonian in your speech," Vic said. "So your lost your Brooklyn accent, too. Tough."

"I took diction lessons," she said proudly. "You have to make yourself over all the time in this business. Like clothes." She put her hands under her breasts and delicately raised them. "Take my busts, for instance. Sure I know they're small, but I pay two hundred dollars for my dresses and they build them up."

Vic got a bang out of being around Jean Ogilvie. He liked to hear her talk. She was talent and he enjoyed the free show which talent always put on during its offstage moments. But he was always very careful not to confuse talent with art, which he really respected.

It was not so much with him an admiration of the skills developed by talent. Rather it was their precocious, child-like qualities that amused him: their total preoccupation with themselves, their impersonal, commercial attitudes about their performances, their bodies, their objective adoration of what they would call their personalities.

"I hate to admit it," Jean was saying, "but one of my breasts is actually lower than the other. My left one." She stroked herself impersonally. "I have to pay thirty dollars apiece for my brassieres, but it's worth it."

A man came by and told her she was sensational, and she thanked him.

"You're so sad and quiet, Vic darling. What's the matter? You been having a bad time?"

"No, I just drank too much tonight."

She had to leave now to do her next show. "But don't go away," she said. "Why don't you take me home? It's only in Sixty-first Street. I'll make you some coffee and we'll talk."

So Vic sat alone and drank while she sang. Then it was midnight and curfew time. The waiter shooed them out into the street.

He stood on the sidewalk and breathed deep.

"Ahhh, this wonderful, dirty town. You know, Jean, when I get away from New York I miss the dirt more than anything."

Jean was looking at a picture of herself on a poster advertising the floor show.

"It says here I'm sensational. Do you think I'm sensational enough for a big radio contract?"

"Quit punching," he said. "You must learn to quit punching. You're a dear girl and I like you, but for God's sakes don't punch so hard."

They walked to her hotel because there were no cabs. Vic rested on the sofa while she made coffee.

"I'm dehydrated," he said. "I can't understand why I drank so much. It was stupid."

"I hope you don't want cream," she said. "There isn't any. Maybe you were just celebrating the new job."

"Maybe. How about you, Jean? Do you manage to keep reasonably happy?"

"I was very unhappy in Hollywood," she said. "The studio loused me up. A man loused me up. I loused myself up."

"Did you want to marry him, Jean?"

"No. He was already married."

"Are you still loused up?"

"Not by him. And this job is a break. It's a sign I'm on the way up."

"There's nothing wrong with talent," he said, "that success won't cure. You'll be okay."

"You liked me, didn't you?" she said.

"I still like you. I don't think you're quite as endearing and sweet as you used to be, but you've gained something too."

She walked over and sat beside him. He was lying back on the couch with his hand pressing his head. The alcohol had finally gotten to his left eye.

"Want to go to bed, Jean?"

"There's no rush," she said. "Stay here and rest a while."

"I meant with me."

She walked over to the window and opened it. "You're sweet, Vic. But I'm getting old. I'm twenty-five, you know. I need a husband, not a bedfellow."

"Good luck," he said. "But if you ever want the latter, I'm at the Waldorf."

"I'm happy for you, Vic. You've got this wonderful new job and everything."

"Wonderful," he said and he made it into an ugly word. "I guess I am drunk. You wanta know something? I hate this job."

"How can you hate it? You've only had it a day or two."

"I hated it before I took it."

"Then why did you take it, darling," she said. "After all, a man of your ability can pick and choose."

"I guess I took it because I'd rather be a winner than a loser," he said, the bitterness mounting in him. "I've felt this way about all my jobs. The men you have to serve. The things you have to do. It makes my flesh creep. Yaahhh."

He stood up and wearily put on his coat.

"What things?" Jean Ogilvie asked, never before having encountered this mood in Vic, and feeling a genuine sympathy for whatever it was that was bothering him.

"It's nothing specific," he said. "This latest job is just a particularly harrowing example. A man cooks up some fat and presses it into a bar of soap. He perfumes it. Wraps it up fancy. Then he needs a barker to sell this miraculous combination of herbs, roots and berries. So he calls me in to bark for him. But not at him. God no, dear, not that. So all I gotta do is bark real good and if he starts needling me, I also gotta be careful to keep a civil tongue in his conference room.

"Yaahhh," he said again. "Ugly word, spit. Ugly word, slave. Ugly word, soap. Or maybe its autos or cigarettes or breakfast food. I don't like peddling and I don't like cringing. And I don't like men who have to think, dream, and yes, by God, eat soap. I just don't like myself."

"You'll get over it," she said comfortably, wisely. "You just got a bad case of war nerves."

Even by trying, she couldn't have said a crueller thing.

"Yes," he said. "Things are tough all over."

He made a luncheon date and left.

"I'll bring some of my records," she called after him, "so you can hear how I sound over the air."

[CHAPTER IV]

"MISS HAMMER," VIC SAID AS HE CAME IN AT TEN ONE MORN-
ing, "I'm afraid you disapprove of my coming in so late."

"Oh no, Mr. Norman. It's just that—well, they start calling
around nine-thirty."

"They?" He hung his hat and coat in the closet. "Who are
they?"

"Well, this morning, both Miss Kennedy and Mr. Paul
Evans called. I'm not criticizing, but, well, I just don't know
what to say to them."

"You just tell them I'm not in."

"Gee, Mr. Norman," Miss Hammer sighed. "It's wonderful, the nonchalant way you take all this. A call from downtown! Why that used to be worse than a five alarm fire."

Miss Hammer was a sexless girl, at least she seemed that
way to Vic. She had lived in Fort Washington all her life,
with strict, church-going parents, and she was more like a girl
who had been brought up in the smalltown manner of twenty
years ago. She had a boy friend in the South Pacific and was
saving most of her sixty dollars a week for a nest egg. But already, at twenty-eight, she was wedded to business.

"Shall I get Mr. Paul Evans now?" she asked.

"Order me some coffee first."

"Oh, heavens," Miss Hammer rushed to the radio. "'Star-
light, Starbright' has been on four minutes already."

She tuned in the soap opera, and left to order coffee.

44

Vic listened and once again marveled at the dramatic taste of the American Housewife. Then the announcer came on with the new business about Love that Soap.

It was working like magic. The more you irritated them with repetitious commercials the more soap they bought. Business was good. The announcer reminded him of the hucksters who used to shout their vegetables in the streets of Fort Madison. Huckster—that was a good name for an advertising man. A high class huckster who had a station wagon instead of a pushcart.

He tuned the soap opera down and took the call from Paul Evans.

"Father wants to set up a meeting today. To discuss V-E Day problems. He thinks Germany might collapse any day now."

Two-thirty was fine with Vic.

"Incidentally," Paul said, "Father is very pleased with the way things are going. I thought you'd like to know."

Then Vic took the call from Regina Kennedy.

She was calling him Vic by this time.

"Hello, Regina," he said. "What's the crisis."

"No crisis, but Mr. Evans would like a meeting today at two-thirty."

"I know. V-E Day. Whatever that is."

"Who told you?"

"Paul."

"I wish Mr. Evans would trust one or the other of us." She was a little upset. "He always tells me to do the same things he tells Paul to do."

"In the soap business we call that check. And double check. See you at two-thirty. Good-bye, Regina."

"One more thing, Vic. I don't like to criticize until you've had a chance to give things a goose. But I still think that Perkins show is off the beam. Scriptwise, I mean."

"The Hooper rating is up. But I'll do what I can."

He hung up.

She was getting as bad as Allison, the Old Man's conditioned reflex!

He buzzed for Miss Hammer.

"You can play those Ogilvie records for me now," he said.

Miss Hammer said she thought Jean Ogilvie was simply sensational and she'd play them right away.

He listened to the records and decided the Old Man would never buy that kind of singer. Not loud enough. He made a note to call Jean for lunch tomorrow.

Then he went in to see Kimberly.

He had good news to report. "Mr. Evans is buying a special newspaper campaign to plug the line 'Love that Soap'. He thinks it's gone over on the radio so well, he wants to ride it."

Kimberly was overjoyed. "How much for the campaign?"

"An extra million two hundred thousand dollars, over and above the present budget."

"No?" Kim almost did handsprings on the Kirman rug. "Vic, you've really clicked downtown. One million two hundred thousand extra, eh? That's one hundred eighty seven thousand five hundred dollars net to the agency. And you did it. Vic, you should feel good. It'll show up in your bonus."

"That's my job, isn't it? To get the old man to spend money."

"Don't be so blasé. I bet he's happy. I mean the way the commercial took hold."

"He's up to his ass in diagrams that show how the sales curve is rising. You know, Kim, he lives only for that damned soap company."

"That's exactly right," Kim, like all people who had been psycho-analyzed, delighted in analyzing others. "He doesn't need any more money or social recognition. He's socially secure. He's also in bad health."

"It couldn't happen to a nicer guy," Vic said.

Kim looked around to see if the doors were closed. Kim was the world's greatest worrier. "I wonder if he really does have spies planted around here?" he said.

"He's getting old," Kim continued. "He has a family that

should mean something to him. You'd think he'd quit and take it easy. But he can't. He tried it once and he can't. Those radio shows and ads, that soap company—it's life to him."

"There but for the grace of God goes the Archbishop of Kimberly," Vic said.

Kim frowned and went into an elaborate rebuttal.

"You're wrong there, Vic. I'll never make the mistake Mr. Evans made. I won't let myself get that immersed in a job. The way I figure it, these three things are important to a man in this order: One, himself. Two, his family, and/or his women. And three, his job. Anybody who puts job first in his life is just a damn fool. And that's what the Old Man has done. He's trapped himself. He's let his job make him a neurotic."

"Look who's calling who neurotic."

Kimberly laughed. It pleased him to be thought neurotic. "Anyway, this million plus you grabbed for the newspaper campaign is great. By God, we still have a chance to be the top agency this year."

"Not how good, but how big," Vic said. He never had the slightest sense of elation over a coup, whether it involved big money, as this one did, or the success of a radio show. He had long ago learned to consider this an abnormality of his, as he knew that most men reacted to even minor business victories as to a shot of adrenalin.

When he returned to his own office, the entire Beautee radio production staff was waiting for a meeting he'd called.

He threw out a good morning at them, then went to the window and gazed down on Rockefeller Plaza. From the sixty-seventh floor, the crowd had grace and beauty; the skating rink was like a puppet ballet.

He idly pulled some loose bills out of his pocket. "It's pretty," he said. "The farther you get away from crowds the prettier they look. It's a good show. I feel like paying for it. How much are balcony seats?"

He threw the bills, a five and three ones, out of the window, but didn't watch them float down.

The group in the office looked a little frightened, not quite knowing what to make of a man who threw eight dollars out the window, just like that.

Vic sat down, put his feet on the desk and gave them a pep talk in reverse.

"I've noticed that everyone around here is too goddam sincere," he began. "What the hell, don't you characters enjoy your work?"

They all looked at him as if he needed a strait jacket.

"You're all so anxious to please Old Man Evans that you forget you're trying to produce radio shows. So what do you do? You make all the music sound like a bad record of Sousa's Band. You make nighttime comedy shows sound like Life Can Be Miserable. And those are just two examples."

The producer of their big musical show said, "I know it stinks, but that's what the Old Man wants."

"The Old Man wants a rating, above all. You can only corn it up so much and the people will refuse to listen. Then you're dead. No, Jack, you gotta satisfy yourself that it's good too. You gotta be a little more insincere about pleasing the Old Man."

"And get our throats cut," somebody else said.

Vic said sharply. "You won't get your throat cut. As far as he's concerned, I'm responsible. Not you. You're responsible to me. Not him. Get it."

He continued. "I been listening to all our shows for a couple of weeks now. And I want to tell you it's been quite a chore because I hate radio."

They all laughed and he said, "Go ahead, laugh. Radio makes me sick to my stomach. I never listen to radio on my own time. I take the position that if a thing is not worth doing at all, it's not worth doing well."

He then went through a critique of the shows one by one, pointing out where he thought they had sacrificed entertainment value to the Old Man's whims.

The radio people listened respectfully to him because he had built so many top rating shows in the past and they accepted what he had to say in good spirit although with an occasional argument.

"Now don't get me wrong," Vic finished. "I don't pretend to be a radio expert. Nobody is. But one thing I do know. You must put something in a show that makes people want to have you visit them next week and the week after. In a comedian that's a little thing called vocal distinction. Our boy Figaro Perkins is good not because he makes better jokes than some other goon—frankly his jokes stink. But there's something in his voice, a kind of distinction, that makes people want him to visit them every Thursday night. And so it goes. Just try to get those sounds out of your talent and you'll be all right. But don't be so damn sincere about it. That's murder."

He then arranged to have the writing staff on a soap opera replaced. "They're reading too many books—getting too cultured," he explained. "Find somebody else. Maybe Joan Wright. She stinks in the right direction."

He had won them over. It was no longer a question of pleasing the boss just because he was boss; they would do their best for him because they liked him and did not want to let him down.

"One more thing," he said, as they stood up to go. "You're all so damn busy. Take your time. Just because some stenographer has been promoted to pushing a button instead of listening for a buzzer doesn't mean everything has to be done in five minutes. When those Wall Street Inquisitors ask for something, take it easy. Plenty of time."

Jack Martin said, "One more question, Vic. Why did you throw that money out the window? All during this meeting I been trying to see your point, figure out your angle, but frankly I don't dig you."

Vic thought carefully, and then admitted:

"I didn't do it for any reason, Jack. I don't really know why I did it. It was just an impulse."

They were certain it had some deep meaning though.

"Forget it," he said, "it's only money."

One man stayed behind for a personal conference—an eager young assistant producer who had been hired as a favor to the star on the Beautee Mystery Show. The boy dissipated ten minutes describing a new idea for a radio show.

"It's never been done before," he finished, "And it's bound to get a twenty Hooperating." He was very eager. "At least a twenty."

Vic looked at the impressive folder describing the show. The boy had spent a lot of time working it out. It was an idea for a dramatic show, using life stories of old-time stars of stage and screen, with the stars cast for their own roles.

"Look, Artie," he finally said. "You're a hep guy—but I don't think you're hep to radio from the ad agency angle."

Artie's crest fell and he asked what Vic meant.

"This show," Vic handed him back his folder. "It could be a good show—it could also stink. It probably would stink. Who's going to write it?"

Artie said any good writer could do it.

"Try to find one," Vic said. "Most radio writers are semi-literate hacks and the few good ones are all tied up. If you were an agent trying to peddle this to me as a package, I wouldn't even listen until I knew who was writing it. Because it's a dramatic show, and writing is the most important thing, not casting. You haven't got a central character who's good enough to make the public forget how bad the material is."

Artie said he thought that what Vic said made a lot of sense. Yes sir, a lot of sense.

"But that's not my point. It's literally a waste of time to think about new show ideas in an ad agency. They pay you dough for different reasons—for helping to put on a well produced show every week, according to a strict formula. They pay me dough because I am supposed to know how to keep the sponsor happy with your work—also I'm supposed to have judgment good enough to throw away the hazardous radio ideas before trying to sell any radio idea.

"Now in radio, like in everything else, good ideas are a

dime a gross. I mean that. We could sit here and in one hour dream up twenty radio ideas. But no idea is any good unless it's first sold, and second properly executed. That goes for this one, too."

Artie looked miserable and said he was only trying to do something for the agency.

"Sure," Vic said. "I know it. And thanks." The phone rang. "Not in," he said. "Do you know how many new radio shows went on the networks the past two years? Don't guess. It's almost two hundred. Now somebody thought each one of those shows was a killer-diller, or it wouldn't have gone on. And do you know how many got over a ten Hooperating, which is, you'll admit, a fairly low rating. Don't guess again. The answer is four. It's fun to dream up ideas, Artie, but in radio it doesn't pay. Personally, I'd rather own Edgar Bergen's contract."

Artie said Vic had personally developed a lot of radio ideas.

Vic denied it. "I just wrote and produced more of the same old crap, using Doctor Norman's famous switch system. Right now of course, I wouldn't be caught dead writing or producing anything."

Artie asked for God's sakes, why?

"So I write a show? Or produce one? And I take it down to Old Man Evans, or any other sponsor. And he asks, in your judgment should I spend a million dollars a year on this show you created? See, Artie? Actually, I'd have no judgment. I wouldn't be in a position to criticize. In short, I wouldn't be an executive. More radio executives have lost their jobs trying to tell actors how to act, or trying to write, than for any other reason. See?

Artie saw.

"So my advice to you is, concentrate on putting the right kind of crap in the show you already work on. It ain't art but it's good radio. Then when you want to create shows, get out of the ad agency business and go into the radio package game."

Miss Hammer came in to tell him two people wanted to
see him, a talent agent named Greenberg with whom he had
made an appointment, and a Lieutenant Walters.

"Do I know a Lieutenant Walters?"

She said no, he wanted to talk to Mr. Norman about a job,
but that she would brush him off to personnel. He told her not
to do that.

"I feel guilty about those guys. Send him in and ask Greenberg to wait. Be seeing you, Artie."

Lieutenant Walters was thirty-one. A life insurance salesman when the war started. Two years of college. Also a purple
heart and a bronze star from Anzio beachhead.

"I just can't go back to selling life insurance," he said. "It's
not very exciting, And I just sort of figured that maybe I could
get started in radio."

Vic asked him what kind of radio work and he said, "Oh
anything. Radio appeals to me, that's all. Announcing, directing shows maybe. I did some dramatic work in school. Not
much, but some."

Vic said, "If you were younger and could risk one failure
I'd try to get you a job flunkying for some station or network.
That's all you can do at first, flunky. But you can't afford to
spend five years doing that, and especially so when your
chances of making good in radio are very meager. It's a tough
racket, everybody wants in it, and especially you guys who
have been turned ass-over-appetite by combat and don't want
to go back to dull, tasteless jobs. You can't afford to take a
chance on failing in radio at your age, Walters. You're thirty-
one."

The soldier looked disappointed and ill at ease.

"You say you're restless. Got a wife or children?"

"No. Thank God."

"What did you do in the army? I see you're with the Engi-
neers."

"Construction work, moving up supplies, the usual stuff."

"Like it?"

"It was okay."

"Suppose you could get a job with a big construction company? Suppose you specified work abroad after the war—China, Europe, South America. The kind of thing that keeps a man on the move."

Walters said he'd like it all right, but he couldn't wait that long for a job.

"Maybe you wouldn't have to," Vic said. "I know a man in that business. Let me scout around for you and see if you can get started with a good outfit now, and train yourself for a bigger thing when construction starts up again."

Walters said that would be swell. He hadn't thought of himself as a construction guy, but actually he knew more about it than anything else.

"That's just one reason for keeping in it," Vic said. "You also got to be damned sure you like it. A man has to feel like somebody. He has to be functional and get a kick out of his work or it won't mean a damn thing to him. Right now, radio seems glamorous and wonderful to you, but maybe that's just because you don't know anything about it. Maybe if you knew something about it you wouldn't want it."

Walters got up to leave after Vic took his name and address.

"I'm already excited about the idea," he told Vic. "I'd love to spend the next few years knocking around the world building things. I guess I am kinda restless. I got to tone myself down a little, I guess."

"Why?" Vic asked critically. "I don't believe in a guy curbing his restlessness. I think it's a good feeling to have and I think a man should exploit it."

A lot of them coming back wanted radio, or advertising, or the theatre—anything exciting—but few of them had the talent or the time to develop the skills and it was a sad thing usually to talk them out of it. But this time, Vic felt good because he was sure he had done a sound thing for this lieutenant.

Then Greenberg came in and said, "Vic, I think I got a new package Mr. Evans will go crazy for."

"What is it?"

"An entirely new quiz show—a show that's got class and well, everything. It's bound to get a twenty rating in a good spot."

Vic said, "This is going to be the second twenty rating show I've turned down today." He had the audition record played. When it was finished he said, "I think it's absolutely unsensational." Greenberg misunderstood him and was happy, then understood him and was unhappy. "You're making a big mistake, Vic. Mr. Evans will be crazy for this one. What about it don't you like?"

"I honestly don't know," Vic said. "I either feel good about a show or I feel bad. I don't know enough about radio to tell you why. I only know I feel bad about this one."

Miss Hammer came in and helped him get the agent out of his office.

She also brought in a big pile of mail. Vic looked at it distastefully.

"Miss Hammer," he said, "today I'm starting a new system. I don't want to see any more mail."

"You have to read the mail," she protested. "Some of it has to be answered."

"That's my new system. *You* have to read it and answer it too. I don't like to read mail or dictate letters."

She was properly flattered by the new responsibility and reminded him of his luncheon date.

"But I will have to show you Mr. Evans' memos."

"I can't wait," Vic said.

"Before you leave, will you sign these, Mr. Norman?"

"I wish you'd call me Vic, so it would give me an excuse to call you Louise. I always think you're talking to my father, when you say Mr. Norman."

"He must have been some character, too, the way you always quote him."

"He was. You know, I was seventeen when I left home, and I guess my mother must have asked him to put me wise to some of the facts of life on my last night at home. So he comes into my bedroom, clears his throat and says, 'Vic, your mother thinks I should tell you some of the things I found out when I started my war against the world.' Well, Louise, he thought and thought and I was beginning to figure that the poor old guy had never really found out anything about life worth telling me when he finally said, 'Well, Vic, all I can say is, beware of redheaded women who wear black underwear!' I discovered later that it was the best advice anyone ever gave me."

Louise blushed and said, "What did he do, your father?"

"Why he was an old colored rabbi down in Atlanta, Georgia, and he used to fight the forces of intolerance. He always said Irishmen, Jews and Frenchmen were every bit as good as Negroes and Englishmen."

Louise Hammer thought that was just awful and she knew he was just making it up to shock her.

She handed him his pen and said, "You'll be late for lunch. Now sign these, Vic, please."

He did not look at them. "Give me a fast briefing."

"It's a petition to George Blaine's, Mr. Blaine's, draft board. He's been called, you know."

"So what? Many are called. Many are chosen."

"Well, you don't want him to be drafted, do you? It would seriously weaken the account. He's our top commercial writer."

"Too many George Blaines would seriously weaken the country," Vic said.

He looked at the papers. They explained to the draft board that Mr. George Blaine was in an essential occupation, radio, and that it would seriously impair this great purveyor of national morale if he were yanked into the army.

"It's his second call," she said. "He got out of the first one."

He signed the petition and said, "Whom is criticizing who? So he wants to stay out of the army. So we'll help him do it. Can't let poor Mr. Evans run short of commercial writers."

He had lunch at "21" with the head of a market research company. This man was convinced that the soap business was run in a most unintelligent manner and that the only way to

make it intelligent was to set up a consumer panel so you'd
know what was happening to the market.

Vic's interest in market research was almost zero so he pretended to listen but didn't.

"The panel will be two thousand families," the man explained. "An exact cross section of the U. S. Census. And exactly what happens to every ounce of soap in those two thousand homes will be carefully charted. We'll know the brands
they buy, and how often they switch. Now I appreciate that
Mr. Evans runs his business by hunch. And his hunches must
be pretty good. But once you really know the soap habits of
people you can—"

"Say," Vic interrupted, "excuse me, but I've got a great
research idea."

"Now you're talking," the market research man said heartily. "What?"

"Let's do consumer research on sex habits. We'll find out
how often married people have sex relations inside and out
of the family. We'll find out whether blondes are more
promiscuous than brunettes. We'll know how long the average
service wife stays true to her husband. It should be a very
comprehensive survey, broken down by age groups, and of
course all three sexes."

"You couldn't compile stable data on the subject," the research man objected. "How would you determine the mis-
representation curve? And besides, who would want it?"

"It'd be a hell of a lot more interesting than a lot of figures
about soap," Vic said.

He left the fellow to make his two-thirty date with Evans.
You couldn't keep Evans waiting, but of course he could keep
you waiting.

He waited at Regina's desk, in that sea of desks. She was
just back from lunch herself and was dabbing Beautee toilet
water on her ears.

"Well, what do you think of us, now that you've been
around a while?" Regina wanted to know.

"Well," said Vic, "you're the first client I ever had any desire to sleep with."

She laughed, "I meant Mr. Evans, really."

"He's quite a character. From what little I've seen of him, I like him. He's a great showman, too."

"He's really a great genius. I've worked for a lot of people, the ten years I've been in this business." (Nine of which, thought Vic, had been as a typist.) She rattled on, "But he's the most inspiring man, he really is. Such simplicity, such great simplicity. It's the best education anyone could have just being around him."

Regina was a great believer not only in education, but also in charm. She used both as much as possible on the Old Man.

Paul Evans came over and sat with them. He reported that his father was now back from lunch and would see them shortly.

Paul was the heir apparent, but was a disappointment to the Old Man because he had no sense of showmanship or any feeling for radio or advertising. In the Old Man's opinion, you hired people to make soap and do the other necessary work—it was up to the president to promote and sell it properly.

Paul could have been very competent in the manufacturing end, and he was a fish out of water in advertising. But his father was going to make him an advertising genius or know the reason why.

"Have you mapped out a sales trip yet, Mr. Norman?" he asked. Vic realized Paul was the opposite of the Old Man, even to the point of being deliberately opposite. He dressed conservatively, as if he were making a physical effort to counteract the Old Man's straw hat and bandanna handkerchief. He wore glasses and was nondescript in a sort of high class Harvard Club way.

"Miss Hammer keeps harping about a sales trip," Vic said. "But I still don't know what she means."

"It's policy," Paul explained, "for all the advertising people to take periodic trips with our salesmen. To get the feel of the actual sales problems, you see."

"I see."

"Then you write a paper for us, giving any ideas you might have gained from the trip."

Regina explained that now, in wartime, the salesmen really didn't have much to sell. That was taken care of through jobbers. So not having much to sell, Mr. Evans had conceived The Movie.

"What movie?" Vic asked.

Even Paul was shocked.

"You mean to say the agency hasn't told you about The Movie?"

"I told you they needed to be goosed," Regina said.

"Why the salesman just goes into a store and puts on a show for the customers. You know, our radio stars plus our selling story. You must see it."

"Last year, our salesmen showed it to nine million consumers," Regina said. "And it repeats our slogan fifty-nine times."

A harsh and strident buzzer sounded. Paul and Regina jumped as if goosed. Simultaneously Allison rushed up.

"Hurry now, everyone," he said. "We can't keep Mr. Evans waiting."

They filed nervously into his office.

It was always there, the feeling of fear. It hung in the air in the office of Evan Llewelyn Evans. He was reading a document and never looked up. They waited and watched. He put the paper down and they all leaned forward. He picked it up again and they settled back. Finally he said, "It's too damn complicated. Get Brown to boil it down to one page, Allison, then I'll study it. Bureaucrats, ruining the country!" It was almost a snarl. He wiped his face with the handkerchief from his sleeve. "What's the topic, Allison?"

"V-E Day, sir." Allison never sat down in the Evans presence. He had a fixed battle station back and to the left of the Old Man's chair. "Victory in Europe, you know. The other one is going to be called V-J Day!"

"V-E Day. Right. Well, Mr. Forman." By now, Vic was sure his mispronunciation of names was deliberate. "I'm not blaming you personally, because you're new on the account and got to get acclimated. But what in hell is the agency doing that they haven't brought me a plan for V-E Day?"

Vic thought it best not to answer. He just looked interested and Mr. Evans pursued the thought.

"One of these days this fella Eisenhower is going to say the Germans have surrendered and all hell's going to break loose on the radio. But does anyone try to figure out how we're going to handle our five shows during that period? No. I have to figure it all myself. I say, let's chin-chin. Let's spin the compass and find out where north is. Then let's get on the beam. Right?"

He waited for the echo to bounce back at him. He looked steadily at Vic, who returned the glance, but who would not bring himself to share in the vigorous chorus that repeated the word. "RIGHT." Then the Old Man's eyes focused again on the mahogany desk top and he leaned forward into the business at hand.

"I guess you weren't with us when I planned the invasion problem. You know, Normandy. What day did they call that one, Miss Kennedy?"

Miss Kennedy explained that it was D-Day and that Mr. Evans' ideas had won them immeasurable good-will from their consumers.

But Mr. Evans said that was all water over the dam . . . no sense in looking backward. The problem now is V-E Day.

"Now take our music show—we'll play nothing but fast marches—and we'll play 'Happy Days are Here Again' four times. Repetition—that's the stuff." He paused. "No we can't do that, dammit. This maniac Roosevelt ruined the song."

Vic said the OWI position on V-E Day was that the war with Japan must go on—and they urged sponsors not to celebrate too much.

"Bunch of damned bureaucrats. They can't tell me how to run my shows," was all the Old Man had to say on that score.

Regina asked Vic if he could get any generals, and if not how about a few winners of the Medal of Honor.

"We could spot them around on all five shows," she explained.

But Mr. Evans wouldn't buy the generals or the heroes, either, "unless it was MacArthur or Eisenhower. And they're both busy. Besides, those fellows are always after you to cut out commercials." And he'd be damned if he'd cut out one second of commercial. "Not even for the Second Coming," he said. "If the networks want the time let 'em take it and pay for it."

"Talent, too," Paul said.

"Let's take it show by show," Vic suggested. So they worked all afternoon and by five p.m. Beautee soap had V-E Day all planned. The rest was up to Eisenhower.

"I'd still like to shortwave the Paris Canteen for the Tuesday night show," Regina kept insisting. But Mr. Evans couldn't see why the French should interfere with his radio shows. "That fellow DeGaulle," he snorted. He never did understand that it would be American soldiers in the Paris Canteen.

Allison then shooed Regina and Paul out of the office, so that Mr. Evans could have a confidential chat with Vic.

He wanted to know what Vic thought of his people. Vic said so far, very good.

"They're not really any damn good at all, but my good men have been drafted. My son Paul can't tell the difference between a slogan and a prayer. And that Miss Kennedy is no bigger than a six thousand dollar a year clerk. Oh well," he took off his straw hat and patted his bald head. "It only means I got to do all the thinking myself."

He then asked Vic about some of Vic's people on the account.

One of them, a commercial writer named Blaine, impressed him. "What do you pay him?"

Vic said ten thousand and the Old Man thought it over.

"I'd raise him to twelve five. Somehow or other I always think of people in the ten thousand bracket and under like they were animals. Buy 'em, sell 'em, fire 'em. Better get Blaine out of that class. He's a good man."

Vic whipped out his notebook and wrote "Blaine".

The Old Man again removed his hat, wiped the sweatband with the handkerchief in his sleeve and settled back. He fixed his intense blue eyes on Vic.

"Mr. Norman, people think what little success I enjoy is due to whatever talent I may possess for making the cash register ring—sales and advertising wise. But most of them overlook an equally important part of my philosophy of how to run a business. By that I refer to a single word 'Organization'. I pride myself in having built an organization that's trained to do things right—and by right, I mean just the way I want it. I don't condone and won't stand for mistakes."

He paused to let silence and slow time work on Vic, who thought, well, he's started. He's trying to terrify me. I wonder what mistake he's talking about. Vic sat there, looking straight into the Old Man's eyes, and waited.

"Miss Kennedy has brought to my attention a mistake that occurred on the Mystery Show last week. I believe you reported it to her."

"Yes, sir," Vic said.

"She tells me that a change in the commercial which should have been teletyped to Hollywood the day of the show was through some error in your office not teletyped and as a result did not appear on the show."

"That's correct." Evans was referring to a sentence which originally read: "*Remember folks, Beautee Soap has not sacrificed one-millionth of one percent of it's pre-war quality. What other wartime product can make that statement?*" On the day of the broadcast it had been decided to add the one word "fine" to the first sentence, so that it would read: "*fine pre-war quality.*"

"You understand, Mr. Norman," the gleam in the Old

Man's eyes was baleful now, "that I hold you personally responsible for each and every aspect of the account."

"I understand."

"I believe you told Miss Kennedy that the change had been typed by your secretary, given to the teletypist who put it on the machine, but that for some reason of carelessness the slip of paper fell behind the machine and as a result was never sent to Hollywood."

"That's correct, sir."

"I consider that a major error on your part, Mr. Norman."

Vic decided to be sincere about it. "I do too," he said. "Naturally it's my responsibility and I accept it. But once done I can only say that I have made every effort to see that such an error cannot happen again."

Evans leaned forward, planted his elbows on the desk. "Did you fire the teletypist, Mr. Norman?"

"No, sir. I did not."

"Then fire her. If you're ever going to have a trustworthy organization up there, you have to set the example. Fire her."

So this was stage two in the Indoctrination of an Account Executive. It neither frightened nor angered Vic. He knew Kimberly would have given Evans the old Yes Sir. But it was the accumulation of such things that had thrown Kim into permanent shock around the Old Man. So Vic said:

"She's our best teletypist. I'm sure you know that in these times, they're hard to find. I don't think I could replace her with one half as good."

"Fire her, Mr. Norman. She made a mistake. She should pay for it."

"I should pay for it, sir. It's my responsibility. You said that."

"What's her name? I'll call Kimberly. He'll fire her."

Vic gave his reply a well-timed pause.

"I don't think I'll tell you, Mr. Evans."

The Old Man sat and glowered. He was pink and his jowls trembled. A long time passed in silence. Then he said, very quietly, "Mr. Norman, no doubt you have good reasons for treating me in this cavalier fashion. I choose to overlook them at this time. But I can only say to you that if another mistake of any kind occurs anywhere in your organization then I shall be forced to recommend to Mr. Kimberly that you be removed from the account."

With no hesitation and showing no more anger or concern, Evans picked up a telegram from his desk. He seemed to have completely forgotten the incident.

"The second and final subject which I have to discuss with you concerns the success of my campaign on 'Love that Soap'. Listen. . . ."

He read a wire from the manager of the western division:

QUOTE LOVE THAT SOAP UNQUOTE RUNNING US OUT OF STOCK. THANKS A MILLION BARS FOR THE LATEST OF MR. EVANS SENSATIONAL SELLING IDEAS. IT'S RIGHT OUT OF THE TOP DRAWER.

"You see," he said, "we followed the formula. We charted our course, we found out where we were going. Then once we knew where we were going we gave it the works. Already, they tell me, eighty-three million Americans know that Love that Soap refers to Beautee soap. Little children say it in the streets. Radio comedians on other sponsors' shows make jokes about it every night in the week. Free advertising, that's what the damn fools are giving us, free advertising."

He wiped his forehead and his neck again. He grinned impishly at Vic.

"You know," he said, "that's the kick in this business— knocking 'em dead with a great powerful, rhythmic sales idea. By God, I get a real thrill out of selling like that. No premiums, no bonuses, no kowtowing to salesmen or dealers or customers—just knocking, 'em dead and asking no favors. But even the best idea won't work unless you repeat it again and again and still again. My stockholders should thank God our competitors have never figured that one out yet."

No question about it, the man was a born salesman. That

was his life and his wife and his children as well as his job. And here I am, Vic thought, a synthetic salesman, supposed to tell him how to sell.

The talk then shifted to business in general and Vic said he'd be glad to see the day when you could measure advertising results by sales, as well as by Hooperatings.

That thought made Mr. Evans sad.

"If it ever does us any good," he said. "These bureaucrats have got us all by the throat. It's like this," he drew doodles on a pad. "They take away your incentive to make money with ridiculous income taxes. Then along comes the OPA and puts a ceiling on my finished product, but not on my manufacturing costs which keep going up. So they limit and damn near eliminate my profit. But is that enough? Not for those bureaucrats. Next the WPB comes along and won't let me use but so much paper. If I can't package, I can't ship. So in addition to cutting out my profit and yours, they cut my volume. So what's the use of fighting? I can't make any more soap, and they wouldn't let me make any more money if I could."

Vic said he was sure that was only a wartime measure, and Mr. Evans shook a warning finger at him. "It's a trend," he said. "A bureaucrat trend." He paused, untied his red bandanna and mopped his face again. "But we'll fight back, by God. And how will we fight? By making every advertising penny count double. They may lick us, but we'll keep selling our heads off until they do. We'll make it . . ."

He paused in the midst of lighting a cigarette. Held the match to the box of matches sticking out of the ashtray. They flared up in a blaze of sulphur and phosphorus.

"We'll make it hot for them," he said. "See what I mean?"

[CHAPTER V]

LIVING IN A HOTEL UPSET VIC. WHY, HE DID NOT KNOW, UNLESS it was the hotel look which rooms even in expensive hotels have. So he went through the arduous wartime process of renting an apartment, luckily finding one in Sutton Place South.

Saturday morning he called Jean Ogilvie. "I'm buying furniture for my new place," he explained, "and I need company."

Jean looked very beautiful and it gave him a bang to walk along Fifty-Seventh Street with her. He decided he really was very fond of her that morning. He liked the overall effect of her egocentric chatter, although he seldom listened to what she said. "You know what you are," he said, "to me you're just a sound effect—a sound effect with red hair and one breast lower than the other."

As they went from one antique shop to another, looking for furniture, she was throwing her red hair around and going on at a fast rate.

"I don't see what you see in antiques," she said. "Now if it were me, I'd put a beautiful white rug on the living room floor, and get some of those mad curved sofas and things, all modern and bright with big mirrors."

"I can see we'll never be married," he said. "I'd cut my throat before I'd live in one of those decorator salons."

"And the prices you pay. Five hundred dollars for that old beat-up sofa. Who is this character Sheraton anyway? And

eight hundred dollars for a wormy old foyer table. I don't
see why you want to live in an apartment. You'll need a maid.
And all that bother."

Vic did not actually know why he was doing it either.
He felt so homeless, so rootless, living in the hotel, he halfway
thought that he might have a more settled feeling if he established a home. Besides, he liked furniture, and he knew something about it, so there was satisfaction in fixing up his own
place.

"Let's go upstairs," he turned in at a building. "I heard
they had some Provincial bedroom furniture here."

"I thought men didn't care what their furniture was," Jean
complained. "I thought women were the only ones that cared.
My feet are killing me and I got to practise my new routine."

He finally wore her out on Third Avenue.

"If you buy that awful Chinese lamp, I'll simply go mad,"
she said. "Two hundred dollars, too. You're a mad character,
darling; you spend money like a drunken advertising man."

Vic said he gave up. "I'll buy my own damned furniture
after this. Come on, let's get a drink."

"The only reason is because all these junk shops are closing. Admit that, darling."

They sat in a bar and he heard about her new routine.
"I had to do something, Vic. That comedian who's on before
me tells such dirty jokes he just ruins my act. I'd have to tear
off one of my legs to get a yak, after him."

She was always stroking herself, patting her breasts, feeling
her legs, straightening her dress with long sweeping movements of her hands.

"When you get your apartment finished, are you going to
have a housewarming?"

"Sure. You're the only one I'm going to invite, though."

Jean sipped at her martini thoughtfully. "Seems to me
you're not very mad about me any more."

"Why?"

"Well, for one thing, you haven't asked me to go to bed
since that night you were drunk."

"I only ask a girl once. Then to hell with her, I always say."

Jean pouted. "I don't want you to say to hell with me, darling."

"I'm afraid of you, to be honest."

"Afraid? Silly. Of what?"

"You make noises like you want to get married. I'd love to sleep with you, except I'm afraid you'll want to get married."

"Is that bad? So what if I do?"

"I'm too old to get married," Vic said. "Too set in my ways."

"You're not either. You'd make a wonderful husband."

"I make a wonderful bedmate, but I'd be a lousy husband."

Jean put her hand on his arm. "Oh Vic, you can have me. You know that. But you can't blame me for wanting you. Permanently. You are a very attractive man, you know."

"I just wanted you to understand," he said carefully. "I don't want you to feel that I'm giving you the old romantic one-two or anything. It isn't very important anyway. To hell with it."

"Some day, Vic." Her eyes filled with tears and made the mascara run a little. "Some day I hope you find something that is important. I really do, darling. I really do."

"I wish I had some dough," Vic said.

"I always think of you with money running out of your ears."

"I mean heavy dough. The only time I ever get an impulse to make lots of money is when I see something like that El Greco at Korner's. God, I'd like to have it for my apartment. That's when I curse my unbusinesslike qualities."

"Don't worry, darling." She patted him on the cheek. "You poor thing. In another year you'll own that advertising agency and you can pay forty thousand dollars for your old El Rancho Grande."

"Like hell I will. Not even for an El Greco. If Kimberly were to walk in tomorrow and say, Vic, it's all yours, I'd tell him to get lost. I wouldn't saddle myself with characters like Evans for all the art in the Louvre." He was thoughtful for a second. "It's a funny thing how extraneous little gimmicks affect a man's life. When I was young, just out of college, I started newspaper reporting. And I saw there was no money and little success in it so I got into this racket. It didn't take me long to find out I was allergic to business—I can't tolerate the whole principle of making products and then going through all the motions necessary to make money from them. Even so, I learned what it took to make money. So I said, 'Ten years of it and I'll have enough to tell them all to go screw.' But you know, just when I started making that kind of money, the government started taking it back. I'm not the type to gripe about income taxes, but it is a funny thing how they have doomed me to work or steal or hustle all the rest of my life. And I don't like it. Not one teentsie-weentsie goddamned bit."

Of course Jean had stopped listening to him way back. "I heard that horrible Steele dame on the Figaro Perkins show. Darling, she stinks. But clear out to Dubuque she stinks. What a vibrato. Ughhh."

"Her Hooper has fallen too," Vic said.

Jean said she'd heard about Hooper ratings ever since she'd auditioned for a kid trio on Station WRIX Brooklyn, but she'd never actually understood what it meant. So Vic explained.

"Nothing matters in commercial radio but a Hooper, or Crossley rating, whichever one you happen to read. All success is measured by them; most jobs are lost on account of them. The ratings are figured like this. Research people in all the big cities call telephone numbers, picked at random out of the local phone book. When somebody answers, they say 'Is your radio tuned in?' If the answer is yes, they ask what station and what program and what product is advertised."

"Nobody ever called me," Jean said. "I think it's a fake."

"They only have to call a few thousand people to get a fairly accurate percentage of the whole country, just like a presidential poll. Anyway, if eleven percent of the people answering their phones say they're turned to the local station

that's broadcasting the Beautee soap show, starring Figaro
Perkins, that means we get an eleven Hooperating."

"Is that all?" Jean was brushing up her lips and admiring
herself in a pocket mirror. "Sounds like a lot of fuss over
nothing."

"Well, if the research people who figure out things are correct, then an eleven rating means eleven million people are
listening to your show—a million people for each Hooper
point. On some shows, like Fibber McGee and Molly, as many
as forty million people listen. That's why radio can never be
an adult art form—too damn many people to please."

"Vic darling," Jean said dreamily, having stopped listening
again. "When are you going to get me a job on the radio?"

Vic picked up the change from the tray and held her coat.
"We could use a singer on that Perkins show. One who could
stooge for Figaro as well."

"What would it pay?"

"Oh, five hundred or so a week to start, then a raise every
twenty-six weeks if we decided to keep your options. A thousand, then fifteen hundred and so on up to twenty-five hundred dollars a week over a five-year period."

"And I work in that upholstered sewer every night for a
stinking two-fifty! Darling, can't you please get this weird
character Evans to listen to me? Pretty please?"

"He wouldn't buy you if he heard you. He likes loud gutsy
singers, not croony little crotch singers like you. I guess he's
a little deaf."

"For that kind of money I could sing loud, louder than
anybody."

They were walking towards Jean's hotel in Sixty-first
Street. Vic chuckled. "You gave me an idea. I should be a
talent agent, God help me. Tonight, I'll telephone Wiley
Warren and tell him to put just that in his column."

"Just what?"

Vic delivered the item in Wiley Warren's worst style:
"Titian, patrician Jean Ogilvie, Casablanca moaner, flung out

a chesty challenge today. I, says the well-ogled Ogilvie, can sing louder than anybody. Evan Llewelyn Evans take notice!"

"Yes, but I can't sing loud. It's not my style. Nobody sings loud anymore."

"You can take your style and you know what. Leave this to me. It's a plot but I won't tell you the ending."

"You sly fox of a darling," Jean kissed him. They were in front of her hotel. "You don't miss many bets, do you."

"So far, I've missed you, honey. But I'll keep trying."

"You won't have to try very hard. You know that, darling."

"Say when."

"Soon. Tonight." She pressed her hand hard against his cheek. "Let's go to bed tonight, darling."

"Don't rush me," Vic said. "If I went to bed tonight with you, I'd have to disappoint a friend. But you've got a sound proposition there, very sound. I just think I'll disappoint that friend anyway."

Jean kissed him again. "I've got to run, darling. I'm late for the dinner show already. God, it'll be wonderful just to work once a week. It'll give us lots of time, darling."

The doorman found him a cab, earned his quarter, and Vic rode back to the Waldorf.

There was a call from Kimberly. Urgent.

He dialed the number. A woman answered. She called Kim.

"Vic?" Kimberly sounded a little drunk. "I hope I didn't disturb you."

Vic said no, of course not.

"I wonder if you'd like to talk a little business, Vic. Not much business, just a little. And in case you don't want to talk any business then I say to hell with it. It wouldn't disturb you to have a couple of ladies present, would it?"

Vic said no, in fact he'd like that.

"As a matter of fact, Vic, one of 'em's yours. All yours. Bought and paid for."

Vic got the address and went over.

He was somewhat surprised to find Kim with a couple of

whores. Not that he objected, but he could never understand the necessity for a man to use them, amateurs being a dime a dozen these days.

Kimberly was quite drunk, in his shirtsleeves, lying on a couch in the living room.

"Vic," he said morosely, "I hope you're not shocked and disgusted."

"Don't be silly."

The girls, like the apartment, were neat, well-kept but not high class. One was named Gladys, the other Bobby.

Gladys brought Vic a drink and sat on his lap.

"Honey," she said, "any friend of Kim's is a friend of mine."

"Don't be shocked and disgusted, Vic," Kim pleaded. "I'm just tired. Tired and a little drunk."

"He's a sex maniac," Bobby said.

She was the older girl. Kim said she was Miss Oklahoma City of 1925.

"1927," she corrected. "I'm not that old. And it wasn't Oklahoma City."

"And I object to being called a sex maniac. My psychiatrist says satyriasis is not mania."

Gladys thought he was awfully cute when he used those big words.

"Vic is my business associate," Kim said dreamily. "In fact, he's next to me in the New York office. Anything Old Vic wants is on the expense account. Anything at all. And don't you worry, Vic. These are good healthy fifty dollar whores, compliments of K and M."

"Please do not use that vulgar word again in my presence," Gladys said.

"What vulgar word, fifty dollars?" Kimberly lay back on the couch. His eyes were closed.

"You know what word. It's so coarse." Gladys, to Vic's relief, got off his lap to put a cushion under Kim's head.

"Poor dear," she said.

But Kim had fallen asleep.

Bobby thought she had better be going. "Unless Vic . . . ?"

Vic said, "No, thanks very much. I think I'll just sit this one out, if you don't mind. I have an—er—appointment later. I'll let Kim sleep a few minutes while I finish my drink, then I'll wake him up and we'll go home."

Bobby said, "Good-bye, all." She left.

Gladys was a fairly pretty woman in her early thirties. She was given to all sorts of queer little refinements of speech.

"You sure you don't want to indulge in some frivolity?" she asked.

"No thanks. No offense. It's just that I'm very tired."

"Well, let's just sit here and have some nice conversation."

So they sat and had some nice conversation. She came from Brooklyn and had gone all the way through high school.

"Then I modeled. Brassieres. My breasts are very photogenic. They always cut my head off and put somebody else's head on though. But the breasts were mine."

She thought Kim was so wonderful. And such a gentleman. "You know, he's not like some of them. Disrobing all over the house and everything."

Vic asked her if she had a boy friend.

"Not in New York. I got a wonderful friend in Detroit though. He comes to see me every single time he comes to town. A real gentleman. You never hear a vulgar expression out of that one."

She pulled her robe around her and her eyes brightened.

"Someday he's going to buy me a shop. A dress shop. And not one of these lower priced shops either. I'm going to sell only the more expensive garments—sixty-nine-fifty, eighty-nine-fifty—you know, the best."

He asked her when she expected to go into the better dress business.

With great confidence, Gladys explained that right now, well, his taxes were so high he couldn't afford it. "And he's got a wife who's sick a lot and the doctor bills are simply awful." But after the war he was going to do it for sure.

"Gee, honey, I walk along Park and Madison looking for locations all the time. Shopkeepers think I'm crazy, always going in and asking how business is. I can't wait until I'm running my own place." She sighed and refilled his drink.

"You seem to be doing all right in your present business," Vic said. "Minute for minute you make more than I do."

"Yeah, but a girl gets to be forty and she's through. Me, I want a little business that earns money while I sleep. The last time my friend was in town he said maybe if there was enough money after the war, he'd also put me in my own apartment all expenses paid."

"How long have you known him?"

"Oh, he's been coming to see me for eight years now. He's old, over fifty, but he's a sweet gentleman, a real sweet gentleman. He was almost ready to do something about the shop in 1939, but conditions were bad, he said."

Kim stirred on the couch, and Vic awakened him. He was one of those men whom a twenty minute nap completely revives.

"Dammit Vic," he yawned and took a drink from Gladys. "I shouldn't do this. You'll probably think I'm an alcoholic to boot."

"I wish you'd stop thinking of me as the next to the last Puritan, Kim."

"I wonder what the Old Man would say if he knew we were lying around all day Saturday in a whorehouse?"

"Kim," Gladys said, very much hurt, "it's unlike a gentleman of your type to use that vulgar expression."

"Sorry, dear." He looked at his watch. "My God, ten o'clock! I haven't checked in for two hours. Maybe he's been calling me."

He started to dial. "I hope you don't mind my calling Mrs. Kimberly on your telephone, dear."

"Of course not, honey. Please do."

"Hello, Maggie lover," he said. "I'm with Vic Norman. We're still working. Is Kimmy all right? Good. Any calls?"

He sat up in bed and looked shocked. "He did? How long ago. Thanks, dear, I'm sorry I awakened you. I'll call him right away."

He nervously dialed another number. "The Old Man must be on the warpath. He's been trying to get me for an hour. Maggie's been calling all my clubs, saloons and joints. Was the show lousy tonight?"

"It's Saturday night, we don't have any shows," Vic said.

"Good." Into the phone he said, "Is Mr. Evans in? Mr. Kimberly is calling. . . . Hello, Mr. Evans, sir." There was real fright in Kimberly, so much so that Vic was shocked. It's only money, he thought. It's just a business association. How can fear be planted so deep . . . why would Evans go out of his way to inject fear into his satellites, and why should his satellites stand for it anyway? Was an apartment on Park Avenue and a country home in Connecticut worth it? How far can a man go just to have the price of a mink coat in his pocket? Kimberly had said once that Evans had him pretty well staked out. With platinum chains, by God. And yet this demanding old man, who carefully pressed every disadvantage, thought of himself as a protector of Kimberly's, as the one person who had done most for Kim, who had made Kim what he was today. Vic shivered a little. . . . There was a trap down in Wall Street . . . a trap filled with desks and slogans about courtesy and Beautee Soap . . . a trap set by an Old Man who did evil things to the men his money purchased . . . and the pitiful, stupid, ridiculous fact was: the evil did not stem from badness or lack of goodness, it was an evil that unconsciously and perhaps even accidentally had grown out of an honest desire to sell soap that would make the customers clean and sweet and beautiful, customers who in turn would make the salesmen of the soap rich and sleek and powerful. He'll try to plant fear in the pit of my stomach, too, thought Vic. He knows I don't give a damn now, that sharp, cool, crafty, conniving Old Man. I've got to examine his techniques, I've got to be on guard, or he'll get me the way he's got Kimberly and Brown and Allison and all the rest.

Then he thought, Jesus, I sound strictly from desperation, maybe he's started on me already and I don't know it. Watch your step Vic, old man, keep one eye on the ball, the other on the clock and forget about that El Greco. It's bad to want El Greco in a spot like this. Weights a man down.

Kimberly was talking into the phone. "My deepest apologies, sir, for not returning your call sooner but you left word to call back, regardless of the hour. . . . As a matter of fact, Mr. Evans, I've been working with Mr. Norman. . . . Discussing the over-all strategy of the Beautee company. He's here with me now. No, we didn't hear the Wondrous Theatre Tonight. Too busy to listen to the radio. Who? . . . Just a minute, I'll ask him."

He covered the mouthpiece and whispered, "Do you know a comedian named Buddy Hare? Evans said he heard him do a guest spot on the Wondrous Theatre tonight."

"Sure," Vic said. "He's a former burlesque ham. He's been doing comedy bits in B movies for several years."

Kim went back to the phone. "Yes indeed, Mr. Evans. Norman knows him well. . . . Oh, he did? Great! . . . Maybe he's just what we're looking for. . . . Just a minute, I'll put him on."

Evans said: "Norman, I just heard this chap Hare. Seems to me I have to do all the talent scouting for the company, but I'll pass that at this time. I think Hare is great. Sort of a Bob Hope and Jack Benny combined in one. Check?"

"That would make him pretty good," Vic said.

"Well, Norman, I think we ought to give the compass a whirl and see if this chap Hare is headed in our direction. North. I don't want you fellows to miss the last bus to Hoboken. See what I mean?"

"I'd suggest we slap an option on him right away, sir," Vic said. "I'll get a record of the Wondrous Show tonight and we'll study it at once, so by Monday we'll know whether or not we want to build a new show around him."

"Don't miss the bus to Hoboken, Norman. You sound like

a good operator and I might as well tell you I'm not interested in any other kind of operator. Now give me Kimberly."

Kimberly talked to Evans a while, mainly with Checks and Rights and On the Beams. Then he finished dressing.

Gladys said, "Was that Evan Llewelyn Evans?"

Kim was wary. "Why do you ask?"

"Oh nothing. I used to know him."

"Really? When? Where?"

"Oh, it was back when I started in this business. I was seventeen. I worked for Madge Minter when she had that beautiful place on Park Avenue. He used to come there. God, Madge had one big bedroom with a circular bed in it—twelve feet in diameter. It was beautiful."

"I understand he was quite a playboy in those days," Vic said.

"Playboy?" Gladys wouldn't quite call him that. "I don't ever talk about my own clients, but I guess I can talk about Madge's. He used to get roaring drunk and take over the joint. There'd be eight or ten girls there and he'd be alone in the place for three or four days. No other clients were permitted when he was there. Then when he was ready to leave he'd wreck the place. Pull down drapes, cut up the oil paintings, tear up the silk spreads, break the lamps—it was terrible."

"Sounds expensive," Kim said, interested but trying not to show it.

"He did it on an average of once every three or four months, Madge said, and Madge invariably sent him a bill for five thousand dollars. For damages. He always paid it without a word too. And, funny thing, with the money, he'd send a great big case of Beautee soap. He'd get awfully angry if there wasn't Beautee soap in every bathroom when he came to see her."

"Sounds like he was nuts," Vic said.

"No honey, he wasn't nuts. He's a very brilliant business-man. It's just that you don't understand men. They all have, well, different ways of expressing themselves sexually. If you think he was nuts, you should see the things some of them do. Even I can't figure some of them out."

"Please don't get personal," Kim said.

As they left, Gladys, who was real pleased to make Vic's acquaintance because it was always a pleasure to meet a real gentleman, said, "I don't think you're the type who requires any personal services, but if you ever do, here's my number."

Vic wrote it down out of courtesy. He threw the note in the street.

Walking crosstown, Kim said, "So she doesn't think you're the type. And I guess you're not."

Vic said nothing.

"Well, I'm not the type either, but what the hell can I do?"

The poor fellow was simply a fugitive from Old Man Evans and didn't know it. But Vic said, "You don't really have to, you know. You could have the best dames in town for free."

"No, I couldn't, Vic." Kim was sad at the thought of all he was missing. "I can't afford to get involved with any amateur who has less to lose than I have. Besides where would I take them? No, it'd cost me a hundred grand for the buyoff and half my clients if I chased women in public. I envy you."

"Well, don't tear up any brothels," Vic said.

"The Old Man thinks you should leave for the coast Monday to wrap up the Hare deal. Better start working on reservations."

"Check," said Vic. "I'll stay right on the beam. I'll either know where I'm going or I won't. I'll goose the goose that laid the bar of soap."

He said good night to Kimberly who asked him please not to be so bitter in public. "I got my problems too, you know, Vic."

Vic decided to say something that had been on his mind for days.

"Sometimes, Kim, I think you'd be better off to resign the Beautee account. I think you might even get more business out of the time you'd gain. And it's a cinch you'd be happier."

Kim said he wasn't ready for a drastic step like that. "The

Beautee account is a great influence on other clients," he explained. "I wouldn't want to jettison my ship only to find out I was really making it sink."

He said good night and then followed Vic into the lobby. "I forgot one thing. This Buddy Hare. Is he any good?"

"I thought it was about time for you to ask that question, Kim. And here's my answer. Put a big name to support him, buy a good time on NBC or CBS, and get the best writing money can buy and we might—might, I said—get a seven or eight peak winter rating."

"Oh God," Kimberly shook his head and looked more morose than ever. "Is he really that bad?"

"As I said, I thought it was about time for you to explore that subject. Dammit, Kim, do we ever tell this guy when his great ideas stink?"

Kim shook his head. "No. Flatly no. That's the hell of it. We've even got a formula for it. We always say it's a great idea."

"Doesn't he realize that a flop radio show costs close to one million dollars of his own dough? I mean before you can tell it's a flop. And does he take credit for his bad ideas as well as everybody else's good ones?"

"If the show flops, he'll blame us, don't worry. But he won't fire us. If we tell him his idea stinks now, he'll fire us and get some other goon to tell him how good he is."

Vic laughed. "It's only money. His money. So it looks like we're going to stink up the airwaves with the new Buddy Hare show. Sixty-eight laughs in thirty minutes . . . all sight gags."

"But don't underestimate the Old Boy's mind," Kim said. "In some ways he's a genius. I'm convinced of it."

"Me too. But not at building comedy radio shows."

"You see, Vic, that old man can get hold of one good idea out of maybe a hundred mediocre ones. And when he thinks it's good, he'll spend millions just harping on that one thing. All the other advertisers want you to change ideas every six months because they get tired of them. Mr. Evans knows the public is just beginning to be aware of ideas by then . . . so he keeps repeating, repeating, repeating them until everybody goes crazy. That's why Beautee soap is top dog."

"Love that soap," Vic said. "Good night, Kim, I got to stop by and lay a friend."

"Good night," Kim said. "I wish I could join you—what am I saying? I couldn't if I wanted to. Haven't the strength."

Vic sat in the lobby and read the papers until time to pick up Jean. He stayed out of his room as much as possible now, loving the thought of moving into his own home.

[CHAPTER VI]

VIC DID NOT GO DIRECTLY TO THE OFFICE ON MONDAY MORNING. Instead he went from Jean's hotel to inspect his new apartment in Sutton Place South.

Some of the furnishings had already been delivered, and he wandered through the paint-smelling rooms mentally decorating them.

He set up the fireplace brass and admired its shining colonial splendor. He decided to buy that Sheraton table in Kirby's, after all. It would look good with his jade lamp.

He shoved his desk from the foyer to the living room where he could better inspect its patina in the morning sunshine. He hoped the inlaid sandalwood would not pop out, as the desk was newly arrived from England and not yet acclimated to steam-heated apartments.

There was so much to do before you could really call this expensive rabbit warren a home. The thought of going to Hollywood right in the middle of the job made him indignant. He wanted to move in now; he wanted to be around objects and in surroundings that gave him pleasure to feel and to own; he wanted to be settled down. He needed a refuge from Radio City, Wall Street and El Morocco. He wanted a place to go to because he was tired of going places.

He left abruptly and went to the office. Kim's eager secretary flagged him as he passed her door. Mr. Kimberly had been looking all over for him, she breathlessly reported.

He said all right, and asked her to tell Miss Hammer to bring his coffee in to Mr. Kimberly's office, please.

Kimberly was thoughtfully gazing at two tiny medicine bottles, the only extraneous objects on his monumental desk.

"Sulfa or benzedrine, I don't know which I need most," he complained. "I feel rotten." He reached in his vest pocket for his thermometer and stuck it into his mouth.

Vic lay down on the sofa and closed his eyes during the enforced two minutes of silence.

"At least I won't have to listen to you talk to Maag in Hollywood as long as that thing's got your tongue," he said. "I feel lousy too. I'm hung-over, drained dry, beat up, and knocked out. I was up all night with a friend. A very healthy friend whom for security reasons I call the barracuda. It'll be a relief to go to Hollywood for a rest."

Miss Hammer tiptoed in with his bottle of coffee. She poured a cup for Kim too. Vic asked her to make an appointment with Jean Ogilvie, and she tiptoed out. She was gradually conditioning herself to Vic's unbusinesslike ways, although her expression made it plain that in her opinion no Account Executive should sprawl out on the President's sofa, even if nobody asked for her opinion.

"Only two-tenths of a degree," Kim reported, disappointed not to find it higher. "I guess you think I'm the world's worst hypochondriac, Vic."

"I'd like to make a helpful suggestion for the good of the entire organization," Vic answered dreamily. "I think this outfit needs a GU specialist on the staff. If you lack space, I'd be glad to donate a corner of my office for a prophylactic station. It'd be very convenient. What's the crisis this morning, boss?"

"I just wanted to talk with you before you left for the coast," Kim said. "What train you taking?"

"Obviously the Century. Is there any other train?"

"Then after our private meeting I'd appreciate it if you'd sit in on a conference with the Plans Board. You're supposed to be a member you know. We're discussing a new business solicitation."

"I'm not interested in new business," Vic said. He unfastened his tie and collar and settled back again with a sigh of comfort.

"I am," Kim said almost curtly. "God, how I'd like to get a two million dollar account!"

"So you could tell Old Man Evans what to do with his soap factory, bar by bar?"

Kim was stung. "There you go again! Needling me to throw twelve million dollars' worth of business out the window. You can't trade two for twelve in this business." He paused, decided to get off the defensive. "Incidentally, old chap, I don't mean to cavil, but what does cavalier mean?"

Vic laughed. "So the Old Man called you already. You going to fire that teletypist?"

"Would you let me?"

"Nope. Not unless you fired me too."

Kim waved it off. "That's what I thought. No, he'd cooled off. Spoke of you with guarded respect and only slight venom. He envies your ability and I think he admires your guts."

"Check! Right! I either know where I'm going. Or I don't. And frankly, I don't." Vic looked for a cigarette, couldn't find one; Kim offered him one and held a lighter for him. Then Kim went to the phone. "Miss Richards, I won't take any calls. Except you-know-who, of course." He paced around the office, trying to begin.

But when he spoke he still avoided his subject. "I only say this because I love you like a brother. When the Plans Board comes in, can't you sit up and strike a pose like an account executive for just a few minutes? I don't mind, you know that, but those stuffy pseudo-Yale bastards resent your easygoing, go-to-hell attitude."

"Tell em to go unprint themselves," Vic said. "You know my motto?"

"No. What?"

"Screw 'em all but six," Vic paused. "And save them for pallbearers."

"Now about this Hollywood trip." Kim sat at his desk and

Vic half sat up to face him. "You know Maag. He spends six months a year out there, managing all our coast radio shows. And six months back here conferring with clients on general matters as well as radio."

"Yes, you told me that once."

Kim said, "Do you know Maag well?"

"Only to say hello."

"What do you think of him?"

Vic said carefully, "He's a good front man. Sponsors ought to like him."

"He's a good man," Kim said. Then he came over and sat by Vic. "We're as different as night from day."

"He's got a breezy side, all right," Vic said.

Kim laughed in relief at the implied criticism. "I tell him, just as a joke, that the difference between him and me is that he likes horses and I like women."

"Oh well, some sponsors must like horses too, so it ought to work out all right."

"Sure it does," Kim took a deep breath and took the plunge. "I want you to consider this a top secret, Vic."

"You know I'm not a talker."

"Frankly, there's a certain amount of conflict between Maag and me."

"Hell, honey, that's the very essence of any partnership. And the history of what I call the ad agency game."

"I know. I know." Now that Kim had started it, he was impatient to get on with it. "A lot of the conflict is subconscious on Maag's part. But it's based on a very real condition, a condition of which we are both highly conscious. As you know, I've a certain interest in psychoanalysis and I'm hypersensitive to these hidden conflicts and desires in Maag's mind."

"Sure, sure," Vic said expansively. "You know as much about psychiatry as most psychotics."

"Seriously, I work under certain handicaps in New York. We have a twelve million dollar client whom I control lock, stock and barrel. But we also have twenty-one million a year that comes from smaller clients whom I don't control. It's only because I have no time to give them. Of course, I take other clients out for an occasional lunch or cocktail, but I mean working time. Well, our account executives on those accounts handle them all right, but when Maag comes back he spends all his time with them. As a result, he's the man at the top to them. He's the symbol of Kimberly and Maag."

"You mean the Old Man demands, and gets, one hundred and twelve percent of your time. Which leaves minus twelve for the rest of your business."

"Exactly." Kim started to pace again. He was beginning to seem older than forty-two. His face had a clouded look which was making a bid to stay there permanently, and he was flushed from too much drinking. "Now when I saw how beautifully you handled Old Man Evans as well as the business end of the operation, I became very, very happy. Heretofore, whenever I found a man who knew how to run the business, Evans didn't like him . . . and when I found a man whom Evans liked, he didn't know a goddam thing about running the business."

"Evans doesn't like me."

"He respects you. Maybe that's just as well. Anyway, we'll see. But you know, the Old Man has a strange fix on me. It's not affection, God knows, but there's something intuitive and instinctual—I sometimes worry a little about it because it seems almost like a homosexual jealousy."

"In four letters, shucks," Vic said. "You'd better stay away from those dreambook guys or one of these days you'll be adjusting a strait-jacket instead of yourself."

"The point is," Kim said, "he won't give me time to solicit new business. I can see how Maag might take advantage of my vulnerability."

"So Evans calls you up and uses words like cavalier. I'm sorry, Kim."

"It's no fault of yours," Kim protested. "You see, Evans can't find anything to criticize about your operation. You're too damn slick for that. So that means he can't come to me and say, 'Your man Norman is mishandling the account. Fix it up yourself.' But he's determined that I'm not going to get away from him. You know, Vic, everytime we get a new account here, he blows his top and hints that he's going to find a new agency. He doesn't want me to get so big I can afford to drop him. And whenever he finds out I'm in a meeting with some other clients he immediately invents an excuse to call me up and give me hell."

Vic poured another cup of coffee. "He's bad for you, Kim. Very bad."

"Take this morning. He called me at eight. Seems he can't get enough cardboard to package his soap because the War Production Board limits his allotment."

"Those bureaucrats," Vic quoted. "I wonder if the Beautee Soap Company will ever formally recognize the government of the United States of America?"

"So he demands that I go to Washington, with orders to stay there until I somehow talk the Board into raising his allotment."

"Are you an ad man or a factory manager?"

"He won't send a factory man, who can talk production intelligently to the WPB. He's making Brown go, to counsel me on legal matters, but I've got to finagle this thing through the Board. And for one reason, mind you. To prove to me that I'm still his little boy Kimmy, despite my title and other clients."

"You certainly are at his slightest beck and command."

"Daddy, what did you do during the war?" Kim mimicked a child with mocking disgust. "Oh, I made a heroic assault on the War Production Board for Beautee soap, son. Goddammit to hell. I'm ashamed of myself."

"It'd be a great business, if it wasn't for clients."

Kim drank a glass of water as if removing a bad taste. "Well, that's my problem, and you're the only one I'd trust with it." Miss Richards came in, handed Kim a note and he said severely, "Miss Richards, I told you I would only take calls from Mr. Evans. No! Let Smith handle it."

Vic said, "I think I understand your position. And Maag's. But how do I fit?"

"Well, I know now I can't escape the Old Man. But I think you can. Not right now, but as soon as we find a good man to replace you. Maybe in six months or even sooner. Mr. Evans will always trade in a rugged individualist for a cringing sycophant, regardless of merit. So I wanted to ask you if you'd protect my interests with other clients if as and when I can cut you loose from Wall Street."

"Thanks," Vic said. "I'm not flattered but I am touched by your confidence in me. It's a very serious problem you have."

Kim's native enthusiasm began to sparkle. "I can see an important future for you in this agency. You're so much bigger than Maag. He's not in the same league with you." He laughed and slapped his desk. "Give you a year as executive vice-president in charge of all New York Accounts except Beautee soap—and I'll bet ten to one you'll be ready for a full partnership."

This was, of course, the heavy dough, the El Greco kind of dough. Kim probed Vic's face for a reaction but found nothing there. It was a mask, as usual. His eyes were lifeless and uncommunicative, as usual. And when he answered, his voice was at its usual impassive flat level.

"Do you mean a full one-third or a full one-half, Kim?"

Kim shook his head and grinned with honest admiration. "You cold-blooded sonofabitch," he said. "You are a cold-blooded sonofabitch, you know. A genuine, gold-plated sonofabitch. Poor old Maag won't know what hit him. A full one-half, of course. Fifty-fifty."

"I'll have to think about it," Vic said. "Let's get this stupid Plans Board meeting the hell over with."

The top men of Kimberly and Maag came in and took their places. In an advertising agency, the management group is called a Plans Board. At K and M it consisted of the Copy Chief, the Art Director, the Radio Director, the Research Director, Kimberly, Maag when he was in town, and Vic.

One of the big automobile accounts was unhappy with its present agency and was secretly looking for a new one. Kimberly had been invited to make a solicitation, which was already complete, except for a decision on one element.

Maag had discovered that one of the high-rating radio shows could and would break its contract with its present sponsor. The comedian who owned the show was willing to option it to the agency and some of the board felt it should be offered to the Detroit company as a lure to get the account.

The old-line ad men of the group, who thought in terms of printed advertising and radio commercial messages, but who did not understand the entertainment end of radio, were suspicious of the idea.

The Copy Chief was spokesman for that point of view. "Goddammit," he said, "we're ad makers not talent agents. These people in Detroit need good salesmanship first and that's the basis on which we should talk to them. I think Kimberly and Maag should be sold on its merits as a business firm, not as a peddler of radio comedians. It's a cheap business and I don't want it."

The younger men disagreed, saying that radio was here to stay and the best damn commercials on the air were no good unless you had an audience to talk to.

Kim listened and pondered and finally asked Vic for his opinion. So far Vic had said nothing. He considered the Plans Board a reliable but dull group of men who, as a group, carefully examined all sides of every problem and then invariably thought things through to the wrong conclusion.

He did not answer Kim at once but walked over to the desk, where he found the ubiquitous ruler which, along with scissors is standard equipment for every advertising man.

As the Board watched curiously, he carefully took the measurements of the desk—width, length, depth—and painstakingly noted them down in his book. Then he said, "Kimberly, it's very plain to me what you need. You need to get your ashes hauled. This morning. If you went out and got your ashes hauled right now, it'd do wonders for you. I'll let you have one of my phone numbers!"

The Board looked annoyed and Kim laughed heartily.

"You guys talk like a medical society," Vic next said. "All this professional crap about highclass business versus lowclass business. Christ, we ought to face it. We're hustlers. We don't steal, probably because it's bad for business, but we sure as hell do everything else for clients. And I say if a radio show helps us get business who are we to stick up our noses?"

He put the ruler back into Kim's desk. "Kim, the very next raise you give me, I'm going to offer you thirty-five hundred dollars for this little number by Mr. Chippendale. I've always wanted to scratch up the top of a thirty-five-hundred-dollar desk with my feet."

Kim made the decision which supported Vic's view, and the meeting broke up after he instructed the Radio Director to negotiate an option for the radio show. Then Kimberly's buzzer again began buzzing and the president resumed his normal position as the Man with the Phone.

Back in his own office, Miss Hammer had big news for him.

"They got a cancellation and switched your reservation from that awful train to the Century."

"Natch," he said. "Louise, what's that letter doing on my desk? I told you that the mail was a personal matter between you and your typewriter."

"That one's personal all right," she said. "From someone named Marguerite. I thought—"

"You answer it," he said. "What's she want? Blackmail?"

"No, just to see you sometime." She sighed. "What a man. Other people stand in line for weeks just to get an upper berth. Overnight you demand compartments on the Century and the Chief. And then you just say 'Natch'."

"Natch," he said again. "But I distinctly specified Super Chief. Tomorrow's Tuesday, you know. Now you'll have to change the reservation out of Chicago."

That, said Louise Hammer hopelessly, was all, brother.

Vic explained that he was not the Chief type at all, that only talent agents and kept women rode the Chief. But if Miss Hammer wanted him to ride the Chief instead of the Super Chief, then he would do it, but only out of love for her, and just this once.

It was of course all in fun, but there was a kind of serious snobbery involved too. Now that airplanes were impossible to ride without priorities, it was again fashionable to ride the Twentieth Century Limited and the Santa Fe Chief or Super Chief for the trip between coasts. All the radio and movie people spent a lot of time, thought and bribe money finagling space on those deluxe trains.

One of the reasons was that you traveled with your own kind. Especially on the Super Chief, which was a sort of exclusive club for the Hollywood-New York commuters. It was one of the symbols of the entertainment fraternity, like gold Dunhill lighters, glossy women and hand-painted neckties.

"Were you able to reach Miss Ogilvie?" he asked.

"Oh, certainly. She's here now. Been waiting for fifteen minutes. She's very—uh—striking, isn't she?"

Jean made her entrance. She kissed him. "Darling," she said, "what a mad character you are. But really mad. You leave me at nine-thirty saying nothing, and two hours later I'm summoned by a secretary, just like I was an AFRA scale choir girl."

Vic said he'd been in a meeting all morning and to shut up, he had great plans for her.

"I don't know why I go to all this bother for you, anyway. You're such a horrible girl. Those clothes you wear, too. Awful."

It was a stunning black faille suit and her hair seemed brighter than usual. "You look, to invent a new word," he said, "sensational."

"It's so mysterious," she said. "I figured you must have a contract all ready for me to sign. A big, fat, juicy contract, done medium-rare and two inches thick. Ummmm."

He was phoning Jack Martin, the producer, and he told her to keep her panty girdle on until Jack came.

"I don't like to repeat myself, dear. So when Jack comes in you'll find out all about it."

He introduced Martin, and told them he was leaving for the coast. Jean was hurt.

"You could have told me, darling," she pouted. Jack looked interested. He'd wondered about Vic's taste in dames. Not bad.

He ignored it. "Jean wants to change her style. She thinks she can sing loud, and fast, so I'm going to spend some of my dough—charge it to me, not the agency—to make some audition records of her in the hopes that a certain hard-of-hearing old gentleman whose name I won't mention might go into a lather over her and sign her up for a radio program advertising a soap whose name I won't mention."

"How loud, coach?" Jack asked.

"The highest level you can get on a high fidelity record. Don't use acetates for this. Jean, you should sing as loud as you can without breaking. Also keep your voice as hard and clear as you can. Most of it will be a recording trick if you follow instructions."

"Darling," Jean said. "I'm not a coon-shouter. Even if Wiley Warren said I was. Incidentally, you're a wonderful press agent, darling."

"You are too a coon-shouter," Vic said. "Now I'd cut three songs, and use a ten piece band playing melody straight and in unison. Heavy rhythm, no modern licks. Very corny. Don't let the balance get below sixty-forty in favor of the voice but make the music sound loud too."

"I getcha, coach," Jack said, grinning at the scheme. Jean asked what three songs.

"Three old loud fast songs. I don't care what songs they are so long as you sing *Crazy Rhythm, Over There* and *Some of these Days.*"

"Christ, honey! I don't know them. That was before my time."

"Quiet. Make her sing on the beat, Jack. Now she sings a little after it. And every end note of every phrase must be a screamer. And fast, as fast as she can go. The faster the better. Jean, give Jack your keys on those three songs and he'll have Manny do the arrangements. Rehearse all you want to, but have a good loud fast record waiting for me the day I get back from Hollywood."

"I dig you, coach," Jack said. "Please give my secretary your phone number, Miss Ogilvie, and I'll handle everything."

"Jean," she corrected. He left and she said, "I'm scared, honey."

"It's normal to be afraid. Everybody is. That's what's wrong with people."

"I know you're trying to make the kind of record that Mr. Evans will buy. And I want a big radio job. But dammit, honey, I'm a singer. I got pride. And I got a style."

"Singers are like piccolo players. They all got their own style, too," he said. "And if you don't like one piccolo player there's always another one with a local 802 union card."

"But, Vic, the whole trend of modern singing is opposite to what you're doing to me, honey. Dinah, Ginny, Jo, Helen, Georgia—they all sing sweet and sexy and ad lib, the way the people like it."

"We're not doing this for the people," Vic reminded her. "We're doing it for one man. An old man with a checkbook. An old man whose tastes were formed back in 1910. Take it or leave it, Jean. But that's what I advise you to do. And I want you to know it's the first time I ever connived with talent against a sponsor."

"I appreciate that, Vic."

"It's only because I'm very fond of you, dear, and I want you to get in the big time. You've got a lot of wrong thoughts about what it takes to put a singer in the big time. You think it's just because she can sing."

"Well, that's part of it, isn't it?"

"Yeah, but far more important is how many people know what her name is. You could spend years crooning in night clubs and on sustaining radio shows, and nobody would ever know your name. But a few weeks out in Hollywood on the Figaro Perkins show, with all the publicity build-up the Old Man will give you, plus your own press agent, and each week twenty-five million people will know your name. You'll be a personality."

"Yeah," she gloomed, "and all twenty-five million of 'em will say I stink—but clear out to Dubuque."

"Still, they'll know your name. That comes first. That's why I'm trying to hustle you a contract at seven-fifty a week to start."

"Seven-fifty?" Her face lit up. "You said five hundred the other night."

"I've raised the price. So for seven hundred and fifty fish a week you sing two songs loud and fast, aided and abetted by the boys in the control room. And you also make with the jokes, just as good as any talking dog. So by the end of your first thirteen week cycle you're known all over America. Then you know what you'll do if you're smart?"

"I'm not smart. You know that, Vic. What do I do?"

"You gradually slip back into singing in your regular style, which is, incidentally, a damn good one."

"But will that awful old man let me?"

"It'll give him apoplexy. But you won't know it, because he never sees or talks to talent. Finally he'll become infuriated to the point where he'll say you've become too big for your britches, and he'll cancel your contract at the end of twenty-six weeks."

"That's great." She glumly stroked her breasts and smoothed the skirt over her thighs. "Out of radio back into night clubs in twenty-six weeks."

"You really aren't very bright. In twenty-six weeks you'll own a name that can command big money. You'll get another show, like that! And you'll be able to sing in any style you damn please. This is simply a device to get you in that position, fast."

She brooded about it a moment and then said, "If you

say so, okay. I'll cut the record the way you want it, and you'll
try to get me a contract with Evans. Okay?"

"Okay."

"I'd be a sucker to go against the advice of a smart character like you, that's how I figure it." She patted her stomach.
"Let's have lunch. I'm starved."

He told her he had a million things to do before train-
time. "Including a trip all the way down to Wall Street. Sorry,
but I'll have to skip it."

"I'll be waiting at the gate to say good-bye," she said.
"The Century, I suppose."

"Yeah."

She came to him and kissed him again. "You're such a
pretty little boy," she said.

"And you, dear, are the prettiest little barracuda I've ever
met."

She laughed. "You act just like a little boy. A handsome,
mad little boy. I love you. Do you love me?"

She embarrassed him a little. He said, "It was a wonderful
weekend. I'm sad at having to leave you so soon. But it'll be
wonderful when I come back. You're very wonderful. Something good to come back to."

"You're the one that's wonderful. You're such a wonderful
mad lover." She pouted. "I wished you loved me. I wish you
wanted me bad enough to want to marry me."

Vic thought she should leave these delicate things unsaid.
"I'm sorry," he said. "I'm afraid I've let you in for a bad
time. If it's that way with you, it isn't worth it, dear. We'd
better call it off quick before you really louse yourself up."
He went to the window and looked down. "I can't explain it
to you—I can only tell you that marriage is not for me. And
I tell you this, because I care more for you than any other
woman in the world."

She stood beside him, looked down at the skaters and said,
"Right at this minute, you mean."

"How can we ever say such things honestly, except right
at this minute?"

She kept her eyes fixed on the street below. "I think you made up your mind not to fall in love with me from the minute you decided to go to bed with me," she said. "I think you're not permitting yourself to fall in love with me. You won't give a single inch, will you, darling."

"You're quite a thinker," he said. "My father used to say that thinking never got anybody anywhere."

"Maybe you're so final about not marrying me because I'm a Jew," she said. "Is that the reason, Vic?"

He seized her by the arm and roughly drew her back from the window. He released her arm and looked steadily into her face.

"Don't hurt me, Vic," she said.

"I want to hurt you." He did not raise his voice, but his eyes seemed to burn into her eyes. "I despised you when you said that, Jean. It was a cheap, dramatic, rotten thing to say to me. You can't help thinking things like that, I suppose. But you can help saying them. And me, I only know myself, and no one else, to me it was unjust, uncalled for and untrue."

She walked to the sofa and sat down with her head bowed and her pageboy hair covering her face.

Vic stood alongside her, not touching her. He continued talking, the words hitting like stones.

"How dare you throw your race or religion or whatever the hell it is into my teeth? I thought you knew me better than that. How could you misjudge me so? The only Jews I happen to be intolerant of are those who are stupid enough to think that I might be concerned with their Jewishness. I know this preoccupation is a deep thing with all of you. Bnt please have the grace not to let it enter into our relationship. And try to understand that I have no hatred nor love for Jews, Irish, Welsh, Abyssinians, Seven Day Adventists or any other group. I only hate or love individuals. And, by God, I'm insisting on my right to hate or love them as individuals, not as members of some symbolic cult.

"You raise this question of love and marriage," he said. "You really want to know why I harden myself against marriage? I'll tell you. I don't want to take the responsibility for luring any woman into the same trap that I'm in. I've made up my mind that I've got to find my own salvation before I ask you or any other dame to share it with me. Remember that, Jean. Always remember that. And if you don't like it, then walk away from it."

Whether or not she understood him, she cried a little and was sorry. He apologized. "I'm sorry I lost my temper," he said. "I only do when I'm personally assaulted. I usually have better control of myself." They kissed again, she made up her face and left.

Vic ate a sandwich at his desk, accepted Miss Hammer's usual acid remark about ulcers, and hurried downtown for a last meeting with Evan Llewelyn Evans.

Allison told him not to take too long, that he'd scheduled meetings with lawyers for Mr. Evans' personal tax problems.

"He'll chin-chin all afternoon about advertising if I'd let him," the assistant to the president said. "But I'm not going to let him do it. Not today."

Vic said, "I'll bet he's got plenty of 'em. Tax problems, I mean."

"It's a problem for him just to make living expenses. He can't do it on a salary nowadays, the way the government takes it away. But he's closed his country place. That helped a lot."

Allison thought it was a damn shame that a man had to change his living habits at Mr. Evans' age. "He had twenty-one servants at that country place. He had built his own artificial trout brook on it, too. I never did know how many rooms in the place, but it looked like a hotel. Now he's stuck in that Fifth Avenue house with no place to go to cool off. And all those Rolls Royces are just sitting in the garage. No chauffeurs, no gas. It's hard on a man his age."

The buzzer buzzed, Allison jumped, and Vic was ushered into the fear-irradiating presence of his client.

The Old Man was sure that Buddy Hare could get a thirty rating with no trouble at all.

"No trouble at all," he repeated. "He's got everything. That funny voice! Like a mouse! See what I mean?"

Vic said he'd do his best to build a good show.

The Old Man said it was Vic's entire responsibility from here out.

Vic didn't want that rap pinned on him.

"But he's your discovery," he said. "If he turns out well, I don't want any credit I don't deserve."

Evans fixed that baleful glare on him. "Let's get this clear," he said. "I discovered Buddy Hare, true. But when I discussed it with the agency, I found out you fellows were as enthusiastic about him as I was. Right?"

"Correct," said Vic.

"I therefore take that to mean that you, representing the agency, recommend him just as much as I do. Check?"

It was too late, the whole thing had gone too far, for Vic to be anything but very sincere at this point.

"Yes," he said. The crafty old sonofabitch!

"The agency has to take certain responsibilities," the Old Man said. "Otherwise they wouldn't be interested in turning out a good job."

Mr. Evans took off his straw hat.

"I want to be able to take off this hat to you, when I hear that record," he said.

Vic asked if Miss Kennedy knew about Hare.

"I don't know how much you discuss talent deals," he explained. "I've always found that the fewer people in on them, the less chance for leaks!" Evans said he didn't discuss them with anybody but his top people, which was a good idea because once the word got around that the Old Man was after something the agents began doubling the price on everything.

"By the way, Mr. Norman," Evans put on his hat again. "Miss Kennedy is not being critical, simply trying to be constructive in the best interests of the Beautee Soap Company.

But she's been complaining a little about how some of the details are handled at the agency. In fact, she said you had a wonderful creative mind, but like all creative people you paid no attention to the little details."

Vic said he didn't know exactly what she was talking about, but he certainly could disprove her statement about all creative people.

"How?"

Vic pointed at Mr. Evans. "You," he said. "It isn't just flattery to call you one of the great creative minds in radio and advertising. It's on the record. And you, sir, certainly do pay attention to all the little details."

And he left on that note, which was not a bad note to leave on. He walked over to say good-bye to that bitch, Kennedy.

"If you have any little details you want handled," he said, "I'll have Mr. Evans, who assists me on the account, take care of them for me."

"You should be on the radio," she said, and Vic realized that if he wanted to handle Beautee soap for very long, he'd have to figure out some way to get rid of her. Certainly, she didn't want him as a competitor for the Old Man's favor.

He spent the rest of the afternoon in his office seeing his assistants and then stopped in to see Kimberly.

"I'm on my way to the train now. Any last minute instructions?"

Kim said no. "I hope you're more bullish about Buddy Hare, though."

Vic said he could only hope that Buddy Hare would drop dead and get them out of the jam.

Kim's optimism flashed briefly. "Do you suppose he might?" he said. "No, I'd never be that lucky."

"But maybe you can make a good show out of it anyway," he finished hopefully.

Vic told him there wasn't a chance. "It'll sound all right. Good jokes, laughs, I'll pack the script with boffolas. But hell, the guy's no radio comedian—period. He's fair on burlesque routines that he's been practising for years. But not on material you have to change once a week."

Kim was worried. "It's the kind of thing that can prove disastrous. ELE will certainly do a fast switch and claim we discovered Buddy Hare and made a bad choice. He always does when his discoveries flop."

Vic said, "He went out of his way to tell me I was responsible, not him. I've got a great idea. Let's tell him we have discovered a greater comedian than Buddy Hare."

"Who?"

"Old Man Evans himself. Hell, he'd be sensational on the air."

Kimberly looked to see if all the doors were closed. "Somebody's going to hear you talking like that one of these days and report you. I wouldn't be at all surprised if he had spies planted in the agency. Have you run into anything suspicious?" he asked.

"Don't worry, Kim. Besides, he would be wasted on radio. I'd rather have him for television. That straw hat alone is worth ten Hooper points."

Kim said he was sorry Vic had to go on this wild-goose trip. "But make it up to yourself. Spend the firm's money on whores. Have a good time."

Vic wanted to know if he could go as high as fifty dollar whores and Kim said sure, that man was not made of wood and besides, what were expense accounts for?

"But don't tell any vice-presidents," he warned. "Whores on the expense account are only for partners and potential partners."

"You know, Kim," Vic said, shaking hands, "I'm really fond of you. Most presidents talk about money and think about whores, while you talk about whores and think about money."

As they stood in the open doorway, Kim said in a low voice, "Spend a lot of time with Maag. Find out his weaknesses. I want a full report."

"That won't be necessary," Vic said. "I already know them."

He closed the door and stood in the hallway a second. A

lot had happened today. He had a lot of thinking to do.
A partnership with stock profits subject only to capital gains
was worth—at the present rate of earning and taxation, he
roughly figured—at least a million dollars in seven or eight
years, in addition to a hundred thousand a year he could
take out of the company for salary. It wasn't hay. But seven
years was a long time. Maybe too damn long. If he had to
spend seven more years with the smell of this business in his
nose, he feared what it would do to him. And seven might
easily run into seventeen or twenty-seven. That's what happened when business seized a man by the throat. He didn't
know what to do. Kimberly's deal was so damn big. A smaller
chunk would be easier to throw away. But this. It could be
a way to buy time for him—and it could be a way to dissipate
time. It could be a trap or it could be a way out of the trap.
He had always been appalled at the fast hysterical pace
with which businessmen marched toward death and the end
of time. And yet he didn't honestly know how a man, how
he, personally, Victor Norman, should use his time. He had
only the sense of thus far being a spendthrift with it, and the
unexpressed urge not to fling it away so extravagantly, not to
tip, as it were, employers with it. How in this brief life, this
life that had been gadgeted and gimmicked half to death,
could a man use time? Where could he hunt and savor time
eagerly with zest and purpose, the way men around him
hunted money and security and power and position?

Yes, it was quite a pass that Kimberly had made at him
. . . and with the best of intentions, all mixed up with friendship and esteem. But it must be thought out with impersonal
clarity and sharp savage understanding. What was meant to
be a brotherly pat could well become a knockout blow.

Louise Hammer was waiting with the intelligence that
Miss Kennedy was on the phone. Urgent.

"Tell her to hang on until I get back from Hollywood,"
Vic said. "Not even Miss Kennedy is going to make me miss
the Century. Did the boy leave for Grand Central with my
bags?"

He left her wailing that she couldn't tell Miss Kennedy
that.

[CHAPTER VII]

VIC STAYED IN HIS COMPARTMENT AND READ THE AFTERNOON papers until the Twentieth Century Limited was an hour out, hurtling along the magnificent Hudson. The news was good. The Germans were doomed. Vic skimmed through the pages rapidly, and realized with a somewhat guilty feeling that he was no longer a student of the war, just a headline reader.

Then he went into the club car for a drink. He spoke to some people he knew, a writer named Bennett, and an agent whose name he'd forgotten, but avoided sitting with them. Most of the Hollywood group would stay in their compartments for this leg of the journey, not coming out until they boarded the Super Chief.

The car was dominated by a drunken major who shook every newcomer's hand, saying, "I'm Oscar Skiboosh. What's your name?"

He tried to buy everybody a drink and he kept telling about how he had been overseas for twenty-seven months and now his wife didn't love him anymore. When an Army Air Force Captain came in, the Major said, "Hello, Ninth Air Force." And the Captain was given the Oscar Skiboosh routine. Then the Major announced: "This officer, ladies and gentlemen, has on his chest certain ribbons and decorations. Can any civilian in this car identify those ribbons properly— for ten bucks?" Nobody said anything, and the Major repeated the offer, adding, "We earn our ribbons the hard way, don't we, Ninth Air Force? And these goddam civilians don't even know what they are."

A woman cleared her throat and said in a tiny, appeasing voice, "The first one's a DFC." And the Major stumbled in her direction. He bowed extravagantly and said, "My compliments, madame. Now for the benefit of those civilians present who are unaware of the meaning of the decorations which this officer wears so modestly, may I translate. Besides the Distinguished Flying Cross with two oak leaves, the Captain wears the Air Medal with three leaves, the Purple Heart, a European Theatre ribbon with fifteen combat stars, and an Asiatic theatre ribbon with three stars." He then sat down by the woman and was telling her about enduring twenty-seven months overseas, but all the time thinking about coming home to his wife and then he did come home and look what happened! She was his second wife, he said, and he really loved her. The steward came in from the dining car and cleared the air by telling the major that his place was ready. He had to be helped through the lurching car.

The man beside Vic said that there was going to be a lot of that now, and it was a hell of a problem. Really a hell of a problem. "I've got two boys over there," he said, "and you just don't know what to expect when they come back. One's in Germany, and the other's in Italy."

Someone turned on the radio. It was a spot announcement on Love that Soap. With great disgust the man parroted to Vic, "'Love that Soap. Beautee is as Beautee does. Hollywood's favorite bar.' Jesus, I get tired of hearing that crap. They should force them to take those commercials off the air. Or at least change them once in a while."

The only trouble, Vic explained, was that they sold soap. "Seems like the more you irritate people, the better they remember your brand. And that's half of selling." He told the man about the Beautee sales curve.

The man was impressed but thought the American people were a bunch of suckers to fall for it. "But they do, I know that. I own a soft drink. It's called Yumola. It's very big in

the midwest and we're planning to expand it to a national
brand after the war when we can get sugar. And I suppose
we'll be doing the same thing."

Vic told him he should use radio, and said he should buy
a big rating show right off, not try to build one. "Incidentally,
you have a wonderful product in that Yumola, and that's the
first insurance ad men look for."

Mr. Yumola was very interested in radio, especially network shows. "We use local spots," he said. "But spots always
seemed smalltime to me. You kinda have to apologize to your
friends at the club when you use spots. But when a product
comes on the air with a big half hour radio show, coast to
coast, that's bigtime stuff."

Vic foresaw some future business for Kimberly and Maag,
or maybe it would be Kimberly and Norman by then, so he
was very nice to the man. He explained why he'd recommended that Mr. Yumola buy a big established star with a
high-rating show, rather than try to build one. "New shows are
a fifty to one gamble. And it costs a million a year to gamble,
including talent costs. You're not playing with marbles when
you get into network radio."

"I'll be glad when this war's over and there's sugar and
plenty of help and trucks and everything's normal again,"
Mr. Yumola said with passion. "'Yumola presents the Bob
Hope Show!' Man, wouldn't that be sumpin?"

"It would," Vic said, "except that Bob Hope has a ten
year contract with his present sponsor. You'll have to struggle
along with some other name."

Mr. Yumola was very naïve, an ideal sponsor for an agency
to have, if you protected yourself against him. Infatuated
with the glamor of show business, and why not, thought Vic.
After all, a man spends his life carbonating water and collecting bills and needling salesmen—then all of a sudden, overnight in fact, he can become an impresario with his company's money. He can buy and sell talent, and call his friends
in once a week to hear his man make jokes over the radio. He
can call his agency next day and say, "I think the performance

was good, except for that fluff at the end, but the script was lousy. Incidentally, Mrs. Yumola thought so, too." He can pick up the jargon of radio and offer suggestions for improving the stooge character in the middle spot. He buys himself an excuse to take frequent trips to Hollywood. He can attend parties given in his honor by his star. He can go back home and casually remark, "Last week on the coast the ——s gave a party for me. And Greer . . . Miss Garson . . . told an anecdote I think you'll enjoy."

Then as he gradually grows hep to this colorful new world which is selling his product like crazy, he can discover new stars, he can fling a new singer into the air because he likes her bedstyle and to hell with her singing style.

He can wear sharper clothes, louder ties, be less conscious of his wife, because he is a showman, and everyone, including wives, know how showmen are.

And, if his agency happened to be bright about such men, he would never be in a position to really louse up his show, unlike Mr. Evans who insisted on control of all elements of the Beautee shows. No, for the Mr. Yumolas you simply buy a star-owned package, and he'd sign a contract giving the star control of the script. That way you could listen to Mr. Y's helpful suggestions and make sympathetic sounds, but you wouldn't have to put them on the air.

Mr. Yumola asked about Vic's firm and was visibly impressed to learn that K and M had twenty-three radio programs on the air at present. "The big time," he said reverently. "I know how busy you must be, but do you think you could spare me the time to talk some more about Yumola postwar radio when I'm in New York? I'll give you plenty of advance notice when I come."

He considered it a favor when Vic said, "Of course. Delighted."

He then realized they had forgotten to introduce themselves so they exchanged cards. Mr. Yumola apologized for leaving, but said he was traveling with an important customer and had to get back to his quarters.

After dinner, Vic sat in the club car and listened to the chatter of the travelers as they tried to impress others. He tried to think of a good idea for the Buddy Hare Show, but his mind wouldn't sharpen. Beside him, one gin rummy player told another: "Personally, I'd rather have luck than skill. You gotta have luck. I know a man who wrote the book on how to play gin. A best seller. He always loses. Sure he's a good player, but he's unlucky." And on his other side, a man was saying: "The next war'll be fought with rockets. And whoever starts it won't make Hitler's mistake. Hitler told everybody he was going to fight. Next war, you know what? One day, New York, London, or Washington'll be wiped off the map, without warning, by thousands of tons of rockets. The war'll be won before anybody knows there's a war going on. I been thinking I oughta get me a farm. Get out of the city. They won't bother to aim rockets at farms."

"Rockets are just primitive things," his friend said. "It'll be something that makes rockets seem like the Fourth of July. This is only the beginning of a race to develop weapons which can destroy the world. I won't talk specifics for security reasons." He seemed very mysterious and moody about the whole thing. Then he said, "I'm a man of scientific training. My father used to say that the science of yesterday was the superstition of today. But me, I'm beginning to think that the comic books of today are the science of tomorrow. I get cold chills whenever I see those *Superman* and *Buck Rogers* books. Things will come that'll put even them to shame."

Vic knew that he was speaking truth and recalled a drunken conversation with an indiscreet general in Paris. Vic's feelings about the future, when he permitted his mind to dwell on futures, were dark and gloomy. The peoples of the world seemed to him to be writhing and moiling, as the earth itself had once shuddered and heaved up and reformed itself. There was yearning after security and struggling against that yearning, there was a raw primeval urge to destroy all security; he had witnessed the children of that harsh parent, Europe, lose all faith in the men who led them, the gods who once com-

forted them, and finally, and oh how inevitably, in themselves.
We all wanted to go places, but there was no place to go, and
always the mob beckoned, the reckless, turbulent, subhuman
mob. Then he told himself that his own restless spirit had
befogged his vision of the life about him, that things were
bad now, but perhaps it was only a bad period, and the time
would come as it always had before, when a man could look
on himself and others with respect and love and joy. And
then, as usual, when his thoughts carried him into the world's
slime, he deliberately drove his mind out into the prosaic
present, where it was soothed and occupied by the simple
sights and sounds of human beings frantically inventing de-
vices to help them pass the time away.

The one old lady traveler remaining in the club car sought
out the Ninth Air Force Captain who was sticking strictly to
his drinking. "Well, how does it feel to be back, Captain?"
. . . "Fine. Great." . . . "I guess you've been in quite a bit
of it." . . . "A little." . . . "You heading for the Pacific? My
grandson's in the Pacific." . . . "No, ma'am, I'm on leave."
. . . "Oh, I'll bet you'll be thrilled to be home again." . . .
"Yes, ma'am." . . . "Married?" . . . "No, ma'am." . . . "I bet
you've got a girl waiting for you. A handsome young hero like
you." . . . "I wouldn't say that, ma'am."

The feeling of the train, of being remote and lonely in the
crowd, of not belonging to it or anything, of only being a spec-
tator and not a participant, became unbearable to Vic and
he walked back to his compartment. As was his unfortunate
lot, he slept hardly at all on this, the first night of his journey.
Unlike most of his kind, he would have nothing to do with
sleeping pills, so he fought during the long night a losing
battle with the aft starboard wheel of the Twentieth Century
Limited.

In Chicago, as Vic left the Century, he saw Donald Worth
walking ahead of him. Don was a talent agent, member of
Talent Ltd., a huge corporation that handled orchestras, movie
stars, radio stars, ice shows, Broadway plays, and night club

floor shows. The firm was not quite a monopoly, but was in there pitching for it.

Talent Ltd. was Buddy Hare's agent, and Worth the man assigned to handle his business. Vic had of course not mentioned Evans' interest in Buddy Hare, in fact had not known that Worth was in New York. Vic hoped he was going west on the Chief, instead of the Super Chief, since it would give him a chance to sneak in a casual option and keep the prices down. If he had to go out of his way to call Talent Ltd. in Hollywood, Worth would of course immediately become suspicious that it was an Evans order and would jack up his price and terms accordingly.

Vic did not appear to notice Worth, but hurried past him and let the talent agent discover him.

Worth caught up with him and seized his arm.

"Look here, old boy," he said. "Don't try to brush me, just because you're cutting in on that easy Evans dough. How the hell are you, honey?"

They shook hands and Vic fancied finding Don in of all places Chicago.

Don Worth was a clever little man, about forty, who was classified as sharp. Talent Ltd. was known as the sharpest group of agents in the business, and Don was one of their best, that is sharpest, men.

He was English and he somehow managed to give the impression, without actually saying so, of being the younger son of at least a duke. A lean, distinguished face, framed in grey at the temples, manners every bit as good as Mike Romanoff's, real graciousness, too, nothing phoney.

Don, being English, still clung to a few rightos and old boys, and many a movie starlet whose career he'd guided had first learned her eyethers and neyethers from him. Not that his speech, like his dress, did not reflect his years in show business. He was, in fact, a rare and curious combination of Hollywood, Broadway and London.

He wore fine flannel suits discretely tailored for an English gentleman. He was one of Hollywood's few hat-wearers, usually a grey homburg.

But his accessories were six thousand miles from Bond Street: today his tie was apple green hand-painted with orange-yellow carrots; his white silk shirt had a loose, casual collar, and of course, but natch, he produced for Vic's cigarette a gold Dunhill lighter that cost one hundred and fifty dollars, not including twenty percent war tax.

"So you've graduated to the gold ribbed model," Vic said. "You must have something on Dave Lash. I doubt if his recent interest in philanthropy extends as far as you."

Lash was Worth's boss, and the head of Talent Ltd.

"Honey, I thought I'd have a stroke when I heard about you taking the job buttering up the Old Man. I never figured you for the type." Worth waved to a girl surrounded entirely by airplane luggage. "Hello, lover. See you on the Super Chief." Worth called all men "Honey" and all women "Lover."

She said, "Not if I see you first," and he cheerily responded with "Righto."

"You don't know it, but you're saving at least two hundred and fifty bucks by going on the Super Chief instead of the Chief," Vic said.

"Really?"

"Sure. I'm going on the Chief and I had planned to pay my way out with gin rummy winnings. You should give me a hundred dollars now just for not riding with you, and we'll call it square."

"I lost eighty dollars to Sally MaGuire last night on the Century," Worth complained. "You can't go on the Chief, old boy, I have to make my money back someway."

He then did what Vic hoped he would do—asked him to change reservations.

Vic said no. "I got a compartment on the Chief. I won't take any chances of sitting up in the club car for two days just to clip you at gin."

But Don had an angle. "For twenty dollars I can get you a compartment on the Super Chief."

Vic pretended to be dubious, then he said:

"Okay, I'll take it. It only leaves me two hundred and thirty dollars profit, but what the hell. There's a war on."

Vic waved a greeting at Mr. Yumola, whose name happened to be Turner. He agreed to meet Worth at the gates at five-fifteen, and Don promised to bring the ticket. He wanted Vic to have lunch with him, but Vic claimed he had an appointment. He could only stand so much of Don Worth.

Or Chicago, either. The big, dirty, ugly, hard-drinking, hard-working, fornicating city always depressed him. The ambitious men, the complaining women, the intense concentration on business, the rubber-stamped suburbs . . . he had no feeling for the thing Chicago was trying to tear out of life in such big chunks.

At five-fifteen he stood in the crowd waiting at the Super Chief gate and watched for Worth. It was a neighborly group, many of whom he knew. The men still wore their business suits and loud ties; but Vic knew that once on the train they would change into the Hollywood uniform: a sports jacket or shirt, no tie, slacks and moccasins.

In the main, these were not the handsome, glamorous, acting, starring people of Hollywood. They were the producing, writing, directing, distributing, financial people—the permanent part of the town, the ones who hired the others to go before the microphones and cameras.

Many had with them their glittering, gesticulating, shrill and glossy women, who had gone back east for some new clothes and the ride and perhaps to keep an eye on the husbands.

They had seen the hit plays, possibly bought one or two for pictures; they had gone on an eating spree and rattled off names like Al Schacht's (the french fried onions melt in your mouth and that marinated herring!!), the Colony, Chambord, Voisin, but above all Twenty-One and Toots Shor. (That was a good one Toots told Sam 'I've seen your pictures' ha-ha-

ha.) (I always leave New York with Toots' graham cracker pie running out of my ears.)

A man with a typewriter brushed by Vic. "Hello Bernie," he said. "Got another picture job?"

"Yes, dammit. My play flopped and I need the dough."

"Be seeing you on the train."

Don came by. He had the ticket, but it had cost him forty dollars bribe.

"I won't pay it," Vic said. "Thanks anyway."

"You can afford it better than I," Don complained. "I only get ten percent of my gross, and you get fifteen percent."

Their compartments were separated by several cars, so Vic left Don after agreeing to meet later.

"Before you go," Worth said, "and confidentially, just what brings you out to the coast?"

"It's a nice trip. I like the ride. I want to sleep with a few old friends."

"Evan Evans discovered something new?" Worth was probing for a clue.

"Confidentially, I'm looking for a singer on the Figaro Perkins show," Vic threw him a curve, but that's the way you had to deal with agents.

"Good. We've a splendid lot of singers, honey."

"We'll talk it over in Hollywood. No use working all the time," Vic said. "Get out the deck. I'll be back."

The Super Chief pulled out of Chicago. Vic hung up his suits and brushed his teeth. He decided to put off the card game with Worth, and went back to the club car for a drink.

The travelers were just beginning to drift in. Not the hep characters, the Hollywood commuters; it was too soon for that.

He ordered a drink and successfully avoided a conversation with a man who kept talking about business conditions in LA which war production had made but terriffc. The wolves began to prowl through the train looking for unattached women. A pretty, actressy girl finally showed up. The wolves stared at her, in that slow, insulting head-to-foot way that must be infuriating to women.

Then one of them went over and sat down by her, on the pretense of looking at a newspaper. He gave the paper a thorough-going five-second glance and then made with the conversation.

Vic remembered the girl, but pretended not to notice her. The wolf was given a few unrewarding answers, but he was persistent, and insisted on paying for her drink. She kept looking at Vic, busy with his paper, then crossed over to him.

"Excuse me," she said, "but didn't I meet you in Italy?"

"Of course," he indicated the empty chair beside him and she sat down gratefully. The wolf left the club car. Strike one.

"Your name is Miss Constance Linger and you were with a USO group," he said. "I saw you brush a baldheaded colonel in the Medical Corps at a party given by Al Swift. You do a drunk act that laid the boys in the aisles. I'm Vic Norman. Do you really want to talk to me, or was that just a way of getting rid of that character?"

"Of course. I mean I do want to talk to you. When did you get back?"

"Last month."

"Those horrible men," she sighed. "I feel like kicking them right in the—teeth."

"He was a little obvious, I thought. Wait, I'll get your drink." He did so.

"If I thought it was my sultry beauty," she said. "But it makes a girl kinda mad to see those guys go right after the old fat ones, too."

"It's the train that does it. The Super Chief is definitely an aphrodisiac. Even to me, old and beat-up as I am. I get that feeling in my blood the minute I step on this train. All the hidden mysteries of the orient can't compete with high-pitched laughter locked behind a strange compartment door."

She laughed. "You're old and beat-up! A man like you shouldn't have to hunt for women these days."

It was true what he had said about trains. A man wants a woman. Is restless for a woman. It is a much stronger feeling than any other travel feeling. So men drink, play cards, talk their heads off—but none of it helps the loneliness for women. That is why it is hard to read, impossible to work, on a train. A man says the shifting light is hard on his eyes, or that he hates being cooped up, but the fact is, he wants to concentrate on a woman and nothing else. He is only happy on a train with a woman. The best relief from his longing is gambling, but even gambling for higher stakes than he can afford is a poor excuse for not finding a woman.

Connie was going out to do a musical.

"It's the silliest one I ever heard of," she said. "About a jungle. They want me to do my drunk act in a jungle. They're talking about having me drink something out of coconuts. Fantastic."

Don Worth came in, looked at Connie, and said, "I say old boy, you do work fast." Then, "Get out the deck, honey." He had a man with him. "This is Mr. Al Lash. Mr. Norman."

Vic introduced Connie. They moved to a table for four.

"Are you related to Dave Lash?" Vic asked.

Al Lash said no, thank God, and then he told a story.

It was about a man who came to Hollywood and finally ran into a friend who lived out there. The friend asked the man what he had been doing.

"Oh, the guy says, Monday I went swimming with Gable. So the friend asks, *Clark* Gable? No, no, no, the guy answers, *Max* Gable. Then Tuesday I went swimming up to the Gold-wyns'. So the friend says the *Sam* Goldwyns? and the guy says no, no, no, the *Irving* Goldwyns. But last night, the guy says, I had the best time of all, I went to the Lashes for cocktails. So the friend says, the *Dave* Lashes? And the guy says, yes."

"Honey, you are talking about the hand that's biting me," Don complained.

"I'm a unique character," Al said. "I tell 'em right to their face. The biggest ones. I told that story right to Dave Lash's face. He laughed."

"What did you expect him to do?" Vic asked. "But why are you a unique character?"

"Everybody says I'm a unique character," Al explained. "I

know 'em all. I'm the guy who slugged the executive producer of Global Pictures when he tried to ban me from the lot. They don't get by with nothing, and the bigger they are the less I let 'em get by with."

"Why did he try to ban you from the lot?" Connie asked.

Lash began a boring story which Worth interrupted.

"All right, unique character," he said. "Let's cut for deal."

The gin game started. Connie was very good at it. She blitzed Lash.

"Before we start the next game," he said, "just one question. Do you cheat?"

He turned out to be a very offensive character, too. He questioned the addition, noisily quarreled about rules and was so obnoxious that Vic said at the end of the second game, "I'm too tired to play."

"I think I'll go back and freshen up for dinner myself," Connie said. "See you later."

Lash left soon after. Then Vic and Don played one more triple game.

"Got any singers in mind, Vic?" Worth was still working away. "I knock with six."

"You're beat. I play my queen and seven and that leaves four points. Oh, anybody'll do, as long as she sings loud. You know the Old Man." Vic dealt. "By the way, who you handling now?"

Don named a dozen people, including Buddy Hare.

"I liked that Buddy Hare's last guest spot. He might go places," Vic said.

"He's got a lot to learn, honey," Don said.

"I could teach him. The way to do with a ham like that is get him on a cheap show, but make the writing good. Then if he flops you're not out much."

"Care to sign him? It's my deal," he said. "Talent Ltd. would be delighted to build you a little package."

"I don't think that much of the guy. It's getting so a man can't even make a little conversation with you."

"You know," Don mused, "Evans might like a chap like

Buddy Hare: He might appeal to him. He likes comedians with squeaky voices."

"I doubt it," Vic said. "I knock with ten."

It was so silly, this innuendoing around, but it was the best way to get the kind of contract you wanted. The minute a big spender like Evans looked hungry for a piece of talent, then the restrictive clauses poured in and the prices went up.

"I'm leaving. Connie and I are having dinner together."

"I guess you don't want to be disturbed for the rest of the trip," Worth said. "That'll be forty-three dollars even, sir, and thank you very much."

"It's only money," Vic said.

"Expense money, at that," Worth cracked. "Chargeable to Kimberly and Maag."

Vic looked at him coldly. "I resent that, Don. Gambling money is my money."

Worth said, "Okay. Okay. It was just a gag."

Vic knew it was just a joke. A very old, corny one to boot. But he was tough about it because he didn't like Worth. One time in a radio deal, he'd had his secretary take notes on Worth's conversation, just out of curiosity to see how many checkable lies and exaggerations the agent would make. The count had been fourteen lies in forty minutes.

That was one good thing about New York business—at least the bluechip, Wall Street kind of people that the big advertising agencies dealt with. There was a tradition and an ethic in their world of mass production and mass selling. When a man gave you the nod, that was it. The contracts could come later. Not that these well-bred men could not clip you as hard, or harder, than the sharp ones. But they wouldn't renege, once they gave you the nod. Old Man Evans spoke for them when he'd told Vic, "A contract is a contract. A man's word is his word. That's how the Beautee Soap Company operates. It's not that way with talent and their agents. A contract, or a spoken pledge, is something they try to weasel out of the minute they find it not to their liking." That was why the Old Man had long ago made it a firm company policy never to

deal directly with talent or their agents, and insisted that all
such matters be handled in his name by his advertising agency.

Vic felt he had said enough to Worth about the Buddy
Hare deal. It would normally be a simple thing to get an
option on a piece of talent like Hare, and then work with the
talent agency to build a show around him. But the magic
name of Evans made it complicated. In the first place, if Worth
knew that Evans had issued orders to sign Hare, he would
double the price. So the trick was to get a thirty-day option
on Hare at a reasonable price. Otherwise Vic would look
stupid to Evans. Then, also, if Worth knew of Evans' interest,
he would refuse to give an option on Hare alone, but would
try to control the other elements of the show: the orchestra,
stooges, writers, singers and actors. That way, Talent Ltd.
could collect ten percent on everybody in the show, not just
on Hare. So it was Vic's problem to extract a simple option
letter from an unsuspecting Worth, stating that Kimberly and
Maag had the right to use Hare in a radio show for a stated
amount of money. That way Vic could cut Talent Ltd. completely out of the package, which was the way Evans liked
to operate.

The voices in the club car were beginning to shrill a little
drunkenly, and Vic said he was going to make one sober trip
to the coast, this one, and he left Don Worth and went forward to his compartment.

He tried to read a book. He noticed the Super Chief was
passing through a small city. He took a longer look; sure
enough it was Fort Madison. He'd spent seventeen years of
his life there, had returned only once—to bury his mother. He
looked briefly at the landmarks which he could still identify,
lost interest, then leaned back and closed his eyes.

He opened his eyes and saw a child in the doorway watching over him. A brown boyish boy with yellow upstanding
hair.

"Hello," Vic said, still lying down, accepting the boy with
no demonstration.

"Hello," the boy answered.

"Sit down," Vic invited.

The boy said thank you and sat down.

"My name's Vic. What's yours?"

"Hal."

They shook hands carefully.

"Hello, Hal."

"Hello, Vic."

Vic sat up.

"Been reading?" Hal asked gravely.

"A little."

"What?"

Vic turned the book over.

"*Strange Fruit*," the boy read. "Mother read it. I started it. Didn't like it."

Vic asked him how old he was. "Eight," Hal said, "but I'll be nine in eleven months. Then I can join the cub scouts. And hey hey I can go out in the forest and carry a knife and a hatchet and if a wild animal comes at me I can hey hey skin 'em and bring the fur home."

He began to speak very fast and the hey hey was simply a punctuation device to keep the conversation firmly in hand while thinking over his next statement.

A little girl ran down the corridor, saw Hal, and came to the compartment. At first shy, then coming closer. "My sister," Hal said. "Ellen."

"Hello, little Ellen," Vic said.

"My not 'ittle Ewwen, my big Ewwen," she said.

"She doesn't talk very well," Hal explained, gravely. "But if you want to know what she's saying just ask me. I'm the only one that understands her. Not even Mother understands her half the time. And Martha never knows what she says." He explained who Martha was. "Some of the kids call 'em governesses. But she's really a nurse."

By this time Ellen became very voluble. "Tell me a stowy," she commanded. So Vic told her a story.

"Hey hey," Hal said, "do you like comic books?"

"Tell me anuya stowy."

"I should say not," Vic said. "Not until you sing me a song." By this time she was leaning against him, and he put an arm around her. What a beautiful, beautiful child! She was about three.

"My be seeing you," she sang in out-of-tune, penetrating magpie notes. "My be looking at the moon but my be seeing you. Tell my anuya stowy."

The nurse came by looking for them. She succeeded in luring Ellen away, but Hal stayed on.

Vic asked him where he lived.

"In New York, darn it."

Hal didn't like New York. "You go to the park, and you can't climb trees. You go out of the playground and they try to send you back into the playground. It's not like the country. Hey hey," he said, "I'd like to live on a farm, and have my pony and dogs. Lots of dogs. Not these little ol' dogs either." He said, "Big fierce dogs. Hey hey, I just wish I could get my mother and daddy to buy a farm. I'd help with the farm work too."

"But you go out into the country every summer, don't you?"

"Oh sure, we go to Connecticut and other places. But it's not like a real farm. It's almost like Central Park, with the gardner and everything but hey hey Daddy has to work in New York to earn money as soon as the war's over and he gets out of the army so I guess I'll have to live there."

Vic asked Hal what his father did in the army.

"He never tells us," Hal said. "I guess it's a military secret. He's a lieutenant colonel. He's been overseas a long time, but he's coming back soon."

Hal was going to be either a detective or a doctor when he grew up. Not a farmer. "Hey hey," he said, "do you know what to do if a crook's pointing a gun at you." He stood up. "You fall on your knee and draw your gun." He demonstrated this. "Kakkkk, Kakkk, you're dead. Hey hey, you see I ducked and your bullet went over my head," he explained.

Vic played at being a crook. He was killed four times.

Another woman came to the door. "You're awfully good

to play with him," she said. "but really, Hal, you'll wear the gentleman out."

"Shhh," Vic said, "I'm really dead. Inspector Hal had a derringer up his sleeve."

She called the nurse and told her to take Hal back to his own compartment. "You're being very nice, but I know how other people's children affect other people. You probably want to be by yourself."

"No, I'm quite gregarious. I wouldn't want this bruited around, but I'm really the man who invented gin rummy. Just to bring strangers together. I live on the royalties."

She laughed and made as if to move on. "Please sit down," he said. "You see, I know so much about you, I feel as if we were old friends."

"About me?" She was surprised.

"Certainly. You live in New York, but you go to Connecticut in the summer. And you also live near the park but that doesn't really mean very much, because you can't climb trees in the park. It's not like a farm."

"Hal didn't waste any time telling you all our problems, did he?" She sat down now.

"He's a wonderful, fine boy. So grave and self-reliant. And Ellen. I've fallen in love with her."

"It's just that you like children."

"I've never really been around them very much. But your two, it was love at first sight.

"You'll forgive me for talking," Vic said. "I'm usually the shy, sullen type. But sincere. Every once in a while, however, I go on a talking jag. By the way my name's Victor Norman. I'm one of those hustlers who commute between New York and Hollywood. Sort of a radio ham."

"Oh are you on the radio?"

"No, thank God. I just heckle the people who do go on the radio, Mrs.?"

"Dorrance," she paused. "Kay Dorrance."

"Ellen looks like you. And I can't think of any better way to tell you how beautiful you are."

"You're just saying that, young man, because I'm older than you."

"Wanta bet. I'm thirty-five. And I regret every year but the first five."

"You don't look it. But if you won't tell anyone I'm thirty-two."

"And undoubtedly prettier than you were at twenty-two. You're the kind of woman who is."

In a way it was train chatter and in a way it wasn't. Kay Dorrance had the regal kind of beauty that was far more than a camera angle. It was a sexless feeling Vic had about her, but he was strongly attracted to her, just as he had been attracted to her children.

The children came rushing back to them and climbed over Vic, as the mother watched with a tolerant smile.

"Ellen," Vic said, "let's get married tonight, and go to the moon in a rocket for our honeymoon."

"Un," said Ellen.

"She means yes," Hal translated.

"My not mean ess, my mean un," Ellen said.

"If it just so happens that the moon is made out of honey, that would be a real honeymoon," Vic said.

"Un," said Ellen. "Tell me anuya stowy."

"Hey hey," said Hal, "Do you ever listen to the Shadow on the radio? The Shadow knows. Ha-ha-ha-ha."

"Why does the Shadow know?" Ellen asked, and the mother told the nurse to take them away again.

Constance Linger looked in. "Excuse me," she said.

"Come in, Connie. Miss Linger, Mrs. Dorrance."

Mrs. Dorrance said she had to go back and help Martha with the children.

"You know it's much simpler giving birth to them than to try to take them from New York to the coast. Especially these days."

Vic stood up. "May I spend some time with them tomorrow? I don't mean to be pushy—but I never saw such children. It'd be a big favor to me."

She began to say no, then changed her mind and smiled. "Of course. They certainly are attracted to you. They've never done that before with strangers."

When she'd gone, Connie said, "So you like children? She is beautiful, isn't she? And that dress—a Schiaparelli original if I ever saw one."

"Let's order a drink and play anagrams," Vic said.

"Okay on the drink, but anagrams? I always thought they were something like canapés."

"My favorite game, next to you-know-what." He reached in his bag. "I never travel without my anagrams. I'll teach you."

She looked at him with teasing eyes. "I bet that's not all you could teach me."

The Super Chief plunged forwards and rocked sideways into the night, a long twisting aluminum pot, boiling with the noises that people make to impress, to distress, to flatter, to seduce, or simply to pass time away.

"How do you ever stand Hollywood? Such a dreadful place! It's like Larchmont, only three thousand miles from New York."

"Nonsense! It's okay if you're successful, horrible if you're not—just like New York."

"Beverly Hills is like a big hotel where they're holding a trade convention. They should pin buttons on the inhabitants, just like they do salesmen at a convention. All they talk about is their business—movies, movies, movies!"

"I met her in Santa Monica one night, and I fell in love with her. But madly. But her husband's overseas with the USO and I won't make passes. Dammit to hell, you can't take advantage of a guy who's gone overseas. Just make it straight, Eric. A little more, please."

"So Sam says to Walt, the picture flopped for one reason. I tried to cram a message into it. Hereafter, on my lot, all messages will be delivered by Western Union. Ha, ha, ha."

"She reached down and slapped me on zee forehead wiz what you call ze heel of her hand, and she say, 'don' do zat. Eet is unAmerican.' Ho, ho, ho!"

"Personally I prefer the Chief. This train goes so fast and rocks so much it gives me flight fatigue."
"Try a seconal, honey. My doctor says they're very mild, almost harmless."

"No real New Yorker likes the coast."
"Why?"
"Oh, you know, the theatre, the art galleries, the food—you know."

"I've got a letter to a big executive at Fox. I'll start as anything. Script girl or anything."

"So he asked me for a treatment on spec. I said, Bert, when it comes to writing, I'm a whore. I won't lay a finger on my typewriter unless I get paid for it—in advance."

"No record company is any bigger than it's artists. Don't forget that, Joe. I'm warning you."

"This is what Hollywood needs. This script's got America in every line of it. Cheap set, too. You can do it for peanuts."

And once Connie held him furiously and whispered madly to him, "Don't think I'm wanton, Vic darling. Please don't think I'm wanton."

[CHAPTER VIII]

THE SUPER CHIEF WAS WELL INTO COLORADO WHEN VIC MADE his first effort to climb out of bed. He dressed and went into the dining car, still almost filled with the late breakfast crowd. He looked up and down—Kay Dorrance and her children were not there. Connie was eating with a Navy lieutenant. That obnoxious character, Al Lash, was telling a table of four why he was a unique character.

He read the Denver *Post* and ate his usual breakfast of orange juice, one soft boiled egg, toasted muffin and coffee. One of the things he missed most about New York were the newspapers. Especially the *Times*. He always tried to read the *Times* thoroughly, then during the day he scanned four or five other papers.

He went back to his compartment. As he came through the Dorrance's car, he glanced at the door but it was closed.

He waited in the aisle until the porter made up his bed, then sat down to finish *Strange Fruit*, but kept the door open and occasionally his eyes strayed to it when he heard the noise of someone approaching and passing.

Don Worth came in.

"I thought you might want to get your forty-three dollars back, honey," he said. "Get out the deck."

"That was a come-on," Vic told him. "Now I want to raise the stakes, just like the ocean-going gamblers do to their suckers."

Worth said, what stakes?

"Four cents a point, take it or leave it."

Worth thought it was pretty steep but agreed to play. Vic ruled the tally columns on a sheet of paper and over Worth's column he wrote DON, while over his he wrote BIG WINNER.

"I'm going to use psychological warfare on you," he warned Don, picking up the first hand. "Give me the right card and I'll knock with nine."

Worth gave him the right card and was at once convinced that Vic had the old hex on him.

Next hand Vic said, "I'm waiting for my gin card, Don. Better unload." He got his gin card three discards later and in three hands rode roughshod over Don with a triple victory.

While he was totaling his winnings, Don said, "I been thinking about Buddy Hare, old chap."

"No wonder you play gin so badly. Thinking about that ham would ruin anybody's game."

"I think you're right. I think you might get a good middle rating out of a low-price Buddy Hare package," Worth said reflectively.

"And furthermore," Vic said. "I frankly don't like your attitude about this game. It seems to me you want to win, to make money. It's a rather sordid, contemptible point of view, if you ask me. Now me, I only play because I'm fond of you, Don. I like your company. I don't even think about winning or losing money. Why down where I come from, people who think about money are considered crass, commercial folk a person wouldn't even consider inviting into the hospitality of his plantation."

"Would Kimberly and Maag finance an audition for a Buddy Hare package?" Don said. "For about four thousand investment you might have a show that'd make you a fortune."

Kimberly and Maag did not happen to be interested in any Talent Ltd. packages at this time, Vic informed him. "Your deal."

Worth asked why.

"Because they hired me, and if any packages are going to be built around a new comedy name, why the hell should they let Talent Ltd. build it, louse it up and collect ten or more percent commission on everybody in the show, that's why? No, Don, if you're trying to interest me in Buddy Hare, it's as one performer in a show I'd build myself."

Worth said he thought the other way was best.

"But would Buddy Hare think it was best, if you cut him out of the chance of a bigtime radio spot just because you couldn't control the entire package?" Vic didn't think he would, frankly. "You see, Don, you're in the middle between your own talent and the ad agencies. We can go to talent direct you know. Talent doesn't like to be pushed around by you agents."

Worth shrugged and said, "Jesus, honey, the cards you deal me. This must be your day."

It was. Vic was incredibly lucky. "What price would you quote on a Hare option?" he said, dealing again after a quick knock.

Don figured you could get him, if you approached him right, for about fifteen hundred a week.

Vic put down his hand. "Where d'you get the idea I was stupid?" he demanded. "If you're going to do business with me, ever, Don, you got to stop thinking I'm stupid. I'm really not stupid at all. I'll bet you five hundred dollars, right now, that I can get off at Albuquerque, phone Buddy Hare direct, offer him $750.00 and get a yes in two fast seconds. I bet he'd say yes without even consulting Talent Ltd."

"Let's say a thousand for him and call it a deal," Worth said. "You expecting someone?"

"No, why?"

"You keep glancing out the door all the time."

"I have a shill out there to tip me off on the cards you're holding. It's nothing, really."

"I'm beginning to think Al Lash asked a fair question last night. Do you really cheat, honey?"

"Sure," said Vic. "But I wouldn't demean myself by cheating a man that plays gin as badly as you. I only cheat good players. How's three?"

Three was wonderful and worth two blitzes. Vic, figuring his winnings, heard the children coming down the aisle and he then admitted to himself that he had been watching for them all morning. He hoped the mother would be with them, too, and she was.

"Game's over," he said, as Hal and Ellen came rushing in. "You owe me one hundred and ninety-one dollars. Good morning, Kay, Hal, Ewwen. This is Mr. Worth."

"I bet you had them planted out there all the time, just to break up the game the minute you'd made a killing," Worth complained. "Hello, Mrs. Dorrance." He gave her a double take and then said, "It's an amazing likeness. Amazing."

"What?" Vic said.

"Look at her," Don said. "She looks almost exactly like Ingrid. Same coloring, same features, everything. Amazing. I must tell Ingrid about this."

"I forgot to tell you, Kay," Vic explained, "Don is what we call in Hollywood a name-mentioner. There are two types of name mentioners, A, those who mention the full name, and, B, those who mention only the first name. It is their intention to show you that they are on speaking terms with celebrities. Don is a type B name-mentioner."

"I'm really quite flattered," Kay said. "Look, we just dropped in to say hello. Don't stop your game."

"Tell me anuya stowy," Ellen said.

"I'd much rather tell Ellen anuya stowy than take money away from this character," Vic said. "Be seeing you, Don."

Worth paid up. "Well, old boy," he said, "as long as I have to lose, I must say that I'd rather lose to you than anyone I know. It's a pleasure to—"

"Look, Don," Vic said, taking the money. "You really are at your most annoying today. If there's anything I hate it's a good loser. Don't be so damn cheerful about it. Act the way you feel. I like bad losers."

Don was ready to leave. "Be seeing you," he said. "Want me to close that deal at a thousand?"

"Nope," Vic said, "I've lost interest. So long, Don."

The porter removed the table and they all sat down. Vic was dominated by the children, of course, with Ellen climbing all over him and Hal drawing beads from all angles.

Kay said, "They've been teasing me to death about visiting you. I hope it's not too much of a burden."

Hal said, "Hey hey, look, this piece of paper looks like a butterfly." He tossed it in the air.

"Like a flutterby," Ellen said and Hal corrected her. "No, Ellen, butterfly."

Vic liked Ellen's word best. "Sure, we grownups call them butterflies, but where's the butter?" he asked. "And they certainly don't look like ugly old flies. So what do they do, they just flutterby you. Ellen, it's a wonderful word."

"Thank you," she said, "tell me anuya stowy." And Hal said Vic hadn't even told one yet, and besides he'd told the last one to her and it was his turn to hear a boy story.

"Hey hey," he said, "does a catbird really sound like a cat?"

Vic told him just a little bit like a cat, and Hal said, "Anyway they sound funny."

"Not to another catbird," Vic claimed. "Only to human beings. Catbirds sound very good to each other."

"I don't get it," Hal said. So Vic said, "Ever been to the Bronx Zoo?" Hal said sure. "Well," Vic said, "ever see the hippopotamus there?" Hal said sure, both of them. "I guess a hippo looks ugly to you?" Hal said, "Terribly ugly." "Well," Vic said triumphantly, "did you ever stop to realize that a hippopotamus looks beautiful to another hippopotamus?"

"A hippopotamus," Hal said reflecting, "would make a fine watchdog . . . they're so ugly they'd scare all the burglars and crooks away."

"Point killer," Vic said. "Besides you'd have to call him a watch hippopotamus."

Kay said, "It's hard to tell which is the oldest, you or Hal."

"Now it's my turn," Ellen commanded. "Anuya stowy." She had a shrill voice that sounded like a bird who had been trained to talk but not very well. She was a thing of wondrous beauty and very affectionate with Vic, kissing him all the time. She would kiss him and say, "That's a weal loud one, isn't it?" She stroked his hair and patted him lovingly.

Kay said, "Hal wants to be a detective when he grows up. . . ."

Hal said, "I haven't decided yet. I may be a doctor, or an engineer, or maybe a deputy sheriff. I haven't made up my mind."

"Anyway, I don't think there's going to be any doubt about Ellen," Kay finished. "She's already studying to be a Lana Turner."

"My love Vic," Ellen said, feeling the lobe of his ear. "My ittle Vic," she crooned.

"Well, don't love him to death, dear," her mother said. "Now we have to go."

"Anuya stowy," Ellen demanded.

"Let me tell them one story," Vic pleaded.

"Hey, hey, tell us a story about an airplane," Hal said.

"No, I wanna stowy about a flutterby," Ellen said.

"Well, this is a story about a man who watched a flutterby and it gave him an idea," Vic began. "He was with his brother on a hilltop covered with blackeyed susans and a flutterby fluttered by and he said to his brother, 'I'm sick and tired of traveling on the ground all the time. I wish I could fly like that flutterby.' So his brother said, 'Maybe we could build us a machine that would let us fly.'

"They both thought that was a good idea, so they studied and worked and built all kinds of strange looking things. And you know what the neighbors did?"

"What?" Hal asked.

"Tell us anuya stowy about what the neighbors din," Ellen said.

"Well they watched these two young men working away and they laughed and laughed. Because they thought these two brothers were crazy, see. 'Ho ho ho,' they laughed, 'those two idiots think they can fly. Like birds, or flutterbys," he added for Ellen's benefit. "Now I can't tell you their names, yet, because that's still a secret, but you know these two brothers finally moved down to a little town called Kitty-hawk, in North Carolina, and—"

"Oh, I know," Hal said, "it was Wilbur and Orville—"

"Don't tell Ellen," Vic said. "And I suppose you know how all the people stood around that Sunday and laughed at these young men, and called them crazy, and stood by just to see them fail. But they didn't fail, their machine did fly, and mankind was given still another way to destroy itself."

"Sure, I know," Hal said. "The first airplane. The Wright brothers."

"Yeah, but did you know what the people standing around laughing themselves sick at these poor fools did, once the poor fools succeeded? Well, sir, they all went to the Wright Brothers and said, 'Oh, what smart men you are. And we knew it all the time.'"

"Then why did they laugh at them?" Hal asked.

"Because, that's the moral of this story. You see, Hal, I always put a moral into my stories when the mother is around."

"Thanks," Kay said.

"What is the moral?"

Vic told him. "If you ever get a new idea and people start laughing at you and calling you crazy, as they always do, don't pay any attention to them. Be like the Wright brothers. Just go ahead and do your work, and let them laugh."

"A wonderful moral," Kay said. "Come children, time to go."

He kissed Ellen and shook Hal's hand, then threw in for good measure a salute, which was snappily returned.

"My love nu," Ellen said.

"She means *you*," Hal translated.

"My do not mean you," Ellen spoke the *you* very clearly, "my mean *nu*."

"She clings to her mother tongue, whatever it is," Vic said;

"she won't give up to an upstart language like English. Won't you stay, Kay?"

Kay said she really couldn't.

"Why not, I'll teach you how to play anagrams."

"Anagrams? Really? I love the game." She said she could never find anyone to play anagrams with and promised to come back.

She was very good at the game and they finished with Vic getting twelve words to her thirteen. Then they talked casual traveler talk about this and that. And Vic learned a few things about her.

Her husband was the famous lawyer, Francis X. Dorrance. Vic associated the name with an old, wealthy New York family.

"Hal's very proud of his father's silver oak leaves," Vic said. "But very mysterious about his duties."

So was Kay. "I only know he's in the O.S.S. He won't tell me what he does."

"Do you know where he is?"

That she could tell him. "In China. And he's coming back soon. He cabled me to go out to California and wait for him. That's why we're making this trip."

"Did you have trouble finding a place to stay?"

"I tried to rent a house," she said, "but California seems to be overcrowded now, so I reserved a cottage at the Sunset Hills Hotel."

Vic told her she was lucky to get even a cottage. "I'm stuck in a suite at the Beverly Plaza. At least you've a fine swimming pool and some palm trees around you."

The palm trees she could forego. "They always seemed to me the ugliest of trees, forlorn and unfriendly and snobbish with their shade."

She was a very comfortable person to talk to. They did not try to impress each other with the warmed-over wit and humor of the day, and there was no struggle to make conversation either. He told her about the part of the war he had seen, and something of his work.

"Just what do people do in advertising agencies?" she asked. "So many of my friends are connected with them, but I never really knew what they did."

Vic explained that the work was very specialized, artists, writers, salesmen, radio people, and various other skilled workers being part of a modern agency.

"In general, however, I would say that an advertising agency is at the intersection of Wall Street, Main Street and Sunset Boulevard. Because of its radio duties, it touches on the glamor of Hollywood and attracts that rather repulsive group known as bright young men, who want to combine their alleged creative impulses with the earning of fancy money. It is, however, a life of insecurity, as ad men float from one agency to another, just as they float from New York to Hollywood and back again, making different sets of sounds for the different groups from whom they extract their livings."

"What kind of sounds?"

"Pleasant-to-client sounds. For example, you never say to a client 'I have a great idea.' No. You make him think it's his idea."

"Are you one of those bright young men?" she asked.

"I was. Being thirty-five, I am now an old advertising man. By the time you're forty, if you don't own a big chunk of some agency, you're gradually squeezed out by the newcomers, preferably from Yale, who being less cynical can sound more enthusiastic about the sensational new ideas they hatch every half-hour on the half-hour. Actually, I'm ready for either a partnership or the junkheap."

"With your intelligence, I prophesy a partnership," she said.

"Oh, everyone in the ad game is intelligent. They have to be. You see, ad men are half-creative. For example, disappointed novelists do very well in what I call the ad game. So they have liberal ideas. But since their life consists of keeping reactionary old men who control bluechip companies happy, they have to be smart enough to keep those ideas well hidden. They voted for Roosevelt last election, on the one hand, while on the other hand they made their clients feel they were going to vote for Dewey. That sly little victory was won by keeping a well-polished stock of anti-Roosevelt jokes on tap at all times."

"My," she laughed. "You are a cynic, aren't you? If you think big business is so terrible, why don't you do something about it?"

"Big business isn't terrible. And the men who run big business are only accidentally bad. But that's another sermon, dear girl. Right now, the ad man has other worries. And the greatest of these is prosperity."

"I should think he'd love it."

"Not in wartime. Advertising is non-essential, so he literally has nothing to sell, which frustrates him. Yet because of the excess profits tax, his clients spend money like water because it only costs them ten cents or less on the dollar. So he gets the feeling he's in non-essential work. He also feels guilty about not being in the war, although he's so welded to his symbols of living that he usually pulls every string to stay out."

"Do you feel non-essential?"

"Yes, but not because of the war. I felt that way long before the war. But I'm different." He paused a long time, gazing thoughtfully at the New Mexico hills. "Seriously," he confessed, "I don't get any kick out of success. And most ad men glory in success. Somehow or other I have a disdain for the kind of cheap, sensational mass advertising appeals it takes to sell goods. Just as I feel a kind of contempt for what you have to put on the radio to get a lot of people to listen to your program."

"I know you've been speaking half in fun," she mused. "But I've been watching you. You wear a look that is not good."

"Well," he grinned, "I guess I have let my personal appearance run down a little, but—"

"You know I don't mean that," she said. "You're very handsome and you know it. I mean your look. Your face, it's like a mask. Nothing impresses it very much. Your eyes, they're totally lacking in expression, they don't light up. And when you laugh, it's a muscular laugh, and it leaves your face in an instant and there is no feeling of gaiety at all. You seem to be remote, a man who sits with people but is not ever a part of them in anything. It's . . . but I guess I sound pretty silly."

"I don't know," he said soberly. "I really don't know whether you're talking nonsense or not. I hope you are. You just made quite an indictment of me. I realize I don't get too much of a bang out of things. And I certainly don't like this hustling business I'm in. But that's probably my fault. Lots of people like it. I know a whore named Gladys who doesn't like whoring. But she knows what she does like. She wants to own a dress shop on Park Avenue. I know a man who likes to sell soap. I don't. I guess all I really know is what I don't like. I don't have the vaguest notion what I do like. I suppose you'd call me socially unconscious as well as socially insignificant. A genuine minus mark."

Kay was still thinking about what she called Vic's look.

"But when you play with children, mine at least, you do, well, light up is a poor way to describe it—but you seem to get an inner pleasure that doesn't show up any other time."

They gazed out into the New Mexico scene without speaking. A tiny town flowed by their window.

"In my world," Vic said, "America is a place called Hollywood and a place called New York. There are cities and places in between, but to me and my world they are total abstractions called markets, important only for the curves they make on sales charts and Hooper rating indices. The two hubs are connected, now that you can't fly without the danger of being hopelessly set down in a total abstraction like Memphis or Kansas City or Cincinnati, by the New York Central and the Santa Fe Railroads. Or to be completely specific, by the Twentieth Century Limited between New York and Chicago, and by the Chief, daily out of Chicago and Los Angeles, and on Tuesdays and Fridays only, by the Super Chief. . . .

"That little town we just left," he said. "That one little

store. Martinez's Market. One case of Beautee a month. Love that soap. Love that Mr. Martinez."

"You know what," she said suddenly, "I think you're an artist and don't know it. A writer, maybe."

"No," he said. "I've written enough radio stuff to know' I'm not a writer. I could be a good commercial radio or movie writer but I'd hate myself *every* morning. I have a kind of disdain for writers, too. Not the few good ones. But I'm not of that class.

"You see, Kay, a real honest-to-god artist has an easy out—his ivory tower. It's we characters who haven't any ivory tower to run to that are really trapped. And we find out too late that a thousand dollars a week won't help us much either."

She kept right on, trying to find some place where he could fit into the world. "Why don't you try a serious piece of writing? You could do a wonderful satire on radio, knowing it so well. With your sardonic slant it could be a fascinating caricature."

"There's no need to caricature radio. All you have to do is listen to it. Or if you were writing about it, you'd simply report with fidelity what goes on behind the scenes. It'd make a perfect farce."

"Then why don't you do it?"

"I told you I am not an artist," Vic said. "I don't feel like an artist. I don't have any position about life that is even slightly artistic. And worst of all, I don't burn to capture some interpretation of experience. Having a flair for words is no yardstick. You either feel as an artist or you don't."

"I guess the whole world is unhappy," she said.

"You, too."

"I wouldn't include myself, but only because I'm self-conscious. I don't like to talk about myself."

"You'll get along great in Hollywood," he said. "You'll be so different."

"Tell me about Hollywood."

He said there was nothing to tell. Outside of certain deviations from the norm, it was like any other place. She asked for an example of what he meant by deviations and he thought carefully, and said, "Well, Hollywood is a place where people fall in love for reasons other than love."

She said love had often been used as a ladder to social or business success, that it wasn't peculiar to Hollywood. They sat in silence. She concerned herself with what made Vic tick.

"So you don't like writers either," she much later said. "You're a strange man, Vic. What do you like?"

"I wish I knew. About writers, it's their pretense I dislike. Most of them are semiliterate folk who have acquired a certain meagre skill at stringing words together. So they begin to look on themselves as being something special. And then they get pro-Freudian and anti-Fascist and make with all the fashionable chatter about the writer's position in society and I just think they're a bunch of not very convincing poseurs. No, Kay, like me most of them have no art, just talent."

"Well," she said, "if you won't be a writer, at least you can be an intellectual."

"Smile when you call me that," he said. "The American intellectual is the world's most outrageous example of sterility."

"Why? Or should I say how?"

"Well, he considers himself a leftish liberal, but actually through years of rigorous training he has got himself trapped in ideologies. He is totally incapable of considering his own personal interests objectively."

"I'm afraid you'll have to draw pictures for me," she said.

"Easily. Take any political act or idea. Does the American intellectual consider it from the point of his own interest or of his country's interest? Never. He always feels compelled to accept it or reject it on the basis of Soviet interests. Always. Whether the issue is good, bad or indifferent."

"Why?"

"Probably because his failure as an individual has made him reject individualism. So he clings with fanatic devotion to all mass things, the farther away the better—and he believes that individuals should never have any rights, only masses. You see, the intellectual has discovered Freud, invented neuroticism, and discarded God. In short, he has lost faith in himself, as a man, so he pins all his faith on some remote mass of men, possibly as a substitute for his discarded god.

"What am I saying?" Vic demanded. "And how did I ever get started talking this way. I don't even understand myself."

Bennett stuck his head in and said, "Did you hear about the man who spelled Serutan sideways?"

"Come in," said Vic, "and defend yourself. I was just giving writers hell, Mr. Bennett is a writer, Mrs. Dorrance."

Bennett said, "According to the New York drama critics, I'm no writer. According to the Global Studios I'm a two grand a week writer. Me, I don't know."

"Let's not talk about your play," Vic said. "I saw it, unfortunately."

"Don't mind this El Morocco misanthrope, Mrs. Dorrance," Bennett said. "He's really a very nice guy. I worked with him once."

"On a radio show?"

No, this was for the government, Bennett explained. "I was on the Writers War Board. He was with OWI. We were all looking for a good horror story—and then Lidice happened. It was a small town, so people could grasp the unity and simplicity of it. And the Germans killed everyone in the town, total war, total brutes, you know. It was just what we'd been looking for, we knew the people would go crazy, and we had all our writers steamed up about it. But we ran into a snag and Old Vic got us unhooked."

He explained that, too. "We couldn't get our plan to the President. Some of those fascists around him didn't think it was big enough. We knew the President would see it instantly, but somebody had to angle past the outer guard and get to him. Which Vic fixed. He's really got a good heart, Mrs. Dorrance."

"Propaganda," Vic said, "is like washing dishes. Necessary but distasteful. I know what it takes to get people steamed up, but personally I'd rather shoot a fascist than write impassioned pieces against him."

"I should warn you, Mrs. Dorrance," Bennett said, "that Vic is not only against fascism, he is also against people who are against fascism. In short, he's against people."

"I simply don't happen to be the type who groups and regroups groups for fashionable crusades. Hell, everybody's against fascism. So am I. But I don't think the death of Hitler is going to usher in an era of utopia. Somebody'll just coin a new word for fascism, that's all."

Bennett said, "Move over." He sat down. "Incidentally, Mrs. Dorrance, I suppose lots of people have told you you look very much like Ingrid Bergman."

"He's the type A name-mentioner," Vic said.

Bennett looked out of the window. "Desolate, isn't it?"

Vic said, "Quote it's beautiful to ride through and look at, but God, darling, can you imagine people living out there unquote."

"Speaking of slogans, did anyone ever think to call Jello or some such thing the Great American Dessert?" Bennett said, picking an idea off the landscape.

"You should get a new writer," Vic said. "Your material stinks."

"I write my own stuff," he said and Vic thought that made it completely unforgivable.

The Super Chief pulled into Albuquerque and Vic went out with Kay to stroll and stretch. He amused himself buying Indian trinkets for the two children. Connie, still with her Navy man, came up behind him and said, "Darling, how are the children, anyway?"

He liked Connie. She was like a man. If she wanted to go to bed, she went to bed and then forgot about it. No problems, no dealing in futures, no regrets. And for that reason, Connie was a more desirable woman for him than Jean Ogilvie, who had caused him considerable worry since their last meeting. He felt responsible for the torch Jean carried, and wished he had not been the cause of her getting involved and mixed up and unhappy.

Kay said, "That was a very beautiful woman who spoke to you. Is she some movie star?"

"Sort of," he said and then they laughed happily together at an overheard remark, when a girl told her friend, "My agent said I simply had to get a mink coat or the studio wouldn't respect me."

[CHAPTER IX]

THE SUPER CHIEF, DEAF, DUMB AND BLIND TO THE TRAVELERS
who paid its way, rushed relentlessly towards Hollywood, alive
with motion, pushed and prodded by that old railroad watch,
time.

For Vic there was dinner with Kay, fond good nights to
her children, and later from her a polite but firm refusal to
sit and talk further into the Arizona night. There was also for
Vic a good feeling in being involved with this traveling trio,
three-fourths of another man's family. And later, when *Strange
Fruit* was done away with and lay deserted on its back, there
was a tap on the door, but he told Connie that he had a split-
ting headache, and she went, probably back to her navy
lieutenant. Then there was sleeplessness and that restless man,
Vic, put up his blind and lay in his bunk watching the moonlit land which had been set in motion by the Super Chief.

The moon was blacked out by a cloud bank, and Vic, no
longer able to see, pulled down the blind and tried to sleep.

He did not toss, turn, punch pillows, or kick off blankets.
But after a time, he again switched on the light, climbed out
of bed, found his pen and a pad of empty telegraph blanks,
and half sitting up in his bunk, wrote rapidly. Once he
stopped writing to raise the blind and peer out the window,
but there was only blackness, and he lowered the blind to
continue his writing.

This is what he wrote:

137

Restlessness swells into a lump that aches as throb-bingly as any tooth. And during the climax of the pain, restlessness has an urge to cure itself by expressing itself.

At that instant in restlessness, all men behave as artists. There is a compulsion to describe in some creative form the area of restlessness through which one is traveling.

The sufferer seeks to define the cause of his restlessness, which is usually one of the hungers: love, hate, fear, and above all, loneliness.

He is inclined to stare savagely into the leisure of the night and consider with brief terror how his life is spent.

He may blame his restlessness on externals, such as traveling, or peering out at strange horizons. He loses con-tact with old familiar things; even his homeland seems remote and abstract. To a restless man on a train, for instance, America becomes only a ribbon stretching from his window to the hilltops or the horizon, whichever comes first. The Palisades are back of him, and Lake Michigan and the Tribune Tower of Chicago. Then the farmlands, the corn and hog lands, the black loam lands, the small white house and big red barn lands. And on into the flat wheatlands, sand colored—and out of those Kansas flat-lands into the Colorado hills, sloping sharply upward to the pass at Raton. Mountains far background, red gullied bone dry soil foreground. Adobe shacks, too. The other houses, barn red or railroad yellow. The earth now all sides and tops. Flat topped, slabsided, snow topped, jagged shapes of the west. Truly a godforsaken land. Mesas, buttes, arroyos, gulches and so on and so forth. Flora, or is it fauna? One is mesquite, the other greasewood, but the man on the train doesn't know which is which. The roads lead-ing like intestines into the hills.

Yes, it's a great country all right. Yes sir. A fella has to travel through it to appreciate it.

And the man on the train looking into the Super-Chief-dominated night, looking hard, with concentration, thinks: yes, this is America I am passing through, this is my own

*my native land, its people are my people, its god my god
. . . and it is my great loss that I am so restless and unful-
filled in the midst of all its glory. I can only say to myself
and to no one else, only to myself in this Super-Chief-
imposed Arizona solitude, that I wish I could have a more
profound feeling for my country, my people, and myself.
I do not, in all truth, seem part of you, or do you seem
part of me.*

*And then the man on the train tries to console himself
with this thought: Maybe I'm just one of those in-be-
tweens. Maybe I'm the man who stands to the left of the
patriot who says, "My country, right or wrong," and to the
right of the character who even now is practicing how to
say, "The Earth expects every man to do his duty." Or
perhaps I only drank too much coffee for dinner.*

*At this point, the moon left Arizona and the restless
man on the train, aching-eyed, pulls down his blind, knowing that tomorrow he will hear someone say, "California,
here we come," and someone else say, "It's good to be back
in God's country," and also knowing that the last hour,
sliding alongside the orange groves and looking into the
blue-green depths of the hills above them, will be, as it
always had been before, the longest hour of the journey. . . .*

Vic put aside the pad on which he was writing, turned
off the light, and being too fagged to appreciate the cure his
restlessness had urged upon him, fell asleep with miraculous
speed. And once asleep he kept at it until midmorning.

He saw the telegraph pad while he was shaving, and the
lather on his face dried while he self-consciously read his essay.

Shaking his head in amusement, he carefully tore the
sheets to pieces and went back to his razor.

By the time he had dressed and breakfasted, the Super
Chief was well into the last hour. Passing the door of Kay
Dorrance's compartment, he again found it closed and again
resisted his desire to knock on it.

Anyway, he'd see her at the station, and he had some fast business with Don Worth.

The agent was packing.

"Okay," Vic said. "Let's make a deal for Buddy Hare. We haven't much time left."

"Righto," Worth said. "For a thousand a week?"

"Okay," Vic said. "A thousand, you robber. Are you authorized to sign an option letter on him?"

"Sure, honey. But what's the rush? We can do it in Hollywood."

"Nope," Vic was definite. "It's now or never. I figure I can cut a suitable agency audition on Hare and look good to my new boss, Kimberly. But I'm not going to any more trouble than necessary and I'll be damned if I go to the bother of sitting around with you Talent Ltd. characters for two or three days while you work up one of those big formal legal-eagle deals. All I want is a simple option letter now, take it or leave it."

Worth appraised Vic silently, then gave him the nod. "Okay, honey, he's your baby. I'll send you a letter this afternoon. And don't think Lash won't give me hell for not building our own package around him. He'll swear Old Man Evans sent you out here to get Buddy Hare, too."

"Why Don," Vic said chidingly. "How could you be so suspicious? It's not at all like you. Not much, it isn't."

The train had stopped at Pasadena, where many of the Beverly Hills people got off, and was just pulling out when Vic saw Kay, the nurse and the children on the station platform. He waved and tapped the window, but they did not see him. He turned back to his business, but with a sense of loss, which he overcame at once as he realized that it was a train friendship and the closeness that he felt for the Dorrances was artificially induced by the confinement on the train. It was something to be forgotten the minute the traveler's foot touched solid ground again.

"No need to send me a letter," Vic said. "I'll write it here and we'll both sign it."

"Oh forget it, Vic," Don said. "Why bother? Let our lawyer draw it up."

"I know more about law than most bricklayers," Vic said. "Where can I find Bennett?"

He borrowed Bennett's typewriter and, as the Super Chief pulled into Los Angeles he was typing:

> Don Worth
> Talent Ltd.
> Hollywood, Calif.
> Gentlemen:
> This letter of agreement gives Kimberly and Maag, Inc., an irrevocable, exclusive option on the services of the performer known professionally as Buddy Hare, said option to . . .

[CHAPTER X]

KIMBERLY WALKED IN CIRCLES AROUND THE INFORMATION DESK
at Penn Station. It was seven minutes before train time. He
had arrived punctually eight minutes earlier. But Maggie, as
usual, was late.

It was five of when she finally arrived, yoo-hooing at him
from yards away. Kim didn't like to be yoo-hooed at in public,
either.

The porter took her case and Kim pulled her after him to
the gates. He had no percent of patience left.

"It's very upsetting, Maggie. You have no right to upset
me this way."

She said she was sorry, darling, but that Kimmy had
started bawling as she went out the door, and she just couldn't
tear herself away until she had quieted him down.

"Mrs. Holmes is simply helpless around him," she said.
"I don't think he likes her at all, darling. There's some kind
of conflict between them. It worries me."

"It might help if you'd worry about catching trains." He
was still unrelenting.

They were on the train in plenty of time, of course, and
Kim immediately said, "I need a drink. I'll be in the club car,
unless you want to come along."

Maggie did want to come along. She knew Kim was so
terribly, terribly busy all the time, and she overlooked no op-

portunity to spend a few minutes with him whenever his frightful old schedule permitted.

"And don't be cross, darling. You won't enjoy your dinner if you let yourself get upset like this," she called after him as they crossed from the parlor car to the club car. He wished she wouldn't screech at him that way.

They were on the three o'clock to Washington and would eat dinner at the hotel. Kim hated train meals, especially nowadays in the wartime travel jam.

They found seats and ordered drinks. Maggie said she didn't want any, but Kim said he'd drink hers if she didn't.

"Do you realize, darling, that you haven't told me why we're going to Washington."

It was unimportant, Kim said. He spoke so inaudibly she had to strain to hear him. Just some dull business about priorities. He didn't want to talk about it.

"Don't drink so fast, darling," she said. "It's a four hour ride. And you said we might have to stay for a week, maybe. It must be important, to take you away from Mr. Evans for so long."

"That's all right, Mrs. DA," he said. His second drink had relaxed him and he felt better towards, one, the world, and two, his wife. "The reason I'm going is because of Mr. Evans."

"Well, I did find out a little something, anyway," she said. "I wonder if all men are so closemouthed about business as you are? With their wives, I mean."

Kim didn't know. He also did not understand how any woman in her right mind could possibly be interested in such things.

So Maggie explained it to him. "I think a wife wants to and can be a help to her husband in his business, darling. A woman has a kind of, well, I guess you might call it intuitive way of approaching problems that a man hasn't. A man's mind is more orderly and logical. But sometimes I think business decisions have to be made on instinct. Don't you, darling?"

"It also helps to have a little information too," he said.

"I like these little bottles they serve you on trains. You can drink doubles without people thinking you're a dipso. Why are you wearing your brooch, lover?"

"It does look awful with this suit, doesn't it?" She felt the brooch lovingly. "But I have a surprise for you, darling. The most scrumptious dress Hattie Carnegie ever turned out. Ummmm," she said. "And it just cries for my brooch."

"I hope it's a black dress," he said.

"Of course it's black," she cried. "And simple. But really clean and simple. Just the way you like my dresses only more so. The brooch will be the one touch of ornament. Hattie thought a long time before she'd even consent to letting me put the brooch on it."

She was going to change into the new dress at the hotel then they could go out to dinner and he could be proud of his well-dressed wife. "Look, darling," she said, "here comes Irving Brown."

She called and motioned to the empty chair beside her. "Hello, Irving, I didn't know you were on this train. How nice."

"Didn't Kim tell you?" Irving sat down and Kim said, "Drink?" Irving could just stay for one. He had to read some legal papers.

"I've spent all my time in Mr. Evans' office lately on this manufacturing problem," he explained. "I'm way behind in my work. And this expedition is not going to help me catch up either."

"What are you betting on our chances, Irving?" Kim asked. Irving said it was yes and no, fifty-fifty. "It all depends on developing a friendly feeling with the Board. We have a borderline case that can legitimately be decided either way."

Maggie said it sounded very mysterious to her. "You know, Irving, that Kim never tells me anything. About business, I mean. Do you ever tell Pat anything? How is that wonderful wife of yours anyway?"

Irving said Pat was fine. Then they talked about his house in the country and what income taxes were doing to Irving's way of life. "I'm not objecting to them, understand," he said, "it's more like a joke with us, learning how to economize. Pat always thinks of things that save thirty cents a week."

"Maggie always thinks of deductions that are against the law," Kim said.

He sat and chattered brightly with them about country houses, knotty pine playrooms, impudent servants and a lot of other things, up to and including the story about the head-waiter at the Colony, the woman with the low decolletage, and the two warm spoons.

And when Irving prepared to return to his legal papers, Kim said, "Don't go yet. I seldom get a chance to sit down for a friendly chat with you, Irving. You're always so damned busy."

But Irving had to go, much as he would have liked staying with Maggie and Kim in the club car.

Maggie said, "At least you can have dinner with us to-night, can't you Irving? We'd love it."

Kim laughed heartily, "Maggie has a new dress she wants to show off."

"I'd love to," Irving said. "And I promise to admire the dress, Maggie. I'll make a note to remember to give Pat a full report on it. Thanks, you nice people. It's lonesome eating alone. What about the Embassy Room at the Statler at eight-thirty?"

"It's a date," Kim said.

Irving left and Maggie said, "I'm so glad we thought to ask Irving to dinner. He was lonely and dying for an invitation."

"You asked him," Kim said, waving at the porter and pointing at his empty glass. "I didn't."

Maggie was shocked. "Darling, you seconded it. I heard you."

"I didn't ask him, and I didn't want to eat dinner with him," Kim said. "I haven't any new dress I want to show off, and besides, I don't like Irving Brown."

Maggie was amazed. "You don't like Irving? Why you were always very fond of him. This must be something new."

"No, it's nothing new," Kim said.

"I don't understand you at all, today," Maggie complained. "Something must be bothering you. But anyway, I'm sorry I asked him, if it annoys you."

"Forget it," Kim said. "Everybody can make a mistake. Even your intuition. I'll just write it off to a faulty intuition, and deduct it from my income tax."

Maggie made several attempts at conversation but Kim did not respond so she read *Coronet* and he silently drank his way to Washington.

As Kim was tipping the bellhop and ordering ice and soda water, Maggie went into the bedroom and said, "I'm famished. I'll change in a jiffy, darling."

Kim asked if jiffy was still a synonym for two hours. "And even if it is, it'll take a strong wind at your back to help you make it," he said.

The bellboy chuckled and left. Kim opened his bag to get a bottle of scotch.

"Don't drink too much," Maggie called. "Or you won't want any dinner."

He stood at the door with the bottle in his hand. "And no fair peeking," she said. "I won't let you see the dress until I'm ready to model it for you."

Kim drank while Maggie dressed. He was very gay when she did make her entrance. "Lover," he said, getting up to walk around her. "It's a knockout. You look positively sleepable-with in it."

"It's still a size twelve," she bragged. "See how beautifully it fits around the hips."

He ran his hand over her hips. "It's a hell of a fitter around the hips," he said. "How do you manage to squeeze into it?"

It was done with zippers, she explained, demonstrating. "You don't think the brooch is too gauche, do you darling? Hattie was afraid it'd be a little gauche."

He didn't think so at all. "I don't think a diamond brooch that cost twenty-two thousand dollars wholesale could ever be gauche, lover. Come here."

He stroked her lovingly. "I always did say you had the most magnificent construction on all of Park Avenue, lover. You're really very, very sleepable-with."

"I'm very, very hungry," she corrected. "Let's go downstairs. Irving is always ten minutes early to everything."

Kim had a better idea. "Let's get drunk first; Irving is much easier to take when I'm drunk." He poured himself a drink. "You're not drinking," he accused. "Have a drink."

"I want to show off my dress," she pouted. "Come on, Kim, let's go downstairs."

She didn't want a drink, either. "How do you suppose I'd stay size twelve, darling, if I drank all the time?"

It wasn't that at all, he said. "Drinking makes you sexy. You just don't want to be sexy. You're trying to sex-starve me."

She said she was too hungry to be sexy. That would have to wait until she'd had some dinner. Kim finished his drink and flung himself on the bed and closed his eyes.

"Poor tired darling," Maggie sat beside him and put her fingers on his eyes. "Something's bothering you, Kimmy love, and you won't tell me what it is."

"Nothing's bothering me," he said.

Maggie tenderly stroked and patted his hot flushed face. "What is it, Kim? Dear, please tell me what's bothering you? Is it something about Mr. Evans?"

He reached out his hand, groped for the bottle, found it, sat up to pour a straight drink. "The only thing that's bothering me," he drank, then settled back down on the pillow, "is your frigidity."

She was shocked. "Darling! Why, darling! You never said that before."

He said, no, but he'd thought it before. Many, many, many times before.

"Many's the time I've made love to you," he said, waving

the glass, "when I felt I was imposing my body on yours. It's getting worse, too. When we were first married you used to be like a mink. A size twelve mink. But now you get older and colder."

He sat up again. "I guess I'm a little tight," he said wearily. "Maybe I can't remember those first days very well. Maybe you were just putting on an act. Was that it, lover? Were you just putting on an act? And then you got kinda tired of acting, is that it, lover?"

Maggie stood up and put her hands to her temples, pressing hard. "Quit picking on me," she cried. "So that's what's been bothering you? So that's what you've been thinking about —and drinking about too, I suppose!"

"Okay, okay," he said. "Let's make a deal. No more acts. Okay, no more acts. So it's been an act, all these years, lover?"

His inflection on the word *lover* was most insulting.

She said in a flat, defeated manner, "Yes, if you insist. I guess it has been an act. Not all of the time. Not even now all of the time. But if you must know, I can't jump into bed every time you say 'jump.' And—oh, I'm not like you," she cried. "And I can't be like you. I've tried so hard to be and I can't be. With you, love is like drinking. It's something you do to forget things you don't want to think about."

The things she was saying shocked him, but they seemed so true to him, and her dilemma so understandable, that he became compassionate. He sat on the bed and looked at her solemnly.

He said now gently, "I do want to understand you, Maggie. I love you and I don't want to force myself on you. It's just that I thought you liked it too, the way I did."

"I do, Kim, I do," she cried. "But not any minute of the day or night. I can't help feeling frustrated sometimes. Don't you understand?"

"Sure," he said. "Sure. I understand." He mixed another drink. "Come here."

He lay back again and she snuggled beside him, careful

not to muss her dress, and they were tender and morose, thoughtful and bittersweet and comforting to each other. He held her hand and stared at the ceiling.

The last drink had burned the clarity out of his mind and it was a confused mixture of past and present selflessness and selfishness, hope and hopelessness. He felt like a heel, not only for what he'd said to her, but for how he'd treated her, for how he'd acted with her and with other women. He guessed he'd never recover from being a minister's son. He'd tried to change his conscience, but it always flaunted him with the stern, unforgiving maxims of his early presbyterianism.

"I didn't mean it," he said. "I'm a little tired, that's all. I'll try to understand you better," he promised. "From now on."

"Poor darling," she crooned, tender and motherlike. "I understand you so well. It's not what you think it is at all."

He dropped her hand. "What do you mean, it's not what I think it is?"

"Oh, darling, admit it. I was just an excuse. What's the use of going to psychiatrists if you don't learn to probe into the real reasons?"

She had broken the contact with him. He said:

"That should be interesting, what you think are the real reasons."

"It's business, darling," she explained. "That's what's made you upset. You're worried about something and you won't tell me what worries you. So you transfer your worry to some other object . . . in this case, me."

The resentment rose like gorge within him. He said nothing.

"If you'd only confide in me, darling," she said. "You'd feel better. Just talking it over, with a lamppost even, would make you feel better."

He abruptly left the bed and found the bottle.

She stood up, too, smoothing her dress about her. "Now you're annoyed again, darling," she said. "What have I done this time?"

"No," he said. "You haven't annoyed me. I think it's wonderful that you're so interested in my business worries. You're what I'd call a helpmeet."

"You are, too, annoyed," she said.

He drank. "As a matter of fact, I wasn't worrying about business at all. Business is fine. Never been better. Well, it might be a little better after I've hypnotized the War Production people. But anyway, Kimberly and Maag is in great shape. Are in great shape," he corrected.

"Then why are you worried?" she said.

"I said I wasn't worried. I've been thinking, that's all. Seeing Irving Brown on the train simply started me thinking about the real secret of my fabulous success."

"Oh," she said. "We forgot all about poor Irving waiting down there."

"Are you interested in my business problems or are you interested in Irving Brown?" he demanded. "I'm trying to tell you something."

"Please do," she said. "I want you to tell me."

"I've never told you the secret of my fabulous success," he went on. "Been saving it for my autobiography. But since you're so interested in the business I guess I should. I guess I owe it to you."

She could not quite follow him or make much of what he said, so she said, with rare intelligence, nothing.

He continued, speaking in a style which was painstakingly simple, as if he were explaining advertising to a young neophyte.

"I was a young, dumb kid, hot out of Princeton, and not smart enough to pour piss out of a boot. But an old friend and parishioner of my father's, a man named Harry Atlee, owned an advertising agency. Strictly from charity he gave me a job."

"Darling," she said. "You really don't think I know much about you, do you? I know about Harry Atlee giving you a job. I read about it in *Who's Who*."

"That's right," he said. "It's nice to know you keep up with your reading. But I bet *Who's Who* didn't say that the

Beautee Soap account was the cornerstone of Harry Atlee's business, did it?"

"Darling," she said, "pour me a drink, please. If I'm not going to eat, I might as well drink."

He fixed her a drink, saying, "If you'd rather eat . . ."

"No, dear, not at all. I really do want to hear the rest of your story. Please go on."

"Thanks," he said. "Harry Atlee was worth a lot of money, having disdained stock speculation. So when the market crashed the second time in 1933, it was only natural that the boys from Beautee would come to good old Harry to borrow cash to pay off their market losses."

He sat down in a fake Louis Quatorze chair and slumped back, looking at the ceiling and talking, still drinking too.

"And I doubt if the *Who's Who* piece on Irving Brown told about Irving calling up Harry Atlee one day and putting the bite on him for ninety grand. Again to pay off his brokers."

"Irving Brown is not in *Who's Who*," she said. "Mr. Evans is, but Irving isn't. I looked."

"Even if there was a *Who's Who* piece on Irving, I doubt if he'd submit copy on that point," Kim said. "Anyway, by that time I'd become the assistant contact man for Beautee soap and Harry Atlee was very pleased with me because my courtly, old world, Princetonian manners had appealed to the Old Man and he was saying nice things about me, even needling Harry to raise my salary. I was poor, you see."

"That was before I met you," Maggie mused, sipping her drink distastefully. She didn't like liquor, and always went through elaborate pretensions of drinking it. "You always had oceans of money, ever since I knew you."

"Evans money," he said. "But at the same time that I had earned the right to quake before the Old Man's wrath, during the first days of the depression, Beautee was involved in a big patent suit that had been fought clear up to the Federal Court. There was a good chance that the company would be fined the maximum, twenty million dollars. And it was touch and go whether Judge Delehanty, the federal jurist trying the case, would give them the limit. All this was going on when Beautee stock was depreciating insanely and the company was in a critical spot. Am I boring you?"

She hurriedly told him of course not, it was a fascinating story and she was flattered that he'd take the time to tell it to her.

"No trouble at all," he said graciously saluting her with his glass.

"So one day Irving Brown calls Harry Atlee again. On the private wire, of course. He was very mysterious. He told Harry a very important personage, whose name he couldn't mention, needed four hundred thousand dollars cash. For you know what, he said."

"What?" Maggie asked.

"Those were Irving Brown's exact words to Harry. For you know what. What would your intuition figure from that?"

She thought about it and said, "I'd think that the important personage was Mr. Evans. And that he wanted Harry Atlee to loan him money to pay off his stock losses."

"You're terrific," he said. "That's exactly what Harry Atlee thought. So, following Irving's instructions, he certifies a check for four hundred thousand dollars, payable to bearer, and waits for the messenger Brown said he would send right up from Wall Street."

"How exciting, darling. It's just like a story. And you tell it beautifully."

"So the messenger comes and guess who it is?"

Maggie had no idea who the messenger was.

"Well," he said, "I guess anybody's intuition can fail once in a while. The messenger was Judge Delehanty's bagman."

Maggie had not the faintest idea what a bagman was.

"He's the man who picked up the bribe from Harry Atlee, lover. It was the pay-off to Judge Delehanty. And the following week the Judge decided the patent case in favor of the Beautee Soap Company and they weren't fined twenty million dollars after all."

"Really? Then what happened, darling?"

Kim drank some more. "Oh, nothing much. The FBI traced the bribe down, and the government indicted Delehanty, Atlee, Brown and Evans. Harry Atlee was enraged at the Beautee Soap Company for involving him, an innocent man, in this sordid mess and it actually looked for a time as if he would be sent to jail. He told the U. S. District Attorney the whole truth, however, and the federal grand jury finally believed and exonerated him.

"But Evans did not think Harry would mention Brown's name and tell about the previous loans and he in turn became enraged at Atlee for what he called a double cross.

"And now our hero—that's me—comes on the scene, summoned by Evans for a conference. He said he liked the cut of my jib. He said I was on the beam and he thought with his help and good advice I could stay on the beam. So he offered me the entire Beautee soap account on condition I would open my own agency. I gave the matter a lot of thought, spending probably eight full seconds on it before saying, Yes sir, Mr. Evans, and gee, thanks." He drank again. "And that was the beginning of Kimberly and Maag."

"What did they do to Mr. Evans?" Maggie said. "I should think, they would—"

"He claimed total ignorance of the entire deal and Brown took the rap, testifying that he had engineered the deal without Evans' knowledge. The court fined Brown, reversed Delehanty's decision, and poor Irving got a jail sentence, which was humanely revoked before he ever served it. Judge Delehanty got ten years but never served either. He committed suicide."

Kim stopped and there was a bit of silence while Maggie digested all this.

Then she said, "You know, it's perfectly amazing the way those FBI men work. What I can't understand is how on earth they could ever trace a certified check made out to cash. That judge must have made some slip. Is that what happened, darling?"

"He sure did," Kim said. "You fascinate me, lover. You

show a burning desire to know what happened to everybody in the case except the one man who was betrayed by it."

She had to unravel this one. "Oh," she said. "You must mean Harry Atlee, don't you, darling? What did happen to poor Mr. Atlee?"

Kim walked over and threw himself on the bed. He was very tired tonight.

"Jesus," he said wearily, "you really are interested in my business, aren't you, lover? I guess I should talk about it to you more often. I really should."

And then he said, "How the hell should I know what happened to Harry Atlee? He never spoke to me again."

"Darling," Maggie sat down beside him now. "You poor darling. You are tired, aren't you? It's a shame we have to meet Irving Brown." She looked at her watch. "Oh darling, it's eight-fifty. We're late."

"No," Kim said thoughtfully. "I don't really care for Irving Brown. I guess I'm not what a person like you might call fond of Irving." He yawned. "Ol' Vic Norman hit it right on the barrelhead when he described Irving. He sure did."

"What did Vic say about him, darling?" Maggie asked.

"Ol' Vic just said, 'There but for the grace of God, goes the Archbishop of Kimberly.'"

"Get some rest, darling," she implored. "Please rest. I'll go down and tell Irving you're not feeling well."

"I don't want to rest," Kim said, turning away from her hand. "I want to go to bed. Do you understand, helpmeet? I want you to come to bed."

Maggie stood up. Kim's face was turned away from her, so he could not tell whether his eyes were open or closed.

She delicately held the almost empty bottle of scotch and poured a glass about half full, letting the whiskey run into the glass very quietly. She then turned her back to the bed and drank the whiskey, forcing it down, gulp by gulp, making tears come to her eyes, but not choking over it.

She put down the glass and her fingers felt for, found and slowly removed the diamond brooch from the Hattie Carnegie dress. They placed the brooch silently on the table and then reached slowly but unsurely for the side zipper that made the dress fit so well over her hips.

"Of course, darling," she said.

CHAPTER XI

VIC HAD BEEN IN HOLLYWOOD THREE DAYS AND BY NOW WAS thoroughly slowed down to the more leisurely coast tempo. He had accumulated all the standard equipment for visiting New York executives: a rented drive-it-yourself convertible roadster, a suite at an approved hotel, doeskin slacks and a peach-fuzzy camel hair jacket, a slightly red nose from lounging at swimming pools, the visitor's office in the Hollywood quarters of his firm, and a borrowed secretary named Norma who was dying to learn all about radio.

It was eleven a.m. and the office was just beginning to show a little action, as producers, writers, script girls, and agents began to saunter in to spend a dreary hour or so.

Outside Vic's office, the music arranger on the Figaro Perkins show was hotly telling Wyn Byars, the show's producer, that, Mr. Evans or no Mr. Evans. you couldn't play Laura in march tempo no matter what you did to the arrangement. "Besides, it'll make me the laughing stock," he cried.

The producer, happy to bow to higher authority, brought the arranger in to get a decision from Vic, who as account executive outranked him.

"I'll be the laughing stock, Mr. Norman, if I do a thing like that. The laughing stock!"

Vic laughed and told them both to get lost. "Figure it out between yourselves," he said. "I'm a fish out of water on music. I don't even know what an arrangement is."

156

The teletype from New York had begun its clattering, and Norma brought in a fresh stack.

"The account men in New York are just getting back from lunch," she explained. That was due to the difference in time.

In Hollywood you were very conscious of time being three hours earlier than New York. For example, Kimberly usually phoned Vic at ten or eleven New York time, thereby waking him up at seven or eight Hollywood time, to mouth a bunch of sleepy or hungover yesses or nos to Kim's chatter.

Not that it made any difference what he had said to Kim. To date, there had been nothing important to talk about— the Old Man was well and excited over Buddy Hare's possibilities; Washington had raised Beautee's paper allotment and Kim was a hero in his joust with bureaucracy; Kim had discovered a new babe, but a sensational one. No, Kim had no actual reason for phoning as yet, but since he had become accustomed to a midmorning chat with Vic, and being telephone-happy, he refused to let long distance tolls or differences in time change his habit.

Vic shuffled the teletypes sourly. With Kimberly and Maag, as with most agencies, the big radio shows were controlled in New York, where the sponsors were, but produced in Hollywood, where the stars were.

The teletype was the link between them. Scripts would be written in Hollywood and feverishly teletyped to New York, right up until show time—and a man standing beside the New York teletype might rewrite or edit under those conditions, not forgetting to dictate caustic comments on how lousy the material was. Also, all bad news from sponsors was clattered from coast to coast.

It was no wonder that Hollywood radio men considered the teletype a horrible instrument of inquisition which rejected scripts, or sensational new ideas for shows, or guest star suggestions, or gags on commercials . . .and at the next minute imposed impossible demands on producers trying desperately to keep both their stars and the New York office happy.

The teletype had created perhaps more occupational ulcers than straight whiskey or hastily eaten ham sandwiches. It was so damned impersonal, totally lacking the human touch. Standing beside the machine in Hollywood, the producers always visualized a starched, pin-striped, stuffed-shirt of a New York executive wracking his brains to make life difficult for the Man with the Show. And the New Yorker, desperately trying to teletype his client's policies and reactions, thought of the Hollywood man as an indolent fellow in a loud shirt who had long ago forgotten how to think, write, be funny, or even understand plain English.

Norma came in again to report that Buddy Hare and his agent were outside. This being Hollywood, where business manners are more casual, they were not outside in the waiting room at all, but standing right back of her.

Vic told them to come in and Don Worth said Hello, honey, and introduced him to radio's next great comedian, Buddy Hare.

Most comedians look like golf pros or clothing merchants, but Buddy Hare actually looked like a comedian. He smoked a large cigar, he wore a houndstooth suit cut very much on the sharp side. He was small, with a smooth, boy-face that somehow managed to carry a tired forty-two-year-old look on it.

"Buddy's all excited about the show," Don said. "He's got a lot of good ideas for you, too."

Buddy Hare almost sat down, then stood up and became brisk. "I been taking the trouble to listen to the radio," he said. "Been listening very careful." His speaking voice was not his professional voice. It was high, but clear and hard, not at all squeaky and raspy. "Got a lot of new ideas . . .

"Cigar?" he said, then began to give Vic his lot of new ideas.

"The trouble with radio," he criticized, "is that it all sounds alike, unnerstan? Now that's a fact with comedy shows especially. All the gags are alike. Unnerstan what I mean, Mr. Norman?"

"Call him Vic," Don said. "There aren't any misters in radio, honey."

"Yes, Buddy," Vic said, "I certainly do understand what you mean."

Buddy Hare did not pace. He flitted. He would sit in a chair, then buzz to a sofa. He was like an insect. He was up and down darting from corner to corner. Vic would not have been at all surprised to find him crawling on the ceiling.

"Unnerstan, Vic," Buddy Hare said, "radio needs originality. It needs originality because when you stop to analyze radio what is it? Nothin' but show business. That's all! Show business! Me, I been in show business twenty-seven years, unnerstan?"

And he had been doing some thinking about radio. And his thinking had given him some ideas for his radio show.

"I haven't had time to go into his ideas yet," Don told Vic. "I'm hearing them for the first time, just like you."

It was Don's way of saying that if the ideas were lousy, not to blame him, he'd had nothing to do with them.

Buddy Hare spoke again, from a fighting crouch in a far corner. "Now unnerstan, they're just ideas. A little rough, maybe. I'm no writer, unnerstan. I leave it up to you fellas to put it into words."

His first idea was a lulu. "A lulu," he said, circling over Vic's desk before lighting on a corner of it. "Listen. What kind of jokes are the best jokes? I'll tell you, dirty jokes. Unnerstan? And what kind of jokes last the longest, for generations even?"

"Dirty jokes," Vic said.

"You get the idea," Buddy Hare exclaimed in triumph. "Now here's my idea. Every comic gives the short dirty jokes the old switcheroo, cleans 'em up, unnerstan. But no comedy show on the air ever made a *feature sketch* out of a cleaned up *long* dirty joke. Unnerstan what a sketch is—with actors in all the parts and everything?

"So I figure a feature spot on each and every program should be a three, four, even five minute sketch based on a famous old *long* dirty joke. Everybody'll listen, unnerstan, and everybody'll know the joke, see, and they'll be expecting something dirty—but we'll make a terrific switch on the pay-off and they'll laugh like crazy. Unnerstan? They'll listen every week to see what dirty joke we're gonna feature."

"I understand," Vic said, "but will the network censors understand, and even more important will the sponsor's wife understand?"

"Take any of the long, dirty jokes—you know, the ones with long buildups," Buddy Hare said. "Wonderful sketches. Like the undertaker joke, you know: double suicide at the Park Central Hotel—all hell broke loose, we were in the wrong room —or the three honeymooners, unnerstan—or that new talking dog one, it's the first time I ever had a quarter—or that old one about the man who found out a safe way to murder his wife, she's only got three more days to live—wonderful material for a thousand radio programs, wonderful."

"Old chap," Don Worth said gently, "it is a great entertainment idea, but it won't go on radio. Radio is talking to young punk kids, innocent girls, all that crap. They won't stand for stuff like that on radio."

"I'm afraid Don's right, Buddy," Vic said. "But it's still a great idea."

"Well, I got a lot of other ideas, too," Buddy Hare said. "Just as great, too. Unnerstan?"

Norma came in with the two writers Vic had hired to do the show. They crumpled on the sofa and the first story conference began.

One of the writers, Max Herman, specialized in gags; the other, Georgie Gaver, in what is called situations. Together they combined laughs with story, or plot. Max already worked on three shows a week and grossed twenty-five hundred dollars every seven days. Writing was a soft touch for him, because he used the same jokes on all three shows. Georgie Gaver only worked regularly on one show. He was a private in the army, stationed in Hollywood and assigned to the Armed Forces Radio Service, and the army would only let him do one commercial show a week. So Georgie had to struggle along on a lousy seven hundred and fifty dollars a week, which is a starvation wage in Hollywood.

Vic said, "This is for an audition which the agency is making in the hopes that we can sell it to one of our clients."

"He means Evan Evans," Don said miserably. "New York teletyped me that Regina Kennedy let the word drop at a cocktail party last night. You louse."

"He must be quite a character," Max said, "Is he as bad as they say he is, Vic?"

"We plan to build a gag comedy show, starring Buddy Hare. So I want you writers to spend as much time with Buddy as you can, to capture his style. Maybe he'll run through some of his old routines for you."

"Like when I was in burlesque," Buddy said happily. "I got some lulus."

Vic said, "I see the show was having a normal gag-comedy format, that is, an opening spot, music, a middle spot, music, and a short closing spot. We'll drop the commercials in the usual places. I think you might fool around with a fast-patter monologue opening for Buddy."

"I got some great monologues," Buddy Hare said. "I can . . ."

The writers lounged and listened, looking very bored.

"But if you use a monologue, for God's sakes make it different. Don't bring in any of that old craperoo the boys throw out to GI audiences.

"Now about the character of Buddy, on which all the comedy situations should be based. I see Buddy as a kind of old, beat-up confidence man. Strictly a carnival hustler, see—but each show in a different kind of situation. And he's always cooking up some deal to con somebody and make a fortune, but he always loses."

"I gotcha," Herman said. "And I agree. It's the only kind of character he'd be any good at."

Buddy looked downcast. Vic continued. "So what the stooges do is obvious. I've optioned Jerry Kilmer as Buddy's assistant in crime—and Ellie Scoville as the female wolf."

"Honey," Don Worth said in a hurt voice, "why don't you use Maxine Young? She's a much sounder choice than Ellie."

"Sounder for Talent Ltd." Vic said. "I can't help it if Ellie belongs to another agent, Don."

"It's good voice contrast," Georgie complimented. "You might have a hell of a show there, Vic."

"We might, if the writing is good," Vic said sourly. "Joan Dexter is the singer. She can read straight lines and get wolf calls from the audience. She can also foil Ellie."

"Why don't we set the first show right in the carnival?" Max suggested. "Then we could use Buddy as a barker. Might get some boffs out of that."

Vic didn't think so. "It'll be a better example of the format not to put the whole thing in a carnival. You might start the opening spot there, though." Then he reconsidered and said, "How about this? Here's the carnival con man in the off-season. Idle hands, you know. So somebody tells him about psychiatrists charging fifty bucks an hour to interpret dreams. Well, he buys a ten cent dream book, rents a Park Avenue office and sets himself up as a psycho-analyst, complete with beard and fake accent. Then Ellie comes in, a fake society dame who's having trouble with her . . ."

That started them off, and they all began to spark, each man knocking himself out with his own gags and waiting impatiently for the others to finish spouting their ideas.

Buddy Hare even wanted to have a sign on the door of the psychiatrist's office, reading "Batteries Charged".

"But, honey," Don pointed out, "it's not television. People can't read signs over the radio."

In an hour they called Norma in and Vic dictated the entire storyline to her. This sort of thing was fun for him. He realized it was just rearranging the same old crap. But it was fun anyway, at this stage. Later, if it ever got on the air, he knew he'd listen to it and be humiliated at ever having had a part in it, but now it was kind of fun.

He passed out copies of the storyline to the writers, and

gagged that for protection he'd get it copyrighted at once, since a Talent Ltd. representative was present.

"We'll probably hear this on one of Don's shows next week," he said. "I also want a finished script in," he looked at his watch, "exactly one hour and four days."

Both the writers howled, as writers usually do, at the deadline and begged for more time.

"You just can't turn it on and off like a faucet," Georgie pleaded. "You know that, Vic."

"The hell you can't," he said. "Four days, no more, no less."

Then he remembered one more thing, a little safety measure. "Oh, incidentally, Buddy, will you sign this option letter before you go. It's the one you signed on the train, Don."

"Sure, sure," Buddy Hare signed with Worth's grudging approval and said it was a pleasure to do business with Kimberly and Maag.

As they all left, Max called back, "Hey you forgot to tell us, can the orchestra leader talk?"

Max came back alone and Vic said, "No more than two one-syllable words in succession. It's Johnny Levine."

"Great," Max said, "his music is in this world."

Then he said in a low voice, "You'd have a good show here, Vic, with another comedian. This Hare character can't sustain a half hour of comedy. He just ain't got it."

Vic said, "Let's write him a good show anyway, Max."

"It's a waste of time," the writer said gloomily. "Not mine. I'm getting paid. But brother, you are certainly wasting yours."

"I've been wasting time for thirty-five years, Max. I see no reason why I should stop now."

When Max opened the door, Vic heard the hearty, pleasant voice of Anthony Maag spreading good personnel relations among the secretaries.

He hoped Maag would not come in. He particularly did not want to eat lunch with him today and he felt he had to accept if Maag asked him again, because he'd turned down an invitation three days running.

For some reason unknown to Vic, the West Coast partner of Kimberly and Maag was giving him a big play. And sure enough Maag opened the door and came in.

"Son," he said, hospitable as an open door. "I been waiting for you to finish with Buddy Hare. How about puttin' on the feed bag?"

"It's a little early, isn't it?"

"Maybe early for you late-sleeping New Yorkers. But for an old ranch hand who was up at the crack of dawn it's late. How about it, son?"

Vic said, "Okay, Tony. Where'll we eat?"

Maag thought the Brown Derby could spare them a booth. Vic looked unhappy. "I've eaten half my meals there. I'd like to go some other place just because it's some other place."

Maag suggested Lucy's or the Players.

Vic had an idea. "Let's drive out to the Sunset Hills hotel. The food's good there and it's far enough out not to be crowded."

But the Sunset Hills was too far out for Maag. He had a date on the Paramount lot right after lunch.

So they went to the Brown Derby.

As they waited for a booth, Maag kept his hand in easy waving position. He knew almost everyone in the place.

The loudspeaker announced, "Call for Mr. Donald Worth. Mr. Donald Worth, telephone, please."

Vic said, "I wonder if the Brown Derby'd sell me time signals? How's this for copy—*It is now twelve-thirty-one Victor Norman time.* I'd like to buy all the spots following the Don Worth announcements. That'd probably run into eight or ten commercials a day."

Maag laughed. "A lot of them really do have their secretaries page them here for free publicity."

As they sat down, David Lash, the head man of Talent Ltd. came over. "Hello, Tony," he said. He pretended not to recognize Vic. "Is this a new sucker of yours, I mean, sponsor?"

"I'm his new lawyer," Vic said. "And my first legal advice was never to talk to Talent Ltd. without a lawyer present."

Maag went along with the gag and pretended to consult Vic. Dave Lash said, "Hello. What's your legal advice?"

"Don't answer," Vic said, "He's probably got a dictaphone planted somewhere. How are you, Dave?"

They shook hands. Lash said, "You got a great prospect in Buddy Hare, Vic. I been planning to build our own package around him. But you beat me to it. Don was crazy to give you that free-wheeling option. Especially for a buyer like Evan Evans."

He refused a drink and went back to his own table.

"Dave likes you," Maag said. "He told me so."

"I'm very fond of Dave, too," Vic said. "It's always a pleasure to do business with such a really contemptible fellow."

"He respects you," Maag said. "As a matter of fact everyone in this business does. How do you do it, son?"

"It's because I'm so sincere," Vic said.

"I'm glad to hear you say that, son. If more business men had more sincerity there wouldn't be so much trouble in the world."

The man was really a hell of a straight man, he really was.

"You're looking a lot better, now that you've had a few days of sunshine, Maag went on. "I didn't like your look at all when you first got here. You were downright peaked. I call it the New York pallor. You just got to admit it, son, this is God's country. I feel like a horse cooped up in a boxcar whenever I have to go back to New York."

"That was spoken just like a native Californian."

Maag said proudly, "I'm a western boy all right. Oh, I originally came from Ohio, but this is my real stampin' ground. I know those Broadway characters make fun of the wide open spaces, but son, you don't really begin to live until you surround yourself with a little fresh air."

Maag described his ranch out in the valley. He bred horses. "I take a fast ride every morning. Before breakfast. Afterwards I take a dip in my pool. In the raw, when Mrs. Maag don't catch me at it. Then I go in to breakfast and eat like a horse. Can you do that in New York?"

Vic said he liked New York. "But I must admit it's an awful place to visit," he said.

They ordered some lunch and then Maag had a great idea. "You could too do it in New York."

"Do what?"

"Live like a man ought to live. Of course it would cost money, but you're going places with our outfit and you won't have to worry about money."

Maag thought Vic should invest in a little ranch up Connecticut way.

"Hell, after this war's over you can commute by helicopter," he said. "And I can start you out by shipping you a couple of my horses. It'll make a man out of you, riding every morning before breakfast."

Then he said compassionately, "That is if you can ride, son. Your health—I understand you're 4F."

Vic said it was nothing serious.

They ate at their shrimp salads and then Maag said gloomily, "I'm 4F—and over-age to boot. I was a shavetail in the last war. Infantry. But they wouldn't take me for this one. I told those brasshats to come out to my ranch and I'd outwalk, outride and outswim any man jack among 'em. But it didn't do any good. They just said this was a young man's war and offered me a commission to ride herd on a desk in Washington. Public relations. Naturally, I refused it."

He sadly gnawed on a hard roll.

"Of course we handle a lot of war plant business out here. We help keep the personnel on the job. It's something. But by God I envy my son. He's a Navy divebomber pilot."

His eyes brightened, "You ought to let me take you through some of these west coast plants," he said. "Make your eyes bug out. I could get us passes to go into any of 'em, seeing's I'm on the Manpower Commission. Ever see an aircraft assembly line?"

"When I was a Californian," Vic said, "we only had tourists and movie mills out here. Times have certainly changed."

He figured the remark would be right up Maag's alley.

"Son," Maag said prophetically, "I'm going to tell you something. Southern California is going to develop into the greatest goddam postwar industrial center in the world. It damn near has already. You easterners are going to have to change your whole concept of distribution and marketing. The swing's westward, son. Hell, do you think for one minute that all these workers who came out here from the east will want to go back to those dirty, cold cities? Not on your life. There's millions to be made out here. Millions."

"I'd say it's a good thing K and M's got a full partner out here, if what you forecast comes true," Vic said. "Not only for radio, but for business in general."

It was what Maag wanted him to say. He did not like the feeling of being a branch office partner.

"I'm glad you said that," Maag said. "That's what I call thinking in a straight line. A partner out here keeps us on the ground floor."

"Kimberly knows that, too," Vic said.

"How is the old bastard?" Maag spoke like a buddy, shook his head and chuckled. "You know, Vic, that Kimmy's some character, all right. Sitting in that big stuffy office, surrounded by telephones, going down to see that Old Man. Like pulling teeth." Maag leaned earnestly over his ham and eggs. "Son," he said, "I been looking forward to this. I been wanting a chance to know you better. Heard nothing but good about you. And I personally like the way you operate."

"If a thing is not worth doing at all," Vic said, "it is not worth doing well."

The switch went unnoticed. "That's the beauty of the ad-agency business," Maag continued. Vic thought, he doesn't have to sell me anything, I only work for him. I'm no client.

"Take a young fella like you. Fast on his feet. In an ordinary business—I mean a business based on products and not ideas—you'd wait years for the old fossils to die before you could move into the big money. Into a management position. But in the agency business a man can rise right up to the top in weeks, days even, if he's got the stuff. And I think you've got the stuff."

"All a man needs is control of accounts," Vic said.

"Now son, that's what I like about you. You think in a straight line. It's so simple, really. And I like the way you put it. All a man needs is control of accounts.

"By the way, I worry about that Kimmy Boy," Maag said. "He's not at all well. The poor sonofabitch works too hard. Evan Evans takes too much out of him."

Vic ate and listened.

"I understand you got that Old Man eating right out of your hand, son. That's great."

"Not exactly," Vic said. "If he ever did, I'm sure I'd lose my arm all the way up to the elbow."

Maag chuckled. "That's the attitude that'll sell the Old Man and keep him sold. I always did tell Kim he was too wishy-washy with that client."

Vic wondered if Maag really knew Evans. "Do you ever have any dealings with him?"

Maag hesitated, then decided to be frank. "To tell you the truth, Evan Evans and I don't see eye to eye. I saw him a few times, but I was a little too blunt, I guess. That was years ago."

That was something Kim had neglected to tell Vic. So Maag was *persona non grata* on the Beautee account. No wonder he needed Kim, or someone like Kim, to hold on to that business.

Maag steered away from the ticklish subject.

"You know, Vic," he said, "a smart feller like you is a sucker to work for a salary. I'd like to see you try to set yourself up so you don't have to give all your money back to the government."

He explained about stock. How you could declare capital gains on stock held over six months, and only pay a twenty-five percent tax on it. Also how you could let cumulative stock, such as K and M stock, just sit and increase in face value until one day, you woke up with a fortune on your hands.

Vic of course knew all this, but he asked, "How does a man get in a spot to make a soft touch like that?"

"By being on the team, that's how."

"I thought I was on the team. Well, anyway on the beam."

Maag laid down his fork and patted Vic's arm. "You are, son, you are. But if you really set your mind to go places with us there's no limit. That's my point."

This doubletalk was very amusing, and Vic decided to draw Maag out further.

"I'd like that," he said. "What's the first step?"

Maag said, "Vic, I like you. You're my kind of folks. I guess I feel kind of like a father to you. Of course, I'm only a few years older than you, but somehow if you came to me for advice, I'd feel obligated to give you the same advice I'd give to my own son if he was in your shoes."

"And what is your advice, Tony," Vic said, very sincerely.

Maag thought it all out before he said, "Well, in the first place, it'd be a great thing if you could relieve Kimmy Boy of the responsibility of holding the Beautee soap account. It's too hard on that boy."

Vic wondered if Maag had any idea just how great a thing it would be, if Kim's plan went through.

"But who would relieve me?" he asked.

Maag laughed his hearty salesman's laugh. "Son, you wouldn't want relief. You'd be in clover. A twelve million dollar account in your hip pocket."

Vic said, "I shouldn't think that you and Kim would want an account man to get too strong a hold on the Beautee account. He might walk out with it."

Maag said, "You know, son, I've spent this time with you for a purpose. A purpose that might be interesting to you as well as constructive to the future of the agency."

Vic drank coffee and listened to the big, bristling words.

"I wanted to find out, personally, what your caliber is.

You're a big man, and you can be a hell of a lot bigger. You've got the stuff, son. You've got what it takes."

"Thanks," Vic said.

So Maag wanted to tell him something in strictest confidence.

Here it comes, thought Vic, as Maag leaned across the table, after glancing around cautiously.

"The truth is, Vic, that Kimberly and I haven't been seeing eye to eye lately. It's a basic conflict on the policy level, if you get what I mean."

Maag leaned closer. "Of course, you must know by now that Kimmy Boy's real value to the company has not been in the field of creative advertising or radio—it's more or less hinged on his setup with Old Man Evans. And he's always been too occupied with the higher politics of the Beautee account to develop in the new-business end as he should, as any president should. Now I don't want you to get the idea I'm trying to sabotage Kim. He's like a brother to me."

He cleared his throat and plowed on.

"But in terms of the Agency's over-all interests. I was just thinking—well, if you really got solid with the Old Man, you know, really solid . . ." He paused, not wanting to be more concrete. "Care for a brandy?"

"No, thanks," Vic said. "I wouldn't want to split the agency in two."

Maag protested he wasn't thinking of that at all. Not at all.

"Besides, you wouldn't. Don't ever get the idea I'd do any harm to Kimmy Boy. I'm thinking of him, too. After all, if you look at it straight, it's for his own good. That boy is not well. Not at all well. He's cracking up. You know that. And I've tried my best to get him away from that bottle, and on to a horse or something. But he won't listen."

If Maag had tried to talk Evan Evans on to a horse, Vic thought, it was no wonder he wasn't accepted down in Wall Street.

"No, son," Maag said, "don't worry about Kimmy Boy. I

know what," he snapped his fingers. "Kimmy ought to be Chairman of the Board. He deserves that title. He's earned it."

"Doing what?"

"Oh, general policy work. Over-all strategy. Things like that. But first that boy needs a long rest. I'll make him take it," Maag said sincerely. "Afterwards, maybe he could take a whirl at trying to drum up some new business."

Vic said he thought Kim would be good at that.

Maag thought so too. "But of course, every tub has to stand on its own bottom. He'd have to produce or we as his partners would not be acting in the best interests of our company to let him just hang on, drawing income but producing nothing."

"I see," Vic said.

Maag spun out the remainder of his thoughts.

"We'd be a great team, son," he said. "With that kind of setup, it's you and me who'd be running with the ball. And we'd go places, I can tell you. Once you got Evan Evans in hand you could work in other fields, too. You could even service the other New York clients. Not like Kim," he said, a contemptuous tone entering his voice for the first time, "he doesn't work in anything but soft soap."

Then he asked Vic again to keep this entire conversation under his Stetson.

"I just wanted you to know what direction I think you ought to take for the good of the agency and for your own good too. You asked me for this advice and I gave it to you." As he finished his coffee, he became most enthusiastic. "I can see the day when I never have to go to New York," he smiled happily at the thought. "I'll be on my ranch. You'll be on yours. New blood! Kimberly, Maag and Norman."

Then he explained . . ."Of course, as far as you personally are concerned, and me personally as well, that's probably only the first phase of our relationship."

Vic said he'd honor the confidence, but why didn't they just let things ride along as they were for a while and see what happened. "The whole picture might change overnight," he said, chuckling inwardly over his choice of language, and also thinking of Kimberly's counter-offensive.

Maag interpreted it to mean that Vic would play ball in his court.

"Okay," he said heartily. "You let me know the picture as it goes along and we can decide later on the timing. I am damned glad we had this talk, son. I always like to put my cards on the table."

Vic felt a little sorry for Maag. He was a bit naïve for the kind of coup he was trying to engineer. Especially against a slick operator like Kim. The New York clients would accept Maag on radio matters, but in the New York business sense, he was just a cards-on-the-table westerner and didn't really belong, in the way that Kim belonged. Kim was one of them and Maag was an outsider, an important consideration in a business that completely depended on personal service and friendship. If Maag really made this move, all by himself, he would be crucified one fine afternoon over cocktails at the Princeton, Harvard, Yale, Racquet, University, or Union League Club.

They were ready to leave when Vic remembered something.

"I hate to bother you with this, Tony," he said, "but that hotel I'm staying at is awful. No service, no nothing."

Maag said, "We'll have to do something about that, son. We sure will."

"Could you get me a villa at the Sunset Hills Hotel?"

Maag said it was a tough order. "They're reserved weeks in advance, you know that. I can get you a suite at the Ambassador, though."

Vic said he never considered Tony the type chap who would let a little thing like reservations stand in his way.

"You wouldn't for a client," he pointed out.

So Maag said, all right, he knew the owner and would give him a buzz. He made a note of it. "Consider it done," he said. "You've got yourself a villa . . . partner."

Then he paid the check, saying, "What difference does

it make whose expense account it's on? It all comes out of the same pocket."

Maag also sounded the parting note.

"I think we're going to go places, son," he said. "I think we'll make a hell of a team."

Vic watched him bustle down Vine street. Kimberly and Norman . . . Maag and Norman. Either way it sounded like a vaudeville team. One thing, if he ever teamed up with Maag it wouldn't take long to change the name to Victor Norman, Inc.

That is, if a person were the type person who went in for that type thing.

[CHAPTER XII]

VIC REGISTERED IN AT THE SUNSET HILLS HOTEL AND MADE THE usual request about laundry service, receiving the usual answer of one week to ten days. Things were tough all over Southern California, most crowded and inconvenient of all the country's war production centers.

He casually inquired for the Dorrances and the clerk said "Villa fifteen, just three doors beyond yours, Mr. Norman."

He followed the bellboy out of the hotel proper and down the palm-lined walk towards the villas.

The afternoon sun had broken through and the bright green water in the swimming pool sparkled pleasantly. He looked carefully around the pool—there were only a few brown bodies stretched on the sand, and no children.

His villa was pleasant, too. It had a terrace, a living room, two bedrooms and a kitchen. All around there was the brilliance of California gardening: pepper trees, acacia, canna, fiery rambler roses, with eucalyptus helping the neatly groomed palms dominate the park in which the villas were set.

Vic inspected the bedrooms, selected the most cheerful one, and unpacked, hanging his suits in the closet. He gave his laundry to the bellboy, and walked into the little kitchen. Like any new tenant, he opened and shut the refrigerator door. Then he went to the living room, phoned the operator he would be at the pool if there were any calls, removed his shirt and put on a T-shirt, and walked down to the pool, cheerful at being in the sun.

He had the Los Angeles *Times* with him, and read about the war. Occasionally a newcomer would walk down the steps to the pool and each time Vic glanced up for one sharp look.

Of course he was looking for the Dorrances and he felt rather silly about it. If I want to see them, I should call them, he told himself accusingly. But though there were phones at the pool he did not call them.

Several times he thought: to hell with this, I'm going down to the office. Then he looked at the time and figured Ellen had probably napped late, so he stayed on and was at last rewarded by the sight of Hal and Ellen and the nurse, and there was a happy reunion of the three friends as the air was filled with requests for anuya stowy, hey-heys, and vocal gun shots.

Hal wanted to show Vic his crawl. Ellen sat on Vic's lap, patting and stroking him, and he watched Hal swim, calling out compliments on the boy's form.

"A terrific flutter kick," he said as Hal climbed out of the pool.

Hal said his left arm didn't bend right yet, and he wasn't so hot on breathing either, but his instructor thought he was going to be all right.

Ellen said, "My all wight, too."

Hal said, "That Ellen! She doesn't even know how to dive yet."

It was after five and Vic felt he should go downtown to check on the New York teletypes, but he wanted to see Kay. Hal said she was up at the villa.

Vic told the children good-bye, promised Ellen a surprise, assured Hal that the surprise included him too, and walked back to Villa Fifteen.

After he knocked, he found himself trembling with, well, he thought it probably should be called eagerness. He hadn't

had such a feeling since his first high school dates with Fort
Madison belles whose names he had long forgotten.

The notion made him smile and then Kay Dorrance opened
the door and he knew that whatever this feeling was, it was
certainly worth it.

She was in shorts and her blonde hair was down. On the
train she had worn it up, coiled in braids. She looked different
—not so elegant, but softer and even more beautiful.

"Vic," she said, greatly surprised. "Do come in."

"I just saw the children," he explained. "They said you
were here."

They sat on the terrace and she served tea, after Vic refused a cocktail.

She said, "Last night when I was putting them to bed, Hal
and Ellen had a violent argument about which one you liked
best. It was never settled."

"Not even Solomon could settle that one," he said. "I like
both of them best."

Then he said, "How did you train them to be so independ-
ent and with such poise? To most children, life is such a struggle. They have so much assurance."

"I remembered my own childhood and it seemed to have
a lot of tragedy in it," she said. "People tugging and pulling
at you, emotionally I mean. Parents loving you, but not letting you develop independence because they loved you. I
consider my duty as a mother not to create such issues in their
minds. It does give them assurance, I think."

After a silence, he said, "I'm your neighbor now. I live
down there. Just moved in this afternoon."

She looked at him briefly, a somewhat startled look, then
glanced away.

"The children will be delighted," she finally said. "How
long are you staying?"

He told her probably another week, until the radio show
he was working on was safely preserved in wax.

Then he said, "I hope you don't think I'm intruding, Kay.
That other hotel was just impossible."

Of course she said, "Of course not."

He turned his face up to get the sun, leaning back and closing his eyes.

"I feel good," he said. "I don't know whether I should say it. But it makes me feel so damn good just to sit here with you."

She said, "Hal read about your arrival in one of those gossip columns. He's been bragging about it for two days."

Vic opened his eyes. "I feel like getting personal. Do you mind if I ask you a few personal questions?"

She hoped she wouldn't mind. "Only I told you how terribly self-conscious I am. Usually, I can't even talk to strangers. They frighten me and I freeze right up."

"One," he said. "Where were you born?"

She didn't mind that one at all. "Rome."

She explained that her father had been in the diplomatic service and that Rome happened to be his assignment at the time.

"That answers question two as well," he said. "So here's number three. What are your interests?"

She said. "My family. It sounds very dull and housewifey to say that. But it isn't really dull at all. Not to me. I'm a very simple woman, you know. And I've been alone so much, since the war. . . . A married woman with a husband overseas is scarcely a social asset, you know."

"Yes," he said, "I know your family is your big interest. I meant your other ones. You don't have to answer if you don't want to. I'm just an old busybody for prying into your affairs."

She smiled and thought a while. "I'm trying to think of something that will impress you and make me sound glamorous," she said.

"Don't," he begged. "The more glamorous you make it sound, the less I'm going to be impressed."

"Before I was married I wanted to be a sculptress. I studied it—oh at several places. I still like it. You have a head that would be interesting," she said, studying him. "Bronze, I think would be best. And very expressionless."

"No wonder you talked about my look, back on the train, I see you're a student of looks."

She'd done many heads of the children. One of Hal was supposed to be good. By critics, she meant. "Actually, I'm not good, or bad either. With me sculpture is more like needle-work with some women—it's fun, it passes time, you know."

"With some women it's occupational therapy," he said. "Your hands are beautiful. I like lean, hard hands on women."

"You just like women."

He thought about that. "Not particularly. Most women are so fakey. I enjoy the spectacle of watching their fakeries. And I enjoy them as women—or as my father used to say, the opposite sex. But I haven't ever really been deeply attached to any one woman. At least not since my love affair with my second grade teacher."

"You will," she promised. "As they say in the magazine stories, you just haven't met the right one. I fancy you're a very warm, gentle passionate man beneath that frozen twentieth century mask of a face."

He asked her why she thought so. She didn't know. "Perhaps it's the way little children kindle your eyes."

He said, "Why twentieth century mask of a face?"

"Because it's a godless face," she said. "You are godless, aren't you?"

He supposed that he was.

"Well, as you pointed out somewhere in New Mexico," she said, "that's a characteristic of the true twentieth century man and woman. Godlessness. Don't you see it in their faces? They have nothing outside of themselves to go to."

"Yes," he said. "I've seen it. No refuge for the refugees. No place for the displaced. Are you godless, too, Kay?"

"I don't know," she said. "I suppose so. I have no sense of ever having had or lost any kind of god. But I do have a force outside of me and yet part of me. And it seems as bound-less and mystical and beautiful as anybody's heaven, or promise of it."

"Your family," he said. "Yes, I know. You're very lucky,

Kay. And very wise, too. Not many women have the luck or the wisdom to find in their families the things that you do."

"Or men either," she said, and he looked quickly, almost hopefully, for some disquieting sign, but found none. Her face remained calm and peaceful.

"Is that your villa?" she pointed. "Where the bellboy is rattling the door?"

It was. He called to the boy who told him there was an urgent message for him to get in touch with his office at once.

"The telephone's in there," Kay said.

Norma said, "Vic, I hate to bother you, but Mr. Kimberly said to get out the FBI if necessary." She read the teletype:

MR. NORMAN FROM MR. KIMBERLY

    TRIED TO FONE U BUT LINES ALL BUSY. JUST LEFT JB REEVES WHO TOLD ME HIS AGENCY IS PICKING UP THEIR OPTION ON BUDDY HARE. SAID DON WORTH SIGNED THEIR OPTION THREE WEEKS AGO. THEY WANT HARE TO GO ON AS SUMMER REPLACEMENT FOR 17 WKS, WHILE JIMMY PICHER IS OVERSEAS WITH USO. REEVES WOULDNT KID ME SO THIS MEANS WORTH GAVE HIM AN OPTION, THEN FIGURED REEVES WOULDNT PICK IT UP, SO WHEN U ASKED FOR ANOTHER OPTION WHICH HE HAD NO LEGAL RIGHT TO GIVE U, WORTH GAMBLED AND LOST. A TYPICAL TALENT LTD. TRICK/EXCLAM/PLS. T-TYPE EXACT WORDING ON OPTION WE HOLD. THIS IS BAD, VIC. NATURALLY IVE SAID NOTHING DOWNTOWN AND ON THE FACE OF IT WE ARE NOT GUILTY OF ANYTHING EXCEPT WORTHS DUPLICITY. EVEN SO, WE MUST FIGURE OUT SOME WAY TO HOLD HARE TO OUR DEAL OR MR. EVANS WILL BLOW HIS TOP/UNDERSCORE BLOW HIS TOP/IF U CAN IN UR OWN INIMITABLE WAY FORCE TALENT LTD. TO SETTLE WITH REEVES IN SOME OTHER WAY AND GO AHEAD WITH OUR OWN HARE AUDITION THEN QUOTE I TAKE OFF MY HAT TO U UNQUOTE. END OR GA.

MIN. PLS.

    MR. KIMBERLY FROM H WOOD

        MR. NORMAN NOT IN. TRYING TO LOCATE HIM.

HWOOD FROM MR. KIMBERLY

    GET ABOVE T-TYPE TO MR. NORMAN IF U HAVE TO GET OUT THE FBI. END.

Vic dictated his answer:

    KIM, PLEASE TELETYPE HOW MUCH TALENT REEVES BUYS AT PRESENT THROUGH LASH, ALSO AMOUNT WE BUY. AM PUTTING HARE OPTION LETTER ON TELETYPE. LUCKILY, HARE SIGNED IT TOO. WILL MEET WITH LASH AND WORTH SOONEST AND SEE IF I CAN SHAME AND/OR FRIGHTEN THEM INTO BUYING OFF REEVES SOME OTHER WAY. DONT FORGET HE HAS THE PRIOR OPTION. MAYBE WELL HAVE TO CUT BUDDY HARE IN TWO WHICH MIGHT IMPROVE HIS COMEDY STYLE. TAKE A BENZEDRINE AND RELAX. NO USE YOU GETTING COMBAT FATIGUE YOU CAN DO NOTHING IN NY. END OR GA.

Norman put it on and read back Kim's answer.

DEAR BOY, WHOS WORRIED? HAVE FULL CONFIDENCE IN U. DELIGHTED U ARE DEALING DIRECT WITH THAT GREAT PHILANTHROPIST DAVID LASH. (UNDERSCORE GREAT PHILANTHROPIST). END.

Vic called Dave Lash. "Dave," he said, "can you and Don Worth see me right away?"

Dave hedged a little then said, "Well, if it's important. I'll have to cancel a cocktail date. Can't we do it tomorrow?"

"It's important," Vic said. "I'll be over in ten minutes."

Lash said okay, ten minutes sharp. He then called Don Worth in his office and said harshly, "Well, I guess Reeves let the cat out of the bag. Get one of the lawyers and come back in ten minutes."

Vic joined Kay on the terrace.

"I've got to go, Kay. Thanks for the use of your tea."

"It was nice to see you again," she said.

"May I see you some more?" he asked.

She hesitated.

"For dinner maybe?"

"We'll see," she said. "Later. You run along and take care of your business now. I'm an incurable eavesdrip. I heard you say something about ten minutes. I don't want you to be late."

"I planned to be late," he said. "It's the kind of meeting where being late is one of the dramatic effects."

She moved inside and stood holding the door open.

"How about dinner tonight, Kay?"

She shook her head. "I halfway promised some people."

"Then you can still unpromise them."

"Vic," she said, "I'd love to have dinner with you. But . . ."

"But what? I promise not to eat you, make passes at you, or tell off-color after dinner jokes."

"You make me sound like Queen Victoria," she said. "It's just . . ."

"Just what?"

"You're a little frightening, Vic."

"Don't flatter me," he said. "We'll dine out at that place on Malibu Beach. Charred shrimp. Pheasant. Why am I a little frightening?"

"I don't really know, Vic. I'm not accustomed to . . ." she paused.

"Who's frightening whom?" he demanded. "God save me from cryptic women who leave sentences dangling hopelessly in midair." He walked from the terrace to the walk. "This meeting is over in Hollywood. It shouldn't take more than an hour. I'll come back here as soon as I can. We should start early. It's quite a drive."

Vic frowned thoughtfully as he drove to the Talent Ltd. offices. What had happened to Kay? On the train, he would have bet that nothing could have changed her cool, assured composure. Especially in the simple social act of entertaining a guest. But she seemed so shy and worried, not at all at ease.

The notion of being with her tonight gave him a strong

feeling of pleasure. He wanted to outdo himself to show her a good time, to impress her. He knew how it was with women whose husbands had been away so long. They were starved for companionship and gaiety.

Could it be that she was suspicious of his intentions? One of the first things he must do tonight would be to assure her that he had no designs on her. She must be made to understand that he was not a man to go around disturbing marital relations between wives and husbands, especially husbands who had gone overseas to fight.

She probably remembered Connie Linger and assumed he was that way with all women.

He must put her mind at ease on that point.

[CHAPTER XIII]

DAVID LASH DID NOT LIKE TO BECOME ENTANGLED IN THE NIGGLING
conflicts that make up a talent agent's little day.

He preferred to sit in the background, a man of mystery.
and all his men were instructed to keep him out, as much as
possible, of what in his business were always called deals.

He was a thinker who could think up ways to extract ten
percent commissions out of each and every part of the entertainment industry, but of late years it was his policy to send
his boys out with his thoughts and don't come back until the
contract is signed.

Furthermore, Lash was a big man now, and he did not
care to dwell on the twenty years of dealing that had made
him a big man. Sometimes, not often, someone with a memory
would lay down his gin rummy hand and recall the old David
Lash, hinting mysteriously at some anecdote that involved
the three B's of the Twenties: Bootlegging, Bribery and Blackmail.

And sometimes (even today with all its fine socially con-
scious business ethics) the antics of the men who worked for
Lash would cause a little profane talk, but in those antics
Lash was seldom personally a party of the first part.

No, not David Lash personally, who had so many millions
that he was now more interested in philanthropy than business, if such a thing were possible.

Quite by accident, Victor Norman had been with Dave

that great night when the talent tycoon first discovered that no-man-is-an-island; he had been a witness, so to speak, at the wedding of David Lash when he took Humanity for a bride.

David Lash's feelings about these things were honest and sympathetic, and Vic respected them that night (it was on a plane) although he could not help but think with amusement on how some of this humane money had been collected, and, knowing Lash so well, of how it would continue to be collected.

In his office, Lash said impatiently, "He's ten minutes late already."

With him were Don Worth and the lawyer, a nervous twitchy man named Sam Hoffman.

"It's a good option letter," Hoffman said again. "I don't know where the sonofabitch learned how to write them, but it's a good one."

"Can't we make Reeves drop it?" Don Worth asked. Don was miserable. "Hell, Reeves as much as told me in New York that his sponsor did not like Buddy Hare. He told me that the day I left."

"He didn't give you back the option letter," Lash said pitilessly. "You should know sponsors better than that. The minute they think somebody else wants a piece of talent—they wouldn't drop an option on a deaf-mute. Now if Reeves knows it's Old Man Evans who wants Hare, you couldn't buy him off unless you offered to trade Bing Crosby and Bob Hope even up."

Vic came in and was introduced to the lawyer. He sat on the sofa, pulling a chair over and putting his feet on it. Lash asked him if he was enjoying his trip to Hollywood. Vic said yes. Worth asked when he was going east, saying he wanted to get back that gin rummy money. Vic said, maybe tomorrow if this Buddy Hare deal was loused up the way he thought it was.

"Don's sorry about that," Lash said. "Reeves said no dice, verbally you understand, and Don unconsciously wrote off the option. Legally, of course, Reeves had the paper. It was a misunderstanding."

"So legally, you understand," Hoffman said, "Reeves has the prior option."

Vic yawned and decided to lie down on the sofa. He said he didn't understand all that legal stuff. He told them he was just a plain simple country boy with a piece of paper signed by Buddy Hare and Don Worth, his agent.

Lash said, "Did Buddy Hare sign Vic's copy, Don?"

Don answered with a humble nod.

Lash said, "Vic, we're in a jam. I guess I don't have to tell you that."

Vic said no, Dave didn't really have to tell him that.

Lash said, "We're looking for some decent out, of course. A way that will satisfy Kimberly and Maag—and the Beautee Soap Company."

Vic said, "You'll have to dissatisfy Reeves then. We want to build a radio show starring Buddy Hare."

Hoffman again protested that Reeves had the prior option, that legally it was bad to try to cut Reeves out. Very bad.

"Our obligation, legally, you understand, to Kimberly and Maag," he said, "only involves whatever money you've spent so far on the audition."

"It can't be much," Don Worth said. "Can it, old chap?"

Vic rose and went to a chair in the farthest corner of the big office. He said, "I'm going to sit over here very quietly until you gentlemen figure some way to get Reeves out of it. You're not just fooling with a new radio show—you're tampering with a twelve million dollar account."

Worth asked Vic to be reasonable, honey. "The Figaro Perkins contract comes up for renewal next January," he said. "And you know Figaro will do anything we tell him. Wouldn't Old Man Evans rather have a new contract from Figaro than a lousy second-rate show with Buddy Hare?"

"You'd be a hero to the Old Man, Vic, if you went back with a new Figaro Perkins contract in your pocket," Lash said. "And if you'd give a little on this Hare misunderstanding, help us out a little, I think we could swing it for you."

"It's no secret that Figaro is upset by some of the Old Man's directives, Vic," Worth said.

"It's just conversation, Dave," Vic said. "Figaro's too big a boy now for you to push into any deal he doesn't want. If he wants to deal with Evans again, he will. But not because you say so."

Hoffman said suddenly, "Don, is Buddy Hare having any trouble over his script material?"

Don thought. "Now that you mention it, Sam, Buddy did make some suggestions in Vic's office about script material."

"Were they accepted?" Hoffman asked eagerly.

Don Worth pondered. "No, Sam, I guess you could say that Vic turned down all of Buddy Hare's script suggestions."

Hoffman looked at the option letter again. "There's no clause in here giving Kimberly and Maag control of Buddy Hare's script material. Maybe this contract has already been breached. This might be just a worthless piece of paper."

Vic stood up, walked over to Dave Lash, talked direct to him, ignoring the other two. "I don't know your Mr. Hoffman and he doesn't know me. So you'd better tell your man Hoffman not to talk to me like that, Dave. If you want to settle this clambake you'd better tell your man Hoffman not to think up those legal cuties."

Lash leaned over the desk and said in a tight voice, "Sam, you know I don't stand for that kind of thing. Keep that big stupid mouth of yours shut or else . . ."

Hoffman, whiter than a grubworm, began to squeak a little. "You tell me to keep my mouth shut? You, Dave Lash? Why, if I ever really opened—"

Lash said, "Shut up, Sam. That's all. Shut up."

Hoffman stood up, felt his head, weaved a little and half-staggered to the sofa. He collapsed on it, gasping for breath and clawing at his throat.

Vic ran over and knelt beside him. Hoffman looked as if he were having a stroke or a heart attack. He slumped back and his eyes closed. He had fainted. Vic grabbed the carafe and sprinkled a little water on his face.

Back of him he heard Lash. "Don, you got to think your way out of this. You been thinking with your thumbs. Get Reeves on the phone. No, wait. I'd better talk to Kimberly first."

Don half whispered, "Vic did turn down Buddy Hare's script ideas."

Vic looked back at them. They were immersed in the deal, paying no attention whatever to the man on the sofa. He said, "For Christ's sakes, you guys! This man may be dying."

Don glanced over and said, "Oh, he has those fits all the time. You can't do anything, old chap. He'll come out of it in a couple of minutes."

"Maybe we could find somebody else for Vic," Lash said. "Think, Don. Just do a little thinking. That's all I ask."

Vic stood up now. "If you don't get this man some medical attention, I'll slug both of you."

Lash said, "Okay. Okay," and told the secretary to send in a doctor. "Hoffman's had another attack. And get some women in here to sit with him until the doctor comes."

The women apparently knew what to do. Hoffman came to and seemed all right, except weak, and Vic felt no further obligation to help.

Lash said, "Let's move into the conference room where we can finish this. I only got twenty more minutes."

"Maybe," Vic said, "we'll have an earthquake or something that'll really interrupt your business day. I'd hate to die in your office, Dave, might be years before anyone noticed it."

They all sat down and Lash pleaded, "Vic, tell me what to do? These people of mine! How the hell can I get them out of this?"

"I got one little idea," Vic told him. "And it would cost you dough."

He explained. "Reeves is only interested in having a comedian on seventeen summer shows. When Pichel returns next fall from the USO, Reeves won't want Buddy Hare or anybody else."

"So?"

"So you tell Reeves that you'll guarantee a top comedy name for each of those shows—then you'll go out and book him comedy guest stars. Reeves naturally will only be satisfied with the really big comedy names. So you sign 'em up—maybe three or four weeks for each one."

"Their budget won't stand it," Don said. "They only got a thousand a week to spend on a comedian. And the top comics would average five g's a week easy."

"That's right," Vic said.

"So," Lash rubbed his chin. "So you're telling me to spend the difference, four thousand a week maybe, out of my own pocket. Now that's really what I'd call a solution. I love you, Vic."

"It's only money," Vic said.

Lash shook his head.

Vic looked hard at this tough little entertainment tycoon. What besides money would it take to move a guy like that? He didn't want to fail on this deal and besides he didn't like Lash. He hated to see him get away with anything.

Vic said, "Dave. Could Don go out? I want to talk to you alone."

Lash said, "You heard him, Don."

Then Vic said, "Dave, remember that night on the plane, four, five years ago?"

"What night?"

"We happened to be traveling east together. During the night, you told me about the plan you had to put your dough to good use. You'd read something in *Life* about concentration camps. You were very worked up. Remember?"

"Yes," Lash said. "Now I remember."

"Did you ever do anything about it?"

Lash described his current activities with various antifascist and refugee-aid groups. "So far," he said, "I've invested over a half million and I love every penny of it."

Vic said, very gravely, "You'd be wise to put those guest comedians on Reeves' show, Dave. It'll only cost you sixty-eight thousand. And you say you've spent over half a million on charity."

"One is business, the other is charity," Lash argued. "It's bad business to put even sixty-eight dollars in somebody else's radio show. You're confusing the issue, Vic. It's more than just money involved. It's a business principle."

"That," Vic said, "is my point, Dave. You've spent all this time and money and effort to do a good thing. One of the good things you're doing is trying to help the Jews in Europe —and to fight the forces of intolerance against them in this country. I like that in you, Dave. But when this Buddy Hare deal gets out, do you know what some people are going to say, Dave?"

Vic lit a cigarette. "They won't say your boy Don Worth did this dishonest thing. They won't say that Talent Ltd. did this double-dealing thing."

He paused and then said very slowly and softly, "They're going to say a Jew did it. They're going to say that you, Dave Lash, a Jew, pulled this fast one. Yes, Dave, you know there are people who are going to say it just that way. And it'll help tear down what you've been trying to build up. What you've been spending money on to counteract."

Lash was silent. He seemed shocked by what Vic had said. And instantly Vic knew he had done a bad thing. He felt cheap and nasty for what he'd said. He knew that he had no right to say such things. If he himself were Jewish, he might have some right to say it. To say those cruel words. It was true that some people might say them, there were people around who overlooked no chance to say things like that.

He walked over and put his hand on Lash's shoulder. "I'd consider it a favor if you forgot I ever said that, Dave. I was mad at you and I wanted to hurt you, I suppose. I could cut my tongue out."

He walked towards the door.

"Anything you decide is okay with me," he said. "I say to hell with Buddy Hare. Reeves can have him."

He was at the door when Lash finally spoke.

"Wait," he said. "Go ahead with your show, Vic. I'll work it out some way."

Vic said, "I'm sorry I blew my top. I want you to know that, Dave. I want to ask you to forgive me."

"Forget it," Lash said. "You're okay, Vic. I got respect for you."

Vic looked away from Lash and said in a low voice, "This is one time I'd rather be forgiven than respected, Dave."

"You're okay," Lash repeated. He looked steadily at Vic, a stern, bitter unforgiving man. "Yes, Vic, I got respect for you."

"I wish I could say the same for myself," Vic said. "Be seeing you around, Dave."

He left and drove slowly back to the hotel.

[CHAPTER XIV]

HAL AND ELLEN WERE ON THE TERRACE AT VILLA FIFTEEN, waiting for Vic.

Hal told him that his mother would be out in a minute. He stood on his head in a wicker chair. "Hey hey," he said, "why don't you take all of us out to dinner?"

"My wanna go out to dinner too," Ellen cried. "What's the idea? It's not fair."

Vic said, "I guess you've both forgotten about that surprise I promised you this morning."

They spent the next few minutes trying to make Vic tell them what the surprise was, and then Kay came out.

Her hair was coiled around her head the way it had been on the train. She looked very regal.

She said, "Hello." And "All right, children. Martha's ready with dinner. Off you go now."

Neither of them wanted to go to dinner. Hal said, "If I do go to dinner nicely, may I read in bed a while, mother?"

"My wanna wead too," Ellen said.

"That Ellen," Hal said. "She can't even read comic books yet."

But off they went to dinner and Ellen called tragically from the kitchen, "Have a nice time, Vic. Good-bye, my 'ittle mamma."

"Drink?" Kay asked.

"I could use one. Thanks."

191

She served scotch and soda on the terrace.

She said, "The meeting? Was it successful?"

"It was a horrible success. The wheels in my head are still going round and round."

She knew what business tension did to a man.

"Frank used to come home and it would take him an hour, some nights, to slow down to normal. But you don't impress me as being that type."

"Usually, I'm not," he said. "It's just that . . . well, sometimes the heat of business makes a man do things he shouldn't. This was one of those days. I hurt a man unfairly." He took a long drink. "Yaaa . . . the things a man'll do just to be top dog in a deal. Not even money involved. Just to come out on top. The winnah and still louse," he said.

"Now you just relax and forget it," she commanded. "I don't know what it was and don't want to know. But it couldn't have been too bad because you're not a cruel man."

He'd been a fool to ask Lash to forgive him. Not the first time, the second time. Why should Lash forgive him? Would he have forgiven Lash if that obviously premeditated act were reversed? Not that he cared whether he ever saw Dave Lash again. That wasn't the point. It was the nasty aftertaste. What was getting into him? He'd never gone that far before.

"No sense of punctilio," he said. "Excuse me, Kay, for bringing my ill-mannered alter ego to your terrace. And may I use your phone, please?"

He dictated a teletype to Kimberly. "I just traded in my birthright for a mess of Buddy Hare. Show will be produced per schedule, although I personally think the compass is pointing due south."

Returning to the terrace he recalled his scheme to put Kay at ease with him. She was a little better tonight, but still dubious about something. He'd have to think up some polite indirect way to show her that he didn't intend to make any passes.

"Feeling better now?" she asked.

"Just like some food," he said. "Good food. You know, Kay, I can't stand eating alone. I'm very grateful that you consented to dine with me tonight."

"I'm looking forward to it, too," she said graciously. "Of course, I should be home early. I'm rather tired tonight."

"Me, too," he said. "Perhaps we'd better just eat and come right back."

The fact that he said it seemed to give her more confidence, but as they drove down Sunset Boulevard to Malibu she sat rather too far over on her side for comfort.

As she talked pleasantly of the children, telling anecdotes of this and that period of their lives, Vic again marveled at the differences between her and other women he knew. Not just women like Jean Ogilvie or Connie Linger, but women from Kay's own social group. All the little things that women do because they're women: touch you with their hands, brush you with their bodies, rhapsodize over the inconsequential, inflect ordinary phrases with intimacy, strike soft, feminine little poses. This was the most unpretentious woman, in manner, speech, dress, gesture, expression and inner spirit, that he had ever known. And yet the sum total of her added up to the most strikingly beautiful, the most appealing woman he had ever known.

They entered the restaurant.

"The headwaiter out here makes more than I do," he explained, "which obviously gives him the right to look down his bankbook at me. I doubt if he'll condescend to give us a table in under an hour."

But they were seated at once and ordered dinner at the second finest and most expensive restaurant in America, and were served as nicely as if they were Hollywood royalty of the highest marquee rank.

Kay praised each course, but only with words, not with her fork. Vic could not get excited about eating, either. The night somehow seemed too important to him for eating. For both of them, in fact, this exotic, for California, café might just as well have been a hamburger stand.

"Did you ever notice how people talk about food?" he asked. "Especially the A-income groups who eat around a lot. I find myself doing it too. To hear me sound off about sauces and dishes and cafés and gastronomy in general sometimes, you'd think I lived to eat. Actually, it's just a fashionable pose with me. The really memorable food is that of my young, hungry, growing and lusty youth."

"I feel the same way sometimes," she said. "When food's food period."

"I remember," he said, "when I was a kid. Just old enough to be allowed to hunt by myself with a single shot twenty-two rifle, that I earned selling subscriptions to *Grit* and the *Saturday Evening Post*. That would be when I was twelve," he estimated.

"So young? I could never bring myself to let Hal go out alone with a gun at that age, I'm sure. I'd be terrified."

"So was my mother, but my father used to say that it wasn't how old you were, it was how much you knew about guns. He won."

"Fathers always win," she said.

"Anyway, off I'd go, trudging over the Iowa meadows, shooting rabbits, birds, bullfrogs, anything alive. And I'd come home exhausted, barely able to carry my game, and maybe that would be the night my mother baked my special meat pie, with whole onions, whole potatoes and carrots, and God knows what else—everything cooked separately first, then combined in a great shallow pan and covered with a brown, crisp, succulent, thick crust, just like piecrust only better."

"Eat your guinea hen," she ordered. "And stop. You're making me hungry."

"We were always poor," he said, "but on meatpie nights I was the richest boy in Iowa. I don't want any more guinea hen."

"I'm through, too."

"Now that we're agreed that we don't really like fancy cooking, how about a crêpe suzette?"

But she didn't want any dessert and neither did he. He

was now sharing her restlessness and they were both relieved to get out of the place.

He drove slowly along the beach road. She looked out into the night, still worried. He wished he knew some way to put her at ease, but he couldn't be blunt about it and say, "Kay, don't worry. This is something you can write to your husband about, and I won't change it."

It could be he was assuming too much on too little knowledge.

Perhaps it was the husband she was worried about. Possibly no news, or bad news. A canceled leave maybe. He remembered she'd told him the husband was due back shortly. That must be it.

Ahead of them, an amusement park shattered the night with neon.

Vic said, "Look. A dance hall. A genuine amusement park dance hall. Let's go in."

"I haven't danced much lately," she said.

He told her she had nothing on him. "I'm the worst dancer in the world," he bragged. "An accomplishment which I attribute directly to gin rummy. Come on, Kay. Let's go in."

She objected again to his notion, but by this time he was parking the car, and she meekly followed him into the enormous hall.

The orchestra was in recess and Vic led her to the edge of the vast, empty floor and looked fondly across it.

"This is for me," he said. "Plenty of elbow, knee and kicking room. I hate those postage-stamp nightclub floors. Reminds me of when I was a boy, back in Fort Madison, trying desperately to dance the Black Bottom without tripping and at the same time learning how to drink denatured alcohol without gagging."

"It's certainly big enough," she said.

"Big as six barns and dark as a lover's lane," he said.

The orchestra began a new set and the floor filled with jitterbugs, who marched to their positions in a stately manner with serious, intent faces. Once set, however, they suddenly turned the place into a huge bowl of squirming life, as they gravely threw their supple young bodies into a series of rhythmic jerks and spasms.

"Come on," he said.

"All right," Kay said. "But please don't make me do anything like that. I'd fly apart."

"We'll dance with dignity and decorum." Vic steered her gingerly into a deserted corner. "That is, as soon as I know where you propose to keep your feet. Pardon me this one time."

Soon they were dancing smoothly together, although Kay was self-conscious, and very cautious whenever they came within range of the whirling and whirled bodies of the jitterbugs.

"Don't worry," Vic said comfortably, "they sell group hospital policies with every admission ticket."

The music stopped and Kay said, "Let's sit for a while."

So they sat through the next dance, drinking soda pop and watching the frantic dancers almost go out of their senses to the rhythms of a song which Vic identified for her as *One O'clock Jump*. He told her about this orchestra, one of the great name bands that had not yet been in the big money long enough to lose its spirit and its freshness. He taught her to listen for the ad lib solos of the three great instrumentalists in it: a trumpeter, a clarinetist and a drummer. He spoke of this kind of music and of its profound impact on American youth.

"It sends them," he said.

"You have to be young, I suppose," she said. "To feel that way, I mean. Look at their faces."

One O'clock Jump ended with a millenial dissonance.

"Come on," he said. "This one's slow. Just my speed."

This time, there was assurance as they threaded their way through the swirling pool of dancers which ebbed back from the non-dancing hep cats who stood banked in front of the band.

"We're dancing real good," he said with satisfaction. "In two more starts we'll be a fine team."

"It was my fault," she said, as they drifted easily out into the open again. "I was a little self-conscious at first. I thought everybody must be looking at us. Now I'm more relaxed."

"Having fun?"

She looked up at him and smiled. "Great fun. I'm glad we came, now. It's nice to be dancing again."

It was not just a proper social statement, but true. She really was having fun, and showing it.

He could tell by the way she felt in his arms, by the soft fluidity of her body against his, by the gaiety in her face.

"I really believe you are," he said. "I was afraid you were one of those El Morocco characters who wouldn't unbend in the land of colored lanterns, hot music and hot dogs."

"It's not like El Morocco at all," she said gaily. "And I really am."

"Those poor pathetic millionaires at El Morocco," Vic said. "I have only contempt and pity for them. They make dancing a dismal kind of social exercise. This way's fun."

There was a brief pause and the music started up again. "Let's sit this one out," he said. "I feel an old forgotten charley horse kicking around my calf."

"Oh, it's a lovely, dreamy one," she pouted. "Please, Vic, just this one."

"You really want to? I only invented charley because I thought you were a little tired."

She looked up at him brightly. "Tired? You forget what a big strong woman I am." She put her head on his shoulder and murmured, "It's a lovely, lonely song, Vic. What's the name of it?"

"*Long Ago and Far Away.*"

The crooner began to croon the forlorn and sexhungry words and they swayed dreamily to the lonesome melody. "I'd forgotten how nice dancing was," she said. "It's been years, really."

"Does it send you, too?"

She smiled at the incongruous word.

"Yes, it sends me."

They finished the dance in silence, and he led her back to their table. She was flushed and excited. And Vic, who had so wanted her to enjoy this evening, was pleased and happy to see the change that had been brought about by the magic of the dance. And secretly proud of himself for thinking of coming here.

Music again . . . and it was a song from their own youth.

"*Stardust*," she said. "That beautiful, beautiful song."

"We can't miss this one," he said, getting up.

"Do you mind?" she pleaded. "It's the kind of song I'd rather just sit here and listen to. It's so lovely."

She listened raptly.

"It really does send me," she said. "Now I'm beginning to understand what those youngsters mean when they say that."

"Ah, youth," he said. "*Stardust*—a more certain tip-off to middle age than a spread."

But she would not cater to his sophistication.

"Look at them," she said. "That couple over there. So rapt and lovely. Isn't it all so young and beautiful?"

"They're glassy-eyed all right."

She turned to him, impulsively put her hand on his sleeve (so much had the dance affected her, this proper, beautiful woman whose regality had until now been disturbed by some uneasy quality in this new friendship) and she said sadly, "I was just thinking, Vic"—she lifted the meaningful hand to indicate the swirl of youngsters before her—"I missed all that when I was a young girl."

"Why, Kay?"

"Oh, it was living in Europe, I fancy. And being around embassy balls instead of night clubs and country clubs.

"Tonight, for the first time," she confessed, "I regretted missing it. The dancing, the young boys."

"Don't tell me you missed the young boys. I don't see how they'd let that happen."

"I was always too tall," she said. "As a young girl, I was

taller than most of the boys. So I pretended to be critical of them. I must have been hateful."

"I'm glad you never met me as a young boy. I was one of the silliest young boys that ever whistled in front of the Fort Madison pool hall."

"I suppose that's why Frank attracted me," she said soberly, the mood of girlhood not surviving the thought of her husband. "He was a grown, important man when I met him. I was just twenty, And he is—well, you wouldn't exactly call him handsome, but he has such distinction. I still get a proud feeling, after ten years, when he walks into a room full of people."

"I would like to meet him," Vic said.

"If you're still here when he gets back, we can all have dinner together."

"And when I do meet him," Vic said, "I'm going to say, 'Congratulations, sir, on the finest combination wife-and-mother this side of Mrs. Miniver.'"

"Now you're making fun of me," she said. "I thought Mrs. Miniver—at least in the movie—was about as motherly and wifely as one of Mr. Churchill's speeches. But not nearly so believable."

"A stardust melody—the memory of love's refrain"—the girl at the microphone finished her slow, torchy interpretation of the song and the orchestra segued into a hot wild jivey chorus.

But they did not seem aware of this bastardization of their stardust melody.

Vic abruptly stood up.

"It was supposed to be a wisecrack," he said, "but I forgot my original punch word and just threw in Mrs. Miniver from desperation. Look," he said, knowing that the spirit of the dance was lost to them now, "let's go. I'm an old man for this type work."

They drove back towards Malibu, along the beach road. She was again the uneasy companion, rigid and silent, withdrawn and strained. Vic felt very uncomfortable.

He said, "One time in Fort Madison I was sitting in a car with a girl. We were both sixteen. We had been to a dance, as a matter of fact. And I sat, out there in front of her house, in a nervous frenzy."

He paused to devote his mind to passing another car.

"You see, I didn't know whether or not I should try to kiss her. I knew nothing of such things, except what I'd heard from the boys in front of the pool hall. Of course I knew I was supposed to kiss her, but I didn't have courage or knowledge of how to begin and it was driving me frantic."

He slowed down, almost as if he'd forgotten he was driving. "The whole thing was complicated by another factor, too," he said. "I wanted to go home. I had to go to the bathroom.

"Then I realized she was worried too because her conversation made no sense at all. So you know me, I just told her about my problem—the kissing part, I mean—and she broke down and confessed that the same thing had been worrying her. She didn't know if I intended kissing her, and she didn't know what to do if I did."

"And did you?" Kay asked.

"Did I what?"

"Kiss her?"

Vic turned off the pavement and stopped the car, facing the ocean.

"I can't remember," he said. "That's what I was trying to do, remember if I'd kissed her. Let's go down to the beach."

"Do you think we should?" she said.

"Why shouldn't we?"

"It may be damp down there."

"I want to see the ocean," he said. "Come on. Don't be afraid, Kay."

"I'm not. It's just . . ."

But they went down to the beach.

"The tide's going out," he said.

"My shoes are full of sand."

He found a dry log. "Sit here and empty them." He sat

down beside her and they slowly absorbed the wonder of the sea. It was Vic who first spoke again.

"I've always regretted the seventeen years I was an inlander," he said. "Now there'll never be enough time left to look at the sea."

A spanking offshore breeze was tossing some spray at them. He put his topcoat around her and his hands rested lightly on her shoulders for a moment. She shivered slightly.

"The sea is a fighter." It really was as if he were talking to himself. "It must hate the land with some baffled hysterical hate, the reasons for which it forgot a million years ago. It's very punch-drunk, the sea. Strictly fighting on its guts. So in it comes—back for more, as they say—feint, roll, hit—then out again.

"We've borrowed all our rhythms from the sea," he said. "The basic rhythm. Hear it in that surf? That's the sea giving us the downbeat for love.

"And the rhythm of struggle, too. Hear it? Calling all men." He turned to her. "You know, Kay, the real tragedy of my life is that I missed that war they're fighting out there. Calling all men."

"I know," she said. She was a woman again and these things about men were clear to her. "Frank felt the same way. He had to go. You went, too. Don't delude yourself."

"I don't," he said curtly. Then he pointed. "Look. The waves. All lit up. Phosphorescence. Eerie, isn't it?"

She didn't answer. She only looked far out into the Pacific, and as he spoke, she moved slightly away from him.

He said, "Kay, you're very strange. You've lost all your tranquillity, the serenity that makes me feel so—I guess alive is the word—so alive when I'm with you. Something in you, and your children, softens the jagged edges of me. But tonight, it's all gone out of you. You're wary. Resistant. Suspicious. I have the feeling that I caused it. What's wrong?"

He was not accusing or criticizing her of some fault, but she seemed to take it that way and her answer was resentful, sullen, and most unexpected.

"I'm just not gettable, that's all," she said. "I'm sorry if it upsets you, but there it is."

"Gettable?" he stared at her in astonishment, then lay back in the sand and laughed. Laughed until he noticed how rigidly she sat by him, as if in humiliation.

He stopped suddenly. Sat up and put his hand on her arm. "Gettable! Kay, where did you get the idea I was trying to get you? I'm sorry I laughed, but, my God, you must try to understand me better."

He said, very seriously, "You and Hal and Ellen—it's been a revelation to me. You give me pleasure, peace, a sense of wonder at this good thing you have made out of life. Do you think that I would disturb that? I'd cut my throat before I made one move to *get* you, as you put it."

"I'm sorry I said that, Vic," she said. "I don't really know much, about men you know. Things like that. You must try to understand that about me, too."

She was like a young girl, he thought. So naive. So wonderfully tender. Her innocence was wonderful. In his world of hep, glamorous dames, he'd forgotten about the jeune fille, thought she had disappeared from life and certainly from the upper eastside of New York. And here she was, reincarnated at the age of thirty-two.

"You're wonderful," he said. "You're an unbelievable, wonderful, artless, little girl."

"Forgive me," she said again. "But as you were talking a little while ago, about the sea, I was thinking about what some men might think about a married woman who went out and sat on some lonely beach with them. Not you, but some men. And then I thought about my little Ellen and what she said this afternoon."

"What did she say?"

"She came to me and threw her little arms around my neck and just about choked me to death. You've no idea how strong she is. And then do you know what she said? She said, 'My love you so much my stomach hurts.'"

"She does, too," he said. "Let's go home, Kay."

They returned to the car and rode back to Beverly Hills. Kay seemed more at ease and chatted of this and that with poise and assurance. Then she began what was, for her, an extraordinary conversation.

"I've a confession to make," she said.

"I hope it's good. I need an idea for next week's Beautee Theatre of the Air."

"It's about you," the words were slower in coming, and less assured. "You know, Vic, it worried me when you asked me to dinner. And I was going to say no."

"You almost saved me forty-two dollars."

"But then I thought: well, it will probably wind up with him parking by the ocean, and after a lot of obvious, contrived moves, trying—" She paused, then finally got it out— "trying to kiss me."

"I see," he said, really seeing quite a lot. "Just like any two young neckers parking by any old ocean."

She laughed. "It was so amusing, really, looking back on this evening, which incidentally was very wonderful. All night long that kiss you were supposed to attempt just grew and grew, until it became a symbol—simply colossal."

"Watch your language," he said. "You're talking Hollywood."

"Maybe it is Hollywood," she said gaily. "Anyway, The Kiss was going to be The Evidence."

"Then what was I supposed to do, according to your cool, crafty plan?"

"Oh," she tried to say it airily, "I figured you'd work desperately to mend your fences. But to no avail. I was planning to be adamant. Cold. Reserved. It would just be good-bye. That's all."

It was said thoughtlessly but he was sharply aware of the feeling behind it.

"Well, anyway," he said, "better luck next time."

Now they were far away from each other, and the remainder of the drive home was swift and silent.

They walked up the moonlit path to Villa Fifteen.

He held the door for her, and stood silently as she entered
and then turned towards him.

"Vic," she said.

He interrupted her. "Don't say it. I know what you have
to say. But don't say it."

"Vic," she repeated, marveling at this stranger who seemed
to know all her thoughts.

"I won't come back," he said. "Forget it, Kay. Just forget
it ever happened."

He turned and walked to his own villa. He did not look
back or say good-night.

[CHAPTER XV]

WHEN VIC CAME OUT THE NEXT MORNING, DRESSED FOR THE office, not the pool, he did not even turn his head to look back at Villa Fifteen.

It was a deliberate attitude and he was stiffly aware of it, but he was afraid he'd see Kay or the children and he wanted to save Kay a natural embarrassment.

He knew, after the long worried night, that Kay's instincts were profoundly right. Their being together created a catalytic, driving force—and this force kept pulling them ever closer together. By the simple logic of staying apart, that force could be controlled at this point, but perhaps not later.

He wanted to be with her. It was a want that filled his body and his mind. And it was really very bad for her if he gave in to that want.

Driving downtown, he regretted the impulse that had sent him to her hotel, and debated if he should go to another one. No, that would be too obvious. He would simply rush through this Buddy Hare audition as fast as possible and return to New York and let the force dissipate itself somewhere along the three thousand mile journey.

He remembered, too, the surprise he'd promised Hal and Ellen. Actually, he'd intended to give them a big birthday party. It was nobody's birthday, but he knew they'd go wild over the unexpected presents, the cake and the candles.

Now, he worried briefly over the promise and thought of

205

ways he could make good on it without again intruding on
their family intimacy. He decided on nice presents for each
of them. A huge doll for Ellen (they never had enough dolls
at her age) and perhaps a leather-cased knife and hatchet set
for Hal (or something else in case Kay objected to lethal toys).
He would have them sent by messenger.

This was the day set for delivery of the script and the
writers were waiting in his office with it. Buddy Hare was
there too and he'd just finished reading it when Vic came in.

"It's terrific," Buddy Hare said, apparently shadow-boxing,
but finally executing a movement which showed he only
wanted to shake hands. "It's got that old boff, unnerstan?
Punch! The old one, two, three!"

Vic sat down and carefully read the thirty-page manu-
script. The writers pretended not to be interested, but they
surreptitiously watched his face for reactions.

Finally, Vic put down the script.

Max Hermann said gloomily, "It must be great. I didn't
see one twitch out of you."

"Vic never laughs," Georgie Gaver explained. "You know
that, Max."

Vic said, "You got a pretty good start here. But . . ."

"It's still a little rough," Max apologized.

"How long did you guys spend on it?" Vic asked. "All of
forty-five minutes, it reads like."

They protested in harmony. It wasn't that bad.

"You've been a writer yourself," Max said. "You know what
it takes to write a script like this."

"I could write a better script than this under ether," Vic
said.

"Hey," Georgie said. "That's funny. Almost a yak. Let's put
it in."

"It's only funny to writers," Vic objected. "And writers
neither buy nor use soap."

Buddy Hare snapped his fingers and bounded into the center of the room.

"I gotta great gag for that doctor's office spot. A great

gag. A guy comes in to see me, unnerstan? He's sick. He says, 'My stomach hurts. Oh, something terrible.' And I say to him, 'Must be ulcers. What you taking for it?' And he says, 'None of your bismuth'. Unnerstan?" Buddy Hare said pleadingly.

Vic said patiently, "It needs a topper. You're the star, Buddy, I want you to get the laughs. If the gag pays off on bismuth, that gives the stooge the laugh. You wouldn't want that either, would you, Buddy?"

Come to think of it, Buddy Hare withdrew the gag.

"Look fellows," Vic then said, "this is a comedy show. Me, I've got an old-fashioned idea that comedy shows have to be funny. So what do you do? You start out very funny, as you interrupt a carnival con man making his last pitch of the season. He's looking for a winter racket. He gets hold of a dream book and decides to be a fake psychiatrist. So what do you do? You give him a two minute routine satirizing psychiatry. It's not in character for a con man to talk like that and besides it's not funny to people who don't know words like Freud, libido, ego, subconscious. Dammit, you can't put words like that in a radio comedy script. The public won't know what the hell you're talking about. Who you writing for, Park Avenue," he paused and borrowed Kimberly's favorite village to make his point, "or Pessary, Ohio?"

"Well, you said you didn't want the old corn in it," Max pointed out.

"You didn't forget that, either." Vic shuffled through the script. "This gag about Mrs. Roosevelt in New Guinea. I heard that on three shows last week."

"Anyway, they were my shows," Max said.

"And this local yokel joke about the aircraft worker on the crowded Wilshire Avenue bus. I suppose I heard that one on your show, Georgie?"

"Could be," Georgie said complacently.

"And why the hell should a phony psychiatrist tell a wolf joke about GIs? Just because every other radio show has a GI wolf joke on it is no sign we should. The same goes for this gag on the cigarette shortage."

Vic held the script out, weighing it distastefully in his hand, and let it drop back on the desk.

"You've crammed it with every stock gag in the book. The body gag, the old rabbit-skunk joke. And your one and only original about the Marine's helmet under the bed is a sight gag pure and simple. It'll never come off over the air. What'll you do, wave a chamberpot at the studio audience to get a yak? Besides, it's a little dirty, and I told you Evan Llewelyn Evans didn't like blue material."

Georgie was upset. "Well, Max. Looks like we'll have to work another four days."

"Don't be so sincere," Vic said, relaxing with them. "Sure it stinks, but we can fix that. Right here. In less than an hour."

That made everybody happy. And the business of punching up the script began.

"We got a psychiatrist," Vic said. "Maybe we could ring in one of those tough-butch jailbird voices. He wants to know why the cops keep putting him in jail. So Buddy diagnoses him as the shut-in type." He paused. "No," he said, "it's too precious."

Then he said, "How about having the stooge do a running gag? He tries to sell all of Buddy's patients a cure-all Indian herb medicine."

Max said, "He could interrupt with a patter about a combination of herbs, roots and berries. Might be funny."

"Could be," Georgie said. "But how about having him . . ."

They worked out the business on it and threaded it through the script. Then they started dropping in short fast gags for quick laughs.

"I know a good insult gag," Buddy Hare said. "I can toss it at the singer. He sings his song, see, and I say 'Sounds a lot like Bing.' And he interrupts and says, 'Yes, yes, Buddy. You were saying I sounded a lot like Bing?' And then I say 'It sounds just like air escaping from Bing Crosby's tire.' Unnerstan?"

"I like Fred Allen's original version better," Max said.

"Look, Buddy, why don't you go out for a cup of coffee and we'll check this over with you later."

This hurt Buddy's feelings, and Vic said, "Stick around. You've given us some good ideas."

But Max was right. Buddy Hare was no judge of material. He couldn't tell the good from the bad. That was the tip-off. The good comedians knew good material. They didn't depend on anyone else to tell them what did or didn't stink. It was too bad, but Buddy Hare would never be a topflight. He had a tin ear.

Georgie Gaver came up with a usable routine about a woman with a Bronx accent who called on the psychiatrist.

"She never did understand medical terms very well," Georgie explained, "and she's got psychiatrist confused with veterinarian, see."

It was about her pet cat, Bertha, and the psychiatrist (that would be Buddy) thought Bertha was her daughter and he couldn't understand why she hung around alleys all night and came in next morning all scratched up. Or why the dogs chased her. It worked into a very funny blackout.

Vic said, "Good boy, Georgie. Now you're cooking with radar. That'll be the top boff on the show. We ought to get thirty full seconds of belly laughs from the audience. It'll make the record sound good."

They all liked the script now, and had that smug, pleased feeling of accomplishment.

"It's not bad," Vic said. "I'll get the cast together for a read-through tonight and we can fix up the timing. It looks about ten minutes too long, figuring eight minutes for applause, but there are over seventy laughs in it so we can cut out the sick ones and still have plenty."

That was another peculiar thing about radio shows. Studio audiences laughed just as hard at the bad ones as they did the good ones. There was something about getting a free ticket to a radio show that made people want to coöperate to make the show sound funny over the air. But it didn't have any effect at all on the Hooper ratings, that is to say, the home audience.

Just then Norma came in. "Teletype, Vic. I think it's important."

He asked the writers and Buddy to wait, and went out to see what bad news was coming from New York.

MR. NORMAN FROM MR. KIMBERLY

HELLO VIC HOPE UR HAVING FUN. SORRY BUT THERES A NEW PITCH ON THE BUDDY HARE SHOW. JUST TALKED TO MR. EVANS WHO SAID QUOTE I HOPE MR. NORMAN IS NOT WRITING A GAG COMEDY SHOW FOR BUDDY HARE UNQUOTE. WHAT ABOUT IT/Q/ PLS ANSWER SOONEST. GA

Vic said, "That old son of a bitch. No, Norma, don't teletype that." He dictated the answer:

MR. KIMBERLY FROM MR. NORMAN

HELLO KIM. MY GOD/EXCLAM/ DO U REALIZE WHAT U JUST SAID/Q/ OF COURSE WE R PLANNING A GAG COMEDY SHOW. ITS THE ONLY KIND OF SHOW BUDDY HARE COULD POSSIBLY DO. THE SCRIPT IS ALL WRITTEN. WE R READY TO CUT IT. PLS FOR GODS SAKES TELL ME MORE. GA

VIC FROM KIM

HERES MR. EVANS REASONING—QUOTE SOAP IS USED BY A FAMILY. FAMILIES LIKE GOOD CLEAN SITUATION COMEDIES ABOUT FAMILIES. SOAP IS CLEAN TOO. LOOK AT THE ALDRICH FAMILY. ONE MANS FAMILY. ETCETERA. THERE IS A TREND AWAY FROM GAG COMEDY SHOWS BECAUSE THE PUBLIC IS GETTING TIRED OF THEM. ERGO /UNDERSCORE ERGO/ WE WILL TAKE BUDDY HARE AND MAKE HIM INTO A CLEANCUT AMERICAN BOY WITH A FATHER A MOTHER A GIRLFRIEND AND A LITTLE WHITE HOUSE ON MAIN STREET, AND HAVE A HOMEY FAMILY

DRAMATIC SHOW FILLED WITH GOOD CLEAN FUN/UNDERSCORE CLEAN/ UNQUOTE. SORRY VIC BUT THATS WHAT THE MAN SAID. GA

KIM FROM VIC
HAS MR. EVANS CONSIDERED THAT
1. BUDDY HARE IS A RETIRED BURLESQUE HAM OVER FORTY YEARS OLD.
2. HE IS NOT A CLEANCUT YOUNG AMERICAN BOY AND CANNOT BE MADE TO SOUND LIKE ONE.
3. HE CANT ACT IN A DRAMATIC SHOW. ALL HE CAN DO IS READ CERTAIN KINDS OF GAGS AND NOT TOO GOOD AT THAT /UNDERSCORE NOT TOO GOOD/
4. WE HAVE NO WRITER FOR A FAMILY SITUATION SHOW. WE CANT GET ONE. I ONLY KNOW THREE AND TWO OF THEM ARE IN THE INFANTRY. THE THIRD IS SIGNED WITH A COMPETITIVE SOAP.
5. SUCH A SHOW WITH BUDDY HARE WOULD BE A COMPLETE TOTAL FLOP /EXCLAM/
6. KIM U CANT DO THIS TO ME. GA

VIC FROM KIM
I ALREADY RAISED MOST OF UR POINTS TO WHICH HE ANSWERED QUOTE ITS A SIMPLE MATTER OF DIRECTION AND WRITING. IF THE AGENCY STAYS ON THE BEAM WEVE GOT A GREAT NEW STAR IN BUDDY HARE, ANOTHER HENRY ALDRICH UNQUOTE. I CAN ONLY SAY VIC, DO THE BEST U CAN. BRING BACK SOMETHING ON A RECORD AND WE WILL PLAN OUR STRATEGY FROM THERE. REGARDS. GA

KIM FROM VIC
WILL TRY TO THINK OF SOMETHING. I MAY SHOOT MYSELF. END OR GA

IS THAT ALL, HOLLYWOOD/Q/

THAT IS ALL, BROTHER. END

Vic walked back into his office. The writers were ready to go.

"Better stick around," he said. "We got to write a new script."

He explained the bad news.

"I could shoot the character who invented the teletype," Max groaned.

Georgie said, "Who did invent it, Don Ameche?"

"Your material stinks," Vic said, using a gag from his own private stock. "You should get a new writer."

Only Buddy Hare was optimistic. "I can see myself as a young cleancut American boy," he said, bouncing around the room with the idea. "I got the voice for it. You know, maybe this corny Evans character is right. Unnerstan, Vic, I'm not saying you're wrong, but maybe he's right. Maybe the public is getting tired of these gag comedy shows. Maybe there is a trend to drama. And a young cleancut fella in a small town —that's America, see. A fella like that gets sympathy, unnerstan. They laugh with him, not at him, see."

"Well, anyway," Vic said, "whip out a script on it."

Max asked if Vic had any ideas for a storyline.

Vic said he was paralyzed. "I'll buy anything you dream up," he said. "Maybe you can have the preacher visiting this home and Buddy gets into all kinds of trouble. Clean trouble, though."

"It's just like it was when I worked on the Figaro Perkins show," Max said. "That old man back there in Wall Street was always lousing it up beyond all recognition."

"How's his health?" Georgie inquired solicitously. Then, as if having a bright thought, "Maybe he'll die one of these days. Maybe today, even."

They sympathized with Vic and promised to finish the script in three days, rain or shine.

After they left, Vic was able to smile a little at the whole silly business. He only resented the time he'd spent beating his brains out to give the Old Man the best show possible. All that wasted effort.

Norma came in to ask if the teletype meant canceling the audition.

He said of course not, and instructed her to order a studio for the following Tuesday, this being Thursday. She reminded him about tickets and he wrote some copy to print on them, also telling her to be sure that a lot of service men were given tickets, as they made the noisiest and best audience.

"Oh," she said, "I thought all the comedy shows played the camps for patriotic reasons."

"Well, they do," he said. "But those boys cooped up in barracks can make a comedian sound very funny, too. Also a lot of comedians do it to apologize for not being in uniform."

She said, "There certainly are a lot of angles to this business."

He sat and thought.

If he made the show into a real stinker, the Old Man would blame the agency for getting off the beam. If on the other hand he made it too good, Evans might be deluded into putting this abortion on the air. It would not win a good Hooper rating and eventually the blame would again be his. Something had to be done.

Let's see, Buddy Hare had a contract with Global pictures. He called Norma. "Find out if a director named Wally Tibbs is still out at the Global lot. I want to talk to him."

Wally was delighted to hear from Vic again. There was a necessary amount of old home week chatter and then Vic said, "Wally, do you remember a hysterical B picture that just barely got past the Hays office? It was called 'The Runway' and it was all about burlesque."

"Sure," Wally said, "George Graham directed it."

"Wasn't Buddy Hare the baggy pants comedian in that picture?"

Wally had to check that, but finally answered yes.

"I want a print of that film," Vic said.

Wally said he couldn't send it out of the studio. Vic said sure he could for an old pal. He explained he was trying to build a radio show around Buddy Hare and needed the film and it would make Buddy worth more money to Global pictures if he turned out to be a big radio comedian.

So Wally finally agreed to have the film waiting for the messenger Vic said he would send over.

He noticed for the first time on his desk a small advertising calendar, only to be found in Hollywood where talent promoted itself with all the zeal of insurance agents in ordinary towns. The calendar read:

Looking for an ingenue? Call

KAY CANTRELL

Also dialects and character roles

Phone HO9-3100

Vic sat and thought about Kay Dorrance. Rather, the thought of her now became foremost in his mind. It had been lingering there all morning, but the motions of business had kept it in the background. Now, at the first leisure moment, she was up front again.

He wanted to talk to her. To hear her voice. Surely there was no harm in just calling to say hello. Or he could apologize for being so abrupt and walking off without even saying good night.

He followed this impulse and dialed the hotel. But when the operator answered he did a last second switch and only said, "This is Mr. Norman. Any calls?"

She had not left any calls for him. He thought, It's no good. Selfishly, in my own interests, it's no good. If we do follow our instincts, she'll be tortured and wounded by it, and then I'll feel like a heel. And I will be a heel. He knew he would not like that feeling at all.

Yes, from a very selfish standpoint, not considering her or the children, it was in his own best interests to stay all the way away from Kay Dorrance.

He walked out to the teletype machine and dictated:

MR. KIMBERLY FROM MR. NORMAN

AM AIRMAILING TODAY PRINT OF AN OLD BUDDY HARE MOVIE.
THE MINUTE IT ARRIVES /UNDERSCORE MINUTE IT ARRIVES/
PLS SHOW IT TO MR. EVANS. NOT NECESSARY FOR U TO WASTE
TIME SEEING IT FIRST. I WANT HIS REACTION TO BUDDY HARE
IN THIS PICTURE SOONEST AS IT HAS IMPORTANT BEARING ON
RADIO SHOW. REGARDS. GA.

The answer came back at once.

VIC FROM KIM

WILL DO. REGARDS. END.

CHAPTER XVI

THURSDAY WAS FIGARO PERKINS' NIGHT ON THE RADIO, SO LATE
that afternoon Vic went to the studio where the show was in
rehearsal to pay his respects to the star. He also wanted to
find out how much truth there was in Don Worth's statement
that Figaro was fed up with Old Man Evans and did not want
to renew his contract with the Beautee Soap Company.

If Worth happened to be correct, then it could be a very
serious blow to the agency. There would either be the hysterical gamble of finding a new show that would satisfy the Old
Man, or else they would lose the show, and the billing, which
amounted to twenty thousand dollars a week for the talent
and around twelve thousand for the half hour on the network. Fifteen percent of that was a lot of money for Kimberly and Maag (or, perhaps by then it would be Kimberly
and Norman), almost a quarter of a million dollars a year in
commissions!

Vic had been a personal friend of Figaro's for years and
he knew him to be, like most talent, a complaining child, especially so with his agent. So there was always a chance that
he could offer the comedian a piece of candy, striped just
exactly right, which would cause Figaro to change his emo-
tions and therefore his mind.

They were cutting two minutes out of the script, and Vic
stood by until this minor surgery was completed. Figaro, naturally, browbeat the others into taking the lines away from

his most important stooge, and his strongest competitor, a talking band leader who was getting too big a reputation to satisfy the artist in Figaro.

"Vic," Figaro said, "where you been all week? You've been ignoring me. Dammit, let's go someplace and talk. I got a lot of problems."

The producer interrupted with a detail about sound effects which he felt required Figaro's personal attention.

"See what I mean?" Figaro complained. "Nobody thinks around here, Vic." This notion turned him, for a brief instant, into a philosopher. "That's the trouble with people," he said pessimistically. "They don't have thoughts. They just have reflexes."

"That's a very inspiring reflex for the day," Vic said. "Here's an empty dressing room. What's on your mind?"

"Now don't put me on the defensive, Vic. I know you, and you're always forcing people into a position where they want to apologize instead of squawk. These are legitimate problems."

So Figaro talked as a show businessman about his problems, which were in the following order of importance:

Problem 1. Figaro was wearing himself out with all the contributions he was making to the war effort. Something for the boys almost every night! He wanted a summer vacation to give his ulcer a rest. Would Vic please sell it to the Old Man. Vic said he'd try, but the Old Man was sure to say that the only trouble with Figaro was Income Taxitis —that he wanted a vacation simply because he was in the ninety percent tax bracket and couldn't make any more money. Which inspired Figaro's second problem.

Problem 2. Income taxes were terrible. He was not griping, understand, but it's a fact, Vic. I take seventy-five hundred a week out of this show, and I'm broke all the time. Vic tried to look sympathetic, but could offer no solution.

Problem 3. Figaro did not like the agency producer assigned to his show and wanted him removed. You saw what he just did, Vic, always worrying me. The guy's so afraid of Evan Llewelyn Evans that he can't make a decision for himself. Figaro enthusiastically recommended another producer (who turned out to be his current girl friend's brother). Vic promised to think this over, but he knew he would have to do something, if Figaro insisted on it.

Problem 4. For God's sakes, find Figaro some writers! There were six stumblebums on the show now and Figaro personally had to write the script with his own hot little hands. It was no wonder he was killing himself with work. Vic said he'd try to sign Georgie Gaver, but Figaro must know how tough it was. The draft had caught most of the good writers.

Problem 5. And in the name of suffering humanity, couldn't Vic sell the Old Man on cutting out at least half of those commercials that kept repeating "Love that Soap"? They were ruining the show. All Figaro's friends were making fun of him. The listeners were writing him nasty letters threatening to tune him out if the commercials were not changed. It was going to cut five points, at least five, off the Hooper rating. Why Figaro had run into Julie, his ex-wife, the other day, and even Julie said she never listened to the show any more because of those awful commercials. Vic said that if Evans used up the three minutes of commercial time during the half hour which the network permitted him with just simply reading essays about the benefits of Beautee soap, then Figaro would not be worth seventy-five hundred a week. He explained to Figaro that you had to be sharp and even obnoxious with commercials, or they would bounce right off the listener's mind without making any impression. Figaro grudgingly admitted this point.

Vic decided that now was very definitely not the time to talk to Figaro about renewing his contract. He'd have to work the comedian up into a friendlier mood first

"I've got twenty-three minutes," Figaro said. "Let's go out for a bite to eat."

Actually, Vic had nothing to do. And perhaps over coffee, Figaro would be in a better state of mind to talk about contracts.

But for some reason, Vic resisted the idea. He said, "Gee, I'm sorry, Figaro. But I made an appointment."

Figaro said he was sorry too. "But maybe you can come up to the house Monday night. I'm throwing a little party."

"Great," Vic said. "I may have a date, though."

"Bring her along. Maybe I'll like her."

Vic promised to come if he could possibly make it, but not to depend on it. He went backstage and said hello to the rest of the cast, then left with simulated haste for the appointment he did not have.

He drove back to the hotel and was waved at but not stopped by a policeman for driving too fast. He went to the pool for a swim, dressed, returned to his villa, then wandered into the lobby. He stood at the doorway to the dining room, but when the captain tried to seat him he said, no, he was just looking for someone.

He went back and sat on his terrace reading *Variety*. He decided not to go out to dinner, and ordered food from room service. He went to the terrace again, looking at *Variety* but not actually reading it.

The children came out of Villa Fifteen, apparently from their dinner, and made a beeline for him. His presents had been delivered and they were shrill with thanks for them and love for him.

Ellen called him "My ittle Vic" and gave him a series of smacking kisses, after each one asking, "Was that a weal loud one?" Hal had some new intelligence on a secret weapon, sure to end the war. He'd read about it in a comic book.

Vic was playing the game which Ellen called "you be the baby and I'll be the mother" when the waiter came with his dinner.

The nurse was over almost instantly to retrieve the children. "Mr. Norman has to eat his dinner in peace," she told them, but although Vic said he liked noisy dinners, she took them back home.

Probably Kay had been watching, he thought, and the arrival of the waiter had given her a polite and valid reason for retrieving her children without awkwardness.

He finished the meal and it was time for his chore of listening to the Figaro Perkins' show. Afterwards, he caught a news broadcast and then turned the radio off, sitting on the terrace in the cool starry night.

She came out of Villa Fifteen and she turned, not to the left, but to the right, coming towards his villa. Perhaps she was going out for a walk. He looked hard in the darkness and hopefully verified the fact that she wore no coat. If she were going for a walk she would be wearing a coat. It was chilly for a thin dress. But then again, she was a big, strong woman who was probably impervious to a little thing like weather. And, too, she could simply be going into the lobby for cigarettes or newspapers. But she was the kind of woman who would order such things sent to her villa.

He fretted thus until she physically made the turn and did not walk on past.

He rose to greet her. A gracious, friendly, but somewhat impersonal host. "Kay," he said, shaking her hand. "You were thoughtful to call. I was getting a little bored with myself."

She said in a low voice, "I wanted to add my thanks to those of the children's. For the wonderful presents. You shouldn't have been so extravagant, Vic."

"It's only money," he said. "I'm glad they liked them."

"Liked is an understatement," she said, still standing. "Ellen said that as soon as the war is over, she was going to have a baby that looked just like the dolly you sent her. A real live baby. She's known only war, you see, and not having things, including babies, is to her mind always due to wartime shortages."

"The other day," Vic said, "I asked her what she wanted for a present and she said 'a weal live baby' "—he mimicked

Ellen. "So I asked her what she'd do with a baby if she had one. She wrinkled her little nose and answered, 'Oh, when it's good, I'll love it, and when it's bad I'll spank it.'" Kay was still standing so he said, "Please sit down or would you rather go inside? It's a little cool out here."

"Not for me," she said. "I love it. But I really shouldn't. I have so many things to do."

"Aren't the children in bed?"

"Long ago. It's past nine."

"Then sit for just one cigarette."

That seemed to be all right and they smoked a while. Vic was determined to match her silence with his, second for second, and it was she who finally spoke.

"I also ought to thank you for last night." He had to strain to hear her.

"You were so—good. So considerate." She threw away her cigarette. "I appreciated it."

Later she said, "I was silly, I suppose. I don't know. Something got into me."

She walked over and sat on the railing, looking up at the northern hills that hung like mountains over them.

"I've been so restless, lately," she said.

"These are restless times," he said. "For the whole world."

"Yes, I feel like getting into a speedboat, or on the back of a hunter, and riding like mad to burn it out of my system."

"Some people feel like getting drunk," he said. "Your way is better."

"Do you feel like getting drunk?"

"No. I only drink to defend myself from the boredom of people. I never drink alone."

"The hills are beautiful," she said. "I'd like to go up into them, through the canyon. It's so wild and winding. At night you're not aware of those homes they conceal in the wilderness so it really does seem remote from the world."

He brooded over this. He did not really know whether or not she would remind him of his pledge to her last night if he offered to drive her up into those hills. He also did not know if it was the right thing for him to do, regardless of how she felt. But on the other hand, Kay herself was different tonight. Restless, yes, but she had regained her wonderful quality of quiet composure—the quality that gave him such a sense of fulfillment to be with her.

There really would be no harm in it, if they were intelligent about it.

Was it a coincidence that she used the same word, intelligence, when she spoke?

"It's hard to put your finger on the causes of restlessness," she said. "The mind is a funny thing. It's like a spirited horse. Sort of dependent on the intelligence of the rider."

This thought made her more confident and she accepted another cigarette.

"Do you know how long you'll be in Hollywood?" she asked.

He said it was definite now. "I'm leaving next Wednesday on the Chief. I've already started conniving for reservations."

She was surprised. "Next Wednesday? That's only six more days."

Vic perceived that the time-fragment of six days made a strong impression on her. He could understand why. Six days was so precise, so specific, with a clear-cut beginning and an equally definite ending. It did not project her, or rather him, into some awkward future where there could be conflict or confusion with her other interests.

"Six pathetic little days," said Vic. "Six wasted little days. And then the Chief, and then New York, where the little days will continue to scurry away, equally wasted."

"You have a horrifying concept of time," she said. "You make life seem so worthless . . . even the future, which you obviously don't know anything about."

"I can guess," he said. "The future is a phoney psychiatrist, promising a cure for today's hangover."

"I'm different about the way I spend my time," she said. "I have no great pretensions. I spend a day. If I'm happy it's been a good day. I'm not fretful of time the way you are."

"That's because you've done something with it."

"I have not. If I tried to measure my life by achievement, I'd get morbid. You've done far more than I. But you don't have a fix on anything. I do."

"Well," he said, "since you're an authority on how to spend time, why don't you tell me what to do with my next six days?"

"I wouldn't accept so great a responsibility," she said. "I wouldn't even presume to do it for your next six hours."

Just in time, he recalled his promise of last night and censored his next thought before he stated it.

"Gracious," she tried to see her watch in the darkness. "If I don't get back, you'll be well into wasting those six hours just talking to me. I really must be going."

"Please," he said. "They wouldn't be wasted. You know that."

She seemed to appreciate his inability to be specific, and she sat for long seconds gazing up into the black hills banked above them.

And then, as if the notion were sudden and impulsive and quite unimportant, she said, "Let's do drive up into the hills. We both know what we're doing, don't we?"

Vic was sure they were both old enough to know what they were doing.

"And you know me and my children and even if I didn't you wouldn't . . . so why be silly about it? That is if you feel like wasting an evening just driving around with an old married woman."

Vic hastily made the point that he did feel exactly like doing just that very thing. And he agreed absolutely with everything she'd said.

"I'll get my coat," she said, and she gaily ran both ways so as not to keep him waiting.

It was wonderfully restful up in the hills. And happy. Happy because they were friends again, on a firm understandable short-term, six-day basis, and not opponents in some subtle, endless, primitive contest.

She talked with a light heart of the gay, literate, fascinating things in her life. She described hilarious visits to her in-laws on Long Island who had lost everything but the desire to breed fine dogs, ride good horses, and hate Mr. Roosevelt.

Vic told her about radio and teletypes, about comedians and Evan Llewelyn Evans, who tonight seemed to him the most comic of characters. Her laughter echoed loud and long among the North Hollywood hills.

The little car climbed the summit and stopped awhile as they looked on the earth-bound planetarium that was Los Angeles County. They were sorry Hal and Ellen were not there to enjoy it with them, and Vic enacted an impression of the two children upon first glimpsing all this magnificence.

"What's that," he imitated Ellen's high, bird-voice. "Sunset Boulevard? Mummy, my want to take Sunset Boulevard back to New York wiff me. Can I, Mummy?"

And in Hal's staccato, done from a crouch. "Hey hey, I just barely got enough bullets in my machine gun to shoot out all those lights. Follow me, men. Kak-kak-kak-kak."

Tonight, they were not cagey with each other and it was fun. They slid down into the valley and over into Hollywood, and stopped at the first neon sign of civilization where a pretty girl in slacks bought them cheeseburgers and coffee.

There was talk of going to the races together, of borrowing a boat and sailing with the children, of this and that diversion. One night, Kay wanted to go to the Mocambo, not to see the picture stars in their native habitat, but to see the tropical glass-caged birds out of theirs.

But at last the car found itself on the boulevard which inexorably led to the hotel. And too soon, far too soon, there was the uninviting entrance into which the car must turn.

Vic, driving, did not want to turn into that entrance. He did not want thus to end this night of camaraderie.

But the entrance leered at him, moved closer and closer up to him. He gave the wheel a slight turn. He painstakingly looked back to see what the traffic was like behind him. He carefully signaled the turn with his left hand. He turned the wheel ever so slightly again.

And then she acted. Acted and spoke. Her action was a simple motion, of putting her hand on his arm, very lightly. Her speech was but two words, but they were at once words of appeal and words of command.

"Don't turn," she said.

And at those magic words, the car ignored and defied the stern gateway and kept straight on its course. Straight and true it sailed down the boulevard, down towards the sea at the end of the boulevard.

"You did not want to turn in either," she said. It was a confident, true statement and he accepted it calmly.

"No," he said. "I didn't."

So the small, inexpensive, rented vehicle, the frowsy, rattly, war-weary, drive-it-yourself car, bore them nearer, nearer, to the sympathetic sea.

It was chilly. He slowed down and pressed the button which brought the top over their heads.

With windows up, insulated from the world by rubber, glass, tin, steel and noise—the two comrades rolled not merrily but now dreamily along in their six cylinder universe, their animated tinpot which was not in but superimposed on nature, and which had become a cozy, separate little world belonging to them alone. And the two friends were staring and silent as the concrete ribbon unrolled beneath their feet. The movement was a narcotic and it threw their minds into neutral as they coasted effortlessly beside the dark and dreamy hills.

The car was parked and Vic opened the window. "It's a little raw tonight. The spray is coming all the way up here. I think we'd better stay in the car."

But her eyes were glazed and her face was set and savage and she again commanded him.

"Let's go down to the beach."

She walked ahead of him, the tall strong woman. She stood and waited for him as the sea at her back pounded out its rhythm for them. What had he called it: the downbeat for love.

As he came to her, she dropped her coat to the white sands. She grasped his shoulders and fiercely pulled him down to the sands with her.

"My love," she said. "You understand? You're my love."

"Yes," he said. "Yes. Yes."

"Oh yes, my love. Now! Now! Now!"

And love rose dreamily up with them and with them left the sea, and went back with them down the wondrous boulevard.

Kay was afire with love. She was beyond reason and restraint.

She whispered dazedly, "My love." And then emphatically and with conviction, "My only love."

"You're my only love too," he said. "I want you to understand that."

"Just think, my love." She lay limply against him and the touch of him interrupted the words she'd begun. "You're like an artery. Just touching your shoulder. It's like an artery pumping and flowing from you to me and back to you again. I'm so happy. And so lucky. I'm a very lucky girl." Then she repeated, "Just think. In thirty-two years of being alive, I never knew about love. All those years. Fancy not ever being in love until you're thirty-two years old!"

"Lots of people live and die without ever being in love," he said. "Millions of them. All they ever have is a box full of retirement annuities."

"I know," she said. "I see it in their faces. They don't know about love. Their ignorance is in their faces. It must have been in my face."

Her ardor retreated to some deep, quiet, unapproachable haven within her, and they finished the trip in a silent, love-filled car.

Walking with her through the park to the villas, he worried and wondered what it was that had happened to him. He wasn't sure about many parts of it, or of what would come

of it, but he was sure that this was the only profound feeling
of love he had ever known.

And that this fine, tall, strong, quiet woman beside him
could be capable of such an explosion, that she could seize
him physically and without restraint: the night was beyond
understanding, as her action had been beyond understanding.

And then she became understandable to him because of
the feeling that had come into him on this night. It *was* an
explosion, a searing blast that shattered away all her restraint,
all the habits and controls of a lifetime.

This must be love.

If that's what it was, then he had never known love before.
And he believed with passionate conviction that she had
never known it either, not until this night.

So this was what they'd been battling against, almost from
the minute they'd met. This was what had sent him to her
hotel, driven him into a dozen artful little ruses that at the
time had made him seem as a foreigner to himself. Now he
understood himself and also her: the uneasy woman, the
exhilarated girl, the commanding lover. Only love could
create such swift, stirring changes in the innermost character
of this lonely woman.

As they approached the walk leading to his villa, he again
did not know what to do, or how to conduct himself.

He couldn't be the aggressor. He still wanted her. God,
every minute he could have of her, he wanted her. But he
couldn't say, "Come in." Not even for a drink. He had no
rights of love. She must again bestow, as she had already once
that night bestowed on him, the free and unhampered right
to love her.

And he thought: she is not the same woman that she was
on that remote beach. The past was waiting for the wife and
mother at Villa Fifteen.

So he could not guide her, he could not turn in at his own
villa. He must walk right past it as if to take her home.

But she stopped him.

"Don't you want me?" she asked. And he saw again the

glaze in her eyes, the film of love that covered her desperate face.

And helplessly, as figures in a dream, the lovers entered the villa.

[CHAPTER XVII]

THAT WAS THURSDAY NIGHT. AND THEY PARTED FRANTICALLY in the early morning, he standing on his terrace watching her walk alone to Villa Fifteen. Alone and stealthily, so as not waken Martha or the children.

He went to sleep thinking of her and he came awake thinking of her.

The phone had roused him and his love brightened as he heard her voice again.

"Hello there," she said, very brisk and lively. "Awake?"

"Just."

"You're a sleepyhead. It's noon."

She'd been up since nine. The children were now at the pool with Martha, but she expected them back for lunch any minute.

"I thought you might like some coffee," she said.

"I need coffee," he said. "Where? Over at your place?"

She hesitated. "I don't feel up to brewing a fresh pot. Haven't the energy. I thought you might like to meet me in the hotel dining room."

He understood and said, wonderful. He'd pick her up in eight minutes.

"It usually takes me ten minutes to shower, shave and dress. But for you, I'm going to set a new world's record."

She said, "Suppose I meet you in the dining room? I have to go to the lobby anyway."

229

He spied her in a deserted corner of the dining room and put on a little act for the waiter.

"Kay," he said, going nonchalantly to her table. "Fancy finding you here. What a delightful surprise."

"Sit down," she said.

The waiter took his order.

Then she said, "You really overplayed that delightful surprise act, darling. Everyone can plainly see this is a carefully planned rendezvous."

"It was supposed to be a gag," he explained.

They looked steadily at each other until their faces hurt.

"Darling," she whispered. "Do you love me?"

"Yes," he said.

"Say it then."

"I love you," he said. "Do you want a demonstration?"

"Of course," she said. "But not here. I'm so happy, darling."

"So am I, Kay. This is wonderful. You're wonderful. I never knew anyone could be so wonderful. I love you."

She was wonderful. Radiant with her new love. So beautiful. He told her so.

"You're so beautiful," she said looking him over critically. "And you're mine. I don't know how I ever found the courage to get you."

"Courage? It looks like the Russians will reach Berlin before we do." This last was for the waiter, who was serving them.

When the waiter left she said, "You know what I mean. I forgot everything a civilized woman is supposed to know, last night." She laughed.

"You have a wonderful laugh," he said. "Joyous. Bright as a new ensign's buttons."

"How I ever nerved myself to do it," she said wonderingly. "I knew I had to do it, because you wouldn't. But I didn't know if you really and truly wanted me, and I was afraid I'd make a fool of myself."

"I love you for it. You knew I wanted you all right. God,

it must have shone through every minute we were together."

"I suppose I did know it," she admitted. "Even so, it took a lot of nerve. You won't think me a nymphomaniac, will you? I'm not at all."

"No," he said. "You're not a nymph. I know what you are."

"I'm in love, that's what I am."

"Me, too," he said.

"I feel as if I had just been born, right this minute. A new-born woman."

He ate, and looked lovingly at her, and she sat and looked lovingly at him and they talked lover's talk through his breakfast.

"I want to touch you," she said. "I want to reach right across this table and touch you."

"All right. Touch me and see if I care. I want to touch you, too. You're what I'd call a soft touch."

"Don't go to work today. Please don't."

"Maybe I won't. What day is this?"

"Friday," she said. "Friday, Saturday, Sunday, Monday, Tuesday. Five more days and nights. Darling, isn't it lovely to have so much time?"

"Friday," he said. "I do have to go to work. Not that I give a damn about the job, but I've made appointments. People are down there waiting for me. We're doctoring up our mystery show. I'll call you the minute I'm loose," he said.

They walked out into the lobby and she stood with him at the door while the man brought his car round front.

"I love you," she said, leaning hard against him. "Do you suppose it shows."

"At least to the horizon," he said. "I'll call you."

"I'm so happy, Vic. I've never been happy like this before."

In a way, the radio meeting was a blur, but for some reason he was very good, sparking ideas that were really good, and giving the writers a new format that promised to show up in the ratings.

Then he called her at five and she said she'd meet him downtown for dinner. He said he'd drive out for her, but she claimed a taxi was simpler so they decided on a restaurant.

The restaurant didn't make any difference and the dinner didn't make any difference, and they raced through this segment of their evening and afterwards sat in the car parked at the curb outside the restaurant.

"Oh Vic," she said. "Let's go someplace. We have to go someplace."

Vic realized the villa had been all right when they were neighbors but it was not right for lovers. It was too close to the children, emotionally and physically. So he did not even suggest going to his villa. If she wanted to go there, she would have already said so.

"I wish I knew where we could go," he said.

"Oh, let's go to a hotel or something. Isn't that what lovers always do, darling? Go to a hotel and register as Mr. and Mrs. Smith?"

"They do in peacetime," he said. "But not in wartime. You just can't drop into a hotel and get a room, like that, any more."

So the baffled lovers drove around for a long, long time until it grew dark, and they became more and more eager to find a place where they could be alone with each other.

"I never knew before the agony lovers have to endure," she said. "Just to be alone. From now on, whenever I see lovers floating around in public I'll always pity them."

Finally the car found its way into the center of Hollywood and Vic said casually, "The only place I can think of where we can be alone is my office. It'll be closed down for the night. There won't be a soul around."

"Have you a key?"

"Sure."

Kay phoned Martha that she would be out late with some friends and they stole quietly into the Hollywood offices of Kimberly and Maag and stayed until three-thirty in the morning, uninterrupted except for one brief period by a scrublady and that didn't count.

"It's ridiculous," she said. They were driving back to the Sunset Hills Hotel.

"What?"

"This hunting around for dark places to go. Even offices."

"The offices of Kimberly and Maag were never put to better use," he said.

She kissed him. "It was wonderful, darling, and I'm not complaining."

"Then stop running down my employer's offices," he said. "I feel a great loyalty to that brown leather sofa, even if it was too short."

"It's a wonderful sofa," she said. "But I'm thinking about tomorrow and the next day and the next. I just can't keep you out in the open, hanging around cafés and bars and swimming pools and waiting for darkness to fall. You might spoil. And besides, I don't have time to share you with all those people."

"Can you get away?"

She hadn't thought of that, but she answered, "I have to get away."

"Tomorrow, bright and early, I'll try to find a hotel suite."

The idea thrilled her. "We could stay in it all the time. Make them bring up our food. And your old newspapers."

"I can't waste time eating," he said. "Or reading newspapers. Well, maybe just the headlines."

"But it doesn't have to be a suite," she said. "It could be a lovely tiny little room. Anyway, you might get lost in a great big suite and I'd have to waste time looking for you."

"But you've got to think up some plan for Martha," he said.

The plan they worked out was good, they thought. Vic had a trustworthy friend in San Francisco. So Kay would tell Martha and the children that she was going to leave Saturday to visit this friend, returning Monday night late. Kay would leave the San Francisco phone number with Martha in case anything happened; and Vic would phone the friend, instructing her to report by long distance any calls for Kay at whatever hotel he might find.

Kay thought it was a very exciting plan and she couldn't wait until tomorrow. They kissed outside her door and sternly resisted their desire to go back to his villa.

"My love," she whispered. "Get up early, so we can be together longer."

And then she left him.

And for him it was like the night before. She stayed in his mind all through the night. He did not try or want to think her out of his mind, but he knew that even if he did, she would not go away. Yes, this must be love.

The next morning, Saturday, when they met again in the dining room for breakfast, he was gloomy.

"Bad news," he reported. "I've called every first-class hotel in Los Angeles, Santa Barbara and even San Diego. They're all filled."

Kay was desolate. "We have to have someplace to go," she said. "Couldn't you tell them it was some kind of emergency? It really is, you know."

He shook his head. "I even put Maag on the job, and he has a lot of influence. There just aren't any empty rooms. After I tried all the good hotels, I started to work my way down the alphabetical list in the phone book. Oh, I did find one place, but it's an impossible little worm-eaten dump in the worst part of downtown Los Angeles. Down by the tracks."

She brightened. "Well, let's go there then."

He said he couldn't think of taking her there. "Not in a million years. It's a place called the Mapleton. Unquestionably filled with whores, drunks, and small crawling objects. We couldn't go there."

"And why not?" she demanded.

She simply had no knowledge of such things. A room was a room. She didn't have the slightest feeling of awkwardness about it. She didn't see why it had to be a smart hotel.

Finally, he agreed to explore the Mapleton further. "Your

inexperience has triumphed," he said. "If you knew anything at all about going to hotels with men, you'd listen to me."

"But, Vic darling, I'm not going to hotels with men. I'm going with you. That's why any place is fine."

He said he'd reserve a room for today and tomorrow and they'd look it over. "You'll probably change your mind when you see it," he said, "and remember, if you get a bad taste in your mouth, it wasn't my idea."

But she wasn't listening. "Today, tomorrow and Monday," she corrected. "Don't forget Monday. I told Martha I wouldn't be back until late Monday night."

"All right," he said. "I won't forget Monday."

"Now don't dawdle over your coffee," she ordered. "Phone them before they sell that room to somebody else. I'll meet you out front with my bag in ten minutes."

The man at the Mapleton confirmed the reservation, and they drove into the slummy neighborhood, Vic with misgivings, Kay happy as a meadowful of larks.

The Mapleton was emphatically that kind of hotel. Vic had not been in such a crib since his youthful hoboing days. The lobby smelled like a public toilet, and the inquisitive denizens of the lobby were unmistakable fugitives from a flophouse.

A girl like Kay in a place like this was unthinkable. But she stood there, looking particularly beautiful in a green suede suit, and with no outward sign of distaste. For all Vic could tell, she might just as well have been standing in the lobby of the Pierre.

"Look, darling," he whispered. "Let's get out of here. This is no good."

"Are you going to be difficult?" she said. "You haven't even looked at the room. You promised you'd look at the room, darling."

"I give up," he said and went to the desk.

"Reservation for Mr. Norman," he said to the clerk.

"That would be double, sir?" The clerk looked admiringly towards Kay.

Vic felt as if he were committing some crime. He hoped his embarrassment didn't show.

He asked the clerk if he had any suites. The clerk said the Mapleton never had any suites.

Kay came over and said, very easily and brightly, "You said you had doubles, I believe?"

"Yes, ma'am," the clerk said.

Vic said miserably that perhaps they should look at the room before making up their minds.

The clerk said it wouldn't be necessary. He knew just what Mr. and Mrs. Norman wanted.

"We get a lot of people like you," he explained. "Victims of the room shortage. So a few weeks back we fixed up our second floor. Used to be rooms where drummers displayed their merchandise," he said. "Hadn't been used for years. Drummers are too good to come to the Mapleton nowadays."

He said the rooms had been painted and completely redecorated with new furniture. "New beds, springs, mattresses, rugs, everything. Sheets changed every day."

"That sounds wonderful," Kay said, and Vic registered for Mr. and Mrs. Norman of New York City.

It was a long narrow room with one window, of course a bed, a chintz-covered chair and a maple dresser. There were no closets, but the room was new and shiny and faintly paint-smelling.

"Oh, it is newly furnished," Kay said admiringly. "I wonder who decorated it."

Vic looked around distastefully. "Looks like a job by Karl Marx," he said.

But Kay was thrilled with it. "So bright and clean and wonderful," she said, inspecting every corner. "But where's the bathroom, darling?"

"Across the hall," he said, still miserable about the whole thing. "This type hotel room doesn't come with a private bath."

She came to him and kissed him. "Many's the time in Europe I've stayed in hotels with bathrooms across the street," she said. "But darling, you're unhappy. Do you feel sordid about this?" she asked solicitously.

"Don't be silly," he said.

"I know people are supposed to feel sordid, registering as man and wife and all that," she said, "but I don't feel anything but wonderful. How could I feel any other way?" she demanded. "I'm with you. Besides, no woman could possibly want a nicer room. It's lovely."

"You're the one that's lovely," he said. "You're a mad, unpredictable girl and I admit that somehow we got our roles switched. I was supposed to be the nonchalant, worldly one, and you were supposed to be timid and afraid. Anyway," he said, "that's all over, thank God, we're out of that lobby and safely locked in, and I see your point. The room is very, very fine. Do you want me to order a drink? As if you could get room service in a place like this!"

"And dull my senses with alcohol?" she demanded. "I certainly do not want to share you with a bottle of whiskey. I'm going to soberly enjoy every single second of you. Come here."

"You come here," he said.

So they compromised and met each other halfway and the room became to Vic, as to Kay, an ecstatic, beautiful, shimmering place of love.

Saturday, Sunday, Monday. . . .

The two were fused by love and one became like the other. The lovers talked, thought, looked, sighed, heard, felt alike.

The words that were felt and spoken by one were spoken and felt by the other. The inflections of love became special and private, never before made known to any other lovers.

"When did you first know you loved me?" he asked. "What instant did it happen?"

She said, "It wasn't so much when I knew I loved you. The blinding moment was that instant in the car when I knew I had to have you."

"Lovely, beautiful Kay!"

"Lovely, beautiful Vic!"

"Do other people talk this way? Abandon all other feelings of life this way?" one of them asked. "I never knew these words, these silly words, could mean so much."

"You're so lovely. Your body is so lovely. I want to be it. I am it."

"I didn't know. I didn't know the love I could feel for a finger, a toe, the curve of a knee, the sole of a foot—your foot," one of them said.

And the other one said, "I can't sleep. It's sacrilege to sleep. Sleeping is like dying now. But you must sleep, my love. I want to stay awake and love your sleep."

Oh, ecstasy, that hoarse and breathless word, that hot and viscous word.

"Say I love you."

"Yes, yes. I love you. You're my only love."

"You know," she said, "it can't be divided into parts or fragments or even days. What day is this, love?"

"Monday, I think. Yes, it's Monday."

It was turning dark in the narrow room. They were in bed, she sitting up to braid her golden hair.

She said, "I've grown up with you, Vic. I was just a young, loveless girl. And now I'm a woman. A loved woman. A fulfilled woman."

"You've enriched me," he said. "I've found a use for time, and a purpose for myself."

"A week ago, I'd have thought we were doing a bad thing," she said. "Now I'm grown up. I'm a woman and I know this is not a bad thing, but a good thing. How can such happiness be anything but good?"

"It's the best thing that ever happened to me," he said. "Even if it does have to . . ."

He would not finish. He would not think about Wednesday. Day after tomorrow. He would not think about leaving her.

"You know," she said, "I was afraid of you, I thought.

But I fancy I was only afraid of love. We always fear the unknown, I suppose."

She kissed his hand. Bit it impishly. "You don't need that silly hand. May I have it? I was just afraid of love," she said. "But now I know what loving you is, and I'm not afraid of anything."

Not even of leaving it? Of course not! Why should she reject these ecstatic days simply because they couldn't continue? She did not like this thought and shook it out of her mind.

"You're so beautiful," she said, looking at Vic from different angles. "All those women. That awful actress on the train. I hate them all."

"You can't start any arguments with me," Vic said fondly. "Frightful little girl. You are a frightful little girl, you know."

"I am not. I'm an abandoned creature," she said happily. "Didn't I ever tell you I was an abandoned creature."

"Let's have a little abandon," he said.

"You're bragging," she said. "I'll kill you. I'll love you to death."

"I'll either kill you first or die happy."

"Big talker. Braggart," she said. "Your days are numbered," and clenched her teeth for having said it.

"That won't save you," he said. "I'll kill you tonight."

Vic suddenly remembered the Figaro Perkins party.

"You're invited to a party," he informed her, and she said that unless he was the only other guest she was not interested.

"Not in the slightest," she claimed. "You have changed my whole idea of a party."

"Also your conversation," he said. "All you ever talk about any more is what can be done in bed. Don't you realize that there are culture and society and all kinds of high class diversions still hanging around in the world? Don't you realize that two people can't spend their lives marooned in room 209 at the Mapleton Hotel?"

"No," she said complacently. "My tastes are very simple. All I want is this room with you in it. Nothing else. Oh maybe

a meal every week or so, but that's not absolutely necessary."
She looked around with satisfaction. "I could stay in this
room, loving you, until I die," she said.

But he explained there were business reasons for going to
the party and she quickly admitted that she had been dying
to go all the time because she was a secret Figaro Perkins fan.

"He's something or other on the radio, isn't he?" she asked.

"We'll go very late, for Hollywood," he explained. "Most
Hollywood parties break up early. Around one. So we'll eat,
then go to Mocambo to see the birds, and plan on reaching
Figaro's house between eleven and twelve."

Vic was dressed and ready to leave long before Kay, who
overlooked no delaying action.

"I hate to leave this lovely little room," she said. "I'll never
forget it. Never."

As they left, she again said, "I'll never forget this room.
It's so lovely. It's the way a room ought to be for all the
lovers in the world."

"I didn't like it at first," Vic said. "But now I hate to leave."

"Want to know something, darling?" she said. "I really felt
awful down in that lobby."

"Really? You're a wonderful actress, then."

"I had to be. I knew you felt awful, and I was afraid
you'd think it was all so cheap."

"I love you," he said. "Every hour I find something new
to love you for." He closed the door and they stood in the
hall. "Good-bye, room," he said.

"Let's stay just one more night," she begged.

But he reminded her of her promise to Martha, and also
of his business with Figaro Perkins.

Down in the lobby, a sullen whore looked bitterly at
Kay's green suit and again Vic felt compunction for bringing
her here.

They stopped at a drugstore while Kay called Martha,
who reported the children well and that everything was fine
and uneventful at Villa Fifteen. Kay told Martha she'd be

home around one, and then spoke to Hal and Ellen who were just then going to bed.

"I don't really worry about them when I'm away," she told Vic. "Martha is like a sweet, kind grandmother to them. She's been with us ever since Hal was born."

She had often told people she didn't worry about the children when she was away, and it had always been a lie, but she realized that she hadn't really worried about them this time, and she felt a little guilty for almost completely forgetting them.

They drove out to Hollywood and had a long leisurely dinner at the Beachcomber, danced a while at the Mocambo, and then went to Figaro's house in Bel Air.

"If I blink my eyes three times," she warned, "that's a signal."

"What for?"

"It means I can't stand being so far away from you any longer and we have to find a bed quick."

Then she said, "You have changed my conversation. I've learned a new vocabulary since Thursday. You don't think I talk too dirty? I never talked this way before."

"I like dirty-talking little girls," he said.

"I don't want to shock my love."

"Especially you," he said, ringing Figaro's doorbell. "It would take a champion to shock me. You haven't even learned the real dirty words yet. All you've got is the inclination. You're just an amateur dirty-talker!"

Things were as usual in Figaro's house, and they met people who were hits as well as some who were near misses. The celebrities in the game room ungraciously looked up from gin rummy for one brief hello.

Figaro had acquired a new house since Vic's last visit and he showed the newcomers through it. They were followed by a drunken actor who did not like Figaro, for one reason because the actor's current wife had been, among other things, Figaro's girl.

But that was not the reason he gave to Kay and Vic as they dutifully followed Figaro through the house.

"He's supposed to be a comedian," the actor said. "And he's got no sense of humor. That makes him like a thief. He just the same as steals money from that soap company. I got a pet goldfish at home who gives me more laughs than Figaro."

"This," said Figaro, opening a door and turning on a soft light, "is a sort of picture salon."

"This'll kill you," the actor whispered loudly.

It was an austere rectangular room decorated as a gallery and hung with many pictures. At one end, suitably lighted, was a large oil painting of Figaro.

"See what I mean?" the actor said. "No sense of humor. He can't see the humor in this room."

Figaro ignored the actor completely. Vic didn't see anything either at first, but then he got it. All the other pictures in the room were pictures of Figaro, too. Enlarged photos richly framed, in all sorts of poses.

"Show 'em your wine cellar, Figaro," the actor insisted. "It's full of beer, a gift from his last sponsor."

But by this time Figaro was mad and wouldn't talk.

"Show 'em where you store empty bottles, banking for the next depression," the actor said. "Or your Beautee Soap storeroom. Love that free soap. Yes sir, that Figaro is a slow man with a buck."

Figaro mournfully canceled the tour and led them to the living room. He introduced them to the people there, including Helen, the actor's present wife. Meanwhile the actor, whose name was Dick, lurched over to find the signature on a picture painted by Thomas Hart Benton.

He said, "Figaro, that's a nice Benton. Did you paint it yourself?"

"Anyway," Figaro said to the room, "I save my comedy for the radio."

"And if not, who gave it to you?" Dick asked the room. "I can't get the picture of Figaro actually spending real money for a painting by Benton. Or did you pay him with soap samples?"

"An amateur," Figaro told the room. "See how he kills his own gag?"

Constance Linger wandered in from the game room. She glanced appraisingly at Kay and asked Vic if he'd adopted those two children. He asked her about her new picture.

"Oh that," she said.

"Have they shot the drunk act in the jungle yet?"

"Oh, no," she said. "They cut the drunk act. Then they cut the jungle. It's going to be a musical about musicals and I do a snake dance in the middle of a bunch of high-class fag ballet dancers. It's a story about a stage-struck dame, that's Ginnie Gaines, and I'm the sex-starved older sister."

"I'm dying not to see it," Vic said.

A writer named Ronnie Klein said, "I submitted that very same idea to Global three years ago. The exact same idea. They filed it and forgot me."

"It's a lousy picture," Connie said. "It's got no balls. No balls at all."

"When I first came to Hollywood," Helen said to a young actress who was still new enough to ask advice from the old Hollywood hands, "I made all the mistakes there were."

"Such as?"

"Well, for one thing, I slept with all the wrong people."

This revived her husband, who shouted from across the room, "Including Figaro?"

"Don't pay any attention to him, honey," she said to the young actress. "I mean long before Figaro. . . ."

Vic looked at Kay. There had been many of the short earthy words floating around the room. At first glance, she seemed either totally unperturbed by this expected vulgarity, or else she was putting on her Mapleton lobby act. But Vic, now so familiar with her cool surface behavior, also saw that she was somewhat rigid, a little too statuesque.

He was probably exaggerating her embarrassment, but it was there, all right.

Lovely, lovely Kay. In this group, she seemed more remote and regal than ever. He proudly classified her as the most beautiful woman there, and he thought that was probably one reason why these hardened career women were going out of their way to use shocking language in front of her.

The party dragged on drearily for the two lovers. Vic noticed a pretty little girl sitting off by herself. He went over and spoke to her.

She was living in Hollywood, she said, but wasn't in pictures or radio. She'd been here for almost a year now.

"I stay with Helen and Dick," she explained. Dick was still dedicating his evening to heckling Figaro. "Look at him. He's going to have a fight with Figaro, you wait and see. Dick fights too much," she said critically.

Then Ronnie Klein sat with them. "You interest me very much," he said to the girl. "Just what do you do to Dick, anyway? I didn't know there was anything Helen doesn't do better than any other woman in the world. What is it you do?"

"Helen's a good friend of mine," she said. "We're very fond of each other."

The writer later told Vic it was one of those unusual harem plans, one man and two women in the same house. "The women seem to get along very well. But of course Helen, being the wife, has a definite edge on the other girl, and it must create a certain amount of insecurity all around."

"You must have been psychoanalyzed," Vic told him. "People who've been psychoanalyzed are always using that word, insecurity."

Constance Linger was putting on her mink coat, saying she had to be at the studio early. Helen called, "Night, darlin'" after her and then turned to the group.

"Connie must be taking a course in chest expansion. She seems to be developing in that direction."

"Fire one. Fire two," Dick said.

But Ronnie did not think they were real.

"Ask Figaro," Dick said, looking at his wife.

Figaro said they were real, all right.

It was almost one, and the gin rummy players were set-
tling up and throwing a fast "Good night, you lovely people.
Lovely party, Figaro," as they hurried home.

Vic whispered to Kay that he could approach Figaro on
the business matter very shortly now, and she whispered,
"Please hurry, darling."

Dick and Helen were the only other ones left and Figaro
couldn't quite manage to get rid of Dick who was very drunk,
and wanted to stay and needle Figaro. By this time he was
reaching way down for corny insult gags.

He said, "Ol' Figaro's a selfmade man, all right. He's pulled
himself up by his jockstrap."

"That is all, brother," Figaro said, unable to play the silent
martyr any longer. "I wish I had the spitting concession on
his grave," he said to Vic. "At a dollar a spit I could make a
fortune."

The actor had been waiting for something like that and
he made a long curving drunken swing that missed Figaro.
Helen grabbed his arm, and Dick's other girl, who did not
like fights walked sedately out of the room. "What'd I tell you,"
she said to Vic.

Dick then transferred his attack to Helen, but she ducked
his first haymaker and held him spellbound with screaming
abuse for at least forty-five profane seconds.

This gave Vic and Figaro a chance to jockey the snarling
couple out to the porch, and into their car.

"Well," Figaro said complacently, brushing his hands,
"that's that, thank God. You know, Vic, I'm beginning to dislike Dick. He's beginning to get in my hair."

Vic thought it was a very funny pay-off line. "You should
use that routine in your script next week, Figaro. Only change
hair to toupee."

Figaro, pouring himself a glass of milk, said not to worry.
"I will," he said. "Milk?"

"Sure," Vic took the glass. "Where's Kay?"

"I see you two kids are in love," Figaro said. "Anybody

can see it, as a matter of fact. She's a very high quality dame, Vic, very high quality."

Vic called for her and she answered from the game room. "I'll wait here for you," she said.

So Vic and Figaro talked about the contract.

Don Worth had been right. Figaro did not want to work anymore for Evan Llewelyn Evans.

"It's too hysterical," he said. "I like you, Vic, and I'd like to sign a new deal for your sake. But making soap is just a sideline with that Old Man. He's really running an ulcer factory."

"You shouldn't let him bother you, three thousand miles away," Vic said, "Think of me. I have to see him every day."

"Yeah," Figaro said. "You see him, and he lets you have it. Then you let me have it by teletype. Those teletypes, oooh."

"You should see what happens to me when I don't send them," Vic said. "He uses words like cavalier. I still say you don't have to be upset by him, way out here."

"It's not me alone, Vic. It's everybody on the show. We get afraid of commas, adlibs, every damn thing. It's bad for the show."

"I've got it," Vic said. "In your next contract you retain complete control of the script. We won't even let him see the script. He knows you, likes you, trusts you not to get dirty, and he'll sign a deal like that with you where he wouldn't sign with anybody else."

But Figaro said, "You can't change the psychology. He's a mental hazard to me and I don't have to take it any more. I got five firm offers already. One of 'em at ten grand a week."

He sipped his milk glumly. "As if money made any difference. I give my all for the Collector of Internal Revenue. At this minute I owe the government ninety-six thousand I haven't got."

Vic decided not to press the contract discussion any further at this time.

"How old are you, Figaro?" he asked.

Figaro said forty-one, clipping six years off his age just like that.

"You should get smart. You should be planning some way to keep in the big money after you're ready to retire from this racket."

Figaro said it was impossible. "Investments only pay about three percent nowadays," he said. "The safe ones, I mean."

"Just for talk's sake," Vic said, "let's say you don't renew with the Beautee Soap Company. Let's say you don't renew with any sponsor just for a huge salary, because no salary means anything nowadays, after taxes. Suppose instead that you went to some company and said, look here, I'll go on the air for you for a couple of thousand a week plus a big block of company stock. Hell, Figaro, a young, growing company might give you twenty percent of their stock, and you'd be worth it to them. And that stock profit is subject to capital gains, only twenty-five percent tax. Then as the stock increases in value you may be worth millions and you could tell every sponsor to go screw. See?"

"Why, Vic," Figaro said, "that's sensational. Why don't people tell me these things? What's Dave Lash doing to me?"

Vic explained that Dave Lash couldn't afford to be interested in making Figaro a big stockholder. "His business is to make your weekly salary as large as possible so he can collect his ten percent commission."

Figaro said it certainly was worth thinking about.

Vic said, "Then promise me you won't sign any deals until you talk to me. I want to try to convince you to sign with the Beautee Soap Company again, but failing that I may be able to steer you into this stock thing."

He was thinking of Mr. Yumola, the soft drink man he had met on the train.

Figaro promised, and they went to the game room to find Kay.

She was sitting with Dick's other girl, who had been forgotten in the scuffle.

The girl would have stayed with Figaro but he did not want her so Vic drove the girl down to her friends' home.

The girl was feeling very sorry for herself. "It happens all the time," she said. "All the time. They go to a party, get into a fight and forget all about me. They're always leaving me stranded way out in one of these big houses."

She sadly considered her lot. "Oh, well, I guess a girl in my position has to learn to put up with such things. It's that big pink house on the left," she said. "I hope they're drunk enough to be through fighting for the night. I get sick of it. You can let me out here."

"Good night," Kay said and the girl said, "I don't know what's good about it," and walked up the gravel driveway, forgetting to thank them for the ride.

"You're welcome," Vic called after her. Then he said to Kay. "If you consider that one a typical sample of my friends and acquaintances, I know what you must think of me. Come here."

"Poor thing," Kay said. "You mustn't make fun of her."

"Home again," Vic said. "Holding you is like being home. It's the only peace there is in the world."

"Oh my love," she said.

"I don't want to pry into your personal affairs and frankly it's none of my business, but do you still love me?"

"Of course I do," she said. "But we shouldn't park here, right in the middle of this driveway, should we?"

"It's a clean, dark driveway."

"You were right about Hollywood parties breaking up early," she complimented him. "I was amazed. Did you finish up your business with that droll Mr. Perkins?"

"I succeeded in confusing him a little, that's all. But it's very late to make conversation about radio comedians."

He stopped holding her close to him and found some cigarettes.

She said, "I'm afraid I annoyed you."

"Of course not." He lit a cigarette, took a deep drag on it, handed it to her. At some point over the weekend they had gotten into the habit of smoking the same cigarette.

"Why do you say that?" he asked.

But she didn't know why. "I fancy I said it because a shadow fell across your voice just then. I heard it."

"I saw a shadow across your face," he said. "All during that party."

"I was just tired," she said defensively. "I'm a hollow woman. I'm like one of those thin, crackly cicada shells you see clinging to pine trees in the morning. If someone other than you touched me, I'm sure I'd fall to pieces."

"Any regrets?" He was concerned in some amorphous way and it made him want to probe her, to force talk out of her. He knew that this was not very bright of him, but he did it anyway.

"Of course not, darling," she said, handing him their cigarette. "You know how I feel. It's just that I'm tired. I'm sorry."

"Of course you are," he said, the compulsion to probe disappearing. "If you weren't I'd be envious of you. I'm tired too," he admitted. "Tired and dirty. But happy. Like this poor old beat-up suit of mine. I've been wearing it for four days."

"You've scarcely had it on then," she said. Then she smiled reminiscently. "I must tell you an amusing story about a suit. A few years ago Frank put on a little weight and his old dinner clothes didn't fit him anymore.

"As it must to all men," he murmured.

"They were pretty worn anyway," she explained, "so he had his tailor make him a new suit. It came in one afternoon and he had to wear it to a dinner party that night. I took it out of the box and it was wrinkled, so I sent it over to the corner to get it pressed. It was a beautiful suit. I believe Frank said it cost two hundred and twenty-five dollars. Does that sound about right?" she asked.

"If a man shopped around carefully, I think he could manage to buy some dinner clothes for that type money," Vic said.

"Well, not ten minutes after I'd sent the suit out, just by coincidence an old clothes man came by. I love to dig out old clothes for them," she said. "Maybe you find five old dresses, a stack of children's clothes, a couple of overcoats you don't use anymore, and he gives you, oh, six or seven dollars for the lot. I always feel as if I've made a fine profitable business deal. Anyway, among other things, I sold this rag man Frank's old dinner suit."

"Let me finish it for you," Vic said. "You behaved like a typical wife and did an unconscious switch, sending the old tired dinner suit to the presser, and you sold the new expensive job to the rag man for—oh, let's say two bucks."

"What's that word you use?" she said.

"Point killer."

"That's right. That's what you are. I did just that, only the price for the new suit was a dollar-fifty. How did you know that?" she asked.

"It's been dreamed up so often by writers it was bound to happen some day in real life," he explained. "Then the writers always have the irate husband come home, try to get into the old suit, work up a bad case of stage apoplexy, at which point the doorbell rings and the important dinner guest comes in on a note of pandemonium and chaos."

She said her story wasn't that neat. "It just ended right there. Oh, Frank did come home and discover it, of course, when he dressed, but when he found out what had happened he just said nothing. He didn't even laugh," she said. "He just smiled and went on dressing."

"He's certainly not a typical husband," Vic said.

"He was so gentle and considerate, just the way he is when Hal or Ellen do something troublesome. He never even regaled people later. I never once heard him tell the story as a joke on me, the way most husbands do."

"Want a drag?" Vic said. "There's just about one left."

She took the cigarette and finished it.

"He really is a sweet, gentle man," she said.

"He sounds fine," Vic said.

Then she said appealingly, "I want you to know that, Vic. I don't want you to think I'm unhappy or anything. It wouldn't be fair."

"I know that, Kay."

"I didn't want to give you the wrong impression, Vic."

"I never had any other impression but a good one," Vic said. He looked at his watch in a somewhat stagey manner.

"Two o'clock. And you're tired. I should be shot for keeping you out so late."

He started the car and backed out of the driveway. "Besides it may be dangerous to park here. Dick and Helen and that girl may come flying out any minute, right through our windshield."

Vic drove a block or two and then he said with casual care, "Does he love you, Kay?"

She thought about that. "Yes," she said. "I believe he does. Oh, it isn't a white hot flame. It couldn't be. We're not like that, you see. But I guess he really and truly does."

"I'm sorry about the party," he said. "I didn't realize it would be quite so appalling."

"A girl in my position," she said. "There was something frightening about the sad little creature who said that."

They came to the strip and he said, "Want to stop for some coffee, dear?"

"No, thanks," she said. "I've got to get home to my children. I've been neglecting them."

He would not have believed her capable of such cruelty. She felt the impact of it too. He looked at her and her face was set as if cringing from what she had said.

Vic began to speak in an abstracted, even gentle manner. "A really intense love must be a form of insanity," he said. "I think Freud was wrong to pin it down just to the sex urge. The thing that stains and colors all other behavior is love, of which the sex urge is only a part."

She stared at him with concentration, but she did not respond.

"And when love starts twisting its ecstatic daggers inside

you, you soar up to the peaks, the mood of elation is on you. Just like some forms of insanity. And then it may be inevitable that after such peaks you must descend into the valleys, through the mood of depression."

He drove slowly and somewhat jerkily as if he were unaware of the task of driving.

"Love is only a feeling, and like all other feelings, I suppose some persons are affected more intensely than others. And when they are, I imagine you have to expect peaks and valleys."

Then he gave back the hurt to her. Why in God's name he wanted to, he did not know.

"I'm sorry you said that, Kay," he continued in the same mild tone. "You don't have to tell me I have no right to love you. I know I have no rights. I know I'm a trespasser."

"I didn't mean to hurt you," she said, still frozen by the enormity of what she had said, and of what he had said.

He remembered the car, and returned to the conscious act of driving it. "We'll be home in a few minutes," he said.

"Stop," she cried, as if awakening from a frightening sleep. "Stop the car, Vic. We can't do this."

It was a command filled with frenzy and he turned in to the next side street and parked, just off Sunset boulevard.

Then she began to cry and it was as if all her previous cries of love had been distorted into cries of agony.

"Oh my love," she cried. "Vic, my love. I'm sorry. I didn't mean to hurt you. I didn't mean to. And you're not a trespasser. You're not. You know you're not."

She held his head in her hands and looked wildly into his face and her desperate tears ran over his face and into his eyes and mouth.

"I love the taste of you," he said, so tenderly. "I love you, Kay. Do you hear me, Kay? I love you."

"You were right," she said, "it is a depression. But you don't know the cause of it. It's not what you think it is."

And then he did understand and he was contrite, with the

feeling of love and despair hurting his throat and burning back of his eyes.

"That was what made me say it too," he said. "I shouldn't goad you. As long as we're together we should only be happy about it. It's wrong to think about anything else."

"I can't help thinking about it. And I can't stand it. I can't let you go away. Not in thirty-four hours. I counted them, back there in the driveway, Vic, and it's only thirty-four hours. You can't leave me."

"I don't want to leave you," he said gently. "You know that."

"Then stay, stay, stay. In God's name stay with me, Vic." She caressed his face, his hair.

"How long, Kay?" And they both thought sadly of time, of the brief clot of time that belonged to them. And they both thought of the husband coming home from the wars, and each knew the other's thought: that the return of the husband was the basis of her answer.

"Just another week," she pleaded.

And that is how Vic learned that the husband was coming back soon. He erased the idea of the husband's return and said, "I'll try to stay another week. If I can possibly arrange it, I'll try."

"You will arrange it," she said. "I know you will."

"Maybe staying another week will only make it worse for you," he said. "I have to think of you now, Kay. You're my love and I have to think of ways to keep it good for you."

"The Mapleton," she said. "Those wonderful endless hours. I felt I had no body. I felt I was your body. I was floating around you, enveloping you and being absorbed in you. It's just as you said, you were blessing me with your body."

"Now I know what mystics are," he said. "I felt the same thing. It's the difference between skating and swimming."

"You don't have to think up ways to make it good for me," she said. "There's no choice left now. When I'm with you I'm alive. When you leave me I'm dead. I can't soften it, not in any way. That's why you have to stay as long as"—she hesitated and then said—"possible."

"You'll have to figure out something," he said. "Just as I will. Sooner or later."

"But not now," she cried. "Don't make me do it now. If you stay another week, then I can go on living for another week. It's as simple as that."

"Love," he said. "I didn't understand. And I hurt you. Of course I'll stay another week."

"Oh, Vic," she said. "I hurt you first. Oh, why did I do such a thing? It's not right. This is right. Oh, my love, this is right."

"Yes," he said. "Yes. This is right."

CHAPTER XVIII

VIC SAT IN THE CONTROL ROOM LISTENING TO THE REHEARSAL of the Buddy Hare show.

Max and Georgie had turned in a creditable script and everything was going as well as could be expected. The cast read its lines competently, in the exaggerated overplayed style peculiar to radio, where subtleties of performance seldom come off.

All, that is, except the star. Buddy Hare was miscast, misunderstood and generally a mistake. After hours of rehearsal he still read his lines like the heavy in a senior class play. He was completely out of his element and it was too bad. Vic felt sorry for him, but not too much so because Buddy did not feel sorry for himself. If Buddy had one ounce of showmanship in him, Vic reasoned, he would not have accepted this part, this script, or Evan Evans' idea on how to cast him. That was some consolation.

Vic asked the ubiquitous Norma to run over to the K&M office to see if any teletypes had come in. She said it was past closing time in New York and he said he had a hunch there'd be one anyway.

The studio manager reported the audience was jamming up outside so Vic instructed the agency director he'd assigned to the show to let them come on in and, after the warm-up, to go ahead and cut records on the show.

He then went out to phone Kay. She was at Villa Fifteen waiting for his call.

"Hello," he said. "You abandoned creature. Miss me?"

"Every second," she said softly. "I'm mad at you for not letting me come to your old radio show."

"It's not mine. And it stinks. So why should you get a bad opinion of my work when I'm not to blame for it?"

"I couldn't have a bad opinion of your work," she said. "At least the only kind I'm familiar with. It's been very satisfactory."

He said, "Did you call the Mapleton?"

She said yes, of course. "Or, as your friends are fond of saying, 'natch'."

"Did you get the same room?"

"Natch. Two hundred and nine."

"You're becoming awfully goddam cute," he said. "If you had any friends for me to poke fun at, don't think I wouldn't."

"When will you be through working?" she asked.

"In an hour. Do you want me to pick you up at Villa Fifteen?"

"No."

"Where then?"

"You know where?"

"I do not."

"Then guess."

Vic got it. "Oh, you mean the room?" he said.

"Natch. Or to be more specific with some more language I picked up from your friends, is there anyplace else?"

"It's cute," he said. "And you're beginning to sound exactly like a hep dame. About as hep as a cardinal at a commissar's convention. But I'm a little upset about you going to that hotel alone. Maybe you'd better meet me first."

But she said no. "I've got reasons," she said mysteriously. "I'm leaving for there as soon as you hang up."

So he said, "I'll approve the idea on one condition."

"What?"

"That you really and truly love me."

"You know I do," she said.

"Do what?"

"You know what." She couldn't be too specifically intimate over the phone because of the nurse and the children, and Vic was only teasing her.

"I'll see you in an hour or so then," he said.

He went back to the control room. Buddy Hare was waiting for him, jumpy as a flea and filled with typical new show desperation.

"Vic," he said, "they just told me about the warm-up. Hell, we never rehearsed no warm-up. I don't unnerstan it at all. Did you forget to write a script for the warm-up?"

Vic told him nobody ever wrote a script for any warm-up. "Henny Rich, the announcer, will do the usual stuff about applause, then he'll introduce you."

"But what'll I do?" Buddy wailed.

"You adlib a few jokes, that's all. It's easy."

"I'm no adlibber," Buddy groaned. "I strictly work from material, unnerstan?"

The director told the gag about the radio comic who complained that he couldn't adlib a belch at a Russian banquet.

"Tell a couple of jokes," Vic said. "A little on the dirty side. It's traditional in this business to tell dirty jokes before you go on the air because the network censors won't let you tell them after you're on the air. It's what Emerson called compensation."

But Buddy was inconsolable. "I don't know this character Emerson and I'm too nervous to think of any jokes."

"You'll think of something," Vic said. "You don't have to be funny. Studio audiences will laugh at anything."

Buddy flitted away and Vic sat down. From the glass booth he could see both the stage and the audience.

"How do you want to handle the falling-down-stairs music?" the director asked. "Shall we fade it, or cut it off sharp?"

Vic said he didn't really care. "I'm not very sincere about this show," he explained.

He studied the audience, the gay eager audience. Ready to laugh at anything.

"Where do they come from?" he asked no one in particular. "What tragic destiny drives them from studio to studio, pathetically begging for a chance to work their palms to the bone. Free sound effects, that's what they are. Non-union laughs. Where do they go when they complete their sordid work each night?" he asked.

The network engineer looked up from his dials. "The regulars never go anywhere," he said. "Not even home. They just drift from one radio show to another. The out-of-towners, of course, come strictly from hunger."

"Why do they laugh when pointed at, clap their hands when directed, whistle at the pretty girl singers?" Vic said. "Is it really entertainment to their twisted minds, or is it some cruel instinct that denies them rest?"

"It's nothing deep like that," the engineer said. "The whole thing can be explained in two words—Free Show."

Vic sadly agreed, "If most radio shows cost a dime admission, they'd stink to the audience. But if it's free, brother, it's gotta be funny."

His dissertation on people who come to radio shows was interrupted by the double-rich tones of Henny Rich, the famous announcer.

"Henny's a good boy," the director said, signaling him that it was time to begin the warm-up.

"One of the best hucksters in the business," Vic said.

The purpose of a radio warm-up is to put the audience at ease and to start them laughing and clapping so that when the show goes on the air the listener sitting in his home will get the impression that everyone is wildly enthusiastic over the rich and wonderful fare coming out of his loudspeaker. This is supposed to be contagious and in theory it makes the home listener more appreciative of the show's humor, wit, music and so forth.

Henny Rich held up his hands for silence. The audience understood and followed his signaled command. He then delivered his famous greeting, the Rich trademark known to millions of radio fans:

"Good folks evening. This is Henny Rich saying If you Love that Soap you'll be no dope."

Then he went into his warm-up routine which had been perfected through the years into a reflex. He could have done it under water.

"I'm glad to be here, folks. Are you glad to be here?"

Applause.

"Glad to have you here," he adlibbed. "The show you're going to hear tonight is a newcomer to radio. This is a world premiere. Confidentially, we want to sell it to a sponsor so we'll all have more money to buy more War Bonds with . . ."

Heavy applause. Scattered cheers.

"So, I say, you can swoon at Sinatra, whistle at Betty Grable—by the way," Henny adlibbed, "did you ever hear that new song, 'I want a girl just like the girl that married Harry James'."

Laughter.

"Or sigh at Lana Turner," Henny completed his lost thought. "By the way," he adlibbed again, "hasn't Lana got beautiful eyes." Business of stroking chest to punch it into a sight gag.

Very light applause, to which Henny adlibbed, leaning over the footlights and waving at an old lady, "Thank you, grandmother. You appreciate me even if these other folks don't.

"By the way, grandmother," he adlibbed. "Would you mind calling Utter McKinley, the undertaker. I think the audience should be embalmed. It's dead enough.

"Anyway," he said, "we want you all to laugh and cheer and clap yo hands for our great new star, Buddy Hare. How about it folks, let's rehearse our greeting to Buddy Hare?"

Henny began a furious clapping, and audience joined. Henny said, "Louder. I can't hear you." He cupped hands to ears, "Louder, Ahhhh, that's better. That's superfine."

"But get this straight," he adlibbed, "we do not want you

to applaud unless you feel like it. Unless you are really and truly entertained and want to applaud as a sign of appreciation to the performers who are bringing you this show. And for heaven's sakes don't laugh unless you really want to laugh. But when you feel like laughing, laugh as loud as you want to. There is no law agin laughing in this studio."

Laughter at Henny for thinking them so naive as to believe all this horseplay.

"And when you do applaud, beat your hands to a pulp for all I care," he adlibbed. "Like this." He demonstrated.

Applause to prove to Henny that they knew how to applaud, all right, every bit as good as he did.

"Fine, fine. You're so wonderful, all of you. I love you all very much." Henny leaned over again and pointed at a little bobbysocker, "Especially you," he said, "you fugitive from a Sinatra broadcast."

From the servicemen, derisive boos, from the civilians, understanding laughter.

"Now one thing more about applause," he adlibbed. "Now don't think I'm trying to talk you into anything, but just in case," he became very coy, "just in case I come out and do this"—holding hands up high and making an applauding motion—"you will coöperate, won't you?"

Sample of coöperative applause.

"And you will keep it up as long as I keep on doing this"— furiously beckoning motion with hands.

Louder sample of coöperative applause.

"And you will stop gradually as I do this?"—lowering hands towards floor.

Sample of fading coöperative applause.

"That's great," he adlibbed heartily. "Now seeing you GIs in the audience reminds me of last weekend when I was putting on a show for the boys at the Naval Hospital . . ."

Henny told his witty anecdote. It was about a Marine who wanted brown sheets on his bed because he was just back from the Pacific and a little tired of seeing brown bodies on white sheets. Then he adlibbed, "Well, now I want you to meet our new star, a great artist and your friend and mine. . . . give him a big hand folks. Show him you really like him. Here he is folks, BUDDY HARE."

Buddy Hare danced around the microphone, saying, "Thank ya, thank ya, thank ya. You know, when I was on my way to the studio tonight, the craziest thing happened to me. A black cat crossed my path . . ."

Norma ran into the control room with a teletype in her hand. Vic took it.

"Your hunch was right, Mr. Norman," she said. "This is awful."

He smiled at her. Hunch was hardly the word.

MR. NORMAN FROM MR. KIMBERLY

      URGENT

MR. EVANS AND I JUST SAW BUDDY HARE MOVIE U AIRMAILED. RESULTS DRASTIC. HERES THE NET NET. MR. EVANS SAYS QUOTE THIS BUFFOON HARE IS A LOW VULGAR COMEDIAN AND DIRTY TO BOOT. BEAUTEE SOAP IS A CLEAN PRODUCT AND WE CANNOT EVER /UNDERSCORE EVER/ CONSIDER ASSOCIATING A MAN OF HARES VULGARITY WITH OUR PRODUCT. THE BEAUTEE SOAP COMPANY IS NO LONGER INTERESTED IN ANY WAY WHATSOEVER IN ANY RADIO PROGRAM CONNECTED IN ANY WAY WHATSOEVER WITH THIS BUFFOON HARE UNQUOTE.

VIC, IT IS VERY SERIOUS. HE CASTIGATED ME AND AGAIN USED THE WORD CAVALIER TO DESCRIBE U. HE SAID WE TRIED TO CRAM BUDDY HARE DOWN HIS THROAT AND IT WAS A FLAGRANT EXAMPLE OF BAD AGENCY THINKING. OF COURSE U WILL SCUTTLE THE HARE SHOW. AND PLS. COME BACK TO NY LEAVING HWOOD NOT LATER THAN TOMORROW /UNDERSCORE NOT LATER THAN TOMORROW/ AS MR. EVANS DEMANDS A MEETING WITH U NOT LATER THAN NEXT FRIDAY. THIS IS A CRISIS, VIC. WE HAVE NEVER BEEN CLOSER TO LOSING THE ACCOUNT. WHEN WILL U BE LEAVING FOR NY/Q/ AM WAITING FOR ANSWER. GA

MR. KIMBERLY FROM HWOOD

MR. NORMAN AT STUDIO WILL GET MSG. TO HIM SOONEST. MIN. PLS.

Vic tore a page off the Buddy Hare script at his table and wrote his answer:

KIM FROM VIC
LEAVING ON CHIEF TOMORROW. ARRIVING NY FRIDAY AM ON
CENTURY. THINK UR DECISION TO DROP BUDDY HARE SHOW A
GOOD ONE. GOD IS LOVE END.

He told Norma to teletype it at once and she ran out again, dying to read it, just as Don Worth came into the control room to hear how his talent was going to perform.

Buddy Hare was still doing his warm-up, knocking the audience out with that old whirling dervish burlesque routine which he described as charging his batteries.

Henny interrupted Buddy, pointing to the studio clock and adlibbing to the audience, "You've just fourteen seconds to cough."

Vic crammed the teletype in his pocket and started out the door.

The director had raised his arm to come down with that accusing finger which would cue the cast to begin the show.

Seeing Vic leave, he did not bring the finger down, but still holding it aloft, he said with alarm, "Hey, Vic. We're going on. You can't leave now."

"Go ahead," Vic said. "I gotta date."

"But the show? What about the show?"

"I am no longer interested in the show," Vic said. "Go ahead and cut it, if you want to. You can give Don here the record with my compliments and his option letter on Buddy Hare."

Don said, "Vic, honey, you can't do this to me."

"See you in New York, Don," Vic said. "So long."

"Vic," Don Worth ran out and called after him. "Vic. You have to give me an explanation for Dave Lash. You can't just run out this way, old chap."

But Vic was gone.

Nervelessly, the director let his arm drop for the cue. The

music opened with a fanfare, and faded for Henny Rich who, reading from script, spoke brightly and urgently.

"Good folks evening. Beautee Love That Soap presents that lovable, laughable All American Boy, BUDDY HARE . . ."

He then held his hands high and made the applauding motion.

The eager audience filled the microphones with eight seconds of pandemonium.

CHAPTER XIX

THE MAPLETON HADN'T CHANGED SINCE HIS FIRST VISIT, BUT VIC had, and he no longer shrank back from the lobby smell or even the idea, but walked, with all the assurance of a man striding through his own backyard, past the drunks mumbling obscure abuses to themselves, and over to the creaky iron-barred cage that housed the elevator.

Room 209. Utopia redecorated. Bathroom within convenient driving distance.

He knocked and entered. Kay was sitting quietly in room 209's only chair. She wore a heavy chartreuse silk robe and her hair was down. The dim bulb in the bedside lamp highlighted only her cheekbones, and shadows emphasized the gaunt and lovely hollows of her face.

She had never seemed more beautiful, more desirable, more blessed to him.

"You're so beautiful you should be stupid," he said. "I can't understand how you can be that beautiful and smart too."

"I'm not smart to anyone but you," she replied. She stood up and he held her, hard and close, until his muscles ached and his rigid body weaved with hers.

"Oh, Vic," she said. "It's the hungriest hunger in all the world. I'd resigned myself to another half hour of it. You're early, darling. Wonderfully early."

"Sit down before I fall down." He stretched out on the

bed and she removed his shoes for him. Then she sat again in the chair beside him.

"Was the show good?"

"I wouldn't know," he said. "I'm roaring drunk and besides I never stayed for it."

She sniffed. "I don't smell any liquor."

"It's not liquor. It's love. Holding you made me love-drunk."

"You just don't like to stand up. I notice how you never stand, or even sit, if there's a place to lie down."

"Tell me about Hal and Ellen," he said. "I wanted to see them today, but I didn't have time."

"Hal hero-worships you. So he's decided to take up radio for a career," she reported. "Following in your footsteps. He thinks what you do is announce, though, and he practised all day on that peculiar delivery radio announcers affect. I wouldn't know how to describe it."

"It's half-bullying and half-whimpering," Vic said. "If Hal masters it he can make a thousand dollars a week, easy. I hope he changes his mind, though, before it's too late."

"Don't worry, he will."

"He's a wonderful boy, Kay. I just love him."

"I thought Ellen was your favorite."

"She's for my emotional side. Hal's my intellectual companion." He chuckled. "We're just like a couple of old fellow club members. He told me the other day that Ellen embarrassed him in public. You know, the way she runs madly up to him, throws her arms around his neck, kisses his cheek, and croons, 'My 'ittle Hal.' Naturally, he said, he couldn't mention such a delicate subject either to you or to Ellen. A woman wouldn't understand, might get her feelings hurt, all that sort of thing, you know."

"Poor Hal," she said. "Surrounded by women. You're very good for him, Vic. Did you eat?"

"A sandwich. Did you?"

She put her bare foot up on the bed. "Hold my foot, darling. It feels so good when you hold it," she said. "Yes, I've eaten."

"I was worried about your waiting here alone."

"Silly. I've enjoyed every minute of it." She leaned back on the chair and closed her eyes. "I'm a happy, happy girl."

"We're a happy pair of kids. Brave, too. None but the brave deserve the Mapleton."

"Do you know what I did while I waited for you? I used up the time making plans for us and I didn't get restless at all. It was such fun, darling. And now my plans are all made. For seven, solid continuous days I'm going to make you glad that you're my love."

She stood up and walked to the window and back. She came to the bed and leaned over him. Suddenly she sat on the bed beside him and pulled him up to her.

She began to cry, her trembling body contorting as one spastic, agonized muscle.

He tried to hold her to him. He wanted to share his arms and body with her, to comfort her, to participate in whatever shock it was that possessed her. But she writhed away from him, refusing this comfort, and her muscles grew soft as she collapsed on the bed.

So she cried alone. It was a terrible, torturing thing to Vic, watching her and listening to her cries and not knowing what to do or how to stop them, or even what caused them.

She did not cry easily, like a woman. This strong, regal, now-possessed-by-love woman cried as if hysteria were a new, strange and unthinkable experience to her senses. As if the reflex of crying, so intolerable to her mind, were being imposed on her trembling body. She cried against her will. Her nerves and muscles cried with her.

Then the spasm stopped and he moved slightly, touching her shoulder with his, and waiting as she battled with herself for control.

When she was able to speak she said, "I've never cried like that before. I won't again. I promise."

"My love," he pleaded. "Tell me why, Kay? I want to do something and I don't know what to do."

"There's nothing to do," she said. "It was just . . . everything."

"What's everything? What's bothering you?"

"It was just . . . love," she whispered, weak and dizzy from her ordeal. "It was as much happiness as it was sadness."

"Nothing else, darling? Please tell me if it is."

"Nothing else," she said. "I was taken hold of by love. It seized me and I couldn't stand it. That's all. I'm sorry."

She wiped the tears away on the pillow case. "I'll be a good girl from now on, darling. I promise. I won't worry you like that any more. You'll forgive me, darling, but I've never been in love before. I never realized how . . . how shattering it was. And when I did realize it, as it came over me just then, I was overwhelmed."

"Neither have I, Kay."

She was once again herself. "Come now," she said. "Surely you must have been in love at some time. All those awful women. I've seen how they flock around you. Surely you loved one of them."

He shook his head and smiled, relieved to find her rational again. "Nope. No man in love could possibly be the way I was before I met you. Nothing was any damn good. Now I love you and everything is fine. I feel like a man with work to do. I enjoy being alive. I am even fond of the Mapleton Hotel, especially room two-o-nine. I tick like a clock."

She squeezed his arm until it hurt. "Oh, my love. I want you to tick like a clock."

"Somehow," he said, "you've made me young." The mood of wonder rose within him, too, the poetic mood of love. "I feel great things surging inside of me, God knows what. Oh, once in a while I'd get that feeling before I fell in love with you. But then I'd take a drink and wait for it to go away." He tried to think what he had started to talk about and then remembered. "No, Kay, you're my first real love, too."

She snuggled up to him and sighed. The world was perfect. Then she recalled her plan and said. "You didn't let me finish."

"Finish what?" But he knew, all right, and again he did not know how to handle himself.

"Telling you about my beautiful seven-day plan." She sat up, her face eager and shiningly happy. "Oooh, I've the loveliest things planned, darling. Wait till you hear."

"Later," he said. "First you have to kiss me. Come here."

She pouted. "No. I want to tell you now. It's a surprise and I must share it with you."

He had not wanted to tell her, so soon after the hysteria, but now he knew he must tell her. It would be too cruel to let her go on prattling so happily about her plan.

He said, "Kay. I'm sorry, dear. But I have to go back to New York. Tomorrow."

He watched her closely, afraid to touch her. She heard, then she made sure to herself that she had actually heard the words. She sat up in bed, her back rigid, her long and lovely legs stretched out straight and taut.

"Tomorrow?"

"Yes, Kay."

"Must you?"

"I'm afraid so. It's a serious business problem. I had to force myself to promise. I have to leave on the Chief tomorrow."

"You promised?" There was still no change in her position or in the flat tightness of her voice.

"Yes."

"Whom?"

"Kimberly. I couldn't help it, dear. It's a duty. An obligation."

The cross-examination was over, and he had tried to soften it, but there it was. She had been like a patient waiting for the surgeon's knife, holding herself braced against the entering pain. But she would not give in to it and she won the battle, finally speaking slowly and with great fatigue, "I told you I wouldn't worry you anymore. I'm going to be all right."

She turned to him, holding herself on her elbows over his body. "Tomorrow. So it's tomorrow," she whispered.

"You're trembling," he said sharply. "Stop it, Kay."

"It's only from leaning on my elbows," she said, changing her position. "That's all it is."

She lay beside him, clenching her fists, and he put his arm under her head and waited for the trembling to stop.

"I'm all right," she said. "It was from leaning on my elbows."

He carefully planned out what he was going to say, then he spoke. "Kay, if this business crisis had happened four days ago, or even three days ago, I'd have said no, and I'd have stayed with you. Because then, nothing could have been more important than being here with you, as much as possible, as long as possible."

She moved closer to him, but she did not look at him as he continued.

"I must go back tomorrow, Kay, because of you. I want to tell you what is in my mind. And I want you to listen very carefully, because it's the shape of life—our common life—that I'm talking about."

"You're going to leave me," she said. "Tomorrow."

"Please listen," he raised his voice, trying to penetrate her despair. "I want to tell you what I think we should do. It concerns you and me and Hal and Ellen."

Now the lover and the mother listened intently, drowning out the obsession of that frightening word, tomorrow.

"I want you," he said. "Not just for seven more days. I want you for all the days. And all the nights. And I want Hal and Ellen. Your family. I want you three for my family.

"Oh, I know," he said to the silent, aware, hard-listening woman beside him, "I know how deeply you're rooted in your own special life. I know what your husband means to you and you to him. Forgive me for mentioning it, but I must talk about these things. Because I also know you love me, and as you say, you've never loved anyone else before."

"Never," she said, "oh, never. Not this way."

"So whether or not I have any right to ask it makes no difference now. I must ask it." He spoke very slowly, emphasizing every word. "I want you and Hal and Ellen. I want you to get a divorce and marry me."

He lit a cigarette and passed it over to her.

"I've thought it out very carefully," he said. "I don't think it would harm Hal and Ellen. I think I'd be a good father to them. I'd try to be as good to them as . . ." He paused. "Give me a drag, please." After he'd inhaled the smoke he said: "They love me too, you know."

"I know," she said. "They really do love you."

"What I'm asking is a vital thing," he said. "It's not a thing I can bring to you on just an impulse or desire. I have to be in a position to plead with you to break up the pattern of your life. That's not so much because of you but because of the children. I must be able to say, not only, I want you. I must also be able to say, I can take care of you, protect you, give you and your children all the things you ought to have."

He handed their cigarette back to her.

"And that's why I have to go to New York tomorrow. I must tell you that, now, I'm just an employee holding a very precarious job. Precarious because of an old man who might decide to fire me tomorrow, or any day.

"But," he said, "I've been offered a very big thing. A partnership in my firm. And that isn't at all precarious because no one man, young or old, can hurt me then.

"It's also a big-money kind of thing. In a very few years I should have more than enough to quit. We could live anywhere, do anything we wanted to. It's that kind of money."

He laughed without humor. "It's a funny thing. A week ago I'd made up my mind to turn it down. I wasn't willing to make the effort. Now I want to make the effort, and only because I've found you and Hal and Ellen. I've something to work for now, if you say the word, and it's a fine feeling. I'm not a lone wolf any more.

"A family is a remarkable something," he mused. "Here I was, fighting, as my father used to say, my private war against the world. Rather successfully too. But believing in nothing, up to and including myself. And then, wham, it all changes, because of a simple little feeling called love. And it taught me that the big, complicated elements of our lives, the huge mass modern things that people try to fasten themselves on to, are way out on the edge of the circle. While in the heart of it is a simple little primitive group that sociologists call the family unit. And without that heart, the rest is nothing."

"Yes," she said, "I feel it too. You have such right feelings, my love. You're a good man, or you couldn't feel that way. But you're wrong about the other thing. The job thing. It doesn't make any difference whether you're a millionaire or a partner or anything. You should understand that, too."

"It does to me," he said. "Not because of you but because of the children. I've always been a floating, insecure hustler, jumping here and there and responsible only to myself. I'd have no right to say what I just said, unless I fastened myself to a firmer base."

"And I love you for saying it," she said tenderly. "But it would also be a personal sacrifice for you. I know you so well. You hate that awful advertising business and the demands it makes on you. Maybe you'd even start to hate me if I caused you to get trapped in it. Don't make the mistake of thinking that partnership thing makes any difference. That's not the problem."

"If I had you I'd love it," he said. "That's the point, Kay. I've thought it through very carefully. It's the difference between piling bricks helter-skelter, and building them into a home."

She kissed him and she said he was a wonderful human being as well as a wonderful lover.

"I've made it sound very cold and businesslike," he said. "But you understand what I'm asking, don't you, Kay?"

"Yes," she said, "I understand, my love."

"And you also understand that the answer rests with you. You alone. You have to do the big part, the difficult part. And

I know just how difficult it must be. I won't blame you if you say no, right this minute."

He paused and said, "In fact, if you do say no, I'll wire Kimberly that I can't leave Hollywood for another week—or as long as you say."

Now it was her turn to think out and silently rehearse her answer to him.

"Every instinct that I have," she said, "drives me to you. I mean for always. But my nerve ends are raw with resisting them. I guess it's habit," she mused. "A habit that's made deep grooves and channels in me. For ten years I've worked and practiced to form that habit. And now my instincts tell me to break it. It is difficult, Vic."

"Very difficult," he said.

"Doing what you say seems the glorious, wonderful, the only right thing to do," she said. "And it could be so right for the children too. I'm sure it would be."

"Thank you, dear," he said.

"Or is it?" She said violently. "I don't know. Oh, Vic, my love, I don't really know."

"Maybe you do know, but won't admit it, even to yourself."

"Maybe I do," she said. And then repeated, "I don't know. I have to think. And feel. I have to know and believe that my instincts are right."

"Maybe you need more time," he said. "I realize that one week is as nothing compared to ten years. Maybe we're rushing it."

"Maybe that's it," she accepted the idea with relief. "It's not that I need more time to know you. I already know what I want to do. I want to be with you. I can't even bear the thought of anything else. It's just that I need more time to know what I ought to do. I have to look at myself and Hal and Ellen and think, think, think."

"Maybe it's better that I go back to New York tomorrow," he said. "I have to get this business thing settled before I can ask you for your answer anyway. And it'll give you time to think."

Then she said, "And you have to do a lot of thinking, too. Away from me. You have to be sure you want to get involved in something that'll change your whole life. Your work even. Maybe if you're away from me, you'll change your mind. Maybe you won't want it."

"No danger of that," he said. "That would be like not wanting to breathe."

"Yes, there is," she said. "You like to keep things clear and simple. This is rather involved and complicated. It's upsetting to your whole way of living."

"You won't mind so much my going back to New York, on this basis?" he asked anxiously.

She shivered slightly. "I'll mind, of course. But you've promised and I suppose you must. I don't know how I'll stand it, but I will. I'm a grown woman and I must bear it."

He kissed her cheek. "You're such a little girl, really. Sometimes I think Ellen should be the mamma and you the baby. I'll call you every day, and when you've made up your mind you can give me your answer."

"You have to make up your mind, too," she said. "Don't forget that. And please tell me, darling, if you feel just halfway about it. It wouldn't be any good, just halfway."

He said, "Know what? I think you're going to fret and fume over this by the hour. Then the phone's going to ring and it'll be me back in New York telling you that I'm all set, that I'm available for immediate delivery, complete with a genuine gold-plated partnership and a year's supply of Beautee soap. And I think you're going to say, 'I've decided to come to you.' What do you say to that?"

She embraced him with strength and passion. "Oh, I want to be able to say that," she whispered. "I do so want to. Don't you know that, my love?"

"Yes," he said. "I think I know that. Let's not talk about it any more tonight, Kay. Let's forget it for tonight."

"Let's pretend there isn't any tomorrow," she said.

"It's an unbelievably corny line," he said. "But this time it has meaning. Of all the times, this is the right time to pretend just that."

"No tomorrow," she whispered.

He turned out the light and undressed. He lay down beside her. Together in the darkness. Together again.

"Come closer," he said, trying to lose his thoughts, trying to find the fury and the elation from her closeness, trying hard to climb out of the valleys up to the peaks.

She obediently moved towards him. "I was thinking here tonight before you came," she said. "We're not two at all. We're one. And what we have is so simple. So clean and simple when it's all by itself. It's only the things outside us that are complicated."

"Love," he said, "just lie quietly and don't think anymore. Just feel. Don't try to think."

"I'm numb from thinking," she said. "Excuse me, darling, I have to take my arm from under your head. It's fallen asleep."

He fumbled in the darkness and found cigarettes. He lit one for her and then one for himself.

Their bodies were quiet as they lay side by side in the healing darkness, thoughtfully smoking their cigarettes.

[CHAPTER XX]

LOVE THAT CHIEF! AND NEVER MIND HOW I GOT THE RESERVA-
tions. No use spoiling a good thing.

One thing about the Chief, east or westbound, it never changes. That's what a man likes about this extra-fare, extra-exclusive, super-deluxe commuter special that makes Toots Shor's handy to Romanoff's, that connects Sunset Boulevard with Wall Street. The Chief never changes.

A man can depend on the Chief. It's one of the few enduring values left in this unstable old world.

"So you decided to bring your mink coat after all, cutey-pants. Good idea. It's still chilly in New York."

A man just naturally expects certain things on the Chief —and he's never disappointed, they are always right there waiting for him. Of course you can poke fun at that type thing, but when all's said and done, it's the old tried and true, the familiar type things that give a man that real deepdown comfort—that rich, deliciously blended, smooth and creamy comfort that only comes, no matter what type fellow you are, from being among your own type people in your own type world.

Love that Chief! Where else can a man find so many gold Dunhill lighters (the ribbed model) per capita? Or always be within earshot of the cheery and fashionable sound a hand-painted necktie makes? What gathering place, no matter how chi chi, in New York or Hollywood, could be entrusted to provide a man with the gay camaraderie of so many glossy and glamorous women, with just that right, shrill touch of vulgarity that makes a man feel at ease and comfortably wicked?

Oh, gin rummy might come and gin rummy might go—who knows what we'll be playing next?—but the Chief goes on forever.

It was like a play, thought Vic. Every afternoon a new road company leaves town. But the sets, the costumes, the plot, even the dialogue, never changed.

At this performance, continuous for three days, westbound Don Worth had been replaced by eastbound Harry Sanders for the talent agent role. Peggy Donelin was reading Constance Linger's lines. There was a new crew of stagehands, working for the railroad. And all the other familiar types were a triumph of the casting director's art. And it is but very definitely an art, as any casting director will tell you, whether or not you ask him.

I shouldn't be so critical, thought Vic. They are all of them every bit as good as I. They do their jobs as well, if not better than I. Many of them are brilliant, far more so than I. Like me, they are rich and successful enough to afford their own private, handmade, expensive brands of likes and dislikes, hates and loves.

LOVES! Kay my love.

The private subvocal words of love that twisted in his solar plexus and ached in his throat became so unbearable that he left the club car in an aura of desolation and went dazedly forward to his compartment.

He sat there, limp and exhausted by the poisonous fatigue of absence. He tried the words aloud: "Kay! My love." There was some satisfaction in hearing his voice, that seemed so unlike his voice, repeat those monosyllables that have no meaning until love gives them meaning.

Some noisy voices lurched past and he kicked at his door to shut out the voices and be alone with his love.

But he felt different towards those voices. They now were less remote, they were no longer objects of derision or cool amusement, but people. People who had their own loves, even as he had his love.

Looking out at the land, the land that had always seemed so barren and desolate, so unfamiliar and undesirable, he now felt that it must be good because it was loved by people who spent their lives on it and with it. That shacky farm on that furrowed hill—even for him it would be a fine warm wondrous place with Kay to share it.

It was morning now, back in California, and he saw her sitting on the terrace. He saw her as she had sat that night in the darkness. The outwardly regal woman, queenlike in her sculptured dignity—the inwardly young girl, tremulous discoverer of a new empire.

Sweet, gracious Kay. Mad, passionate Kay. Grave, serious, manly Hal. Wild, unearthly little Ellen. The family.

This was the purpose for which the instincts of man had first desired time. This was the reason why the mind of man had invented time. The richest of all time is the time spent in love. No wonder he'd been so restless . . . all that squandered time. That sad loveless time.

The family . . . somehow or other he had missed in his life the meaning of the family. Had until now missed the kind of love that would have given him a family.

Oh, he'd often thought about marriage. The right girl popping up at the right time, as they say. But he'd got caught up in the depression as a young man, when most romances are made, and he'd given marriage the brush because he couldn't afford it.

To be perfectly honest, he'd also brushed it because he didn't want it to get in his way. He'd made up his mind to go places, back in those days.

And after he'd been places, in his middle twenties that would be, there'd been all that excitement of making good, and with it all those easy, clever, beautiful women who go for young men like him who'd made good.

Now he could understand why he'd missed this deep, satisfying value that a family and a permanent, enduring love gives to a man—why, in fact, he'd been unconscious of it for over a decade. He'd found a thousand substitutes for this value, all of them bad.

Then the war, and the years in OWI. For four years the ache of war, as it can only ache to a man who can't get in it. OWI did not count. It was not participation to his mind and he had no feeling of having been part of this most colossal drama of history. . . .

Whose family?

It slugged into him, with savage, devastating fury.

Steady now, Vic. Don't get mawkish, old boy.

Sooner or later he knew he had to look it squarely in the face. The time had come. No use putting it off any longer.

Let's look at the record. Consider the evidence. Examine the bare facts in the case. Your witness, Mr. Prosecutor.

Q. *Your name?*
A. Victor Norman.
Q. *Occupation?*
A. Huckster.
Q. *Are you a returned veteran?*
A. No, sir.
Q. *Overage?*
A. No, sir. I was 4F.
Q. *What did you do during this war period?*
A. Oh, a little radio work. Nothing important.
Q. *What else?*
A. Nothing much. I sold a little soap, I guess.
Q. *(Sternly) What else, Mr. Norman?*
A. I—uh—fell in love with a woman named Kay Dorrance. She had two lovely children. We plan to be married.
Q. *A married woman with two children, eh. Where was the husband when all this was going on?*
A. He was away.
Q. *Away? Where?*
A. Abroad.
Q. *I thought so. And just what was this husband doing abroad*

*during the period in which you stole, yes stole, his wife
and two lovely children away from him?*
A. I—I understand he was in the army, sir.

The prosecution rests. No more questions, Mr. Norman.
You have said all that need be said.

"He really is a sweet, gentle man. I want you to know that,
Vic. Yes, I guess he really and truly loves me, Vic."

"Quiet, Ellen, I want to hear some more stories about what
Daddy did in the war."

"Tell me anuya stowy about the war, Daddy."

"How do you do, Colonel. My name's Victor Norman. I
suppose Kay's mentioned me. Now look here, Colonel, there's
a little something I want to discuss with you. . . ."

What could you tell a man like that? And how could he
possibly understand? How could any man like him, coming
home from where he'd been, possibly understand?

Even so, he'd probably say to his wife, "All right, Kay. I
don't understand, but if that's what you really want, I suppose
you must."

Flash—Victor Norman, agency biggie, is chewing his nails
while waiting for Mrs. Francis X. Dorrance to clear her marital
decks at Reno. Good luck, Vic and Kay, you're both swell
people—Unflash.

"What did your stepfather do in the war? Yah, yah, yah,
Hal's a dope."

And then Victor Norman snarled at Victor Norman, "Take
your conscience and get the hell out. This is no problem of
who won the war? Or of what husbands feel like when their
wives love someone else. This is love. You heard me, love.
And it's now become a simple question of taking it or leaving
it.

"If we leave it, give it up, we've lost everything but a little
pride, a sense of being sanctimonious, and long tragic years
of regret, years of no-love, no-nothing.

"If we take it, we gain the world, our own private world,
and years of happiness, years of love.

"It's not a social situation at all. You can't wear the old school tie and follow the knightly codes. Not in a thing as big as this. It's unfortunate, and nobody wants to hurt anybody, but I can see nothing else to do. The war, and the husband being in it, is just an accident, one of the misfortunes of war. Why should Kay sacrifice her happiness to an accident?"

As if it were something he must do instantly, he seized a telegraph pad and wrote to her, the words sprawling crazily as the Chief rocked and swayed, surged and plunged toward its terminal in Chicago.

A lover's message, with lines artfully fashioned for in-between reading. After all, you can't fill a telegram to another man's wife with the written words of love:

Mrs. Kay Dorrance
Villa 15
Sunset Hills Hotel
Beverly Hills, California
Enduring tiresome journey but eager to reach New York to complete plan discussed with you. Have been think-ing decision over carefully, as you suggested. I want you to know that nothing can change my stated desire. My an-swer will always be the same, now and later. Will phone you for yours the minute I arrive NY. Regards.
                                        Victor Norman

He crossed out "Regards" and scribbled "As Ever" in its place. He reached for the button which would summon the porter who would send the wire, then he stopped.

How could his answer be yes, or how could he promise to call her, until he himself completed his promise to her?

There was no reason why Kimberly would not want to put the partnership plan into operation. He understood now his value to Kimberly and Kim was too good a businessman to be changed by any emotional factor that may have come up during his absence. But he had to make sure.

No, he could not call Kay for her answer, or give her his answer, until he could also say: Here it is, the security I promised you and your children. ·

Maybe I can get Kimberly pinned down the minute we finish smoothing over Old Man Evans, he thought. Surely I'll be ready to call Kay by Friday afternoon. He worried briefly about the Old Man, but not very much. If Evans fired them tomorrow morning at that meeting, things would be considerably changed. But he couldn't believe that such a thing would happen.

He refused to believe that it could happen. The Old Man was in too deep, emotionally, with Kimberly, to want to fire him. And he hadn't yet figured out a way to penetrate Vic. No, they wouldn't lose the Beautee soap account tomorrow. Vic would bet on that.

So aching with love, burning with love, sick from being away from his love, Vic tore up the telegram he wanted to send, but could not send because he was not yet prepared to send it, and tried to find what little satisfaction there was in the knowledge that the minute he arrived in New York, he could take a tangible, concrete step towards bringing Kay to him. He could cinch the partnership with Kimberly.

[CHAPTER XXI]

ON THE RUN FROM CHICAGO TO NEW YORK, THE TWENTIETH CEN-
tury Limited had been sidetracked for troop movements. It
pulled into Grand Central at 10:15 a.m., over an hour late.

Vic went straight to the office. The receptionist said, "Why
hello, Mr. Norman. What a wonderful tan! How was Hollywood?"

He said fine and she said, "Mr. Kimberly left word he
wanted to see you the minute you arrived."

Kim was telephoning, as usual. He waved at Vic, covered
the mouthpiece and whispered, "It's Allison. Where you been?
What happened?"

Vic told him the Century had been late.

Kim said into the phone, "I was just informed the Century
is late, Gerald. It's due in any minute now, so Vic should be
here shortly. Will you please extend my deepest apologies to
Mr. Evans and tell him we'll hurry down as soon as Vic
arrives. Thank you, Gerald." And then in a low confidential
voice, "By the way, what kind of mood is he in now?" Kim
listened soberly, saying "Hmmm."

He hung up, buzzed, told Miss Richards no more calls,
and shook hands warmly.

"Am I ever glad to see you. God, has this ever been a
time." Then apologetically, "I hope you'll forgive the strategic
lie to Allison about your not being here yet. But it was neces-

282

sary. We have to work out our tactics for this meeting before rushing down there."

Vic said, "It's only a meeting. What do we need tactics for?"

"The Old Man's been bellyaching all morning about you being late. He wants us to come down instantly. Had planned the meeting for nine-thirty. Been chewing nails. That damned Century would have to be late this morning of all mornings. He probably blames the agency for it."

Vic sat on the window sill and looked down on Rockefeller Plaza. The skaters were a pleasant, now familiar, sight.

"What's the rush?" he asked. "The old bastard can put off his lecture on Buddy Hare for an hour or two, can't he? It'll keep."

Kim paced around the office. "I'm really worried this time, Vic. He was very bitter about us."

"Us? Or me?"

"Both. What he calls the agency. He says we got no organization. I knew he'd blame that Buddy Hare thing on you. And it worried him because he didn't understand your motive in showing that movie. He can't figure you out. Incidentally, I can't either."

"I figured he'd blow his top when he saw it," Vic said. "We had to face the problem sometime and I still think it was better to do it now instead of later."

"Well," Kimberly was spraying his throat in the bathroom, "that's water over the dam. Anyway, he just thinks we stink and I'm convinced he's calling this meeting for two reasons."

"What's number two?"

"One, he's going to flay us for trying to cram Buddy Hare down his throat. And two, after we've been in the hot seat long enough to satisfy him, he's going to fire the agency."

Vic said he did not for the life of him see how it could possibly be that serious. Kim was sure it was very critical.

"You've no idea what a beating I took," he said. "Brrr. He even said Love that Soap was another bad agency idea."

"I thought sales were up?"

"They're terrific. It's just that with him when one thing goes wrong, everything is wrong. He's got some maniacal notion about that colored maid now."

Kim was really in no shape to think clearly. He was pathetically jumpy. "God, Vic," he said, "your mind is clear, isn't it? Can't you think of something?"

Vic thought they should listen to Evans first and plan the counter-moves from what he said.

"Anyway, I think better in the clinches. Any plan we'd make now is just academic."

So Kim called Allison and told him Vic had just arrived and they'd be down immediately but please, Gerald, allow us a few minutes to get a cab.

Vic said, "I just remembered something." He called Jack Martin. "Jack," he said, "hello. Yes, but I'll tell you about Hollywood later. Did you cut that record of Jean Ogilvie?"

Jack said, "Natch, coach."

"Any good?"

"Good and loud," Jack said. "The little girl has a tremendous pair of lungs on her."

"That's her dressmaker," Vic said. "Send your secretary down to the elevator with the record. I'm in a hurry."

Kim had his hat on. "Here we are," he complained, "about to lose a twelve million dollar account and you talk about some dame's record."

But Vic said you never could tell when a record might come in handy.

"Okay, okay," Kim said. "But let's get going. What a day to keep Old Man Evans waiting!"

Vic had never seen him so depressed before. "Take it easy," he recommended. He looked at the telephone and thought about Kay. He wanted to call her now but of course he shouldn't call her until he'd cleared the partnership deal. And this was certainly no time to talk partnership with Kim. Maybe if he just called her to say he'd arrived safely and wanted to hear her voice again and to expect him to call her on that other matter as soon as possible, probably this after‹ noon . . . no harm in that.

Vic said, "I really should call Hollywood."

Kim groaned. "Please, Vic. You can't do this to me. What the hell do you want to call Hollywood at this hour for?"

"Personal," he said. And remembering the three hours difference in time he admitted, "It is a little early out there. I'll wait till we get back."

"If we get back," Kim said.

"Look, Kim," Vic said. "We can't lose. This is my day!"

"I hope so. Why?"

"I'm in love, that's why. You are looking at a man in love. When I left New York, I didn't have any need for Evan Evans. Now I can use him. And don't think I won't. He's not going to tie a can to us just the minute I begin to need him. I won't let that old bastard do that to us."

"As if being in love made any difference," Kim said. "Come on, let's get started, Vic."

But Vic wouldn't hurry. "It'll do him good to wait. I've one more thing to tell you."

"I hope it's a quickie."

"It is. I need you too, Kim. I need that partnership. I just thought I'd tell you. And I understand that Evans comes first, Kim. I understand that perfectly."

"Yes," Kim said, "Evans comes first."

"Sure," Vic said. "Let's go down to Wall Street."

In the cab, Kim leaned back and pressed his eyes. "If I survive this ordeal," he said, "I'll never take another drink. Or even another benzedrine."

Then he said, "We got to do something, Vic. We can't lose this account now. You were right. Evans does come first. He can ruin all our plans this morning."

"We'll figure out something, Kim. Only don't show so much worry. Or fear. That Old Man can smell it. And it makes him worse. You know that, Kim."

Vic thought about the partnership. If it went through fast, while the Old Man was still willing to let him work for other clients, it would be good for him, but tough on Kim who'd still have to carry the Evans burden.

He'd have to keep a sharp eye on Kim. Yes, he could just see Kim trying to delay the partnership, month after month, in the hopes that Evans would become so attached to Vic that Kim could free himself, leaving Vic stuck with no exit papers. Well, he'd block Kimmy Boy if he tried to run in that direction. Vic had a bellyful of Evans already. And after Evan Llewelyn Evans, the other clients would be a soft touch for him.

He looked at Kim, quaking in the cab, and said, "It can't be that serious. It doesn't make sense."

Kim only said, "Since when has he ever made sense?"

Vic was sure that Kim was exaggerating, that it could not be so hopeless. He also saw clearly that keeping the Beautee soap account was necessary to his own plans, because without it the partnership would not be good business for Kim. In that case, Kim would have to go to Maag and beg for a chance to recover from the blow, and Vic would be discarded.

And it was also a cinch that Maag with his partnership notions had no use for Vic, in fact could have nothing but fear of Vic's swallowing him up, unless Vic had the Beautee account to contribute to the merger.

If the Old Man fired the agency, Vic's partnership plans were hopeless. But if the Old Man transferred his favor from Kim to Vic, the Maag deal was still possible.

No, this was not the morning to get his feet cut out from under him.

"You wait and see," he said to Kim. "I'll be so goddam sincere that the Old Man will quote take off his hat to me unquote. You better by God be sincere too."

Kim sat up and brightened a little. "You know," he said, "that's a good tactic."

"Are you all right?"

"Sure. I mean that word."

"What word?"

"Sincere. It's the key to our grand strategy. I think you've really hit on something, Vic."

"I'm a very sincere fellow," Vic said. "Especially around twelve million dollars."

But by the time they walked into that gymnasium full of desks and mottoes, Kim was in the valley again.

"This may be our last visit to this concentration camp," he whispered to Vic. He paused by the water cooler. "Join me in a benzedrine?"

"Christ, no. And relax. You're getting me Evans-happy."

They saw Regina Kennedy. She was feeling very gay.

"I'm sorry about that Hare thing," she said. "I hope you've got a good story."

She was dying to get on with the execution.

Vic said, "We were lucky even to get an option on Hare. Somebody back here got drunk and spilled it at a cocktail party and Talent Ltd. wired the news to Hollywood."

Her face froze. She wondered whether Vic would consider it to his advantage to tell Mr. Evans about that one.

Vic also said, "I ran into your former boss in Hollywood. He thinks he'll be out soon."

This depressed her too. She knew the war was almost over and she was worried about what would happen to her when her former boss came marching home to the Beautee Soap Company all covered with glory for the radio war he'd fought from Hollywood.

"Well, anyway," she said, "there's Mr. Allison waving at us. We'd better go into the board room."

Irving Brown, Paul Evans and Allison were already there. They offered grave good mornings to Kimberly, Vic and Regina.

Then they talked about the war and asked Vic gracious questions about his trip. He sensed they were being a little too damned nice to him. He supposed they'd gone through this Death of an Account Executive so many times that it was almost routine: the phoney friendliness, the breezy good cheer, the sympathetic side glance.

But the minute that old ax fell, brother, what a brush they'd give you. If today was the Day, Vic would lay odds that tomorrow he couldn't even talk to Allison's secretary on the telephone.

It was not Allison, but Kimberly, who urgently whispered from the lookout position at the door, "Here he comes."

They jumped to attention and the cold breath of Evan Llewelyn Evans entered the board room. He sat down. They sat down. So far, so good. The rite was perfectly executed.

"Good morning, Mr. Norman," he said. "Morning, Kimberly."

"Good morning, sir," Vic responded, and Kim echoed it.

The Old Man sat and thought, never once lifting his eyes from their devout contemplation of the glowing mahogany.

Without looking up, he said, "Cigarette, Allison."

Later, Vic was certain Allison had offered the cigarette before the Old Man commanded it. Was it true what they said, that Allison could read the Old Man's mind?

Vic felt he had underestimated Allison. It would be a good idea to develop his friendship, get close to him, win his confidence. Properly used, Allison could be valuable in forecasting what was in the Old Man's mind.

Vic looked around the table. There was not one relaxed muscle in the group. He lit a cigarette and slumped back in his chair, nonchalantly waiting for the Old Man to begin.

Evans raised his head and his brilliant blue eyes unblinkingly regarded Vic.

"Have a nice trip, Mr. Norman?"

At least, thought Vic, he's pronouncing my name right. He decided to be sincere.

"It was disappointing," he said sincerely.

"You were lucky to get train accommodations back on such short notice," the Old Man said.

"Traveling is rather inconvenient nowadays," Kimberly said. "When Irving and I came back from Washington, for instance . . ."

Not bad, Vic thought. Kim wasn't in total shock after all.

Pretty damn sincere. Kim was of course reminding his client that he had done a good job in Washington only a short time ago, when he'd talked the Board into raising the paper quota. It was another way of saying that the agency, especially Kimberly himself, wasn't all bad.

The Old Man listened gravely. Then he said abruptly, "Did you find anything interesting in Hollywood, Mr. Norman?"

I found love, Vic thought. I found a family. But Evan Llewelyn Evans wouldn't understand a discovery like that. In fact he would say that I had apparently forgotten his orders, given at my first Indoctrination Course . . . that I was hired, and only permitted, to love, sleep with, fondle, or be caressed by Beautee soap.

"No," he admitted with sincere candor, "I found nothing in Hollywood."

Vic leaned forward to put out his cigarette. Kim was beginning to look white and desperate.

"That's too bad," the Old Man said. "Personally, I've never been to Hollywood. Oh, years ago I owned a home in Santa Barbara, but I never actually went over to Hollywood. And I don't ever intend to go there. I see an occasional motion picture and I frankly consider those people rather vulgar."

God, how does he do it? Now who but a genius could think up such a roundabout way of getting down to that Buddy Hare movie? Only a sadistic genius could prolong the ordeal with this pseudo-benevolent approach.

Vic sat back and lit another cigarette.

"You may consider yourself fortunate, sir," he said.

He noticed Kim looking at him queerly. Had he done something wrong? What the hell could be wrong about what he'd just said?

"Allison," Evan Llewelyn Evans commanded, "bring me that letter I wrote this morning."

So that was it. Now, Vic was getting hep to the Old Man's technique. Very subtle. He'd written one of his famous memos. Addressed to Kimberly no doubt. On stationery from the Office

of the President. Dear Kimberly, Your man Norman has once
again proved his unfitness to stay on the beam . . .

Yes, that was it. He'd put it in writing, in crystal clear
epithet to avoid any misunderstanding. And all this preliminary
was simply his way of toying with Vic and Kim before letting
them have the full salvo.

While they were waiting for the letter the old grandfather's
clock in the board room struck twelve.

It would be nine o'clock in Hollywood. She would be having coffee on the terrace at Villa Fifteen. Hal and Ellen would
be leaving with the nurse for the swimming pool. If he phoned
her now she'd be able to talk to him alone, unguardedly.

The Old Man spoke and Vic's mind and senses snapped
back into the board room.

The Old Man was holding the letter in his hand. He read
it carefully to himself, stopping at some places in it and staring
off into space. It was a well-considered letter, no question
about that. Then he placed the letter face down on the mahogany table.

"I take the position," Evan Llewelyn Evans said, "that a
man either knows where he is going. Or he don't. Right?"

"Right," said Vic, leaning forward. And at that instant two
blows struck him: in the brain, back of the eyes, in his ear-
drums, but most powerfully and brutally, in the pit of his
stomach.

The first blow struck simultaneously with the knowledge
that he had answered "Right" before anyone else around that
table. He had been the first. Before Kim. Even before Allison.

The second, and the most horrifying blow was the feeling
that he was now gripped by it. The Fear. He felt it probing
at him, pushing and prodding him every which way.

The discovery, at that instant of discovery, was even more
shocking than the Fear itself.

So that was why Kimberly had looked at him so sharply.
Kim had seen the Fear before he himself had been made aware
of it by that pathetic, symptomatic "Right." It had been there,
all the time. The Fear had been lying sluggishly within him,

and he had not been conscious of its slow awakening, until it had stretched and yawned and shaken itself into a thing of muscle and life, of twitching nerves and furtive movements.

Now he recalled the too too deliberate slumping back in his chair—the unconscious straightening up until the back was rigid—the leaning forward—the holding the guts tight—the lighting of the cigarettes—and then that one pitiful, eager, crisp and craven word, that early word "Right."

He unclenched his fists and painfully slumped back. He made his neck loll a little. Straightened out his tensed legs and crossed the feet lackadaisically. Dangled one hand carelessly on his chair arm.

"I think I told Mr. Norman once before," the Old Man said, "that one of the most important words in life is the word Organization."

He spoke with simulated friendliness, even joviality, but there was an evil kind of warmth in the words, like the evil, repelling warmth of an undesirable, nauseous body lying next to yours on a cold grey morning after a debauch.

Vic would have bet his life at this moment that the elaborate, rococo quality of this attack had been stimulated by another single word, spoken oh how long ago. Cavalier. Evan Llewelyn Evans was now collecting from Vic with compound interest because a poor little teletypist had once dropped a message and Vic had chosen to be cavalier about the error.

Mr. Evans said, "Well, I been thinking about that word, Organization, and I think it applies to one man, one individual, as well as it applies to the Beautee Soap Company, or to Kimberly and Maag. Check?"

Oh no, Evan Evans. You don't catch me that way twice. You tricked me into that other slip, that quaking "Right." You'll get no "Checks" out of me, Evan Evans.

Vic was silent, holding himself slumped back, straining to keep his body in its casual, go-to-hell position that would bravely reiterate his personal creed of screw 'em all but six and save them for pallbearers.

He only nodded.

The Old Man picked up the letter. Put it down again. "It's a little long," he said apologetically. "Like Madame de Sevigny, I'm sorry I didn't have time to write a shorter letter."

Then he said without pause, "Allison, water."

The slow careful staging of the act of drinking. The business of the carafe, the glass. The measured pouring. Vic noticed for the first time that the carafe was monogrammed ELE. What is his purpose in drinking, he thought. What is he trying to do now? Something to me, no doubt. But what?

And then Vic knew. Those bland blue eyes saw. That massive, porous nose smelled. That moist whip of his tongue tasted.

Saw, smelled, tasted the Fear that was in Victor Norman. Victor Norman the man who used to screw 'em all but six.

The Old Man sensed, the Old Man knew, he surely knew of Victor Norman's dry mouth, his rasped throat and cottony tongue. So he drank, did this Old Man, because he knew that Vic's fear would crave the precious water.

And his dry mouth thirsted as Twelve Million Dollars noisily gulped the crystal clear water . . . as a Partnership, and a Love, and a Home, and a Family, and a Haven, and a Security smackingly absorbed the wet, cold nectar.

The Partnership set down the glass with ringing decision and implacably watched Allison whisk it away.

Then he picked up the letter once again.

"So with apologies for its verbosity, and with I hope your sympathetic understanding that I didn't have time to make it shorter, I'll read this letter to you, with your kind permission."

Slump forgotten, now sitting straight, aching to hear the words, not wanting to hear the words, Victor Norman tried to forget his thirst, tried to take it easy, Vic.

The Old Man cleared his throat, hawked and spat in the cuspidor beside his chair, wiped his mouth with the fine linen kerchief in his sleeve, and began to read:

"Dear son," he read.

Dear son. Dear God. What could he not turn into an in-

strument of delayed torture? Into little drops of words that
wear away a man's guts.

And yet it was a relief to hear those sound, practical, true
Evansian words of advice to his second son. A relief, no matter how temporary.

Only, what did the words mean? Vic did not want to
listen, but he knew he must force himself to listen, intently
leaning forward to better understand and isolate the applica-
tion to himself of those corrosive little words.

Evan Llewelyn Evans read:

"Dear son, you have been in the army for twenty-one
months and three days at this time of writing. I must tell
you I detect a profound note of discouragement in your
letters to mother and me. Your general tells me you are
doing your job splendidly, and I know that you have the
ability to do any job splendidly, for the United States
Army now and for the Beautee Soap Company later. He
reports to me that you show a decided genius for organization. But if I may be permitted a father's frankness, your
recent letters sound as if you yourself, Captain Evan
Llewelyn Evans the Third, were not applying to yourself,
individually, that talent which you are apparently applying
to the United States Army at this time. My son, I take the
position that a man either knows where he is going. Or he
don't. And if he don't, he has to think, to chin-chin with
himself and with his associates, to spin the compass and
find north. That is what I call Organization as it applies
to the individual as well as to the company. Have you lost
your bearings? Are you off the beam? You say you want to
stay in England after the war and find something to do
over there . . ."

The Old Man coughed apologetically.

"The rest is personal," he said. "I only wanted to make that
point about Organization, not only as it applies to many people
in one company like the Beautee Soap Company. Or to Kim-

berly and Maag, our present advertising agency. But also as it applies to one man about himself, such as my son."

Vic got the point. He leaned back again. He's going to say that I, like his son, have not Organized myself. That I am not on the beam. And that while he, as a father, would be expected to take the time and trouble to put his own son on the beam, he will not take that bother with some other man's son. Me. He will say an unorganized man like me lacks judgment. Take for example the teletype operator. Or take Buddy Hare. Or take Love that Soap.

"I don't know," the Old Man said, brooding. "I don't know whether he will get the point."

Kimberly said, "It's a beautifully made point, Mr. Evans. Clear as a bell."

"Excellent," said Irving Brown.

"And deeply touching," said Regina Kennedy.

Vic waited for Paul Evans to say something, but the elder son seemed lost in himself.

"Do you think he'll get the point, Mr. Norman?" the Old Man said.

"I'd like to get a letter like that from my father," Vic said carefully, not wanting to say anything that would focus the Old Man on the subject for which the meeting had been called.

Evan Llewelyn Evans rose up painfully and limped to the window. There was an uneasy feeling among the others, the feeling of wanting to rise with him. Vic felt it strongly. Ordinarily, rising meant dismissal. And you were not supposed to remain seated if he stood. But Vic, and indeed all of them, agreed in some telepathic manner not to stand up. It was generally felt that here was an extraordinary situation and the Old Man did not expect or want them to rise with him.

The Old Man opened the window. Allison leaped to help him, but was too late.

He breathed of the chill spring air.

"It's too long," he said sadly. "I didn't have time to write a shorter one, that's all. Whatever good it does, it'll only be a straw in the wind."

He removed his hat and stood there with the breeze cooling his old bald head.

"Just a straw in the wind," he repeated.

Suddenly he flung his old straw hat out the open window.

"See what I mean?" he said, and limped back to his chair at the head of the board table. Allison shut the window and scurried out of the room.

"I'm sorry, Mr. Norman, that you didn't find anything to interest us out there in Hollywood," he said.

Allison returned, with another hat, just like the straw Evan Evans had tossed into the wind. The Old Man placed it on his naked head.

And Vic, desperately floundering for some answer to this criticism—eagerly wanting to prove that he had not come back from Hollywood empty-handed—thinking of his conference with Figaro Perkins and rejecting mention of that as bad news —not wanting to even hint at the Buddy Hare episode: Vic then heard Kim say, "Mr. Norman brought down a record he thought might be of interest to you, Mr. Evans. Didn't you, Vic?"

And now Vic was afraid to play the Ogilvie record. Afraid the Old Man might not like it. Afraid to give him another target to shoot at. But above all, afraid the Old Man might feel, with his crafty animal cunning, the truth behind the Jean Ogilvie record . . . might sense the plot that Vic had made with a singer against him, Evan Llewelyn Evans.

"It's only a singer," Vic apologized.

The Old Man looked amused. "Only a singer you say, Mr. Norman. Well, I want you to know that the Beautee Soap Company thinks singers are mighty important. And I'll tell you why, Mr. Norman."

He opened the drawer of the table and triumphantly held aloft a bar of Beautee Soap.

"Because singers can sell soap, Mr. Norman. Right, Kimberly?"

"RIGHT," said Kimberly.

"That is, if they're the right kind of singers, eh, Kimberly?"

"Right on the barrelhead," Kim said.

And then Vic noticed still another thing. The Old Man had consistently called him Mr. Norman, and Kim he had consistently addressed as Kimberly.

Was that good or bad? Good for which one? Bad for which one?

"Maybe you'll think this girl is on the beam," Vic said, walking over to the record player and turning the switch.

"I'll only think she's on the beam if she is on the beam, Mr. Norman. Go ahead, let's hear some music."

Which of the three songs does he like best, thought Vic. And, suppose this record is no good? I can't tell him I've never heard it. What a hell of a spot Kim put me in, he thought.

So Vic, making a fast judgment, set the needle on Jean Ogilvie's hopped-up version of *Some of These Days*.

Jack Martin had done a magnificent job of recording. It was loud, clear. Fast. On the beat.

Vic kept his hand on the volume control, cheating on end notes, giving the record every possible break.

The effect was like Sophie Tucker, squared. The voice of Jean Ogilvie blasted the board room.

The song ended and Vic stood with the needle arm in his hand, waiting for the Opinion, keeping his face averted to prevent the Old Man from finding there the connivery which had created the record.

"Any more?" Evan Evans asked. There was no hint of the Opinion in his inflection.

But on the second song, *Over There*, Evan Llewelyn Evans began to pound the table. In perfect time, too. And when *Crazy Rhythm* was played, he shook his shoulders and stomped his feet.

"It's hot stuff," he said. "Hot stuff."

"We thought you might like her," Kim said diffidently,

looking for some expression from Vic. But Vic seemed far away and made no sign of wanting to say anything.

"Like her? God, man, she's hot stuff. Guts, that's what I like in my singers, guts. She'll tear the roof off."

He removed his straw hat and wiped his head.

"And you said you found nothing in Hollywood! Mr. Norman, she is really something."

"I found her in New York," Vic said, almost inaudibly. The Old Man chuckled.

"I propose to put her on the Figaro Perkins show at once," he said. "Can you sign her?"

"Yes, sir."

"How much?" Paul cautiously asked.

Vic looked out the window, estimating thoughtfully.

He brought his eyes slowly into focus on the Old Man's face, looked at him steadily and made a blunt reply, "Fifteen hundred dollars a week."

Double what he'd told Jean Ogilvie. Triple what she'd actually have signed for.

Why had he said fifteen hundred dollars? Was he trying to appease himself by getting even on this obscure and ridiculous basis of making the Old Man pay cash money for his fear.

What nonsense!

And then he knew why he'd said it. And he again felt the Fear that the Old Man must know it, too.

He focused his eyes on the window back of Evans and looked slantingly at his face for the criticism that should begin to show there.

The Old Man raised his massive eyebrows. Perhaps in puzzlement. A slight look of astonishment came over his face. And then he smiled gently and said,

"Never mind the price. It's nothing but tax money. Might as well give it to her as to those bureaucrats down in Washington. Put her on the air."

He paused. "That is, unless some of my people are not in favor of this singer that has been recommended to the Beautee Soap Company by its advertising agency."

Paul Evans looked worried but said nothing. The rest of his people thought she was terrific. "But really terrific," Regina Kennedy said. "Such a relief from these slow, low moaners you hear nowadays."

"Excellent," Irving Brown said.

And in Kimberly's carefully considered judgment she was right on the beam.

"She'll sell soap," Evans said. "By God, she'll sell it by the vatsful. What's her name?"

Vic said, "Jean Ogilvie." If the Old Man happened to be familiar with her and her normal style of singing there was still danger of a blow-up.

"Jean Ogilvie," the Old Man said, "Where have I heard that name before, Allison?"

Allison had the answer ready instantly. "In Wiley Warren's column, sir. I clipped it for you. Your name was mentioned."

"Oh, yes," the Old Man said. "Tell Miss Oglethorpe that in my humble opinion she is the greatest singer in America today, bar none."

"And Vic discovered her," Kim said happily. "In a little night club in Hollywood. Four years ago. He's been saving her for something like this."

The Old Man rose. This time, everyone stood. He started out.

"Don't miss the last bus to Hoboken," he warned. "Sign her up today."

He reached the door, turned to Vic who was standing by the record player.

"Mr. Norman," he said softly. "I almost forgot. About that Buddy Hare business."

"Yes, sir." Vic cursed his voice for sounding higher than it should.

"When I saw that movie I guess I was pretty harsh with Kimberly here. But later on I got to thinking."

He put his small, womanish hand on Vic's arm.

"And I think I know what was in your mind when you sent that film back to me."

He chuckled, took off his old straw hat.

"I take off my hat to you, Mr. Norman."

He opened the door and his cruel and fearful presence left the board room.

[CHAPTER XXII]

"GOD, VIC, HOW YOU HANDLED YOURSELF. WHAT A MEETING!" Kimberly was ecstatic. In the elevator he put his arm around Vic's shoulders and gave him an exuberant, masculine hug. Victory was rich and spicy.

He masterfully shouted for and captured a cab.

"Uptown, driver." He made the familiar circle with his thumb and forefinger. "Well, Vic, you certainly called your shot on the way downtown when you said you'd make him take off his hat to you. You made him do just that, Vic—take off his hat to you. And what a meeting. The old so-and-so decided not to murder us after all. Not one critical word did he say. Not one. And he didn't think any, either. I know. He was all sweetness and light. And you know why, Vic? Because he respects you, that's why. He can't figure you out. He won't be able to sleep tonight, trying to figure out why you wouldn't mention that singer. That was very smart, Vic. And because he can't figure you out, he's afraid to give you the whip. He's afraid you'll whip right back at him. And don't think he doesn't know how valuable you are to him, Vic. Don't think for a minute he doesn't know that."

Kimberly could not stop marveling over it.

"By God, Vic, the best decision I ever made in my life was the day I hired you. You've got him right in the palm of your hand. This does it, Vic. What you asked for this morning. This cinches the partnership. We'll cut you-know-who out of the company in less than six months. What a team we'll be. Kimberly and Norman! Together we'll build the biggest damn ad agency in the country. And that means the world. Give us three years and we'll be grossing sixty-five million. Conservatively sixty-five million. Here, let me shake the hand of the only man who ever defeated Evan Llewelyn Evans in his own Board Room." Kim picked up Vic's hand and squeezed it hard. "God," he said. "You're one-of-a-kind."

So Kim didn't know what happened in that Board Room. So you don't think that Old Man can figure me out? He's got me figured out, all right.

"What a session! I need a drink. Let's go back to the office and have a drink before lunch, Vic. By God, we earned a drink this morning. You know, Vic, with me it's more than just a business partnership, partner. You don't mind my calling you partner, do you? Yes, Vic, it's a deep friendship, too. Something that transcends business. I hope you feel that way about me, too. That's the very essence of partnership. Friendship. Men who understand each other. Don't you agree, Vic?"

"Brother. Hey, brother. You said uptown. But you didn't say where uptown. We're in the forties already." It was the cab driver.

"Forty-ninth, driver. Radio City. Sorry! You know, Vic, you gotta respect him. Admit that. He is clever in some deep instinctive way. Notice how he kept calling you Mr. Norman and me just plain Kimberly? Wonder what that means? Oh well, we'll find out soon enough. I really think he's shifting his interest from me to you. I really think he's made a fix on you, Vic. But what the hell, as long as we're going to be partners what difference does it make which one of us he likes best? God, when I left here this morning, I never thought I'd be able to walk back into this office alive. It is a rather nice office, don't you think, partner? We'll fix up one for you that's even plushier. We'll tear out some walls and make you an office bigger than this one even. Scotch or bourbon, partner? Water or soda, partner?"

Vic shook his head.

"I can't drink alone," Kim protested. "Have one anyway.
Then take the day off. Go sign up that dame singer. Spend
the afternoon with her. How is she in the hay? Have a good
time. You've earned it and she'll feel like celebrating too. Here,
have a drink."

Vic was on the couch. Fatigue had set in and his face was
stiff. His eyes stared at the offered glass, refused it. Kim's
chatter raced around the office. "Christ, I almost died when
you said fifteen hundred dollars a week for that night club
singer. You really should cut it down to a thousand Vic. Really."

The flat voice of Victor Norman said, "Kim, you've got to
get yourself a new boy."

Kim was sipping his drink. "Ahhh. Sure you don't want
one?" He set down his drink, shook a partner's coy finger at
Vic. "You mean *you've* got to get yourself a new boy, partner.
Beautee soap is your baby. You're the boss now. Me, I got
other fish to fry. From now on, partner, you'll have to solve
your own personnel problems."

"I'm through, Kim. I mean it."

The drink suspended in midair. "You're joking. Don't make
jokes like that, partner. It scares me."

"It's no joke, Kim."

"You said you needed me," Kim pleaded. "You said you
could use Evans. You said that you were in love. That you
needed all this to get married. Isn't that what you said to me
this very morning?"

Vic did not answer, so Kim went on.

"And you went down to Wall Street and accomplished just
what you said you'd do. You triumphed over the Old Man.
And you earned yourself a partnership with me. You can't
walk out now, Vic."

Kim was in despair. His unfinished drink was on the desk,
forgotten.

"I simply can't believe it, Vic. Do you really mean it?
Really?"

"Yes."

"Listen," Kim urged. "I'll give you equal voting stock. You'll make in this one day what it took me twelve years to accumulate. We'll be partners in every sense of the word. If you don't like to work with Evans you can hire someone else to do it for you. You can be clear of the Old Man in no time."

"No, Kim," he said. "I'm through."

"But why? Why, why, why?" Kim remembered his drink, picked it up. "You've got to tell me why, Vic."

"I'll tell you why," Vic said slowly. "There's not that much money in the world."

"Take a day off," Kim pleaded. "You're just tired. That's it. Take a week off. I'll tell him you're sick. Don't give me a final answer now. Go home and call your lover—your fiancee—talk it over with her. Think it over. Don't be hasty. It might wreck your life. I'll wait for your final decision. You're just going through an emotional reaction, that's all. You're tired."

"No, Kim," Vic said.

He walked back to his office and for a long time looked down on the skaters in the plaza.

The telephone rang sharply and his heart jumped. Could it be Kay calling him?

With hand on phone, he waited for his secretary to answer it in her office. He looked down on his desk at an opened copy of *Variety*. Miss Hammer had blue-penciled a small news item:

REEVES NIXES BUDDY HARE TOO

Hollywood—The morning after Vic Norman of Kimberly and Maag took a powder on Buddy Hare, the Reeves agency returned to Talent Ltd. their prior option on the baggy pants king, with regrets. Looks like no soap, no cigarettes for Buddy Hare, who is now angling for a new sponsor.

The buzzer buzzed. His legs were trembling but he remained standing as he answered.

"Yes, Miss Hammer. Louise."

She said, "Miss Kennedy is on the phone screaming for next week's commercials. Figaro Perkins is waiting for you at the teletype in Hollywood. He says it's a life and death matter. NBC wants to cancel this week's mystery show for a special event. What do you want to do first?"

Vic said, "I left ten minutes ago and nobody can find me."

"You haven't changed one bit," Miss Hammer wailed, but she spoke into a dead phone.

Victor Norman walked out of his office, rode down to the street and hailed a cab.

"Sutton Place South," he said.

His new apartment, cluttered with all the fine furniture of another century, was just as he had left it that morning he, went to Hollywood—could it be only two weeks ago?

The Sheraton sofa stood forlorn and out of place in the middle of the living room. He shoved it along the still uncarpeted floor and placed it against the wall.

He stepped back to look at it, trying to decide whether that was really the place for it, and then irrelevantly he thought: it takes a heap of Sheraton in a house to make it home.

The foyer table had been delivered, and he picked the telephone off the floor and put it on the table. Then he centered the table in the wall space and found the dainty chair which went with it; he turned the chair at an angle so it wouldn't look too stiff.

Then he looked around him and the room suddenly became distasteful. All this junk. What had he been thinking about when he bought it? And what was the point in coming out here now? There wasn't even a bed to sleep in. He should have tried for a suite at the Waldorf.

It was dark and gloomy in the foyer and he took the jade lamp from the desk in the living room and put it on the table. He stooped to plug it in and when he straightened up he discovered that he was dead tired.

Tired. Knocked out. He sat down on the chair and stared at the telephone. He lifted the receiver to see if it had been hooked up yet, heard the dial tone and dropped it back with a clatter.

Tired in his legs. Tired in his body. The fatigue was a dead weight pulling down on him.

He stared at the telephone before him. His hand slowly dropped on the receiver, raised it heavily. Very slowly, he dialed a number: two-one-one.

"Long Distance," the operator said. He listened without speaking.

"What number did you wish?" the operator said.

"Oh," said Victor Norman. "Excuse me. Is this long distance?"

"That's right, sir. What number did you wish?"

He tried to think of the number. "Get me—get me Beverly Hills, California, please."

"Yes, sir, what number?"

He tried again to remember the number. "It's the—the Sunset Hills Hotel. Mrs. Kay Dorrance. She's at Villa Fifteen. I—don't recall the number," he explained.

While the operator was putting the call through, Victor Norman waited at the telephone in the home he had not yet got around to completing, the expensively cluttered, the unfinished apartment on Sutton Place South. Waited and wondered what he would say to her, what she would say to him.

And as he waited the one feeling he had tried so desperately to evade pushed and shoved its way back into him. The feeling of the husband. He closed his eyes and his head swayed as he suffered this staggering feeling of the husband enroute from the wars.

"Please limit your call to five minutes," the operator said.

Her voice came through clearly and his love drove all the smaller feelings back into the nooks and crannies of his senses.

"Hello," he said. "Hello, Kay."

"Hello, Vic."

"Are you alone?"

"Yes," she said, and then she whispered a soft and husky, "darling."

"I just got in New York today."

"I know. Have a nice trip?" she asked.

"Terrible."

"Why?"

"You know why."

There was a pause.

"Ellen ran a splinter in her foot, coming home from the pool. Nothing serious," she said. "Have you missed me?"

"Oh, yes, Kay."

"I've missed you too, darling." Then she said, "Tell me, how was that business thing? Was it a success?"

"A total success," he told her. "So much so that I just quit my job."

"Are you upset about it, darling?" she asked. "If you are, then I'm sorry about it. If you're not, I'm happy."

He said no, he wasn't upset in the slightest.

"I don't even give it a thought," he said. "All my thoughts are about you. I love you."

"Oh my love," she cried.

Again, a silence.

Then he said, "Can you hear me, Kay?"

She said, perfectly.

So he said, "When I left you, we'd agreed that I was to call you for your decision. You had a pretty tough choice to make."

"Yes," she said. "Quite difficult."

"But I'm not going to ask you what it is."

She paused a moment and said carefully, "I haven't made it yet."

Vic said, "Kay. I've made a decision. A very sad one for me. I'm not going to ask you to come back to me."

"Oh, Vic," she said. "My love."

"If we did this thing," he said, "I don't think I'd like myself. And if I didn't like myself I don't think I'd be good enough for you and Hal and Ellen."

"Don't talk like that," she begged. "Please."

"And I don't think you'd like yourself, either," he said. "But

I want you to know that this love is the dearest thing in my life. The very dearest. And I think it always will be."

Her answer came after a long wait.

"It always will be for me, too, Vic."

"It was right and it was good and I'm going to look back on it with joy, not sadness," he said.

There was a long, long pause. The operator said, "Is this call finished?"

"No," Vic said, "it's not finished."

"Please limit your call as much as possible," the operator said. "Others are waiting."

"All right," Vic said. "Kay, are you there?"

Her voice was faint. "Yes." Then she said, "Are you sure we've given this enough time? I can't even think yet. It's all too close to me."

"Kay," he said. "Don't try to think. I tried to think it out and it wouldn't think out. Do you understand what I'm trying to say?"

"Yes, Vic, I understand what you're trying to say."

"I wish it didn't have to," he said.

"Oh, Vic," she cried. "What will we do? What can we do?"

"Nothing," he said. "It had to go this way. I don't know whether I'm a martyr or a fool. All I have is a feeling about it. I don't know. I'll never know."

"What can we do?" she said again.

"Nothing," he repeated.

And then the quality of her voice changed. "The children just came in, Vic. I can't talk anymore. Do you want to say good-bye to them?"

Her voice was thin and tired. Very far away. Victor Norman fought the fatigue that pulled down on him. He tried hard to speak with strength and confidence.

"Yes, Kay," he said. "I want to say good-bye to them."